W9-BAQ-804

CRITICS PRAISE HOLT MEDALLION WINNER
KATHLEEN NANCE!

THE SEEKER

"With tantalizing plot twists and impossible interference, the path to love is a heck of a lot of fun! The fresh premise . . . characters, and complexity of plot result in a sparkling romance!"

—*The Midwest Book Review*

"An exciting story filled with romance, magic and mystery!"
—*Romance Reviews Today*

THE WARRIOR

"An exciting tale interwoven with a fun premise."
—*Romantic Times*

"Kathleen Nance puts a refreshing twist on paranormal romance. . . . Well-executed with amazing romantic and sensual tension."

—*Romance and Friends*

THE TRICKSTER

"*The Trickster* is a magical tale that is fresh and captivating. Kathleen Nance has woven a story unlike anything I have read before and for that I applaud her. She is a true genius."

—Scribesworld.com

"Kathleen Nance spins a unique and clever tale. *The Trickster* is warm, funny and tender."

—*Romantic Times*

SPELLBOUND

Spellbound "will captivate fans and new readers alike with an imaginative world of magic filled with lusty encounters."

—*Booklist*

"Powerful, poignant and passionate, *Spellbound* showcases Kathleen Nance's singular storytelling ability to the fullest."

—*Romance Reviews Today*

"A magically potent romance."

—*Romantic Times*

MORE RAVE REVIEWS FOR
KATHLEEN NANCE!

WISHES COME TRUE

"Kathleen Nance has penned a supremely enticing tale with laughter, intrigue, the paranormal and, of course, a passionate steamy love that comes across in spades."

—Rendezvous

Wishes Come True is "a story of magic, wishes, fantasy, and . . . a lot of spice. Ms. Nance is wonderful. Fantastic! 5 Bells!"

—Bell, Book and Candle

ENCHANTMENT

"Enchantment is a wish come true for fans of genie romance. Ms. Nance creates a world as exotic and intriguing as the characters who inhabit it."

—Romantic Times

"Enchantment was a wonderful reading experience, [with] a great set of characters and a wonderful setting. I cannot say enough about this book except I have a fervent wish for a sequel."

—Romance Reviews Today

MORE THAN MAGIC

"More Than Magic is an undeniable treasure trove of pleasure, bursting with magnetic characters and a bewitching plot that's sure to capture the imagination of fantasy and romance readers alike."

—Rendezvous

"An astonishingly original story in a world which contains far too few paranormal romances, More Than Magic is more than satisfying."

—Affaire de Coeur

A WILD CHASE

Apparently the people in the plane had no qualms about opening fire on a Mountie. Were there any other options besides that stream ahead? Out here on the lake, she was the proverbial sitting duck.

Heart pounding, Day took the sled off automatic and put it on manual. A high-pitched whine protested the sudden release of dampers and controls. She jammed her foot against the accelerator, pressed it past the max point of computer control, past the safety zone. The engine groaned, but it was tuned finer than the national orchestra and kept up the fiery pace.

Shock waves pounded her until she could barely see. Stiffly she rotated her shoulder, unable to bend her aching neck, to check behind. Blood haze impaired her vision, but she saw enough. The plane was gaining. She coaxed out another couple of kph's velocity. The exit stream. She was going to make it!

The plane cut its speed, dropping from above until it flew almost level with her sled, putting her in the direct line of their fire. Of course, that meant they were in direct line with her weapons. She fired, two quick bursts that caused them to pull back, even though she didn't think she'd done any damage.

The river curved just ahead. She could—

A missile exploded in front of her, a phosphorus-white flame that filled her sight with white dots.

Other *Love Spell* books by Kathleen Nance:

WISHES COME TRUE
SPELLBOUND
ENCHANTMENT
THE SEEKER
THE WARRIOR
THE TRICKSTER
MORE THAN MAGIC

Kathleen Nance

Day of Fire

LOVE SPELL   NEW YORK CITY

*For our Canadian neighbors and friends. We are blessed
by your good will. May our common bonds
and the peace of our open borders
never be tested as they are in this book.*

LOVE SPELL®

May 2004

Published by

Dorchester Publishing Co., Inc.
200 Madison Avenue
New York, NY 10016

If you purchased this book without a cover you should be aware
that this book is stolen property. It was reported as "unsold and
destroyed" to the publisher and neither the author nor the publisher
has received any payment for this "stripped book."

Copyright © 2004 by Kathleen Nance

All rights reserved. No part of this book may be reproduced or
transmitted in any form or by any electronic or mechanical means,
including photocopying, recording or by any information storage
and retrieval system, without the written permission of the
publisher, except where permitted by law.

ISBN 0-505-52591-7

The name "Love Spell" and its logo are trademarks of Dorchester
Publishing Co., Inc.

Printed in the United States of America.

Visit us on the web at www.dorchesterpub.com.

Day of Fire

ACKNOWLEDGMENTS

Thank you:

To Pamela Clare, for answering so many questions in so little time.

To Chris, Liz, and Patti, for making this such a pleasure to participate.

And finally, a special heartfelt thanks to Susan Grant. Thank you for your generosity in sharing your world and this project with me, Sue.

Prologue

Canada
Year of our Lord 2176
Post Epidemic Year 106

"Tyranny, like hell, is not easily conquered."

The ancient quote blasted across the Saskatchewan prairie, slicing the predawn vastness like an icy javelin. Settling her hat firmly on her head, Day Daniels studied the source through her sight goggles, then gave an irritated huff.

She was out here at three A.M. following a lead to the No-Borders. She'd expected to infiltrate a clandestine meeting of armed men.

This, she had not expected.

She lowered the goggles, then blinked to warm her eyeballs. Her breath formed a steady white mist in the teeth-numbing cold, while she assessed the situation.

An enormous, concrete moose stood in the fallow wheat field near the TransConnect train station: Mac the Moose, enduring symbol of Moose Jaw, Saskatchewan, all ten me-

1

ters, nine tons of him. His nose was pressed against a green wooden grain elevator, another historical relic. The elevator, newly restored before the first Viral Epidemic, now showed the gaps of neglect. Not so Mac.

Tied to the moose was a sign, a single scarlet word: REVOLUTION. Two teenaged boys, their down jackets a-flap in the freshening wind, balanced on the moose's back. Probably aiming their message to the TransCanada Connect trains, Day decided. The boys' handhelds hung from the moose's antlers, blaring their message into the gray stillness.

"The days of our deliverance draw nigh."

Scraping a nail across the comm patch behind her ear, Day signaled to her backup for tonight, Luc Robichaux. Her body went on hold for a second, until at last Luc returned the signal, sending a faint vibration to the patch.

"I'm a kilom from the Connect station," he said, sounding breathless. Good thing he was retiring next week. "Coming up the rails. What's your situation? Any sign of the No-Borders?"

"I'm looking at Mac the Moose. Couple of lads on his back, maybe hopped up on something, since they don't seem to be feeling the cold."

"We're out in this hibernating cold because of a stupid prank?"

She took another look at the painted sign. "Maybe." The boys might be rash, but their purpose seemed more earnest than prankish. Still, this was not the work of the vicious No-Borders.

"The oppressions of the colonizers have planted the seeds of revolt."

"What's that?" Luc asked.

"Some transmission from their computers." The broadcast voice was strange—sexless, but impassioned; human, but disguised. Compelling and persuasive. Dangerous.

She frowned. Faceless, mechanized messages—espe-

2

cially a lawless message of revolt—meant brewing trouble. Time to find out a little more what prompted this display of teenaged stupidity.

"Wait for me, Day." Luc's cautionary words came before she took a step.

"Sure."

"I'll have your hat if you do this alone."

"Just reconnoitering." Annoyed, she signaled an end to the communication. That's what happened when you worked out of the same Depot for three years: Your backup got to thinking they could predict you.

Annoying as hell when they were right.

Day's boots crunched on the remnants of wheat stalks as she strolled closer to the moose. Reaching its base, she placed one boot on a cloven hoof, then tilted her head back, her braid swinging free. "Hey, boys, what are you doing up there?"

A mix of curses—both English and French—came in response, ending with a fear-filled "Vic, it's a Mountie!"

"She's puck-sized," came the scornful reply from the bigger of the two. "And a chick."

"I don't care if she's short or a woman, look at the hat. She's a *Mountie.*"

She got tired of the chatter. "Yep, I'm a Mountie, boys. You didn't really think we weren't going to be called in, now, did you? A moose this big gets noticed."

"That's why we took it," shouted down Vic, the one who'd called her a chick. "Nobody can ignore us."

"Out here?" she asked, gesturing to the open prairie.

"We Canadians don't gather anymore, but everyone on the Connect trains will see our cause."

"What cause would that be?" She crossed her arms.

"Freedom! For the world! The Voice of Freedom spoke last night!"

"The Voice of Freedom? I assume that's what I'm hearing on your handhelds."

"We burnt it into a chip, so we could play it over and over."

Oh, fabulous. Day rubbed her neck, stiff from looking upward. "You got your message there. Now, time for you two to come down." She glanced around. Except, how had they gotten up there?

The explanation came swiftly. "Our mates took away the ladders. We're not leaving till we have our say." They stood, feet spread and defiant, scowling down at her.

From the corner of her eye, Day could see the first tinge of light in the east. Along the horizon, dust spun in a miniature tornado. Wind bit at her cheeks. She frowned and activated her comm. "I'm going up the grain elevator, Luc. See what I can find out." She needed to be closer. See if she could persuade them off that damn moose.

"I'm almost there. Wait—oh, why do I bother?"

"Join the revolution." The pair kept broadcasting their messenger of sedition, oblivious of the rising wind.

"Like hell," Day muttered back to the impassioned voice as she scrambled inside the dilapidated grain elevator. Anarchy, even when spouted to the ghosts of an empty prairie, was still anarchy.

Not waiting for her eyes to adjust to the gloom, she balanced on the first bucket of the elevator leg, the central shaft that had once conveyed grain from wagons up to the storage bins. She hefted herself upward, arms dragging her half the distance to the next bucket, then her feet scrambling to balance on the swaying rim. Steadily, she climbed, shifting from one bucket to the next. Her breath led the way in white puffs of effort. At least it was still in here, dry and cold and motionless as the inside of a crypt.

Except for that damned voice.

Grain dust—not even the centuries could rid the elevator of it all—tickled her throat, and she swallowed against the irritation. Her fingers and shoulders ached from gripping the elevator, pulling between the gaps of missing or broken buckets, and catching herself from a fall when one shattered beneath her boots. The ache turned to burning as her arms and legs protested the strain, but she kept moving. Her heart drummed against her ears—damn, but she was getting to sound like Luc.

Still, the image of the two boys on the back of a moose, with no way down except a three-floor fall, propelled her up. Once at the top, she dragged air into her lungs. *Be it All, Do it All, Day.*

Steadying herself, she perched in the tiny door of the grain elevator, where once the chute had reached out to the trains stopping for their load of grain. The end of her braid whipped around her neck. The wind was getting worse.

The lads were still standing on the moose. Dear Lord, they were younger than she'd realized. Barely into secondary level.

Vic spied her. "Go away!" he shouted, scrambling wildly backward. "We're not leaving."

"Not leaving!" echoed the other, shivering in the dropping temperature.

Demanding they get off the moose wasn't going to work. Keep them calm. Gain a measure of their trust. Day forced herself to relax against the window frame, even as adrenaline revitalized her muscles. She mouthed to her comm, "Get air rescue here, Luc. And a bounce pad."

"Understood."

Nonthreatening and conversational was the way to start. "Just thought it would be easier to chat up here. What are you revolting against?"

"Why should we tell you?" Vic asked.

"Because with a two-meter-square sign announcing revolution, I'm assuming you want people to know. You might as well start with me; I'm the only one listening."

"Oppression," answered the smaller one. "We're fighting oppression."

She turned her attention to him. "What's your name?"

"Don't tell her," said Vic with a tremble in his voice. "Don't tell her anything. If Mounties get the evidence, you'll be convicted then and there."

She gestured to the moose. "I'd say you two already provided the evidence, ten meters of it. All I want is to know who I'm talking to. First name's okay. Mine's Day." She'd already scanned their images and sent them to Depot. She'd have more info than just names momentarily. "So, what's yours?" she asked again.

"André."

"*Bonjour,* André." She nodded acknowledgment, then bent her knee and propped one foot on the moose's nose. The wooden sill where she perched still bit into her rear as she bent forward. Out of the protection from the elevator, the wind drove the cold against her cheeks and tugged apart her tight braid. She let none of her discomfort show. "Tell me about this Voice of Freedom. Who is it?"

The boys exchanged glances. "We don't know, but the message is exciting."

"I'd have a tough time trusting anyone who distorted their voice and hid from folks," Day suggested.

"It's for safety," insisted André loyally. "Until the strength of the oppressors can be met."

"Who's oppressing you?"

A moment's silence followed.

"It's not *us*. It's the world. We can't ignore the suffering caused by the UCE," André explained.

The UCE, the United Colonies of Earth, Canada's troublesome behemoth neighbor to the south. Day supposed the boys' logic made sense from the viewpoint of a youthful idealist. Discontent *was* brewing in the former US of A, fomented by years of heavy taxes, the loss of democratic elections, and the cruel stranglehold of the current regime.

She gestured to the sign. "So, you're leading a revolt against the Dominion of Tri-Canada?"

Vic snorted. "Canadians don't revolt."

"Then why the sign?"

"To support those who *will* revolt. Listen to the Voice."

She'd had enough listening. Maybe a revolution was coming, but it was none of Tri-Canada's affair.

The world had abandoned Canada in her years of greatest need. 2070. The horrifying year when multiple bioterror agents—a deathly hellish stew of smallpox, Ebola, and anthrax—had been released in Toronto. While the microbial scourge decimated Canada, what had been the world's response? An unbreakable quarantine, established by the plague-paranoid United Nations and enforced by the UCE and UN coalition. Only the occasional air drop of relief supplies got past the borders during the epidemics. Even today, the quarantine was enforced until Canada could prove they were no longer a biohazard.

Except, now Canada had no need of the world. As the nation slowly recovered, Canadian Parliament passed their own strict laws. The border was closed from both sides, a stance upheld by satellite surveillance, rugged terrain, Mounties and border forces, and cold plasma barriers. Canada was an island unto itself; no one and nothing crossed its borders.

In theory. In practice, the long border was getting leaky.

Personally, Day figured Canada was better off isolated, but she kept her opinions to herself. They wouldn't help get the boys off the moose and safe from their misguided idealism.

Jamming her hat on her head, she slid down onto the moose, straddling its nose, and signaled Luc. "Where's air rescue? This williwaw is turning lethal, and the dew slick isn't helping."

"They're almost here. I'm right below you."

She spared a glance down, where Luc paced fussily on the ground. The whir of an approaching chopper sounded.

"You stay right there, Luc."

"And do what? Block their fall with my body?"

"No, direct the chopper. Do you hear that, boys?" She pointed at the now visible aircraft. "It's someone to help you get off here."

"We won't go." The boys each grabbed for an antler, the wind catching their sudden movement. The gust sent André slipping, but he caught his fall. Day's heart skipped two beats, while her stomach tied a square knot.

"Eventually you'll have to." She forced calm to her voice. "You'll have to eat. Or pee."

"If we leave now, you'll take our sign down before the trains come through."

She pondered the complaint. "If you agree to come off, I'll leave the sign on for twenty-four hours."

"You gonna arrest us?"

"Yes. You broke the law." She ignored their twin scowls. "But, I also have the authority to assess your fine."

André paled. "We don't have any money."

"Not that kind of fine. You'll pay off your debt in information. Record everything you know about or hear from this shadowy 'voice of freedom,' for me."

"That's it?" asked André.

Vic stuck out his chin. "How do we know you're telling the truth?"

Anger coursed through her. They might be young, but they should know better. Mounties took only the best. Service in the Corps meant fulfilling your duty with integrity and honor. "The word of a Mountie is not questioned." She curbed her ire. "You knew the law, you knew there'd be consequences. But, you also should know I'll do what I say."

Again a moment's silence fell. The boys exchanged a glance, then nodded and let go of their respective antlers. They both started edging across the moose toward her.

"No! Wait for the air rescue—"

A polar wind swept across the prairie, carrying the frigid

power of a thousand kilometers of unhindered passage. A premature harbinger of winter's gales, the gust staggered her. André slipped, his arms flailing. Day's heart skipped two beats again before he caught himself. Another gust sucked out her breath. Vic plastered down against the moose's neck, hanging on as though his life depended upon it. Maybe it did.

Day slid across the thick nose and over the head. Her jacket caught on a gigantic antler, and she heard it tear as she stretched down the neck toward Vic. She locked her ankles around the antlers for support.

The chopper finally reached them. It hovered above, its side jets of directional air adding to the fury of the williwaw. A ladder descended from the belly of the chopper, and another Mountie climbed down. The currents of wind were too erratic for him to get onto the moose next to the boys, however. Instead, he shouted to the chopper, and they threw down a bucket and rope. He motioned for Vic to get in.

Vic was too frightened to do anything but cling to his perilous perch, shaking his head in denial.

"Get in the bucket," Day shouted to him. "I'll help you."

Keeping her gaze locked with Vic's, keeping one hand on him for reassurance, she helped him slide over until his feet rested safely inside. She squeezed his shoulder, forcing him to look at her. "You're inside. You can't fall. Let go of the antlers and stand in the bucket. They'll pull you to safety."

Vic stared at her, the whites of his eyes huge. He clutched the antlers.

"Vic, take my hand," Day commanded firmly, and he obeyed. "Now the other."

When she had both of his hands in hers, she signaled the chopper. Gradually it moved forward, catching more of the boy; then she let go of Vic. There was a moment's panic in his face, a desperate clutch for her as he realized he was swinging up. Then the air-rescue Mountie had him in hand.

That left André. Day unwrapped her ankles from the antlers, then slid down the neck and across the back of the moose. André must have caught the movement, for he started to come toward her.

"No, André, stay there! Do not let go until—"

André slipped, scrabbling furiously and futilely, trying to stop the inevitable. Day lunged forward, blood raging, and threw herself across the moose, grabbing André's wrists as he slid down the side. His weight yanked her arms with a blazing shaft of pain. She gasped, blinded by the intense agony, and nearly lost her grip. *Be it All, Do it All.* Sheer determination kept her fingers closed around the boy.

The world narrowed. Pain in her shoulders. Straining. André's white face. Fire down her spine. Digging in her toes and sidling backward. The fury of the north battering her. Pain. André back on the moose at last. Air rescue taking advantage of a lull in the wind to close in.

Dimly, Day saw air rescue give her the thumbs-up, indicating they had André secured. One finger at a time, each tiny movement screaming, she let the boy go, then watched him swing up to the chopper.

"We're full here, Day." The air rescue team sounded in her comm. "But the bucket can swing you to the ground."

"I'd appreciate the lift." She forced herself to sit upright.

"Join in the revolution, my sons and daughters who crave liberty!" The Voice of Freedom—a voice of shadows, Day couldn't help thinking—raged on from the boys' abandoned handhelds. As she slid into the waiting bucket and was deposited to the wheat field, Day shook her head.

Where was Luc? She opened her comm. "Luc, where'd you go?"

"I heard something at the station," he whispered. "The

10

No-Border meeting we were expecting, I think. I'm at the container hold building."

"Luc, wait for me!"

"Unlike you, I will. Going silent."

Cradling her abused arms against her waist, she ran forward, comming Depot for more backup. Arms like this, she was virtually useless.

No lights shone in the empty station. The only sound was the Voice of Freedom, still ranting outside. She circled the container hold building, and her feet hit something solid in the shadows. Dropping to her knees, stomach churning, she fumbled for her light.

Luc! Her partner was sprawled on his back, his hat fallen to the side, his throat slashed. Choked on his own blood.

Oh, God. The pain in her shoulders was nothing compared to this.

Outside, the disguised, sexless Shadow Voice continued. *"We shall have our freedom, but beware: We shall lose good men these days."*

Chapter One

One month later

The techbar decor was a throwback—all chrome, black tile, and twisted tubes of colored neon. The only modern touches were the moving nanowall advertising the Can-Ook Pride concert next week, and the games. The games at Flash Point were top technology.

Day Daniels opened her coat and leaned one elbow against the slick bar. Music throbbed from the floor in a driving cacophony of synthesizers and screeches. Four-foot fans pulled in cold air from outside and circulated it, keeping the machines from overheating. The breeze tugged her braid, and Day ran a hand up to smooth her hair. Damn, but she missed her hat.

She eyed the customers at the panels of computers and immersed in the virtual games. Which one was her snitch?

"What'll you have?" The bartender matched the decor—dark hair tied back, black leather, chrome-gray eyes with less softness than the metal, and two spots of color in the

13

electric-blue glass rings piercing the tops of his ears.

On him, she liked the look.

"Root beer with a double shot of caf blend—Lian," she added, noting the name tag.

Lian lifted one thick brow. "Double shot? Never seen a lady your size who could handle that much buzz. Not enough body fat."

"You've never seen a lady like me."

His easy, practiced glance ran from her braid to her boots, then lingered at her eyes. Most people found them disturbing, being different shades and all.

He didn't. "That an invitation? I get off at midnight. Thirty minutes."

She met him square. "Not a chance. Just give me the beer."

He laughed, apparently not the least offended by her refusal. "It's your nervous system." With deft skill, he twirled the bottles of root beer and caf, shaking them into a precise fizz as he assembled her drink.

She paid, then sipped, savoring the cold contrast of sweet soda, bitter caffeine, and bubbles. "Perfect."

"We do it all," he said, pocketing the tip she'd added.

At the familiar phrase, she gave him a sharp look. Be it All; Do it All was the unofficial motto of the twenty-second-century Mounties. Did he know?

Before she could decide, a fight broke out over the legitimacy of a move in Viral Warrior. Seconds later, the combatants were waving laser daggers and sonic prickers. No surprise there. The decor might be from a few centuries ago, but Flash Point was a No-Border hangout. If betting were legal, then Day would be laying odds every patron here hid at least one weapon.

Herself included.

She watched the confrontation but didn't move. Weapons weren't illegal.

14

Lian the bartender wasn't so easy-minded, however. He stalked to the two combatants and, with a few choice words plus a couple of well-placed nerve jabs, had the situation back under control.

Day swiveled in her chair. Turning her back on the bartender, she canvassed the room again, looking for Bart, the man she'd come to see.

They'd never met; Bart preferred it that way. She'd humored him because he was a good source—knew every underground movement in this half of Canada and was always in need of cash to feed his nanochip habit. He'd given her some bad leads on the current case, though, and she figured a face-to-face was needed.

Dude extraordinaire, he'd described himself once. Meaning he was a master of a 150-year-old culture that no longer existed except in places like this bar. *If you're not good enough to figure out who he is from that, Day, then you should be hanging up your badge.*

So, who was Bart the snitch? She dismissed the screen-mesmerized 'puting jocks, including the recent combatants. The chuck at the end of the bar was a different breed, however. Dressed in the current rage—chamois over recycled denim—he was smooth and broody. Hunched over his drink as if it were a pot of true champagne, his body language said "stay away," but it was a mixed command, because something about him drew the eye.

Caffeine blasted down Day's veins as he glanced at her. She'd expected ruggedness, not cruel beauty, in his face.

"He said his name's Rupert," said Lian, leaning against the bar and jerking a head toward the man. "Want an intro?"

An interesting guy, she'd bet, but Rupert wasn't *dude extraordinaire* material. "No, thanks."

An exultant shout from the rapt crowd surrounding the Yeux de Serpent game sphere caught her attention, and

Day strolled over, still sipping her perfect beer-n-blast. Yeux de Serpent. Eyes of the Serpent. One of the toughest games around—if you set it up right.

The Yeux corner was darker than the rest of the twilit room, the glowing, multihued playing field the only source of light. One of the players slumped in his seat, and when she glanced at the tally screen she saw why. He'd been neatly annihilated in a mere five minutes.

No record. Her worst defeat at Yeux was in four.

The winner, a young male about as thick as a wheat stalk, accepted the accolades of his peers as his due. Apparently, he was a celeb in these walls, a guy who'd never been beaten at Yeux de Serpent.

Dude extraordinaire.

She pushed forward as his fans left to get him a beer. "Bart?"

"Name's LaseMan." He gave her an assessing leer. "I'm busy right now, *chica*, but you sit on that couch and I'll join with you real soon. The hands are fast, but the night won't be."

"I'll pass. And you're Bart. No one else in this bar would dare claim the title *dude extraordinaire*." Either from fear of retribution by LaseMan or from utter embarrassment at the silliness of the label.

"So, who's asking?"

She held out her hand. "Day Daniels."

He ignored the hand, and his leer turned hard. "You're too puny for a Stiff Brim."

She didn't take offense—much—at the weak slur. She'd been called worse. Still, it would have been nice if she could have worn her hat, the symbol of her authority. People always took her more seriously with the hat.

"I'm wiry." She resisted the urge to rub her bare head. Instead, she lowered her hand and took a long swallow of her drink. "You want me to flash my badge to prove who I am?"

"In a No-Border techbar? They'd stake me for talking to you. You must be hopped on some powerful drug 'tail if you think I'll talk here."

"Your last info turned bogus. I want the real stuff."

A tattooed girl joined them and handed Bart a beer. He tasted it before answering. "I'm busy now, prepping for a new challenge." He leaned down and gave the girl a sloppy, openmouthed, tongue-filled kiss before slanting a glance Day's way. "Go away. We're done talking."

One of the sycophants laid a hand on Day's shoulder, and the sting from a sonic pricker throbbed across her jaw. Day shook him off and downed her drink in a single swallow, feeding irritation with a dose of the alkaloid. She didn't have any more time to waste with this self-important, stonewalling mucker. Her partner had died; she was charged with finding his killer.

She ran her options, feeling the bite of escaping time. She could put on her hat, make it official, and bring Bart in for questioning. Or . . .

"I challenge you," she said abruptly.

Bart ignored her.

"You chicken? Afraid I'll beat you?"

That got his attention. "What are you spamming about?"

She nodded to the Yeux panel. "I challenge you to a game. Your game. Yeux de Serpent." She lowered her voice, spoke to him alone. "Send your fawners out of earshot, and we talk as long as I keep in the game. I'll even sweeten the deal. No questions the first minute, but after that you answer everything, prompt and true, until it's over. Then I don't bother you ever again about this."

He fingered his knotted goatee. "What's in it for me?"

"Your usual fee, once your info checks. Plus, you're spared the humiliation of your fans seeing you back down from a challenge. By a woman," she tacked on for good measure.

17

He looked her over. "Throw in a kiss when you lose, and you got yourself a deal, *chica*."

"Bring it on."

Bart promptly claimed the Yeux game's Setting chair and turned on the playing field.

Day smiled. Ah, machismo was alive and well, even in the twenty-second century Dominion of Tri-Canada, Day saw.

She sat in the Colors chair, enjoying the double buzz of caffeine and challenge. She laced her hands, stretching her fingers and cracking the knuckles, as she studied the layout.

The playing field surrounded them in a sphere of color. Her easy-moving swivel seat had full range. Standard controls on the glove handsets, but each machine played a little different, she knew. She'd suggested the minute of no questions as much to give herself a chance to get the feel of the controls as to give him a nudge. From Bart's smug grin, she knew he expected the game to be over before that minute was up.

"Do you know the rules?" he asked condescendingly.

"Let's review them, just to make sure one of us isn't playing by a different set. Eyes of the Serpent. Slice off the opponent's eyes before he slices all of yours. Left hand grows your serpents, right hand cuts. No crossing bodies; sliced serpents disappear. Anything else?"

"That's it. Load your settings, then let's play."

She wasn't surprised to see he chose the highest level—max number of serpents' eyes, fastest body speed—but she also saw her choices surprised him. Most people picked a natural scene, letting the serpents swing from jungle trees or slither between desert rocks. She preferred a background of fire.

Four different colors were used. Two—different for each opponent—were the pulsing target dots, the eyes, and two were the machetes drawn to slice each eye. She'd chosen shades of red, her favorite color, at a setting where the differences between the four colors were subtle. And the background made it that much harder.

"Easy to slice your own eye or hit a body." Bart frowned. He'd just stopped taking her lightly.

"Order them back," she hissed, jerking her head toward the gathering crowd. "Or do you want them to hear?"

"Everyone, step back," Bart commanded. "The lady isn't used to playing with an audience."

"I'll offer a little one-on-one action," called someone in response.

Day rolled her eyes. Why did men always assume that she was hoping to open her legs for them? Was it the long hair? The 160-centimeter stature? Or the mere fact that she had breasts and ovaries?

At least the audience obeyed LaseMan's command. Now she and Bart could talk without being heard. Day wiggled her fingers into the control gloves, and the game began.

Bart was good. Damn good. With the unfamiliar controls, she was hard-pressed to keep up with him. Only taking out the eyes behind his back kept him from a quick sweep of her. As the seconds passed, though, Day gained comfort with the controls, giving her fractions better speed as the red lines raced across the holofield. After the first minute, she regained a little space, a little breathing room.

She'd had a lot of Yeux games since that four-minute defeat.

He was better than she was, but then she didn't spend five hours a day playing the game either. Still, Day figured she had two advantages. One: Most men, she'd discovered, didn't like to talk when they competed. Two: She didn't need to win. She just needed to play defensively and hang in long enough to find out what she wanted.

He boxed her in, but luckily he mistook one of his eyes for hers, and she found a corridor to escape. Still, his confident little grin came back.

Wouldn't it be nice to sour that look?

"Minute's up. What do you know about the murder of Luc Robichaux," she demanded.

He didn't answer, his focus on the game.

"LaseMan. *Bart*," she barked. Startled, he looked at her instead of the field. She took advantage, swung her chair and wiped out a corner of his advance with one slice.

"Shit," he muttered, scrambling to regain the advantage.

"We play. You talk. That's the agreement."

"Or what?"

"Or I tell everyone here you're feeding info to a Mountie."

"No-Borders. They killed the constable."

"You told me that before. Now give me solid leads." He swore again as she sliced two eyes. "Enough with the curses, Bart. I want facts."

"I got none."

"You're lying. Mounties always know when someone's lying."

"No-Borders will break my fingers if I talk about them."

"Mounties would go for the wrists, too," she said, just before Bart twisted his hand in a spectacular move that had her silent and scrambling to counter. "Start spewing," she gasped.

"They listen to the Voice of Freedom."

"So does my wolf."

"It's a rallying point."

"It's a sexless electronic voice over fiberoptics."

"There's a message."

"What? Free choice? Stand up to the United Colonies of Earth Imperialists? A better life for all? We Canadians got that message a long time ago." Since their once friendly southern neighbor, the UCE, had helped the U.N. close the borders and enforce the quarantine. "We're the only independent, democratic nation left, and we aim to stay that way."

"Banzai."

It cost her an eye before she realized he wasn't rejoicing. "What's Banzai?"

"Not what. Who. A woman. Spoken of by the Voice of Freedom. The Voice says she brings the ideals of the past. That's all I know." Bart leaned forward, intensifying his push to win.

"That's it? Not worth what I'm paying you. Shall I make my big announcement to your buddies?" She got lucky and sliced four more eyes.

When he saw that he wasn't going to get a reprieve by a quick end to the game, he said, "Talk to Scree, the scavenger. In Winnipeg. Heard he recently made a big sale to the No-Borders."

"And if Scree doesn't come through?"

"Try the Shinook. Word is, there's a connection. Something with their tribe leader."

This she hadn't heard. In the chaotic aftermath of the plagues, the Affiliated Indian Nations had been formed from the regrouped survivors of the old Native First Nations and had reclaimed sovereignty over their hereditary lands. The Shinook were one of the wealthiest of the AIN tribes. They were also staunch isolationists and advocates of the ancient traditions. They kept to themselves and ignored the rest of the country unless it served their purpose. In fact, no one was exactly sure where they were right now.

"What about the leader?"

"His name's Jem, and rumor says he's a man you don't cross. Nobody touches him."

"What's the connection between an isolationist tribe and the No-Borders?"

"I don't know."

"Bart," she warned.

"I swear. I don't." He was sweating now.

She sliced another eye for emphasis.

"The No-Borders got something big going on; the Shinooks have a piece of it. But all I heard was a name. A place. Citadel. That's all I know, I swear."

Citadel. Day stiffened, her lines stuttering on the fire field. Citadel. A place of awestruck legend.

The cheers from the watching audience shook her out, told her she'd almost lost the game. Still, she had the new leads she needed, and all he'd give her. She could quit now. Instead, she bent to the controls. *Be it All. Do it All*. Neither motto allowed for throwing a game.

The match progressed in waves, with Bart pulling ahead and her battling back. Fatigue became a factor, and Day's previously injured shoulder started to burn. She had no doubts about her stamina, but . . .

Suddenly, she smelled it: the unmistakable acrid aroma of UCE tobacco. Illegal as hell for over a hundred years, but making a comeback thanks to the No-Borders' smuggling. She sniffed again, risked a glance off the sphere. There, at the rear of the bar, she saw a door.

And Rupert, the cruelly beautiful man from the bar, was exiting through it.

Abruptly, Day stood. Behind her she heard the click of assorted weapons. Slowly she pulled her hands out of the controls and conceded the game. The move was accompanied by gasps, then the silence of the encroaching audience. She glanced at the field. Oh, hell—she'd been six slashes away from a possible win.

But, the law came first. "You win, lover," she called loudly. Then she leaned over and gave a thorough kiss to the shell-shocked Bart. Never let it be said a Mountie reneged on a bargain.

At the same time, her hand resting on his pressed into the nerves at his wrist, causing him to gasp in pain. His fingers would be powerful sore the next few minutes. She whispered, "Never give me bad info again. Or call me *chica*."

She released him, then slipped into the crowd, who swarmed around Bart with congratulations. On the far side of the back door, she paused in the empty hall and exercised the kinks from her wrists and fingers. Her shoulder felt like hell.

At least the caffeine was working her system. When her hands were limber, she drew her hat from her pocket, unfolded it, activated the nano-fed stiff, narrow brim, and then set it atop her head. Official at last. And back on track. To chase that UCE tobacco.

The tobacco law had been on the books for more than a hundred years, one of the first of the border laws. After the bioterror agents' release in Toronto, the hospitals and Health Canada were overwhelmed with caring for those victims. Health problems from optional behavior like smoking had seemed a luxury Canada couldn't afford, and UCE tobacco was banned. With each passing year since, the border laws had strengthened.

Day liked it that way, but even if she had other sympathies, she'd still be here. Agree with a law or not, a Mountie enforced it.

Cautiously, she advanced down the plush, cold passage, her cloud of breath leading the way. The tiled hall was lined with polymer sculptures and splotch art. The hall twisted past some rooms, none of which radiated that distinct nicotine odor, all of which were empty when she checked them. The hall doubled back before it ended at an exit. The odor was stronger there.

A sound from behind caught her attention. Footsteps? She paused, head cocked, listening and smelling, annoyed that her heart tripped against her ribs. All she could hear came from the bar she'd just left—music vibrations, talk, the ping of games. Must have been the echo of her boots.

That left outside.

The door opened smoothly and silently into a private courtyard. Used for clandestine trysts, she guessed, from the profusion of pornographic statues; the wire lovers twisted into Kama sutra contortions. A narrow tributary of Thunder Creek bisected the courtyard, and behind the thicket of trees lining the banks, she heard indistinct voices. She moved closer until she nudged against a pile of white boxes. Staying in the shadows, keeping one eye on the four men talking and smoking, she crouched down and opened one box. One sniff and taste of the dried leaf inside confirmed her guess. Prime UCE tobacco, ready for rolling and banned for over a hundred years.

This had just gone from a minor smoking bust and a few coins' fine to dealing. Still a misdemeanor, but the fines were heftier.

She wrapped a handful of leaves in her scarf, then pocketed it. The word of a Mountie was enough for a conviction, but a little physical evidence never hurt in case someone demanded an inquiry.

The murmur of conversation sharpened in front of her, but so far the four men hadn't spotted her. No weapons in hand, she noticed. It would take time for any of them to draw on her if they were so inclined. Most tobacco busts went smooth. You arrested the offenders; they paid their fine before the court, and that was it.

Still, she drew her weapon—the mere sight of a Distazer eliminated a lot of pointless bravado and resistance. Long, slow breaths, five of them, gave her oxygen and focus, as she visualized the action plan; then she straightened her hat firmly on her head and stood. The odor of burning tobacco stung her nose. She pressed back a cough and strode forward.

"Evening, gentlemen. That's an illegal substance you're smoking there. Lay down the cigs and put up your hands real slow."

"Shit, a Mountie," snarled one as they sprang apart.

What had happened to smooth surrender? Already this was off plan. Day laid down a line of warning fire, close enough to tingle the hairs on their arms. "Stop! Don't move, except to stretch 'em high. Last warning."

Halifaxing hell, they kept circling—and they were pulling out weapons! Training kicked in with the earlier caffeine. Ducking behind the nearest bush, Day blasted one in the sciatic, one in the shoulder before he could throw a lethal laser dagger. The dagger clattered uselessly to the ground. She got the third in the elbow, and he cursed as his arm flopped nerveless to his side.

A rustle of leaves sounded behind her. She whirled. Rupert! Must have heard her coming and circled. She dove, and the deadly beam aimed at her heart sliced a tree instead. Rolling behind a marble pedestal holding a six-foot glass phallus, she pulled her second Distazer, upped the power on both, and slashed with stunning fire, aiming for the sources of the cross fire that pinned her. She got one.

"Backup!" she called into her comm. "Five shooters in the Flash Point courtyard."

Three smokers and the unseen Rupert scrambled for cover, still armed and firing. The night crackled with silent energy blasts. The fourth smoker tossed the tobacco leaf boxes into Thunder Creek.

What were they doing out here? This misdemeanor bust had gone loco.

One smoker ate dirt, but she didn't bother to celebrate. That still left two shooters, plus Rupert, and they weren't taking turns coming after her. Panting, she spared a glance for her guns and swore. Half charged. There hadn't been enough sunlight to fully recharge the Graetzel cells earlier.

The sculpture above her shattered. Day ducked and rolled. Her hat protected her face, but glass shards sliced and stabbed her arms and nape. They threw off her aim, too, but she didn't stop firing blind into the night. All that kept her opponents back was her resistance.

An enemy blast hit her elbow, paralyzing her wrist and hand. Number-two gun dropped. Blood—her blood—

dripped onto the handle. Where had they moved? She held her fire. Sweat blinded her as she tried to see how the opponents were placed. Her sidearm beeped a low-power warning.

The fourth smoker finished dumping the leaf, then disappeared, probably circling around on her. The other two smokers had used her pause to creep forward. Before she could pick one off, a man burst into view. Lian, the bartender. Great, now she had a civilian to worry about.

"Get ba—" The warning died in her throat. This civilian was packing one of the sweetest-looking Distazers she'd ever seen.

Coolly, he picked off the closest smoker.

Fine-looking gun, and he knew how to use it.

"Day?" he called, ducking back behind the covering of trees.

He knew her name?

"You hurt?"

"Nah," and just to prove it, she took down the third smoker.

That left the leaf tosser and Rupert, who'd shattered the glass phallus and walloped the nerves in her arm.

Before she could shout a warning, Rupert shot at the bartender—who avoided being hit only by an athletic sideways leap. She got in one shot before her gun powered off, but it was enough to keep Rupert from finishing his attack. Day scrambled for her dropped gun, hoping it still had power, as the reckless Lian raced forward.

Rupert must have decided the odds were no longer in his favor, for she saw his shadow join his companion's in a race toward the rear of the courtyard. Day followed. From the corner of her eye she saw Lian run a quick perimeter, making sure the downed smokers were all still out of commission and wouldn't be launching sniper attacks; then he followed her out into the cold, still night of Moose Jaw.

They were both just in time to see Rupert and his companion disappear down into the ancient tunnels beneath the city.

"Stay here," she commanded Lian, the civilian. "You were lucky before; you could have gotten hurt. My RCMP backup will be here in a nano."

He nailed her with a hard glance, and for the first time she felt at a dangerous disadvantage. Bleeding, right hand still useless, shoulder on fire, one gun out of power . . .

"You were outmanned," he snarled. Then, squeezing through the opening in the wooden slats, he plunged down into the tunnels reputed to have once been a haven for smugglers.

Day scrambled in pursuit down the creaking wooden steps and into the first dirt-packed cellar. At the bottom, she choked back a cough. The tunnels—a labyrinth of dirt walls and storage cellars—smelled of mold, rat droppings, and disuse.

"I was bringing them down," she whispered to Lian's back, making a swift reconnoiter to be sure Rupert wasn't looking to ambush them from behind one of the barrels.

"Especially the one aiming for your heart." Lian scanned the other half of the room.

"I had a plan. Lian, get back topside. You're not authorized. You shouldn't be here—"

For a moment, his radiating fury was almost palpable; then the hardness in him morphed into a mocking grin. "Could you at least say thanks for speeding along your plan then?"

Fine-looking weapon, fine-looking man, she realized abruptly—and she'd bet he knew how to use the looks asset as well as the gun.

"Quarry went down here, Day," Lian said. Then he disappeared into one of the branching tunnels.

She turned on her narrow-beam light, before catching up to him in the narrow tunnel. Distazer pointing straight at his shoulder blade, she asked, "How'd you know my name was Day?"

"Day Daniels, I'm Lian Firebird." He glanced over his shoulder. "Point that Distazer somewhere useful. I'm your new partner."

Chapter Two

"Command doesn't partner Mounties with bartenders," Day hissed as Lian sprinted down the corridor in front of her. She knew she'd heard him right, but she didn't understand the scenario—and that she didn't like.

"I'm not a bartender." The thick walls of dirt absorbed his whispered answer.

"You knew how to make a proper caf blend, even to the wrist twist."

"So, the drink order was a test?"

"A small one." The scar on her back was a reminder of when she'd learned that lesson.

"Bartending put me through university," Lian explained.

"You're not a Mountie."

"You know them all?"

"Most of them." The Mounties were an elite, close-knit force. Between Trafalgar's years of service and her own rise through the ranks, she had a lot of contacts.

Their breathed conversation paused as they discovered

29

another cellar and spread apart to secure the area. Day ran her light across the hard-packed earth, looking for a clue as to which branching tunnel Rupert and the smoker had taken. Keeping her Distazer pointed Lian's way, she pressed her comm patch. "Data on Lian Firebird. Claims he's my partner," she whispered.

The answer came back swift. "Superintendent says Firebird's legit. He's on civilian assignment. Orders came from above; no more details handy."

"Thanks." She signed off. Legit, not leading her to a trap. And he knew how to handle a weapon. Other details could come later. She could handle this.

"That way." Lian pointed his light down one of the tunnels, then followed the beam.

"Why?"

In answer, he shone his light back for a second, illuminating the smudged tip of a fresh footprint in the dirt. Damn, she'd missed it.

She followed him, annoyed and not liking the fact that he was tall enough that he had to duck while the ceiling cleared her head by a good fifteen centimeters, and that by him leading down the narrow corridor his broad shoulders blocked her view.

"I asked a friend if I could take his shift when I heard you were coming in," Lian added suddenly. "Your reputation shines, but I wanted to see you in action. To judge for myself."

Another annoyance piled on. He'd been sizing her up, and she hadn't even realized it. Flicking her braid over her shoulder, she ran at his heels, trying to see beyond him, noticing offhand that the bunch and release of his muscled back revealed a man well used to physical activities.

This close, she realized something else. He smelled like fresh sage.

She'd always liked that aroma.

"You're crowding me," he growled.

"You're blocking my view."

"I don't like people breathing down my neck."

"I'm the law enforcement. I should be leading."

"Not in the tunnels."

"Protecting me? I don't need it."

"Protect a Mountie? Hell, no, why would I try that?"

His sarcasm was almost hidden. "You got some better excuse?"

He hesitated, then gave an annoyed grunt. "Because I'm claustrophobic."

"Halifaxing hell, why'd you come down to the tunnels?"

"It seemed the thing a partner would do."

"You're not my partner," she muttered, unconvinced. Civilian advisors were consulted for their specified technical expertise only. Mounties didn't *partner* with civilians. But she did move back a step or two.

Silence descended as they saved breath for the sprint and tuned ears for a sound of their quarry. Their focus narrowed to their endless race through the tunnels, an exhausting moment outside of time where each faint sound or brush of air set off another burst of adrenaline. At each tunnel branch, Lian unhesitatingly chose their route. Without her even voicing, "Why?" he pointed to some faint, obscure sign that he caught fractions before she did.

The man was a good tracker, one of the best she'd ever seen. Better than her, she hated to admit, and she was no slouch. She added that fact to her mental file on Lian Firebird.

The tunnel narrowed; the ceiling sloped down. Day and Lian hunched; then, as the dirt on four sides took on the dimensions of a coffin, they resorted to crawling. The air staled with unpleasant mildew, reminding her that this section had been closed since the Epidemic Years because of hysteria about killer fungi.

Her lungs grabbed for air, and her vision narrowed to the beam of light leading them. If she was feeling the closeness, this must be sheer hell for Lian.

"Are you okay?" she whispered.

"Fine," came his clipped reply.

" 'Cause I don't want you panicking down here, you being claustrophobic and all. Then I'd have to stun you, and frankly you're too damn big for me to relish hauling out of this fine tunnel we're crawling in."

To her relief, she heard him respond with an easy chuckle. "I'll try not to inconvenience you." A beat later, he added, "Thanks."

"Any time."

"You doing okay?"

"Absolutely."

In truth, her shoulder had gone beyond aching to no strength left, her right hand had got feeling back just in time to catch each cut from this rocky dirt, and the air reeked of something dead, causing her to swallow back a gag. Only now, with nothing but crawling and the man ahead for her mind to latch on to, did the miseries distract her. Her narrow light barely penetrated the thick, beneath-ground gloom, and only their laboring breath cut the oppressive silence. Altogether, chasing Rupert ranked down with the time she'd trailed a killer up a spawning salmon stream.

Except for Lian's presence. She reached forward with an urge to touch him, to assure herself that more than ghosts walked these corridors; to feel his warmth in this deathly chill.

She mastered the impulse. Instead, she catalogued what she knew about the enigmatic man in front of her. He had a compact, fully controlled way of moving with sleek mountain-lion-like muscles. His shiny, dark hair would brush past his shoulders if he didn't pull it back with a leather tie. He had a killer smile, nice neck, broad shoulders, and she liked the earrings. From his skin, she'd guess there was a high percentage of Native ancestry. No question that the man's physical package was appealing.

He'd been to university, he knew how to make a caf blend, and he was edgy in narrow spaces. Good start. However, the mettle of the man remained to be seen.

Other facts that popped to mind were disturbing. The Distazer fit his palm too easily for him to be strictly civilian. He'd had training. She should have guessed that from the nerve jabs in the bar. Maybe CSIS. He was a loner, too. An air of solitude clung to him like a fur coat.

All of a sudden, Lian stopped, and Day bumped into him. Shifting back, she asked, "What's wrong?"

"This drops into a storage facility." He vanished, head-first, into the blackness ahead.

Moving forward and looking down, she saw they'd reached tile and metal: the artifact storage area of the tunnel section open to the public. Lian was already prowling the room, Distazer ready. He spared her a quick glance as she shifted in the tunnel, then dropped down feet first the four meters into the room; but he said nothing.

The tunnels were reaching an end. Rupert would be heading to the surface soon.

Or waiting here.

That fast, Day's nerves focused and her mind clicked back to the danger at hand. She began swiftly securing the area. Tall shelves stocked with labeled boxes, barrels, and rolling cabinets that reached the ceiling cluttered the room. Soundlessly, she wove through them, listening.

"*Day.*" Her comm unit sounded, and she recognized the faint voice in her ear as Rich Tesler, one of the other inspectors assigned to the Moose Jaw Depot. "We've got your Flash Point smokers. What the hell happened? Where are you?"

"In the tunnels. We're near the tour sites."

"We?"

"Got a civilian with me. Don't ask."

"I'll send a surface unit over."

"Thanks. Got two gophers down here. If they pop up . . ." She gave a description, then signed off as she met Lian at the far side of the room. He shook his head, silently answering her unvoiced question. She gave back the all-clear, then pointed her light down the two tunnels branching off. Lian's answer was a shrug.

He hadn't a clue which way Rupert had gone either.

In unison, they flicked off their lamps, both listening for a sound, searching for a glimmer of light. A thud vibrated out of the left tunnel. Lights snapped on. Day took off at a run. Damn! Lian was in the lead again.

The tunnel was wider, taller, more cluttered. Pounding feet sounded above her pounding heart. Their quarry was close. She readied her Distazer, then sprang into the tour anteroom. Rupert and his pal disappeared up the stairs to the surface. Her shot just missed their retreating ankles. Rupert fired back. Day's tingling cheek nerves relayed that he'd come close to hitting her.

At the top, Lian kicked open the door. The lobby was vacant, the exit wide open. She raced outside, to the town square. It was almost empty this late at night—except for the new-model trek sled at the far side. Inside it, Rupert and his pal gave a jaunty wave. The sled fired up with a whine, then vanished down one of the streets off the square.

Day skidded to a halt, swearing. The sour taste of failure filled her mouth. The sled would be long gone before Command could get a fix on it with a tracing chopper. Still, she relayed the coordinates, then braced her hands on her knees, her frustrated gasps clouding the night. Her perspiration started to freeze in the cold.

She'd lost them.

Beside her, she heard Lian swear rather colorfully.

Mounties swarmed into the square, Distazers ready. "Raise 'em," shouted Rich.

She spun around. The Distazers were all pointed at Lian.

Not raising his hands, he glanced over at her. "You gonna tell them I'm your partner?"

Partner. She hesitated, stunned by the realization that during the entire chase with Lian, there had been a bone-deep, gut-sure awareness of exactly where he was, what he did. Instinctively, she'd known where he covered and that they had each other's back. Even after three years with Luc, there had never been that easy assurance; yet half an hour with Lian and they'd fallen seamlessly into the rhythm of search and sprint.

She frowned, not sure that was a good thing.

"Last chance," shouted Rich. "Hands up."

Lian nailed her with a steady glance, making no gesture of surrender.

Sorely tempted by the alternative, Day called out, "Stand down. He's with me."

But not for long. She activated her comm again, not caring that she was probably waking the assistant commissioner from a sound sleep.

"Sir, Day Daniels. I have a man here who claims—"

"Lian Firebird?"

An uneasy feeling that she wasn't going to clear this up as neatly as she wanted grabbed her throat. "Yes."

"Meet me at a holopanel in ten minutes. You'll have your orders then. Bring Firebird with you. And next time, Inspector Daniels, check your messages."

"Yes, sir." She switched off the communicator, then rotated slowly to find Lian watching her.

He lifted his brows. "Did the commissioner confirm—partner?"

"We're to confer with him in ten." She clenched her fists in frustration. "Who *are* you? You're not a Mountie."

"I'm a doctor."

She gave an annoyed grunt. "Most doctors I've met don't own a custom Distazer."

"You've never met a doctor like me." He paraphrased her earlier words.

"You're avoiding the question, Lian."

He held out his hand until she took it. "Health Canada," he answered succinctly.

The answer smacked her in the face, and she sucked in a breath. No wonder he'd shown the skill at shooting. And the craziness to head down the tunnels when he was claustrophobic. "Oh, hell. You're a plague hunter."

A Mountie partnering with a plague hunter? Not in this lifetime. Not unless commanded by a direct order from the Prime Minister herself.

Day Daniels was a summer tornado, Lian decided, as he sat by the Mountie Depot holopanel. An energetic whirlwind that ignored obstacles, scorched the air with her unconcealed passionate opinions, and touched down to create havoc for the unprepared. Even when all that force was directed against him, he had to admire it.

After his announcement, she'd dropped his hand as though she'd spotted hemorrhagic plague sores on it. The reaction surprised him not an iota, which was why he'd waited until they were out of danger to tell her.

Most people viewed plague hunters with, at the least, distrust and wariness. Anyone who chose to trek the breadth of Canada, searching for pockets of infection, armed only with vaccine, personal skill, and bravado had to have a bit of craziness in their makeup. Hunters enforced quarantine when necessary, using whatever means it took to prevent the spread of the deadly microbes. They isolated, treated, inoculated, comforted, and buried, while praying their own immunity held.

Sometimes it didn't.

He skated away from those thoughts, preferring instead to watch Day.

She was in a fine temper. After a quick debrief with the unit leader, she had promptly marched to the Mountie Command Depot, brushed off the multiple greetings, questions, and concerns of her fellow Mounties with promises of "later," and then located a holopanel. Now, they were sitting—well, he was sitting; she was pacing—in conference with her commanding officer. Once he'd confirmed Lian was her partner—not just backup, but an honest-to-God share-the-case partner—she'd started reciting the litany of why she didn't need him.

So far she'd gone through: Mounties worked independently, a partner was only for backup situations above a risk level five; he would slow her down, and her trek sled could only hold her and Benton.

He wondered what—or who—Benton was.

Nice package around the tornado, he admitted, stirring restlessly on his seat. He liked her curves and was getting curious about what her hair looked like outside that braid. The way she flicked it back or let it fall to her side or unconsciously wound the end around her finger made the braid as expressive of her mood as a cat's tail.

Short, vibrant, even her eyes—one hazel, one green—were intriguing. He'd studied her blood chemistry through a microscope. Fascinating as her antibodies and T-helper cells were, the woman attached to them was infinitely more so.

She braced her hands on the solid table in front of the panel. "Permission to speak privately, sir."

The commissioner glanced between them. Lian gave him a quick shake of the head.

"Permission denied. Whatever doubts you've got, Inspector Daniels, about this mission, about your partner, need to be out and dealt with."

Neither the rebuke nor the implacability went unnoticed. He thought she'd also caught his signal.

She straightened, stood at attention, her hat tucked at her side. "Very well, sir. Dr. Firebird is a plague hunter."

So, here came the core of her argument. Mounties and plague hunters were antagonistic rivals. Health Canada and the Royal Canadian Mounted Police were the best funded departments of the government, but they both vied for a bigger share of the pot. Not that he gave a rat's ass about such posturing, but there'd been some unpleasant incidents as a result.

Worse, from the Mountie point of view, whenever an infectious element entered any investigation, the Mounties were yanked off the case and Health Canada took immediate jurisdiction and control. Moreover, plague hunters worked by their own rules, outside Mountie authority. For their part, his fellow plague hunters considered the Mounties to be, as a rule, uptight law hounds.

By general consensus, mixing the two groups was like combining powerful bleach and pungent ammonia. Separate, each did their job. Together, the result was noxious and dangerous.

To his surprise, though, she didn't focus on his job. She nailed him directly.

"I checked our records before the link was established," she said. "Dr. Firebird has been involved in at least three known episodes of civil disturbance or infractions of the law." She ticked them off on her fingers, lifting her thumb first. "At the age of seventeen, he received a fine for trespassing and disturbing the peace."

"A freshman prank. The bird was fake," he murmured.

"It was All Hallow's Eve," she answered, still staring straight at her commanding officer. "He placed a raven in front of a rooftop spotlight, casting a huge, eerie shadow. Ten citizens were frightened enough to call us Mounties."

"Twenty told me they loved the atmosphere."

She continued to ignore him. "Two, he was arrested as part of a No-Borders demonstration."

"I don't apologize for my beliefs."

"Thirdly"—she took a deep breath—"he countermanded the order of a Mountie, and as a result, over a hundred people died."

Acid fury licked his veins at the memory and, much as he wanted, he couldn't pretend otherwise. "I was not going to move my patients. It was January, the height of snow gales. They couldn't survive the trek."

"The Mountie had established order and told the infected individuals to move to a quarantine camp. Dr. Firebird stopped the evacuation, and the virus spread through the entire village. Half the population died."

"Don't you think I know that!" He sprang to his feet. By the spirits, he could still smell the stench of vomit and blood, feel the fragile weight of an infant in his arms as the child gasped its final breath.

Coming between Day and the table, he forced her to turn. Even though she had to tilt her head to look up at him, her clear, mixed-color eyes didn't flinch a millimeter at his anger.

"That village was already dying." His words were clipped with the frustration of being too late. "The prodromal symptoms were widespread. By not wasting time with quarantine, by not killing people from exposure to the elements, I vaccinated those who had no signs of disease with temporary immunity and got a few of the natural survivors through the crisis." He might have saved a hundred, but each individual death had carved into his soul. He'd never gotten used to death, never accepted it.

"You *say* you saved them, but we'll never know what would have happened if you'd followed procedure."

"*I* know," he told her with soft, furious assurance.

"That Mountie *died* of the virus." Her jaw set. "For

known infections, the laws mandate quarantine."

"Hang the laws, when it means people die as a result!"

"Quarantine saves lives."

"Not this time."

A deathly silence fell between them as they glared at each other.

The commissioner cleared his throat. "So, Inspector, what is your point in all this? Those infractions are past history."

Day's gaze did not waver from Lian. "Sir, Firebird is not a Mountie. He has no respect for law. Moreover, he is a known associate of a group that, according to recent information, is behind the death of Constable Luc Robichaux. Can we trust him?"

Lian's hands fisted, and he crowded her close. "Do not question my honor or integrity, Inspector Daniels," he warned.

"I'll question anything that could interfere with my investigation." She didn't back away, didn't react by even so much as a blink.

"For the record, you've been assigned to *my* investigation. Exclusively. Not the other way around."

That did startle her. She spun to the holoimage of her commanding officer. "Sir? I can't drop my caseload on some Health Canada whim."

The commissioner coughed again. "Actually, his security clearance is higher than yours. When he requested you, I received orders to agree. Your other cases will be reassigned."

"He requested me? Why?"

"That information I don't have. This is coming from further up the chain of command."

She tossed her hat onto the table. Breathing heavily, she braced herself with white-knuckled fists. "I'm supposed to abandon my investigation into the murder of Constable Robichaux?"

"No," Lian answered. "That's now your only case, and everything the Mounties find comes to you."

"Dr. Firebird will explain everything to you," the commissioner said to Day. "You can use the secure conference room down the hall." He stood, a clear signal of dismissal as he tugged down his jacket sleeves. "Whether you like it or not, Inspector Daniels, you are hereby assigned to temporary duty in the Office of Viruses and Epidemics, Health Canada, and ordered to intersect your investigation into the death of Constable Robichaux with whatever Dr. Firebird's working on."

Day snapped to attention, retrieving her hat and tucking it beneath her arm. "Understood, sir."

The commissioner glanced at Lian, and Lian imagined he saw a measure of pity in the look. "Good luck."

The holoimage cut off, and they were left in a spartan room with two chairs and a table.

Day rounded on him. "Why?"

Lian rubbed the back of his neck. The weight of a long day pressed down on him. He'd learned to recognize the signs of exhaustion, in himself and in others. Right now, he could tell his mind wasn't processing as clearly as he'd like, and Day didn't look any better. She was massaging her shoulder, her face pale and her eyes red-rimmed with fatigue. She still stood stiff and straight, but she'd lost that edge of precision, her body was more pliant than earlier.

Pressing back a yawn, he held up a hand to stop further questions. "We'll talk more in the morning. Tonight, we're both too tired to be effective." And they would need every bit of strength they could muster. "Come to my office in Regina at nine."

"Mountie Command isn't secure?"

"Don't make assumptions. I won't bother to correct them again. There's something you need to see first."

"What?"

"The seeds of my investigation." If they were going to

41

have any hope of success, they had to work together, and that meant blasting her out of her antagonism and fast.

She hesitated, as though she were readying another question, but in the end she jammed her hat onto her head and said, "This had better be vital, Dr. Firebird."

"It is, Inspector Daniels."

As he followed her out of the command post, however, two disturbing sensations blindsided him.

Day Daniels smelled like maple sugar.

And, her braid brushing against her backside as she walked was entirely too enticing.

He rubbed a hand against the back of his neck. This was neither the time nor the woman for such thoughts. Yet, that night, even as he closed his eyes against the memory of that alluring sway of her hips, his body still felt the power of her feminine energy.

Chapter Three

Day arrived at Health Canada at precisely nine A.M., determined now that her temper had cooled to make this enforced unconventional partnership a success. Last night she'd knee-jerk reacted, an unworthy response born of the unofficial but pervasive Mountie attitude toward the plague hunters and her own childhood experiences with them. This morning, she was back in control.

She was a Mountie, one of the few privileged to claim that honor, and she would not fail her assigned duty, regardless of the obstacles. Be It All, Do It All wasn't always easy, but it was the code she lived by.

And, she had to admit, she was curious about what was behind this order.

Lian met her at the front door and saw her through security. He attached the requisite chip on her, his fingers brushing her pulse. The bright orange patch circling her wrist clearly labeled her a visitor. Its digital display began its countdown from 6:00 the moment she stepped through the last set of security doors.

"Six hours is the longest visitor chip available," he explained.

"Will we need more than that?"

"Unlikely."

"Good." She didn't relish the idea of sounding alarms and dropping security doors if she stayed past her allotted time. As he led her to his office, she glanced around. Few people got to see the inner workings of this building.

The Regina headquarters was up to the second in technology. The labs, the offices, even the halls bristled with equipment from nano-run analyzers to high-definition monitors to automated files of storage disks. Within what she assumed was a Level 4 isolation lab, a worker wore the blue, body-molded biohazard suit, the newest in protective gear. And the few people she saw, even Lian, each carried a cytokine aerosol at their waist, designed to stimulate an immune response against any known pathogen.

She rubbed her arms against a prickle of unease. What exactly did they store in all those isolation labs?

The carpeting absorbed their footsteps, but the mostly empty halls echoed back their voices. Despite the inner high-tech, this building shell was a relic. Erected before the first virus release, the extra space was for a time when the population had not been sliced in half, when people weren't wary of congregating, and when workers came to a central location instead of business being sent to home offices and field posts. The wooden doors, the paintings on the walls, the case of Health Canada–sponsored team trophies—all needing polish—gave this whole area a faintly quaint air. Ironic, considering that the department was the most advanced and well funded in the Dominion of Tri-Canada government.

Lian stopped at none of the labs or offices, although he acknowledged the greetings of the few people they passed. Instead, he led her up two flights of stairs, to an out-of-the-way office, which required a retina scan and fingerprint-tapped code to open.

Extra security in an already secure building for what was—she glanced around inside as he locked the door behind them—in essence a very crowded lab suite?

A lab suite with some decidedly odd notes. Not only were there the requisite computers and data dots, but Lian also seemed to actually like reading on paper; she saw several neat stacks of books. A lot was shoved in here, but it was all tidy and organized, even the rows of plants at the two large windows. Their thick foliage looked healthy, without a single dead leaf. Between the windows were glass doors, which led outside to a balcony and a three-foot fir tree.

Despite the clutter and the paper, however, there was a fresh scent about the room, like early morning sage. In the corner, water trickled down a rock fountain, adding the undertones of nature to the hum of technology.

Day strolled over to the wall of glass and the rows of plants. Outside the opened windows was a clear view of the waters of Wascana Lake, right at an overgrown spot where few visited. She pulled in a breath of fresh cold air. "Nice view."

"That's why I asked for this office. The glass."

"I gathered it wasn't for the convenience to the lunch room."

"It also gets a lot of sunshine. Good for the plants."

"What are you growing?"

"This is angelica." He touched a feathery flower, then pointed to a long stem lined with tiny green leaves. "That's astragalus. Both are immune boosters and anti-inflammatory agents."

"These all have healing properties?"

"Yes. Mostly anti-infectives or immune stimulants, my area of expertise. I've found them useful adjuncts to the cytokine aerosols, plasmids, and vaccines."

She stroked the velvety petal of one. "Where did you learn so much about medicinal plants?"

"From our shaman."

So, she was right about there being some Native blood in him. "Which Nation are you from?"

"None for the past seven years."

"That's not what I asked."

"I know." With a lithe movement, he closed the window, effectively sealing them in the closed room, standing so near to her that she could see his eyes were as gray as a winter morning storm, without a fleck of warming gold in their depths. She smelled the traces of wood soap that lingered on his skin.

Despite the illusion of intimacy, the "don't pry" message was clearly given and clearly understood.

Not that she had any intention of obeying.

This close, Lian radiated heat and male strength, but then she'd noticed that in the tunnels. She wondered if he was deliberately using his size to crowd her. If so, the effort was a failed one. A lot of people made the mistake of thinking that being short made her vulnerable. She always figured it meant she could get into all kinds of places closed off to others.

"You come any closer, you'll be stepping on my toes," she told him.

He gave her an easy grin, the one she'd seen in the bar when he'd offered to meet her off duty. "Don't intimidate easy, do you, Day?"

"Nope, Lian." She noticed he'd already slipped into using her first name. Fine by her, since she rarely remembered to use titles. "Growing up with a frontier Mountie was good training. I spent the night on the prairie when I was seven, faced a grizzly when I was ten, and danced a regimental ball when I was fourteen. You don't scare me."

"No?"

She got the distinct impression that maybe she'd said

too much, that somehow she'd just issued a challenge. Uneasily, she ran a hand down her braid, smoothing the errant ends that had escaped, before she caught herself. Talking straightforward did sometimes get her into trouble.

The tension dispelled, however, when he strode back to his desk.

"If I don't scare you," he continued, "maybe this will." First, he wiped his hands with a lemon-scented gel. A disinfectant or a protective? Or both? With an economic motion that said he knew where every last vial and piece of paper in this office was, he pulled a clear biobag from one drawer and a small, flat device from another. He held out the bag toward her.

Inside the filmy plastic was a bloodstained hat. She swallowed hard, not needing to scan the identifying code in the corner, to know whose hat it was or where the evidence came from. The rush of memory of the victim—lying in his own blood, his throat slashed from behind—swamped her, and her fingers dug hard into her palms, trading one pain for another more understandable and manageable. She'd bagged that hat herself, right after she'd handed off those kids on the moose. Luc Robichaux. Her partner, killed one month ago.

"What are you doing with Robichaux's hat? It's criminal evidence."

"You know that anything with possible biocontamination is turned over to our labs. I'm analyzing everything connected with that incident."

"It wasn't an 'incident,' " she said tightly. "It was a killing—of a good Mountie and a better man."

"I know. I'm sorry." For a moment, she thought he reached out, as though he might touch her shoulder, might offer a moment of comforting contact, but in the end he only said, "I'm analyzing all the evidence in the murder of Luc Robichaux."

He held up a flat device. "Do you know what this is?"

When she shook her head, he said, "Lab on a chip, we call it. It does field analysis."

He unsealed the bag, took out the hat, then pulled a thin filament from the lab chip. He touched it to the fabric. Seconds later, red lights began flashing a programmed sequence.

"What did it find?" She leaned forward.

"Smallpox."

"What?" Day leaped backward, unable to control the quivering of her stomach. "Hell in Halifax, what do you think you're doing? Putting it in the open air!"

"This room is sealed."

"Yeah, and we're in it."

"What's here is dried DNA fragments only. Not infectious."

"You're sure of that?"

He gave her an annoyed glance, as he put the hat back in the biobag and resealed it. "I wouldn't be stupid enough to take it out of the bag, or to keep it in my office, if I weren't."

She sat back, partially mollified. After all, it was his health at risk, too. "We've got smallpox here?"

As she said it aloud like that, the implications suddenly hit her.

Smallpox. The mere word grabbed her chest in an unrelenting vise. "My God," she whispered, barely able to speak. "We beat it. *We beat it.* Tri-Canada's been pathogen-free for two months." She paused. "Are you saying Luc Robichaux was infected with smallpox?"

"No. The DNA wasn't in his blood; it contaminated his hat."

"Another pocket's been found?" she asked. "One vestige we missed?"

Lian shook his head. "The DNA fragments don't match the recorded signatures of the released virus. This is something new."

This is something new. The bald statement was a punch to the throat. Hard and terrifying. Stealing breath and carrying pain.

A new virus. A new epidemic.

Could Tri-Canada survive the renewed horror?

As Day visibly pulled herself together, her back stiffening, her jaw firming, a fraction of Lian's tension diminished. His new partner had courage.

Partner. The word felt odd to say. Plague hunting was solitary work, and he'd been alone much before that. Partnership wasn't a concept that sat well on him.

Yet, with Day, it was a word he found himself imagining with some pleasure.

"How did the hat get contaminated?" Good, she'd started questioning, rather than panicking and fleeing. Her commitment to her duty didn't surprise him, not with what he knew about her. Without that core of strength, he wouldn't have risked letting her know.

"That's something I'm hoping you can help me with," he admitted. As she mulled that over, he decided that if he must have a partner, Day Daniels had all the necessary attributes—plus a few unnecessary but desirable ones. A day ago, he wouldn't have listed sweet curves and a tantalizing maple scent among his criteria.

They'd suddenly become essential.

"I'm not sure there's a new threat," he said, forcing himself back to work. "At the time of his death, Luc Robichaux had contact with a new strain of smallpox—that much I know. It's been a month since the exposure, but there are no reported outbreaks, well past the incubation period, so the virus hasn't infected anyone. Yet."

"Could an outbreak be hidden?"

"Not in Canada. Smallpox is highly contagious. Infection would spread, and we would detect it. So, I don't think he contacted active virus." He ran a hand across the back of his neck, feeling the frustration of knowing all the pieces didn't fit. "Our detection systems are so good, I'd have said the DNA fragments were an anomaly, that he'd picked them up from some artifact that once belonged to a victim—except for one fact."

"It wasn't a known strain."

He nodded. "So, did he contact a strain that we missed fingerprinting? Did one of the old strains mutate?"

"Or has someone, somewhere, developed a new strain?" Day concluded softly, a shudder running across her shoulders. "And if so, what are they planning to do with it?"

"Exactly."

The word flopped between them like a dead salmon. Lian saw her cheeks pale, and she swallowed hard. Shadows crossed her eyes, darkness like the one he had lived with since the lab chip had first lit up. Biting regret dried his throat. If only he could have saved her this knowledge, this fear.

He reached out, touched her wrist at the same place where he'd attached her visitor patch, finding comfort in her steady, if accelerated, pulse.

"We'll stop this, Lian." Her dual-hued eyes met him direct, while she laid her hand atop his. For three heartbeats they were in unity, then she sat back, releasing him and their moment of accord.

"Can you work with a Germ Junkie, Day?" he asked, deliberately using one of the pejoratives leveled against his peers.

"Can you work with a Stiff Brim?" she countered.

"I'd have preferred to work alone," he answered honestly, "but I knew the Mounties would raise a stink if I took away the investigation into the murder of one of their own. I'd have met obstacles every step."

"You could have pulled strings to get that information."

"Another layer of people questioning why I'm interested, and I'd have wondered what they weren't telling me."

She tilted her head toward the hidden biobag. "How many people know about this?"

"Me. The prime minister. The director of Health Canada. The RCMP commissioner. Now you." The fewer who knew, the lesser chance of a leak setting off renewed panic.

"Why me?"

"I wanted the Mounties' best officer."

"I appreciate the compliment, but what makes you think that's me?"

He leaned his chair back and rested his foot against the desk. "Edgar Whirlwind told me."

"The Cree Shaman?"

He nodded. "We've studied together. He said you single-handedly rescued his granddaughter when some BC Bud dealers who wanted to grow mj on their ancestral lands kidnapped her. He gives you his highest compliment, calls you a *winyan shungmanitu,* a woman both strong and wise. When the Mounties put you as lead in the death of Luc Robichaux, that only confirmed Edgar's assessment for me."

"How so?"

"Normally you'd be off the case, since Robichaux was your backup that night. But RCMP would want the best investigating this murder. They thought that was you. Besides, you have something else I want."

"What's that?" Absently, she rubbed her shoulder.

"Your blood. Those vials you donate to Health Canada every month. Sweetest little swarm of antibodies and T-helpers I've ever seen."

"Now that's a new line. Most men fall for my charming smile."

"I haven't seen one," he said softly.

She stopped rubbing her shoulder and threw him a sideways glance, laced with suspicion. That quick, the air around them charged as his gaze locked with hers. Tension slipped into awareness; a tingling that had not been there

51

before now filled the space between them. The inexplicable urge to see her smile floored him. Charming, inviting, mocking, teasing—he didn't even care which.

"Is smiling on duty against the law?" he asked.

"No. You just need to give me a reason. Instead of irritating me."

"Like this?" He circled the desk, closing in on her. He saw wariness build in her narrowed eyes and smelled the hint of heat in her.

When he was within a handspan of her, he reached behind her and snapped off a few leaves from three of the plants. He folded them into a piece of paper, then put the bundle in her palm and wrapped her fingers around it.

His large hand surrounded her smaller one, and with that simple, inconsequential touch, an unwanted surge of desire gut-punched him. Her hand wasn't dainty; there was strength in the tapering fingers, but also an incongruous, utter femininity in the polished nails. Sweet scent, sleek hair, curves, smooth skin, a touch of freckles on her nose— each detail assailed him. Involuntarily his fingers tightened around hers, compelled by the urge to keep her close.

Deep in his bones and sinew, he felt so much more of her. The hitch of her breath. The pulse of her life. Every piece seemed so *right*. Only the spreading empathic ache in his shoulder brought back his common sense. Again, he forced himself to release her, then shoved his hands into his pockets. Touching her was too dangerous. Definitely not part of the "partner" scenario.

"Boil those leaves in two liters of water," he said, "then let it set overnight before straining out the leaves. Drink the water over the next twenty-four hours. It will help your shoulder."

She blinked as though she'd been touched by the same insanity and jerked down her hovering hand. "What do you know about my shoulder?"

"I saw you rubbing it. You dislocated it a month ago, and those injuries take time to fully heal." *Remember why she's here. Remember your job.* He unlocked another cabinet and handed her a data dot.

"What's this?"

"My case notes. I'm putting you in charge of our investigation."

"Everything? You'll follow my lead, my directions?"

"No." He perched at the edge of his desk, keeping a safe distance. "You'd expect me to stay in the lab and push the data around. Nope, I'm at your side every step of the way. We share data; we share decisions. Except, anything with the virus, with medical matters, you defer to me."

"So far, this is not sounding much like Day being in charge."

"My expertise is rooting out viruses, not criminals."

A hint of smile twinkled in her eye. "In other words, you're out of leads and you want mine."

"Yes."

She chuckled at his utter disgust with being stymied, and a moment later he joined her. "You're a trained investigator. You've got to have something I don't," he admitted.

"Robichaux was investigating the No-Borders."

"You suspect the No-Borders are behind the murder?"

"Yes. They're planning something, something big enough that they're willing to kill to keep it secret. Do you think that could be a new virus?" She swallowed hard again. "They can be ruthless, but—"

He knew that feeling, the one that snuck up and knocked you off your skates with sheer horror. How could anyone be that ruthless? So devoid of humanity? Nightmare scenarios had plagued him ever since he'd seen that blip on the lab chip.

"But a new virus would slam the borders shut forever." He finished her thought. "Them releasing a virus doesn't make any sense."

"The No-Borders are tied in somewhere. I feel it in my gut. They've grown bolder and more violent."

"Because the ex-pats have taken control." No-Borders were a diverse group, with individual reasons for wanting the borders opened. The most vocal, and most militant, though, were the ex-pats. Expatriates. Descendants of foreign nationals stranded in Canada when the borders slammed shut.

"Maybe they plan to twist the epidemic," Day mused. " 'We've smuggled in serum. If the borders are open, we could get more?' Or, 'Open our borders unless you want to see more of our virus stockpile?' " She wound the end of her braid around her finger. "Insanity, but who knows how they think?" Abruptly her restless fingers stilled, and she looked up at him.

"*You* do," she said flatly. "You were part of them. I have to ask, Lian . . ."

"Fair enough," he said after a moment. He couldn't have her always questioning his decisions, or this partnership was already doomed. "Ask once, and I'll answer you honestly."

"Are you a No-Border? Do you still sympathize with their aims? Could you bring them to justice, even if one of them is your friend?"

Good. Questions he could answer. "I am not a No-Border. I belonged to the group once, but I quit after that demonstration. I sympathized with their goal; I still do. The borders *should* be opened." He held up his hand as she started to speak. "We can debate the issue all you want later. Right now, I'm answering you. I'm no longer a part of them because I abhor their fanaticism. Too often, it led to useless violence. If one of them killed that Mountie or is planning to unleash that virus, it would not matter if he was my best friend or she was my sister; I would do everything in my power to stop them."

"Would you turn a blind eye to their smuggling?"

"Smuggling isn't my concern."

"It's one of mine," she said softly. "Just so we understand each other. I'm charged with upholding the law. I honor that responsibility, and I won't ignore it. Mounties wield a lot of power, but we use it to bring peace and stability. Our duty is to create order out of chaos, and that is essential to this country." She paused a moment, then her lips gave a rueful twist. "Damn, I sound like a recruiting holo, don't I?"

"I was hearing strains of 'O, Canada,' there. Do what you must, Day, as long as your duty doesn't hamper stopping this virus."

"Cooperation's a joint effort, Lian. Make sure your actions don't impede my bringing Luc Robichaux's killer to justice. If you interfere with my official duties there, I will charge you. Do we understand each other?"

"Your focus stays on our mission?"

She nodded. "Yes. Stop a virus and a murderer."

He measured her closely. Day meant every word she said, but her love for Canada was unshakable. Her priority would be this threat. Still . . . "You never answered my question. Can you partner with a plague hunter?"

She tucked the packet of leaves in her coat pocket, then, to his relief, held out her hand. Day would have followed the commissioner's orders with precision, he knew, but she had to trust him, as thoroughly as she trusted another Mountie, for them to work together as efficiently as necessary. Agreeing to be his partner was the first step.

"Lian Firebird," she said, "you've got yourself a partner."

He took her hand, ignoring the surge of emotions stemming from the touch, and gave it a brief shake, sealing their necessary pact. Then, he leaned back. "What's our next step, Inspector?"

"I read over your data then set up a few appointments."

"Anyone you meet with, I'm with you."

"I've been interviewing sources for over four years without help."

"You haven't been dealing with possible microbial contamination at the same time."

She hesitated, then nodded. "I'll get another interrogation of those smokers we nabbed last night. Likely they're No-Borders; they might turn sniggler for reduced jail time. Otherwise, firing on a Mountie puts them away until arthritis sets in." She stood, settling her hat on her head. "I'll send you my notes on Luc Robichaux. If you still have contacts at the No-Borders who might be willing to talk to us, now's the time to use them. Daily comm updates—"

"No, face-to-face. We can't risk a comm interception."

"Then we'll meet for drinks. Tomorrow night. Eighteen hundred hours. Black Badger Tavern in Moose Jaw."

After the rush of orders Day fell silent, and Lian walked her back to security. He retrieved the visitor patch, being careful not to let his fingertips brush against her soft skin. Her mind had been still cataloguing and planning, he decided, for she turned to him at the door.

"One other thing, Lian. Find out what you can about the Shinooks and their leader, Jem. Where they might be. What they're up to. Word is, they're in deep with this." With that, she made a neat pivot and exited.

Leaving him with a palm flat against the window and a hard knot in his gut.

Jem and the Shinooks? What did they have to do with this? He shook his head. *Ah, hell, this has just gotten complicated.*

Chapter Four

Despite Lian's directive to turn all her cases over to other officers immediately, Day had one duty she refused to delegate. This court appearance was too important.

She waited in the musty courtroom for the verdict, while dust motes danced in an afternoon sunbeam and the nearly abandoned building was wrapped in graveyard silence. Solemnly, she stood before the judge's bench, her spine straight, her feet spread. Her hat was tucked beneath her arm, as neatly as her emotions tucked beneath her calm veneer.

Although arrest by a Mountie was a legal conviction of guilt, and Mounties had sentencing authority—two legal streamlines dating from the epidemic rioting—there were safeguards in the system to prevent abuse. One was the rigid screening, training, and oversight procedures for the RCMP, so only the best men and women were allowed to wear the hat and badge. Another was a conviction trial, like this one. Any citizen so judged had the right to challenge their arrest or assigned punishment.

Few did, for they risked further severe penalties for a frivolous suit if they lost.

On the other hand, not all conviction trials upheld the arrest. Criminals were released. Like this man. A border scofflaw and a child pornographer who created the filth he'd smuggled out. Twice, with his connections and wealth, he'd slipped out of a conviction.

That's when she'd been called to investigate, and she'd made sure her case was airtight.

From the corner of her eye she watched the prisoner who'd challenged her. After two reprieves, he now thought himself immune to justice. He'd adopted a casual pose, straightening the sleeves of his silk jacket as though growing impatient. Her stomach churned at his arrogance, but Day kept her face carefully neutral. The guard standing behind the prisoner, however, was not so stoic. Both his distaste for the man and his sympathy for Day were evident.

Obviously, the guard, like the prisoner, expected her to lose.

Day straightened her shoulders as a red border appeared around the judge's holoimage. The jury had reached a decision. The judge studied it a moment, and Day's stomached tightened. She'd done everything right, but juries weren't always predictable. The judge closed his handheld, the snap of it clear even across the holoimage, and stared into the distant courtroom.

"Conviction upheld! Sentence upheld!" The judge slapped his open hand down on the sensor panel, sealing his decision with his palm print and the sound of an electronic gavel. The holopanels of the jurists winked out, their decision rendered.

Yes! Day's fingers curled, the only outward sign of her jubilation. *That slimetoad of a child pornographer would be spending the remainder of his years locked away.*

The well-dressed prisoner slowly pivoted to face her, his

face white. The subtle aroma of his expensive cologne crossed the narrow space between them. "You self-righteous bitch," he hissed. "Nobody dares send me to prison."

"I do," she returned softly.

"Return this man to his cell," added the judge, satisfaction lacing his command.

A panic swept across the previously haughty prisoner's face, as though he suddenly realized what the judgment meant. This trial had been his last chance to slither out from justice, but she'd closed all the exits.

Before the guard could snap on his stasis restraints, with a growl the prisoner lunged toward her, his manicured fingertips like steel rods aiming toward her throat. Day countered with a swift twist, grabbed his clammy wrists and stopped him. Her fingers tight around him, one thumb pressed against his arm nerves. She met his raw snarl with a steady gaze. Only when the guard—between apologies for the incident—had the prisoner's restraints back on, did she release her grip.

As the dirtbag was hustled off, Day's heart tapped a joyous beat. Many of her fellow officers disliked this literal throwback to the concept that every accused had a right to face his accuser, this required appearance in a physical courtroom during the final decision phase of a conviction trial. Not her. This was the most satisfying part of a successful trial: knowing you'd done your job right and kept scum off the street.

The prisoner snarled one final, futile insult. "Poker-assed stiff brim. I'll get you; I got friends."

The guard ushered him out, and the thud of the door silenced him.

Not anymore, she thought. His kind of friends didn't stick around for someone facing a life sentence.

"Nice job, Inspector," the judge said, drawing her attention back to the bench.

"Thank you, sir."

"He's wiggled out of two previous charges. I think your thoroughness surprised him."

She settled her hat on her head. "We don't have many arrests overturned."

"The RCMP knows how to do their jobs," agreed the judge. "And I, for one, am glad of it. Good evening," With that his holoimage winked out.

Her comm patch crackled. "All right, Day!" her colleague, Rich Tesler, crowed in her ear. The whole Depot listened, silent, as a conviction trial was in progress. "Congratulations!"

"Thanks."

"Your record stands," added another. "Not a single conviction overturned. Damn, Daniels, you're good."

"Damn right I am." Grinning, she pivoted and realized she wasn't alone like she'd thought. In the furthest corner, in the shadows, sat a woman holding the hand of a young boy, about eight. One of the slimetoad's victims.

Day touched her comm patch. "You all owe me a beer. I'll be in tomorrow to collect." Then she turned off the comm and her smile faded. She joined the mother and son, Taj.

Sitting down on the bench beside them, she nodded a silent greeting. "You came to the trial?"

"He wanted to see," the mother said, her hand resting on her son's shoulder. "He had to be sure."

"Can he get out?" Taj asked.

Day shook her head, her throat aching at the fear still shadowing the boy's eyes. "No. Lifetime imprisonment, and he can't challenge the court's final decision."

The boy stared at her, his gaze steady, then nodded. "Good." Without another word, he tugged his mother's hand, and they walked out.

Watching, them, Day remembered when she'd first seen Taj during the case. He'd been pale and thin, drawn from chronic insomnia, but it was his eyes she'd remembered most. They'd never stopped moving, never stopped searching for a threat. Now, some of that vigilance had left him.

She never hid the fact she was ambitious, nor that she was proud of her work. She had a stellar conviction record, and she cherished the accolades she'd received. But, in the end, that wasn't why she did what she did.

She did it for nights like this one, where one small boy walked home feeling safer.

The M'Experience provided a range of entertainments. Some were even legitimate, like the virtual reality racing, holoconcerts, interactive surround vids, and exotic techbars. Registered prostitutes and gourmet chefs listed their specialties, while the perfumery provided a sample whiff with the push of a button.

Lian stood in the misty, featureless anteroom and pretended to ponder his choices listed on the vid panel. He frowned for the surveillance eyes, then tapped a code on the unobtrusive pad to the side. The screen flickered and faded. For a moment he feared the No-Border key might be too old for acceptance; then the screen reappeared.

With a few select extra choices. Any mood-altering substance desired, legal or smuggled, was available for a price. The gambling parlor was active. Kinkier sex options of the nonhuman or nonpainless variety also made the list. Lian scanned the tamer options. The latest lounge sensation, Ahanu, performed in 360-degree holo. The fact that the singer was across the border in the UCE, and thus technically banned for import even as a mere holoimage, had not dimmed his popularity.

Lian selected Ahanu, visual mode, front.

Would you like a companion? asked the screen.

The companion he suddenly desired listening to Ahanu was not someone he could ever bring here. She'd be too busy arresting half the staff. Briefly, he considered fash-

ioning her holoimage to share the concert, then abandoned
the idea without regret. No holo could adequately capture
the vibrant essence of Day Daniels, her unique scent, her
stiff spine and wispy braid.

No, he pressed.

Instead, he added a snifter of French brandy. Associating
with Day, he figured it might be his last taste of the smuggled drink for some time. And the concert didn't start for
another forty minutes. He gave his bank chip for the cashier scan, and a soft chime told him when payment was
accepted.

Scanning for weapons, read the screen. *Do not move.*
The faint heat of the radiation scan faded before the chemical sniffer finished vibrating across his skin. When all the
scans were completed, another soft chime sounded. *Clear.*

The spongy gray walls of the anteroom shimmered and
undulated, then a hole spread in one. Music filtered from
the opening, and the aroma of sweetened lavender, scientifically designed for a mellow mood, beckoned him in.
Several tables dotted the area, each occupied by a visual
mode viewer. Many more would be enjoying the performance in nonvisual—unseen by the performer and the rest
of the audience—he knew. He wended his way through
the room. Although the occupied tables were all holoimages, with the audience spread across the world, it was
still considered rude to walk through one and destroy the
illusion. His table was slightly to the side, but still in the
front row. The brandy snifter awaited him. Along with two
chairs.

He'd barely taken his seat and a taste of the brandy when
he felt the prick of a stinger on his ribs.

"Didn't take you long, Falon," he said mildly, not moving. The exotic musk of her perfume was signature enough,
even if he hadn't been expecting her.

"You've got nerve, coming here and using that code."

She swung around and straddled the second chair, keeping her stinger jabbed against his ribs.

"Your security accepted it. And my credit." Falon hadn't changed much. A fuzz of black hair, skull tattoo at the throat, hard athletic body. Personality even harder.

Without lowering her weapon, she pressed a button on her wrist comm. "Add to tomorrow's calendar: Update access codes, starting with the fifth level," she dictated, then released the button. "What are you doing here?"

"Waiting for the Ahanu performance. This is his only venue in Regina."

She gave a snort of disbelief.

"I'm hoping to meet him," he tacked on for good measure. Might as well sow the seeds.

"Never took you for the groupie type."

"I like to compliment skill." He nodded to the stinger. "Put that down and we'll talk. You should know you don't need it with me."

Her thumb upped the power on the stinger and sent him a quick charge. He forced himself not to flinch at the jab of pain, but couldn't stop the residual quiver in his fingers.

"You always were too upright," she said. "I don't trust a man with a conscience; never know when it might kick in."

"Upright? Never been called that before." He forced a low laugh.

"Upright, that's you." She propped one boot on the chair rung, and the stinger relaxed off his ribs. "So, what are we talking about? Don't try to convince me you've changed your mind and want to rejoin the movement. You made your opinions clear at that last demonstration. I always knew you didn't have the heart to kill."

"Must be the medical training," he said easily, shifting imperceptibly to put a few more millimeters between him and her weapon. Falon was twitchy; he'd seen her fire before thinking, and he didn't relish being on the receiving end of a precipitous shot. "I want information. Who killed Luc Robichaux? And why?"

Her cruel smile at the question told him she knew a lot more than she would ever say. "Why would you think I'd know?"

"Because not much happens with the No-Borders that you don't hear about."

"Question two: If I did know, why would I rat out a brother?"

"You're canny enough to know that killing a Mountie isn't smart. Tends to galvanize the RCMP, and they are well equipped and relentless. Any hint you're connected, this very lucrative business is shut down."

"You going to give them that hint?"

"Not if I find out what I need."

She gave him a steady look. "Empty threat, Firebird. Not your style. Besides, you skirt the law, same as me. And you want the borders opened, even if you don't agree with our methods."

"Update your data dots," he murmured. "You might find a few changes."

"No matter, it's an internal matter. We'll handle it and give the Mounties something to close the case with."

"More believable if it comes from me."

Her eyes narrowed. "What's your angle on this? Why do you care?"

He braced his elbows on his thighs, shifting farther away from her. His fingers stopped tingling, and he flexed them. "A woman. Why else?"

She laughed, then, loud enough to attract the attention of the audience, their holotables still winking into the tableau as the starting time neared. Mindful of listening ears, she lowered her voice again, though humor still laced her words. "So, it *was* you who helped that Mountie last night. Lian Firebird in bed with a stiff brim. Hell, next thing you know they'll be announcing the Rockies are free of snow. Tell me, is she that rigid—"

"Don't finish that," he interrupted softly. "Falon, I'll make this real simple." With lethal speed, he whipped out his dagger. Before she could twitch, he had her stinger on the floor, his foot covering the weapon, and his blade pricking her throat. His other hand clamped on her arm, holding her still.

She swore. "Hell, you've gotten fast."

"This is a carbon tube dagger. Hardest substance known to science. Sharp, too." A tiny twist drew out a delicate line of her blood. "And totally undetectable by your security."

"What do you want?"

"Told you. Give me leads to Luc Robichaux's killer, and I'll be grateful enough to tell you how to scan for these. Cross me . . ." He traced another line of blood.

"You don't scare me." The lie sounded in the breath of her bravado. "You won't kill me."

"I don't have to kill to get my message across." He waited a heartbeat, then touched the dagger to her trigeminal nerve. Her jaw slackened from the pain, and the residual stimulation of the optic nerve took her left eyesight for a second.

"Agreed," she choked out. "And I'm changing my mind about the upright part."

"Thought you might." Another flick of the wrist, and he pocketed the knife so seamlessly no one even realized he'd drawn it.

"You've changed, Firebird. Not just speed, you were never this hard."

"Talk. The performance is about to start."

"I'll expect that scanning data by tomorrow." She touched a finger to her blood, licked it off, then cast him a speculative glance. Her look this time held something darker and more inviting.

He ignored it.

"There's a faction within the No-Borders not content with the molasses pace of progress. They aim to speed things up. Killing the Mountie was stupid, but he got too close to something they're planning. They're dangerous."

If Falon thought they were dangerous . . . "Who are they?"

"Not a chance, Firebird. I'll give you one name, though; he's not a No-Border. Rupert Juneau. He was there last night."

Rupert from the bar. The man he and Day had chased. "Who is he?"

"UCE," she answered, enjoying his surprise. "He maintains the UCE's cold plasma grid. Their head man on the system. He's been helpful in the past, enjoys a spot of smuggling on the side. Claims to oppose official UCE policies and want the border opened. He knows all the words. Spouts the rhetoric of the Shadow Voice and says the UCE will deport him to Australia if they catch him."

"You don't trust him." Otherwise, she'd never give up the name.

"Nope. I think he's playing a deeper game than he's letting on. Our faction believes they're using him. I think it's the other way around."

"What's their big plan?"

"I haven't asked." The sound of fear proved her honesty.

"Anyone who might be getting second thoughts? Be willing to talk?"

"If I knew someone, I'd shoot them before they betrayed us." The lights dimmed in the lounge. "Show's starting. Unless you'd prefer to meet me in one of the rooms for old times' sake."

"There are no old times between us, Falon."

"Your loss. Thought you might want some hot memories instead of a stiff brim pucker." She was gone before he could reply.

Probably knew she wouldn't like his answer. He had no regrets about not sleeping with her. Falon was pure poison when she put her mind to it.

The last overhead light faded out, leaving the room in darkness except for a thin emergency strip at the floor. A soft, slow drumbeat sounded at the edge of hearing, surrounding the audience with a barely discerned pulse. One beat at a time, the rhythm picked up pace and volume and complexity. Red lights danced across the ceiling in time to the drum, and the white swirling mist inside the spherical table lights began to glow. Lian picked up the snifter of brandy, savored another sip, then leaned forward, illuminating his face with the glowing orb.

Brilliant white light flashed on the stage, accompanied by a surge of heat and wind and deafening drum. Suddenly, Ahanu appeared in the middle of blackness—all six feet seven, 350 pounds, swirling dreadlocked bit of him. For one beat, his glance darted toward Lian's table, and he gave a nearly imperceptible nod. Then, he began twirling and singing his recent hit: "*Je me suis égaré, Cowichan.*"

Brandy still lingering on his tongue, Lian settled back to enjoy the show.

Ahanu created a show that was part song, part cultural dance, part sensory overload, all exciting and a rare pleasure. Relaxed by the fine brandy, stimulated by the encounter, Lian returned home directly afterward. He set his alarms and privacy scans, then turned on the holoreceiver and sat cross-legged on the floor, waiting for the comm to beep.

He waited only ten minutes.

Without warning, a massive man strode out of the communication wall. He'd taken off his stage costume, but the red breeches, feathered vest, and beaded hair were as colorful. Powerful in looks, despite the holoimage's shimmer, and more powerful in the numbers who followed him, Ahanu Soaring Eagle appeared every inch the leader he was, and nothing like the lounge singer he professed to be. Lian had always wondered how his cousin pulled off the deception, for the UCE was fervent in their hunt for subversives and revolutionaries. Bribes, probably. The casino was extremely lucrative, and as son to the chief of the Shinook tribes in Montana, on the other side of the closed border, Ahanu could access those funds.

He'd met Ahanu only once in person, when he'd undertaken a taxing vision quest across the Rockies, then by kayak down to UCE lands. In that one meeting, though, they had formed bonds beyond blood. Lian stood to meet him.

Ahanu reached out both hands, then pulled back. "Damned holo. Too real-looking, not real enough in what matters. You've been too long a stranger, my cousin."

"I can't return, yet."

"Bah, close-minded Canadian Shinook."

Lian smiled. Though they were relations, there was still a measure of rivalry between their two branches of the Nation.

"You were always welcome with us." Ahanu jerked his head, sending his dreadlocks flying.

"My promise holds for all the Nation," Lian said softly, the ache in his chest catching his breath. "But, the end nears."

"You never answered my last message."

"I've been preoccupied." In truth, even this small reminder of all he'd given up was difficult. "I always knew of your talent, but if I'd realized what a spectacular show you put on, I would have come sooner."

"Thank you." Ahanu pulled a fur rug into view and also sat, his shrewd glance telling he saw the evasion but chose not to challenge it. "The end nears? Does that mean you're coming home?"

"I hope." Unless this new threat turned his desires moot.

"I have some questions, but I'm asking as plague hunter, not cousin."

Ahanu stilled, then turned and reached out of sight. A moment later, he rejoined Lian, his face blank. "My privacy walls are up. I assume yours are, too."

"Yes. The Freedom Fighters. And the Shadow Voice. You're still leader of the Western movement?"

The world's dissidents were called by many names: No-Borders in Canada, Shadow Runners in Asia, Freedom Fighters in the UCE. All though, it seemed, had found a common, unifying banner in the recent call of the mysterious Shadow Voice, the Voice of Freedom.

"Our numbers grow daily. As the Voice says, the actions of the UCE government are no longer the will of the people. We will restore democracy and our freedom. Then we will open the borders once more to our brothers and sisters in the north."

Lian raised his hands. "You don't have to convince me."

Ahanu closed his eyes. "I know. But, sometimes the task seems impossible."

"Do they suspect you?"

"Who suspects a hedonistic wastrel?" He spread his hands, a gesture of innocence.

"Anyone with the sense to really look at you."

"I'm as safe as you are."

"That may not be of comfort to your mother." Lian leaned forward. "Do you know a man named Rupert Juneau? Is he one of your members?"

"I know him, but he's not one of us. In the past, he assisted us, but his price got too high."

"Would you trust any operation he had part of?"

Ahanu snorted. "I would sooner sleep with a coyote. Why?"

"Heard he's planning something with our No-Borders, but anyone who knows what isn't talking. Or is dead. Is your group part of this?"

"No. At least that's one thing we agree on. The No-Borders are Canuck *loco*." He grinned. "Ironic twist on our mutual history, no, when even we rebels think Canadians are too violent? We have heard the same rumor, though, rumblings that they plan to blast open the borders."

"Blast? Literally or figuratively?"

Ahanu shrugged.

The next question was more problematic. "How about the Shinooks? Word is they, and Jem, might be involved. Could there be any truth?"

"The Shinooks here are not. Your blood relations . . . ? I don't think so, but our contact's limited. The UCE has increased their vigilance because of this new Voice of Freedom." Ahanu rubbed his face, suddenly looking tired. "The council of elders stand firm in their isolation. Your brother, Yves, remains impulsive and stubborn, but he cares too much for the people to risk association with the No-Borders. Hakan has taken his seat on the council, but grows impatient that he is often overruled. But I believe he, too, would hesitate to trust outside the Nation. They are the two leaders of the younger blood."

"Thank you. You've confirmed my thoughts." Lian stood, knowing they couldn't risk a longer transmission. Soon, the walls of the room would be blank, the vibrant colors of Ahanu gone. Lost to him as his other relations had been for so long. The inside of his throat ached, and when he lifted his hand he found his fingers trembled. "I have missed you, my cousin."

Ahanu rose, and the holoimage of his hand joined with Lian's, their fingertips blending together. "As I have missed you. May the Voice of Freedom's wishes be fulfilled. May our borders once more be opened and our nation united. Then we shall share fire and meat in the ancient ways."

"May the spirits will it." For one dizzying moment, Lian could almost believe they touched, could believe that

Ahanu gripped his hand with affection and rough pressure. Then, Ahanu stepped back and vanished.

Lian slowly lowered his hand, his fist clenching. At least with Ahanu's confirmation that the Shinook were not involved with Juneau and the No-Borders, he could keep his secret and steer Day away in good conscience. For if she knew who he was, she would insist he lead her to them—and that he could not do.

Seven years ago, the elders had given him a terrible choice. If he fought the plagues with Health Canada, he would go into exile. They would not risk further contamination—either of culture or health. Those of Shinook blood, they said, must be loyal first and only to the Shinook. They did not realize that for any to be safe, all must be safe. They did not understand that his healing skills had to be shared with all of Canada.

Because he understood their fears and accepted their traditions, he'd done as they asked: he'd gone into exile. And he'd given his solemn oath: when next he returned to the Nation, the plague hunter, the non-Shinook, the man of Health Canada, would be banished.

The haunting bars of a flute melody broke through his thoughts. The brief stanza signaled a new message on his handheld. Other messages he checked when he had time; these rare flute-heralded messages he answered at once, for they were from the few Shinook who could access a handheld and would dare contact him.

The message was from his sister Aveline. Her holoimage stood before him, her long, dark hair so glossy that he could almost smell her shampoo. Did she still use the berry-scented one she'd favored as a child? Probably not.

She carried her small son, Perren. Lian reached out, aching to run his hand across the downy head and snuggle the child against his heart. He'd never held his nephew, never seen the boy beyond their infrequent comms.

"Greetings, brother," Aveline said, smiling. "Are they

71

true? The rumors I've heard? That the prime minister is to announce Canada is free of those bioterror microbes? You can come home!"

"Yes," he answered, choking on the single word, though she could not hear him.

With Canada near the landmark announcement that the lingering spores of virulent anthrax, the last of the released bioterror microbes, were eliminated, he stood on the threshold of ending his exile. After the announcement, he could resign his commission with Health Canada, his task completed, and he could return home. His ears could almost hear once again the crackle of the communal fire, while his arms ached for the embrace of his brother and sister and nephew.

Aveline began chatting, giving him news of his people and sharing the events of her day, tidbits that maintained his bonds to his family. She finished with, "Perren's blessing ceremony will come next spring, and he will need a man to stand with him. Will you accept that honor, my brother?"

Stunned, Lian backed the message up, making sure he had heard her right. He had. She was asking him to accept the responsibilities and privileges of a father for Perren.

He swallowed hard, nearly undone by a flood of longing for his family. He had missed so much, had left so much undone.

Only after moments did he regain his composure and record his return message, ending with his answer to her request. "If I am with you then, I would be honored to hold Perren at his blessing ceremony. And more privileged to guide him in the ways of a *wichasha*. Except, this is the right of the natural father. Aveline, you know that. When I return, I will raise the question again, and you can no longer ignore me."

He sent the message, then sat back, thinking. One of his first responsibilities when he returned would be to discover

Perren's father. Not an easy task. It was someone outside the Nation, he believed, for none had come forward to accept responsibility, and Aveline had always been one who roamed far and chafed at restrictions.

There would be other difficulties in his return, too; he didn't doubt that. He was not the same man he'd been when he left.

His people had changed as well. Aveline had been a gangly adolescent when he'd left; now his sister had a son, a child old enough to crawl. Yves, his brother, a serious youth then, was one of the emerging leaders. Lian let out a long breath. The bonds between him and his brother had been stretched too thin; he could only hope they were able to be repaired.

A fire of anticipation lit in his belly. For seven years he'd done what he must. Now, the long-awaited end was in tantalizing sight, an end he'd begun to doubt would ever come. He could only hope the day was not too late to repair his isolated spirit.

There was one more task to finish. One. He had to prove this virus came from an external source, that it wasn't still part of the original epidemic, and he had to stop any scourge from being released.

As Lian padded through his silent, spartan home, each step took him further from the brief moments of community his sister's message had brought. The remote solitude, which had been his only companion all these years, descended once again.

Chapter Five

Day caught up with Rich Tesler at the Moose Jaw Depot. Since she had been reassigned exclusively to the Robichaux case and Lian's investigation, Rich had taken over as point on the smokers of two nights ago.

"How did the interrogation go? They give up anything new?"

"A bust." Rich rubbed a hand against the back of his neck, frustrated. "They claim they were told to pick up the tobacco and take it to a drop in Car Town. We got the address and are checking it out now, but they don't know where the delivery source was. They refuse to name who gave them the order. Either they don't know more, or they aren't talking. With the lie detectors in place, I'm leaning toward ignorance. What about the civilian you were with last night? Is he a lead? Scuttlebutt says he's Health Canada." Distaste laced his voice. "A lab lordling bureaucrat."

Day hesitated, glancing up at the blond, bear-sized man walking beside her, tempted to confide in him. She and Rich went back a long ways. Although he was several years older, they'd graduated from Cadet Training together. He'd gotten that slashing scar on his cheek during a shared case. They'd flirted with the idea of becoming lovers—by any logical reckoning they made an ideal couple. Rich was a Mountie, and everything else Day admired in a man. They had strong bonds—respect, admiration, ease—but they'd never taken their relationship past friendship.

They both knew, instinctively, they were missing a key ingredient necessary for a love affair: passion.

Like that clutch-in-your-chest, fire-in-your-nerves sensation she'd gotten when Lian touched her?

She trusted Rich as much as she trusted anyone. Unfortunately, protocol forbade sharing details on a need-to-know case like Lian had thrown at her.

"He's a civilian adviser," she said at last.

"Can't talk about the intersection with Robichaux's death?"

"Sorry, orders."

"Hey, I understand," he answered easily.

And the truth of the matter was, she knew he did understand. He'd been in the same position before with her. A warm companionship settled between them as they strode through the familiar halls of the depot.

Rich lowered his voice. "Rumor has it, Day, you're up for promotion to Grade-one inspector. If you solve Robichaux's case."

She stopped, stared at him, heart stuck in her throat. When it came to squadron politics, Rich kept his ear to the ground a lot better than she did. "Are you sure?"

"As sure as anyone can be about rumors."

Clenching her fists inside her pockets, she pushed back the surge of excitement. G-1! Few Mounties reached that level. G-1 meant the most exciting, most complex, most difficult cases. Because of his responsibilities to her, not even Trafalgar, her father, had made that honor.

"Don't let this civilian adviser distract you," Rich

warned. "They always think their field is most important. They don't understand Mounties and our priorities."

Unfortunately the threat of an unleashed virus was more than a simple distraction. She forced her voice to calm. "I know my duty, Rich. I'm not going to fail." On Robichaux's murder, or on stopping that virus.

He clamped a hand on her shoulder. "I have faith in you, Day. Just think, you'll be the youngest G-1 on the force. So, Ms. On-Her-Way-to-the-Top, you got time to join us at the Black Badger? Lavinia's coming. I thought this might cheer her up a bit."

"What's wrong?" A single parent with a daughter approaching adolescence, Rich had his hands full.

"Some guy she likes asked her best friend to a dance. Maybe you could talk to her? She likes you. What am I supposed to say? Men are scum?"

"Sounds more believable if it comes from a woman. Sure, I'll talk to her, although I don't know if it will help. I'm meeting Lian, Dr. Firebird, there at six. Time enough to talk to Lavinia *and* beat you in a game of darts."

"In your dreams, Daniels. Oh, by the way, one strange thing. That crazy Rupert who was firing at you? His name isn't matching in any database."

"That's odd." Most Canadian citizens were DNA-typed and name-registered at birth. True, a few slipped through—home births, AIN families who refused the registry, others—but the anomaly was enough to prick Day's instincts. Rupert shifted from the status of sidebar to investigative point, although he was still in Rich's domain. "You might grab an image from the surveillance eyes at Flash Point. Circulate that, too."

"Good idea. Thanks. What's wrong?" he added as she began patting her coat.

Day frowned. "I can't find my gloves."

"Those ratty things? Good riddance, I'd say."

"Trafalgar gave them to me when I graduated." She checked her pockets again irritated. Damn, but she hated to lose something. "I'll meet you at the tavern. I think I left them on the desk," she said abruptly, leaving Rich to return back the way she'd come.

She found the red gloves where they'd fallen to the floor, beside her desk. "Eureka," she crowed, fitting them to her hands. Complete at last.

As she went to join Rich, she couldn't contain the tiny fillip of excitement. G-1. She was up for a G-1!

Lian strode through the lit streets to his rendezvous with Day. The Black Badger Tavern was a rare entity in Canada: a restaurant where people gathered to eat instead of taking the food home. The best one-kilo bison burgers in Moose Jaw, and a location directly across the street from the Mountie depot, made it a popular spot for after-duty Mounties to relax.

He paused in the doorway, letting his eyes adjust as his gaze unerringly located Day. She was in a corner with a group of Mounties—no mistaking the stiff-brimmed hats lining the table—and their families. Several relaxed with pints, while Day played a very old-fashioned game of darts, dangerous pointed tips and all. Standing on the mark, she studied her target. She threw her missile, then punched her fist as her dart hit just outside the bull's-eye. "Halifax!"

Her opponent, a girl that looked about twelve, jumped to her feet. "I won!"

Day slapped the child's upraised palm. "Beat me by a point, Lavinia. Good game."

"Want a rematch?"

"Maybe another day. I've got to rest my arm." Day gave a laugh, slapping palms with her companions, their silent watchfulness of a few seconds prior vanished.

She was utterly at ease with these Mountie friends.

These were not just work colleagues, but the people of her heart, Lian realized, shoving his cold hands into his pockets.

Just as the Shinooks were his. A yearning for all the lost hours and unshared small moments lodged in his hollow chest. Once the exile ended, could he forge again the common bonds with his people? Bonds such as these Day shared with her Mounties? Or was it too late? Had remote solitude become his unshakable lot?

A hulky blond he recognized from the other night—Rich she'd called him—hugged her. "Thanks, Day. Lavinia'll remember this as the night she beat you in darts."

Day drilled the man with a steady look. "She beat me square. I don't play to lose."

Rich hugged her again, closer, and Lian's jaw clenched against an unwelcome wash of possessiveness. He had no rights to it, where Day was concerned, but the startling power was undeniable as he joined her.

She was finishing her mug of beer; her laughter faded as she caught sight of him. The wisp of emotion this time was a chilling withdrawal. He thought he'd grown calloused to being a symbol of potential horrors, but somehow Day awakened the old pain.

"Are you ready?" he asked quietly, retreating beneath the plague hunter's dispassionate veneer.

"Oh, yeah, sure. Is it eighteen hundred? I wasn't paying attention to my chronometer."

The blonde, one hand still resting on Day's shoulder, held out his other. "Hi. Inspector Rich Tesler."

"Dr. Lian Firebird." He shook, briefly, not enjoying being surrounded by Tesler's suspicion. "I'm sharing a case with Day."

"Doctor? You work in a lab?"

"No."

"Which branch of government are you from?"

"I didn't say I was with the government. Day?" He turned to her, ignoring Tesler's frown.

"It's all right, Rich." Day waved off her companions, then gestured to a table in the back. "We can talk there."

After they sat and placed their orders, she leaned forward. "I have an appointment tomorrow in Winnipeg. A scavenger named Scree. I've been told he trades with the No-Borders. You can meet me there at five—"

"We'll go together."

"My sled only holds two, and Benton's going with me."

The mysterious Benton again. The man had better be younger than eighteen or older than fifty if he was going with them. "My sled holds three. I'll pick you up."

"Acceptable." She paused while the waitress brought their food, then sprinkled vinegar on the chips before she popped one in her mouth. "Did you learn anything from your No-Border contact?"

"One fact, but I don't know if it fits in anywhere. The guy from the bar last night. He's Rupert Juneau, UCE citizen and chief engineer for the cold plasma power grid."

Her breath escaped in a hiss. "No wonder we didn't have him on our registry. This investigation's got more layers than an onion." She bit off the conversation, then stiffened as she pressed a hand to the comm patch near her ear. From the corner of his eye, Lian saw the collection of Mounties in the corner sit up in alert.

"What is it?" he asked.

"Expat No-Borders torched a cold-plasma factory in protest against the border barrier. Disturbance spreading. All available Mounties—"

He clamped a hand around her wrist as she surged upward, stopping her.

"What the hell, Lian?" she spat, jerked to a halt.

"Day, don't—"

"Go? I will not ignore a general call."

"You are assigned to Health Canada. Not the Mounties."

She twisted her arm, but luckily he'd caught her off balance with a nerve press, and she couldn't break free. Yet. Likely she had a few moves waiting.

One-handed, she flicked a small Distazer from her pocket. "Let go."

Moves like that one. "When you stop reacting."

Rich paused in his race out the door. "Got a problem, Day?"

"Nothing I can't handle." She didn't take her eyes off Lian. "Dr. Firebird and I are working out the specifics of our partnership. Go, I'll see you there."

When Rich left, she said softly, "Don't interfere with my duty, Lian."

"Right now, your only duties are to stop that virus and find Robichaux's killer. Moreover, you're a hyperimmune. Your blood could be our only source for the antibody template against a deadly virus. You can't take the unnecessary risk."

"Risks are part of the job. Supporting my fellow officers is not unnecessary. I'm off duty, so it's my choice." She leveled the Distazer. "This is on stun, but you're still going to have a big headache. I won't give a second warning. Let me go."

She was going to hate him for this. "Inspector Daniels, stand down!" he snapped, relentless. "You were assigned to *my* case by the Royal Canadian Mounted Police commissioner. You were informed of my security clearance. This is a matter of national health. Therefore, I am your superior officer in this, even if you are off duty. Stand down. That is a direct order."

Her glare could have added inches to the taiga permafrost. Her jaw worked, as if against a bitter taste, before she shoved the Distazer into its holster. "Understood. Sir."

When he let go of her wrist, she straightened and tucked her hat beneath her arm. Looking centimeters above his head, she asked, "Do you have any further orders? Sir."

He pressed his thumb to the bill, paying for the meal they wouldn't get a chance to finish. "Where's the disturbance?"

Her glance flew back to him. "We're going in?"

"No, we're looking for casualties. As a team. Not you harrowing off alone into the middle of a melee."

"Damn it, Lian, why didn't you say that instead of shackling me?" She flipped back her braid, threw on her coat, then settled her hat on her head.

"Because you weren't stopping long enough to listen."

"This partnership will be a lot more genial," she tossed over her shoulder as she raced out the door, pulling on a pair of well-worn red gloves, "if you're not interfering and issuing direct orders."

"Works better if you're not pulling a Distazer on me, too." And it would work perfectly if she wasn't so desperate to race off into danger. "I told you before, Daniels, don't make assumptions."

"Understood. Just don't get to stifling me."

He didn't answer. Because he was aiming to keep her and her antibodies safe—even if it meant stifling her, lying, or breaking the law.

Smoke filled the streets of Moose Jaw, mixing with the vaporous breaths of Mounties as they contained the No-Borders mayhem and cleared the area. Body-heat sensors, nano-derived sniffers, and a tracing copter identified the injured and rooted out the pockets of disorder. Day choked back both frustration and a cough, still fuming as she scrambled with Lian across a rubble of brick and concrete, then scooted beneath a gaping chain fence into Car Town. She should be with *them,* her fellow Mounties, not off on the sidelines searching between an ancient Corolla and a rusting Civic for a wounded No-Border who'd showed up on the sensors.

Despite knowing she was under direct orders, despite knowing the wisdom of not leaving an enemy, even an injured one, at your back, she didn't like it. She'd be more effective someplace other than this eerie junkyard.

Her jaw ached from clenching back anger, and from the nerve jab Lian had laid on her. This team concept needed some work.

"Here he is." Lian knelt down beside the injured No-Border, whose body sprawled at an awkward angle.

Day spared the victim a quick glance, then a longer one. God, he was just a kid, couldn't be more than seventeen. He barely had fuzz on his cheeks. How could one scrawny pipsqueak have so much blood to lose?

She crouched down beside Lian, who had begun an efficient process of repairs. "How is he?"

"He'll live. Now. He would have bled out from that abdominal wound if he hadn't been found on the scan."

Was this what Canada had survived for? Fighting teenagers? She reached out to smooth his hair back.

"Don't touch anything," Lian commanded. "Unless you've got biogear on. I haven't taken the time to scan this blood for contaminants."

She snatched her hand back. Damn, she knew that. But with her hyperimmune system, she sometimes forgot strict precautions. "Sorry. Can I help?"

"I've got it. Just make sure no one's taking potshots at my back."

That was her role tonight. Protection. She pushed to her feet. This place gave her the creeps. All these useless, abandoned autos, their empty wheel shafts poking out like used lollipop sticks. Unlike the nanobottom trek sleds, these relics required tires, and large stockpiles of rubber had been depleted by the embargo.

She prowled restlessly through the surrounding cars. An Ultima balanced precariously atop a Silverado, until the force wave of a nearby pressure cannon set it rocking. It settled down with a screech of metal on metal. Glancing to Lian, she saw he hadn't reacted to the disturbing noise. His focus was on his patient, on stanching the flow of blood.

She'd gained respect for his abilities tonight. His battlefield skill had saved more than one of her colleagues. She'd also seen, though he kept it hidden beneath efficiency, how much he despised traumatic death. Lian Firebird might lack social skills, but he cared about his patients.

Which didn't mean she wasn't still annoyed with him. It just made her a little more willing to listen.

Slipping between cars and making brief forays into side alleys, she kept an eye out for trouble. Some things in life were inevitable. Death. Hockey mania. Health taxes. Tears. Muggings here in Car Town. But Lian and his patient were eminently protectable.

Although the smoke was less visible here, her eyes still stung from the irritants released by the burning cold plasma factory, and remnants of ionized plasma gas charged the air, making the hairs on her arm stand up and her skin prickle. An explosion cracked behind her, and she spun to face the new threat—an old street lamp shattering in a shower of sparks. Cold plasma wreaked havoc on electricity.

A stray thought nagged her. Car Town. The tobacco shipment the other night had been due for delivery somewhere around here. She pulled up the address on her handheld. One block over. Crime-scene techs had done tag and bag on location, but it wouldn't hurt to have a look around. Since she was in the vicinity and all.

After Lian and his patient were evacked. She stiffened with an unexpected stab of alarm. She'd been out of sight for a minute, an eternity for Car Town's mole swarms.

She raced back, without hard evidence, but knowing somehow Lian was in trouble.

"Day—" His voice sounded in her ear, over the comm.

"On my way."

"Be fast." The whine of a Distazer raged behind him.

She swore. The moles had found them. Heart pounding against her self-rebuke, she flew across the broken pavement. "Situation?"

"Brought down one. Three left. One north, northwest. One east. Lost sight of the third. 'Tailheads. Hopped up on something. Sweating, despite it being colder than a reindeer shed out here. Twitchy. If I could see the eyes, I'd lay odds to miosis."

"Translate, Doc."

"Pinprick pupils. Narcotics. Feeling no pain." He swore. "Think the third's above me, but I can't see him."

She pulled up just before she burst around the corner, and peered around a panel truck for a quick reconnoiter. Lian, firing his Distazer one-handed because he was holding a bandage to the patient with the other. Two thugs as described. The third . . . ?

She swung around the truck and fired. The third goon tumbled off the semi behind Lian, landing unconscious on the ground.

If she hadn't been here, if she'd been off with the Mounties, Lian could have died. A terrifying thought. One she didn't have time to examine why it scared her stiff.

"Royal Canadian Mounted Police." she shouted, running forward, giving the others their single warning. "Put down your weapons."

The two surprised muggers spun.

"Hell, she's just a compact stiff brim," sneered one.

His partner, who was aiming a Distazer, didn't get a chance to say anything. Day shot him in the forehead, knocking him out. The sneering one tossed down his weapon. Damn, but she would have liked to give him a headache, too. If only for the "compact stiff brim" comment.

"Are you okay?" she asked Lian as she sealed nanorestraints around the muggers.

"We're fine. Evac's on its way. Thanks for the timely shooting."

"You're welcome." Of course, if she hadn't picked the wrong direction to start her search, she could have taken care of those moles before he ever got into trouble.

The evacuation sleds closed in on them. Day waited until Lian was busy settling his patient in the trek sled before she slid down the street and out of sight.

"Damn it, Day, where are you going?" Lian's tight voice called over her comm. So, he had been aware of her every move.

"I'm taking a look at that tobacco drop point. I'll catch a later evac sled."

"You are not—"

"Just reconnoitering." She turned off her comm before she heard the direct order to desist. Seconds later, she turned it back on. She wasn't stupid enough to be out here without comm. Fortunately, Lian wasn't still issuing orders.

The decaying building reeked of mold and nitro fumes used for picking up latents. She swallowed against a dry throat and cast her light around. The single room, probably serving for storage once, had been picked clean by the techs. Still, sometimes evidence cropped up later. Coffin-like silence surrounded her as she checked the barren room, examining crannies. Nothing popped out at her; no hackles of instinct rose. Another bust. She'd read the tech reports for details.

She turned to leave, when a distant pressure-cannon shock vibrated across the floor. Her light beam quivered, swiping across a glint of metal wedged by the baseboard. A bead, she discovered when she crouched down and played her light across it. She bagged it for the techs, then examined it more closely.

Unusual. The bead was about five centimeters and formed of copper and jade. Into the minerals was etched the shape of a leaf. Or maybe it was supposed to be a wing. She couldn't tell. She pocketed the bead, then exited—

—to find Lian waiting for her, Distazer hanging loose from his fingertips and face cold. "The last evac sled's waiting for you," was all he said.

"Didn't you go with your patient?"

"The emergency doc took him. I came for my partner."

She had no reason for feeling guilty about this, and she would not let him lay that mantle on her. "I was not in danger here; I knew what I was doing." She pressed her lips together, refusing any further explanations or excuses. He had to stop dictating how she did her job.

Chapter Six

Day took a sip of her morning tea, then reached down to scratch behind Benton's ears. "Lian Firebird is more than a lawless plague hunter," she told the silver-tipped wolf stretched at her side. He gave an agreeable yip and turned his head so she could reach a new spot. Absently rubbing his fur, she stared at the screen of her handheld.

Don't make assumptions. After seeing him in action last night, she'd taken Lian's advice, digging deeper and wider into the enigmatic man who'd become her partner—and had found some fascinating, challenging tidbits along the way.

Nothing direct. No early biographical data, which in itself was unusual. A lot of records had been lost in the Post Plague years, but Lian was young enough that there should be records of his birth. Unless he had traditional AIN parents, who kept their own registry. She assumed he was Cree, since he'd studied with Edgar Whirlwind, and the Cree were independent as the Shinook.

What little she found had been through indirect association. For example, that second infraction she'd unearthed: For participating in an illegal No-Borders demonstration turned ugly, he'd been arrested and sent to jail. There he'd served a two-month sentence. End of report.

More illuminating were the facts she'd unearthed from the weekly prison logs. He'd been the only detainee sent to that prison in two weeks. The facility had been under quarantine because of an unexplained infectious outbreak. Six weeks after Lian's arrival, the warden announced they'd found the source. They arrested a guard, an asymptomatic carrier who meted out his own form of justice by infecting inmates.

No mention was made of Lian, but she knew in her gut he'd been sent there to investigate.

Her chest squeezed tight at the thought: A claustrophobic plague hunter who'd agreed to incarceration in order to save lives. Prisoners' lives. Definitely crazy.

Or a man of deep compassion.

She closed her eyes against a dizzying spin, as she admitted an unwelcome truth. He was also a man who awakened a strange recklessness inside her, who called to the wild child she had once been.

The front bell rang, startling her. Too early for Lian, and who else would appear in person instead of vidding first? And at—she consulted her internal chronometer—six in the morning? Benton gave a low growl as he padded next to her toward the door. The wolf wasn't any happier with the unexpected visitor than she was.

She pulled her Distazer from its charger, then checked the viewer. A postal courier. Cautiously, she opened the door. Benton, guarding her ankles, raised his hackles, and a low growl rumbled from the back of his throat—his usual response to anyone he didn't know.

The courier gave a nervous swallow, his gaze darting to the wolf. "Day Daniels?"

"That's me."

The courier dragged his stare from Benton. "I have a package for you." He thrust forward a small bundle.

"Who's it from?"

"Some chap named Trafalgar Daniels."

Her father. "Do I need to register receipt?"

"Here."

A moment later, she was holding the sealed package and the courier was zooming away. Eagerly, Day pressed a thumb across the seal, and the outer wrap opened. Out tumbled two small carved owls and a note. With a cry, Day scooped up the owls, her thumb rubbing against their smooth cedar. After all these years, she finally had them back.

All these years. The past rose up with aching clarity. These owls and the wolf pup were all she'd had in those blanked days between when the last person died in the quarantine camp where she was born and when Trafalgar Daniels had found her.

To this day, she still had no idea how long she had been there, praying to join the others so she wouldn't be alone, scared that God might actually agree to her wish. She remembered snippets. Eating the last scrap of bread. Drinking stagnant water. Nights of cold and days of filth. But she'd been six, with a child's conception of time, and an exact reckoning was lost to the past.

Then, the man with the stiff-brimmed hat had come. Trafalgar Daniels had adopted her, given her a name and a loving home, where people didn't die of strange sores and bloody coughs. He'd given her the Mounties, and she'd had a family again.

Except when they'd readied to leave the quarantine camp, she couldn't find the owls. She'd torn the place apart looking for them. Trafalgar had to drag her screaming and hysterical from the camp. Eventually she'd quieted, but she'd never forgotten.

She placed the two tiny owls on her workstation shelf,

giving them a final pat. Where had they been?

"You won't be lost again," she whispered. Then, she turned her attention to the note, written in Trafalgar's nearly illegible scrawl. She'd never been able to convince him to use a comm unit, a message disk, or even a carbon filament pencil for the nanoreaders.

Discovered the owls tucked away in a side pocket of my old kit bag, the note began. *Remember when you fussed so at losing them?* There was some smudging on the paper, as though he'd tried to erase something. Or a drop of sweat or a tear had smeared the words. It ended: *I've been hearing of suspicious goings-on in the mountains north of Jasper. Could be an invasion force in training. Or a clandestine lab. But I'm thinking it's them expat No-Borders. Might be important to that case you're investigating. We need to compare notes. If you're ever passing by the neighborhood, stop in. Yrs truly, Trafalgar. P.S. Heard you're up for a G-1 promotion. Wouldn't that be a fine event? I'm so proud of you, Day.*

For a moment, she chuckled. Trafalgar lived in Wood Buffalo, on the shore of the floodwaters that had buried the old Nunavut and Northwest Territories. Except for the strip of the Yukon leading to Alaska, Wood Buffalo was the northernmost tip of Tri-Canada. Nobody was ever just "passing by the neighborhood" at Wood Buffalo.

Still, it had been too long since she'd been up to see him. Not in . . . she counted back. Three months. Had it been that long? That he didn't keep a handheld or a holopanel or even a comm unit made no excuse for her lack of attention. Nor did the fact that the TransCanada Connect didn't go that far north have any bearing, since a good trek sled made the journey in a couple of days.

Of course, she could never count on Trafalgar to be there if she did come. Not the way he wandered the country. Still, he might be there now. She glanced at the note again. It was unlike him to ask to see her; he must be worried. Trafalgar's paranoias were legendary among the Mounties, but she'd learned that too many of them contained enough truth to dismiss. She'd head up tomorrow, after her appointment with Scree.

Decision made, she sat back and finished the last of her tea. Then, with dread, she eyed the filled glass next to her tea mug. She'd been skeptical of Lian's herbal remedy, had tried it only because he'd seemed knowledgeable and her shoulder ached last night. The brew had helped, she admitted, giving her shoulder a test shrug. Too bad the stuff tasted so nasty.

She held her breath, downed the last of the medicinal brew in one gulp, and then made a face. "Don't ever let him dose you, Benton," she warned the wolf, trying to work up the saliva to wash out the taste, as she turned off the handheld.

Benton, lolling beside her, rose up on all fours and whined.

"Come on, you don't really want to listen to that Shadow Voice again?"

The wolf looked at her expectantly, his ears twitching.

"What is it about him you like? The cadence?"

Benton gave a low howl.

"Oh, all right." She fired her computer to life, then linked to an Interweb site from a devoted fan who'd captured as many of the intermittent, unscheduled broadcasts of the Voice as he could, then strung them together in a continuous loop.

After momentary static, the Shadow Voice began. *"A panic will sometimes run through a country. All nations and ages have been subject to them. Yet panics, in some cases, have their uses. They produce as much good as hurt. So, my fellow citizens, do not despair."*

The strangely touching words caught inside her chest. Canada had weathered such a panic during the plagues and had emerged stronger.

She paused to listen, curious. The boys she'd rescued from the moose had supplied her with information about this so-called Voice of Freedom. She'd glanced through the data recently, disappointed that it had given her no insight into the No-Border situation and disturbed by its picture of the UCE today. That country, which had once been the world's standard-bearer for democracy, had traded away its core freedoms in favor of world colonization, crippling taxes, military government, and a stable peace. Many were questioning whether the price of peace had been worth the cost.

"*Let us raise a new standard to which the wise and honest can repair. A charter of power granted not by oppression, but by liberty. We have discovered at last the one who can show us that standard. The woman who can lead us back to those principles which founded this great nation. We call to you, now. Return to your country, Banzai.*"

Banzai. Intrigued despite herself, Day leaned one hip against the desk. Benton, lying entranced on the floor, laid his head against her foot. She didn't trust that shadowy Voice of Freedom, but the few details the boys had fed her about Banzai Maguire *had* pricked her interest. Bree "Banzai" Maguire was the female fighter pilot who'd been frozen in time until recently discovered in a Han cave and revitalized. The notion of a woman from the past leading a revolution for the future tickled Day's sense of humor and, in some strange way, lent credence to the brewing revolution. Maybe she should learn more about this Banzai.

Her internal chronometer sent out a faint pulse. Later. She still had to pack for the trip to Wood Buffalo.

The wild called to him. Too restless for sleep, Lian shook off the stifling blankets, then padded naked to the window. He braced against the sill, absorbing the cold predawn.

The flat prairie, undisturbed by a speck of man-made light, stretched before him. Yet, even a long breath of the solitude, even the chill tightening his skin, could not lower the raging desires awakened tonight.

Seeing Day, content within her bonds of fraternity, had disturbed powerful yearnings within him. The yearnings were for a woman. No, for *one specific woman*.

No, they were for peace and for unity, because he could not have the woman he wanted. Yet peace of mind was an illusion given only to those who had not yet learned of the horrors of the world.

Still, unity—for a few short hours, at least—might be possible. The clear unborn morning, with no hint of the gathering storms that heralded winter, beckoned. Unable to tolerate the confinement of the indoors any longer, he shoved on clothes and a coat, stuck his feet into his boots. He retrieved his drum and his pottery smudge bowl—the tools of a shaman—then headed out.

Although he'd been raised in the mountains, he had come to love the vast prairies as few of his people did. He loved the expanse, the unfettered winds, and the absence of human voices. His home was situated beyond the fringes of Regina and faced outward, so views of nights like this could fill the rising emptiness inside him.

Too often of late, the sight was no longer enough.

He strode to the top of a small mound covered with clover, now turning brown with the cold. He took off his boots, needing the connection of skin to dirt, then shrugged off his coat. The wind penetrated his sweater and whipped his loosened hair about his face. No matter; its touch he relished. This vastness, the fathomless energy that man tried to summarize in a single word—nature—had always been his sustenance, his roots. From the time he had first studied his people's shamanic traditions, he could meld the modern tools of medicine with the ancient wisdoms and he had cherished these connections. Even when the other roles were thrust on him and other difficulties raised, he had tried to hang on to this.

Closing his eyes, Lian spread out his arms and dug his toes into the hard ground. Nothing of man could be seen— not voices, not lights, not structures that blocked the elements. Only cold, the prick of spinning dirt, the scents of grain and clover, the taste of clean air, and the rumble of a rising williwaw existed here.

In desperation, he danced the traditions of his ancestors. His body bent to the celebration of life in all its forms and all its goodness and cruelties. Despite the cold, he danced until sweat coated him and his heart raced within his chest. The sensations blanketed him and he surrendered to them, his parched spirit soaking in their vital bonds.

They were no longer enough.

Arid, empty, he settled down on the hard ground and, within his pottery bowl, lit a fragrant clump of sage. Softly drumming and chanting, he watched for the first signs of dawn. He sought the return of the spirits. He prepared himself for the necessary work ahead, seeking wisdom in visions.

Yet, no answers came to his disconnecting soul.

He shivered in the cold. Over the years, during his exile from his people, he had kept to their traditions. If he could not be with his people, then he would share at least this link. But the longer he dwelt apart from his people, the more remote they became. The more remote *he* became.

Now, this link too was lost.

A long howl sounded in his mind; then far across the prairie, he saw a wolf. It was standing and watching him with blue eyes, though at this distance he could not see its irises. Still, he knew they were blue. Reality or a vision?

Day's face appeared in his mind's eye. Lian's numb skin flared with sensation, heat, and a different kind of primitive power. His heartbeat increased, and he tapped his drum in an accompanying beat. The pulsing wildness within him spread outward—to the prairie and the wolf, joining fresh passion to the land that had sustained him.

The first beam of sunshine split the morning. Wolf and woman vanished in a searing explosion of light. Lian's blood leaped in his chest, chasing the fragmented images, tugged by a heart-destroying loss until nothing remained. Nothing at all.

He rose to his feet, alone, feeling only ash inside.

"You're late." Day hefted her trail bag. "Our appointment with Scree is at five, and if we don't hook to the eleven o'clock Connect—"

"My sled can make the station in under an hour," Lian answered absently, glancing around her home. He wasn't surprised to find she was a neat housekeeper. What did surprise him was the half-finished paper and ink painting on an easel. He strolled over to examine it. The black strokes were skillful, demonstrating the fine precision of the art, although he thought the depiction of downtown Moose Jaw lacked the hidden passions made possible by the medium. "You're learning Japanese brush painting?"

"This season's skill."

He lifted his brows in question.

"When I was eight," she explained, coming to stand beside him, her hands at her hips, "I set a goal to master at least two new skills every year. This season it's *sumi-e*—although I don't think it's something I'll be using much." She frowned at the easel. "The traditional method requires ink stick and brush, so that's what I used, but I prefer computer inks."

"Do computers give you the same tactile sense as brush on paper?"

"There's hand motion." Her head cocked as she studied the ink painting. "The scene isn't quite right. See that blot? With a computer, I could remove it for a more accurate outline. Ink and paper doesn't allow for changes. Learning the technique has been an interesting challenge in planning ahead."

"I like the blot." He ran a finger lightly across the paper. "How do you feel about the subject, downtown Moose Jaw?"

"Feel? It was just a scene I chose." She moved away, scanning the room, turning out lights, and readying to go. "I thought the angles and details would be a good test of my skill."

"But art is emotion. Not just technique."

"So, *you* draw?" she challenged over her shoulder.

"Not a lick." He followed her outside to his trek sled, his breath forming a cloud in the cold morning. "I once met an Inuit carver who created wood sculptures of polar bears so lifelike you could see the ripple of muscles and hear the growls. I asked him why he only carved polar bears. Why not seals or malamutes? He said that the bears were part of his soul. Only when that passion fed the necessary discipline of his knife did the bears breathe. Maybe you'd enjoy the challenge of the medium more if you picked a subject you felt stronger about."

"Maybe." She tossed her kit bag into the back of the trek sled, then slammed shut the door. "We're wasting time. It's time to go."

So much for the topic of art. "Here." Lian thrust a bag at her.

"What's this?" she asked, eyeing the package.

"Gloves," he answered succinctly.

"Thank you, but I have a pair—"

"Yeah, I saw them." He figured she had personal reasons for wearing such a dilapidated set, but he didn't like the idea of her with cold hands. "Open it. They come with no strings attached."

She did, drawing out the flexible, red gloves.

"They're liners," he added. "Thin, warm, and coated

96

with an antimicrobial. They go beneath your other pair."

"And they match." She hesitated, then drew them on, wiggling her fingers experimentally. "Comfortable. Thank you."

"You're welcome." He glanced around, curious about their yet unseen travel mate. "Where's Benton?"

"He's roaming out back; I'll get him. The neighbors complain that he howls too much when I'm gone."

Considering her nearest neighbor was five kilometers away, that was some howl.

She tilted her head back and gave a rich, warbling whistle. A moment later, around the corner trotted a runty-looking—less than a meter, and a third of that tail—silver-tipped wolf.

Ah, hell. "We're packing a wolf?"

"I always take him on long treks." She lifted her chin, as if daring Lian to challenge her decision. "He's part dog, so he's less wild."

Less wild did not mean tame.

The wolf joined them, giving Day a nudge with its head, then sat on its haunches at her heels and looked up, tongue lolling, as if to ask, *What's next?*

"What kind of a name for a wolf is 'Benton'?"

"His full name is Benton Fraser the Third—named after my first love, Benton Fraser Jr." Day scratched behind the wolf's ear. "I thought you knew Benton was a wolf; he figures in quite a few Mountie stories. He and I can always go separate in my sled, since I need to go up to Wood Buffalo after this meeting."

Not a chance in hell of them splitting up, Lian thought. At least his sled was bigger than the norm, since he often had to transport patients. The wolf could sit in the far rear seat.

As he rearranged his gear, he gestured to the sled. "He can sit there. How does Benton Jr. feel about siring a wolf?"

"Benton Jr. died when he was eight."

"Oh. I'm sorry." He paused, sending her a sympathetic glance.

"You didn't know. We were the only children in the quarantine camp where I grew up. He caught the virus; I didn't."

Lian tucked his head back into his sled, swearing under his breath. *Way to go, Firebird. First insult her artwork, then bring back bad memories.* "How did you and Benton here form a pack?"

"The day before I started my first Mountie tour, I stayed at Trafalgar's hunting cabin, up in the marshes, enjoying a last night of solitude. I stepped out to watch the moon." She paused, leaning an arm against his sled. Her eyes glazed, looking at a memory, while a dreamy smile softened her face. "I still remember that night, clear as if it were yesterday. So quiet, I feared to breathe, sure that I'd disturb the spirits. The moon was white, full. The air was so hot it erased everything but the sky and that moon. I just sat and stared, transfixed, peaceful. Then an owl flew across the moon, and a wolf pack began howling their song, and I knew to my soul that the night was wishing me well, affirming my choice of joining the RCMP."

Her gaze refocused, back to him and the present, and she slammed shut the trek sled door. "Right after that, a wolf pup came to the cabin. He was scrawny, had a few nips in the fur. I figured the pack I'd heard had kicked him out because he was the runt. I was suddenly reminded of Benton. Maybe because his eyes were the same color as the wolf's. I got the notion that the boy's spirit had gone to the wolf." Her smile turned rueful. "Fanciful, eh?"

"Not to me." Especially seeing the way the wolf hovered at her heels.

He finished rearranging his gear, then opened the rear door for Benton. "Inside," he said softly.

The wolf braced, refusing to move, and fixed a blue gaze

on him. A low growl rumbled at the base of its throat, and the hackles at its back rose.

Lian swore silently. Whatever the danger, he knew what he had to do. He straightened beside the open sled door, only his head angled forward, assuming the position of dominance.

"Benton," Day warned, reaching for the wolf's nape. "We're traveling as three—"

"Day, come beside me," Lian interrupted. Day could command Benton all she wanted; the animal might even obey her. For now. But he and the wolf needed a direct man-to-beast understanding of who was the alpha here.

"I'll handle him—"

"No," he told her, his gaze still locked on the unblinking wolf. He kept his voice low and filled with calm assurance. "Not this time. In Benton's mind, you're the alpha female. Until now, he's believed he's alpha male. He needs to step down for me."

"Oh, really?"

"If he doesn't, then every time you and I are close together, whenever we have to go off and leave him, if I touch you, then he will see it as a challenge. I don't plan on spending this trip with a wolf snapping my haunches and aiming for my nose."

In illustration, he reached out and flicked her braid. Benton's ears bent forward, and his teeth bared in warning.

"Show him you accept me as your alpha mate. Your scent needs to be on me. And mine on you." He waited a heartbeat, guessing that she'd studied wolf behavior, praying she'd see the necessity of the next step.

She did. Slowly, she let go of Benton's fur and backed away from the wolf.

Keeping his gaze on the growling beast, Lian loosened his hair and unbuttoned his coat, letting both spread and wave in the morning wind. He needed to appear as large as possible. When Day reached his side, he set her hat aside before it jabbed his eye, then wrapped an arm around her, tucking her close against him.

Her body, curved with feminine muscles, settled into his. She might be short, but her head fit snug against his shoulder—and spirits, but she felt good. His skin prickled with her heat, while the aching need for more, for bare flesh against bare flesh, gripped him. Quiet fell as her boots scraping on the bricks stilled. His sensitized ears caught the sound of her breath speeding up. That quick, desire speared him; a straight shaft from throat to groin.

He did nothing to quell it.

Instead, he gave in to the urge. His arm tightened around her as his fingers stroked the smooth skin of her cheek. "Touch me. Put your mark on my skin."

Her thumb stroked his jaw, circled his ear, while her fingers combed through his hair. "Like this?"

"Yes," he breathed. He didn't remember when the mere touch of a woman had sparked such pleasure. He ran a hand down her spine, kneading the stiffness in the small of her back. Her braid was as soft and thick as her wolf's tail. He fumbled with the tie.

"Don't even think of undoing my braid," she warned.

He buried his face against the top of her head, suddenly smiling at her level-toned demand and ripped by the contrary desire to see her hair loose and free.

Might as well wish for wolf claws while he was at it. Benton's repeated growl pulled him out of the pleasure. The menacing wolf stalked forward, tail twitching.

Lian snuggled Day closer.

"I don't think you're convincing him, Firebird," she said in an undertone laced with both humor and caution.

"It's supposed to be *mutual* admiration, Daniels."

"Well, then . . ." She cupped the back of his head, her fingers solid against his scalp, spearing through his hair. She urged his head lower, then stood on tiptoe and ran her tongue across his jaw.

She licked him. To Lian's utter shock, she licked him. Openmouthed, sensual, obvious. Her tongue was hot. The dampness left from the stroke cooled at once in the nearing-winter morn. The sharp contrast—burning mouth, cold flesh—tore a jagged edge across his already fraying composure.

"A wolf's kiss," she murmured, then took his lower lip between her teeth. She nipped it, sucked it into her mouth, nipped again.

Something dark awoke deep inside him. Something dangerously wild and strangely possessive: the feral male. His arm snaked around her waist, pulling her flush against him, hip to hip, chest to chest. A lupine snarl rose from his chest as he buried his face against her neck. His teeth scraped the point of her jaw, while his thumb pressed against the skipping pulse in her carotid.

She held him, met him, hands at his head, firm body molding his. God, he wanted her.

A biting yip cut through the haze of his desire.

With a reluctance and a strength he was unaware he'd possessed before now, Lian lifted his lips from Day's neck. He and she turned as one to Benton, desire still keen between them, danger honing each sensation. He took a breath of cold air. The maple taste of Day was on his tongue. His lips were tingling.

The wolf was looking from one to the other of them, ears laid back, eyes squinting in suspicion. It stalked forward, tail twitching. At least the teeth weren't bared anymore.

For a moment, sympathy for Benton played through Lian. Sharing someone you loved was not an easy task.

Then, he erased the thought. Instead, he sought and projected only the inner confidence of the alpha. His body snugged against Day, his arm locked around her, his cheek rested atop her head. He surrounded her with his claim. His gaze met the wolf's—not challenging, simply assuming superiority as his right. His angled body directed the wolf inside the sled, demanding obedience to his unspoken command.

Day remained silent and quiet in his arms, understanding and accepting this vital moment.

Benton was not taking well his relegation to beta status. The wolf stalked forward, his mouth pulled into a snarl. Lian refused to back away, his teeth bared, a matching low growl sounding in his throat.

The wolf circled, sniffing, seeking the scents of fear and submission. He got neither, only the pheromones of desire, male and female melded together.

The beast's growl hesitated. Its ears pulled back. Lian bent slightly and circled his free hand around Benton's muzzle in approximation of a lupine gesture of dominance. The wolf hesitated, then settled down on its haunches. Hand still around Benton's muzzle, Lian waited. With a whine, the beast tucked its tail against its belly and sprawled onto all fours. It butted its head against Lian's foot.

"Good boy." Lian let go of both wolf and woman, then angled his head toward the interior. "Inside," he repeated softly. With each heartbeat he radiated confidence that the wolf would act as commanded. With a huff, Benton rose, stretched, yawned . . . and then entered the sled. Perching on its haunches atop the seat, it cast an expectant glance back.

Solemnly, Lian reached in and rubbed the wolf's powerful jaw, then ruffled its thick fur. "Welcome, friend."

Day joined him, also giving Benton a rub at the throat. "We still love you."

The growl this time was of pure satisfaction. Benton's head rotated in their palms, as Day and Lian shared a mutual caress, before Lian stepped back. Day gave a Benton a final pat, then closed the door. She and Lian settled in at the front of the sled, the thrumming desire between them slowing and muting.

Day cast a sidelong glance at Lian as they headed out of Regina, east toward the Connect Station. "That was primitive."

"You're the one who brought the wolf."

"Benton's never taken to a stranger before."

"Maybe I didn't smell like a stranger to him."

"Ah. He sensed a kindred soul."

Lian gave her a grin. "You saying I'm a wolf?"

"There's at least a touch of the feral in you."

She wasn't too far off in that, he admitted.

"In fact, deep down, I think you're rather uncivilized, Firebird."

"Scratch the surface of most men, and you'll find that's true."

She fell silent, watching him navigate the pitted surface of what had once been a major connection road, just one of many that had fallen into disrepair like so many other things when national resources focused on survival. The sled climbed easily over a jutting wedge of concrete.

Hard to imagine a time when autos traveled this at 130 kilometers an hour. The trek sleds were slower, but their nano-formed bottoms converted as necessary from a surface like all-terrain tires to snow runners to rail wheels, making them more versatile.

Day and Lian reached the TransCanada Connect station with fifteen minutes to spare before the maple leaf painted on the front of the train engine came into view. The Connect engine purred to a stop. Trek sleds going to Regina and vicinity disconnected, while the waiting sleds hitched on with a minimum of fuss.

Some entrepreneurial souls were repairing runways, Lian had heard, and trying to revive the air flights system, although their current business was strictly bush planes. If the borders ever opened, the new businesses would be poised to take advantage of international travel. For the most part, however, Canadians remained suspicious of crowding together. Anyone traveling distances took the Connect. Running the already set path of the old Trans-Canada Rails, the sleek engine allowed the passengers to stay in their personal trek sleds to reach the major cities along the line while covering the entire distance from Winnipeg to Calgary in twelve hours.

Within a half hour, he and Day were sliding out of the station, the blue light on their hitch showing they'd paid to Winnipeg.

Day laid her hat to the side and unbuttoned her coat. She stretched out her feet, then pulled a small, carved owl from her pocket. Her thumb traced it a few moments before she said, "Benton carved this for me right before he died. He liked to watch the predator birds soar, said they were free in a way we could never be. He had that passion your Inuit sculptor was talking about." She turned the owl around in her hand before tucking it into her pocket again. "Maybe that is what's missing with *sumi-e*. Passion. Something I'm going to have to work at. I think I'll make it next season's skill."

With that, she leaned back and closed her eyes. "Wake me in two hours. We can go over our plans before we meet Scree."

A moment later, her easy breathing said she was fast asleep.

Passion. Something I'm going to have to work at. Next season's skill.

Damn. Did she have any idea how provocative that sounded? Especially after she'd given him that wolf kiss? Lian released the wheel one finger at a time and rubbed the back of his neck. The trip ahead was difficult enough, what with the threat of the virus looming, yet with a few words she'd utterly destroyed his focus. With a simple stroke of her tongue, she'd washed away years of discipline. Her sweet maple scent already teased him, and now her husky voice clung to his ears and brought to mind all sorts of carnal scenarios.

She'd claimed he was uncivilized, part feral. Spirits knew, after five hours in the enclosed trek sled with her, he'd be ready to join Benton in a frustrated howl at the moon.

Chapter Seven

Day had trained herself to sleep anywhere—crashed out in a Mountie post, on rocky crags, upright in a chair while a partner took his turn at the surveillance shift . . . Pillow and mattress were optional, and she rarely wasted time by sleeping a night through. Naps wherever the opportunity arose worked just fine.

This TransCanada Connect trip should have been ideal for a refreshing snooze. The trek sled was roomy as far as the vehicles went, and her seat was comfy even if it was a touch close to the driver. Lulling hum of the rails. Fresh breeze from the open window. Benton's familiar snuffs and snorts.

It didn't work out refreshing, however, courtesy of the now alpha Lian. As a rest-disturbing line, "I must outsnarl your wolf" had proved as effective as it was unorthodox.

When she'd finally dozed off, not more than sixty minutes into her nap, she'd hit REM sleep. But the dreams were pure Lian. Vivid. She could still feel the pressure of his body against hers. Energetic. Possibly criminal with so much pleasure. Definitely disturbing. It had woken her back up.

Day stifled a yawn, not prepared to open her eyes and admit that sleep was impossible. Not when her ears caught every rustle and breath of Lian beside her.

No doubt about their inexplicably fierce and rapid mutual attraction. She couldn't deny her body had soundly betrayed her, while his hadn't been hiding any secrets in that embrace either. Her skin had enjoyed the feel of his, and her dreams had intensified her yearnings.

Question: What would they do about it?

Answer: Nothing. Lust was temporary and didn't always need acting on. She and Lian were partners looking for a killer and a rogue virus, and that took precedence over anything else.

So, stop hiding behind your eyelids and do your job.

She allowed her yawn this time, then stretched and opened her eyes. Flat prairie spread on all sides. The wind had picked up, bending the grass stalks in a frenzied dance. Coming through the window, it plucked at her braid with chilled fingers. She tucked the plait beneath her jacket, then snugged up the collar and glanced over at Lian. He was leaning against the transparent side of the trek sled, his eyes closed. The blue of his earrings glowed against the drab scene outside, and against his loosened black hair.

Rest didn't soften him any. Taut muscles, firm mouth, feet planted on the floor as though even in sleep he was prepared for action.

"I'm awake." His low voice brought her attention back to find his gray eyes open and fixed on her. "You didn't sleep long."

"I got enough." They should talk about the investigation, she knew, but she couldn't focus on business. Not yet. Not when her body still vibrated with a need stronger than any she remembered. Not when her flushed skin still felt the imprint of Lian's hand.

She wanted to know more about this man who was jumbling her ordered world, more about the man than his compassion or stubbornness. "What were you thinking about just then?"

"The winds carried the scent of fresh grass, and I was reminded of a story my mother once told me."

"Would you tell it to me?"

He faced her, settling his foot against her seat. "Coyote once traveled far from the mountains, searching for new lands, for he was tired of climbing. 'There are only mountains,' the other animals told him. But still, he wanted to discover for himself. He traveled for a day and a night and a day and a night, up and down the mountains and through the snow, but alas all he found were more mountains. 'I shall never find a land I need not climb,' coyote moaned. 'I will turn around in the morning.' But that morning, when he opened his eyes, he discovered the blessings of Mother Earth before him. A flat land without hill or ice, only vast fields of grain and grass. He raced onto the prairie, as he named it, leaping and running for there was no hill or rock to stop him. Suddenly, the ground shook beneath his feet and Father Sky vanished beneath a plume of dust. The prairie was alive with buffalo, stampeding toward him. Coyote ran and ran, sorry he had gone such distances, sorry he had left the security of the mountains. The buffalo grew closer. Rumble. Rumble. Rumble. Coyote slowed. He could not breathe from the exhaustion. Soon, he would be trampled. The safety of the mountains lay before him, but he could not reach them. 'Help me, Mother Earth, and I will never doubt your mountains again,' he cried. Suddenly a hoof caught him, and he was tossed away, out of the prairie, back to his mountain home. He was safe. The other animals did not believe him, of the prairie and its dangers, yet coyote knew and remembered, for he kept a stalk of the fragrant grass by his bed to remind him."

The mesmerizing cadence of Lian's low voice faded; then he grinned. "My mother intended it as a precautionary tale about leaving home, but to me it was an incentive to find that prairie."

"You became the wandering coyote." Day toyed with the end of her braid, still bemused by the simple folktale and its message. "Do you see your mother often?"

Lian shook his head. "She died seven years ago. My father, too. Along with my two older brothers."

"I'm so sorry." Seven years. He hadn't seen his people in seven years, either. The two events had to be related, but the matter seemed too personal for her to pry. "I didn't mean to—"

"It's okay." He stretched out his legs. "Did your father ever tell you stories?"

"He loved to read to me from a book called *Great Mountie Heroes.*"

"Tell me of one."

She told him the story of "Mule" Brandywine, the Mountie who'd rescued three children from the icy, swollen Yukon. For a time they exchanged such stories, segueing into some of their own exploits, until at last a companionable silence felt between them.

Time to get back to work. "Have you ever heard of Citadel, Lian? Bart told me that's where the No-Borders were planning their action."

"*Citadel?* I didn't think it existed."

"Neither did I, but apparently somebody does." The legend said that Citadel guarded a secret route used by those escaping the first plagues, a place where the borders opened. "If it's real, nobody's used it in a hundred years."

Lian scratched a thumb across his lip. "Citadel has to be remote, isolated. Why would the No-Borders choose it as a location for a demonstration? And how would anyone see it?"

"I don't know. An Interweb broadcast?" Day snapped

her fingers. "Maybe that's the connection to the Shinooks and Jem. What if Citadel is on their land?"

"Why do you think the Shinooks are involved?"

"Bart said there were underground rumblings."

She considered their history, seeking insight. The Shinooks were the richest of the Affiliated Indian Nations. When the Autonomy Treaties were ratified in the midst of the worst of the plague years, the AIN took control of their own destinies, gradually ridding themselves of the twin scourges of poverty and alcoholism by educating their own children and not only in the ways of reading, writing, and arithmetic, but also in the ancient traditions, giving them a solid support to withstand the years of chaos. Their transformation was helped by the land's becoming a source of needed minerals after the embargo, by having savvy lawyers to prevent the reversal of the treaties, and by defending their land with the most modern weapons, not hesitating to smuggle what they needed.

One thing didn't fit, though. The Shinooks were also the most insistent on autonomy, and adhered closely to their ancient traditions. *Why would they be involved with the No-Borders?*

"Wrong link this time," Lian said. "My AIN contacts say no. Until we have other evidence, I say we don't spread ourselves too thin. We should pursue the confirmed leads like the No-Borders and Citadel."

He was right. They had other leads to pursue, at least for now. "All right," she agreed.

Still, her gut told her Bart wouldn't have made the link if there wasn't *something* solid behind it, and she couldn't shake the conviction that an important piece of the puzzle was the Shinook and their leader, Jem.

Tonight, Winnipeg lived up to its reputation as Canada's windiest city. The wind, which started on the prairie and met no resistance until the town's central buildings, buffeted the trek sled as it traversed the rain-damp streets. Lian followed Day's directions to the fork of the Red and the Assiniboine Rivers, shifting uneasily in his seat. The skin at the back of his neck prickled as he read the ominous signs of the evening. Instead of the usual rich pinks and reds of sunset, the sky held an eerie amber cast. A lone hawk soared overhead, its mighty wings flapping as it exited the city.

Dusk was never a good time for business; too many spirits roamed. Too much chance for evil to work. The omens spoke tonight—something bad was going to happen.

"Why a face-to-face meeting instead of holo—" He bit off the question as the sled skidded perilously close to the swollen Assiniboine. With an effort he pulled back, shifting their route to the far side of the empty road. "Isn't Scree strictly an Interweb supplier, a phobic about disease?"

"In the skin was my choice. I can't tell when someone's lying in a holoimage. Can't smell the sweat or see the tics." She cast him a sidelong glance. "Most people don't fool me as well as you did in the bar."

"Because I wasn't lying to you, then. I just wasn't telling you everything."

She drummed her fingers against her knee. "Are you still keeping things from me?"

The woman was more suspicious than a 'tailhead. Of course, her doubts had some merit. "Yes," he said lightly. "How I spent my sixteenth birthday. My first sexual encounter. The list is endless."

He must not have fooled her, for her eyes narrowed. "Don't make the mistake of holding something material back from me."

"What happened to partners and trust?" he asked with a touch of bitterness. And that kiss?

"Trust? There's too much about you I don't understand. I don't even know where you're from. There's no record of your birth. No listing of your nation."

111

His hands gripped the wheel, and not because the sled was skidding. Her digging for his past made him defensive. "I'm who you see right now. Don't ask about anything else. I'm not asking who *your* parents were." He regretted the words even as he said them. That she didn't know who had birthed her in a quarantine camp was a matter of record, and he didn't have to slap her in the face with it. She had never sent a request to Health Canada for DNA matching but that didn't mean she hadn't wondered. Or felt the loss.

He forced his fingers to loosen on the steering wheel. "I'm sorry, that was uncalled for. But I won't keep proving myself to you. I'm not a Mountie. I never will be. You can believe one thing about me, though. If you can find that single speck of unshakable faith, then believe this: I will do whatever it takes to stop that virus. I will lie, cheat, steal, cut off my fingers—and yours if necessary—and rip out my heart if that's the only way to prevent the scourge of another plague. If something is important to your investigation, I'll tell you. Can you believe that much?"

Her mixed eyes studied him. "Yes. I think I can."

He switched to Native Common. "Believe also this. I will never lie to you in Native, Day—either in my own language or in this common language used among the AIN. Do you understand?"

"*Hanto's,*" she answered in the Common tongue. *Yes.* "So, there is a limit, something you will not do."

"Yes. A weakness of mine."

"No. A sense of honor I can respect."

He paused, then admitted, "I prefer your take." Switching back to English, he asked, "So, how'd you get a germphobic scavenger to meet us in the skin?"

The ends of her mouth quirked up. "Told him I was investigating the death of a Mountie, and gave him a choice. Meet us here, or at Regina HQ. I did let him pick the time."

"The no-choice option." Surprisingly, he found talking

to Day like this, as companion and partner, helped quell the previous snappish, ominous mood. "But didn't he have the right to refuse unless you had an order of command?"

"He neglected to ask about that. The law doesn't state I have to tell him." From the corner of his eye, Lian saw her lean back, her hands behind her head as she added, "I can be persuasive. It's the hat, you know."

Despite his unease at the evening, despite the tensions between them, he laughed. "Day Daniels, if I've got an honor you can respect, then you've got a deviousness I admire. You know no one refuses or questions a Mountie's official request."

"Not true, I've dealt with resisters often enough. Not everyone cares about appearing lawful—but when I'm investigating the death of my partner, I don't feel like being too nice."

Lian grunted, the only response he could manage as a blast of wind skimmed their sled along the riverbank. Benton gave a loud bark as the rear of the vehicle hung out over the edge, and Lian looked down at the water, the only thing beneath him. With a jerk, the sled's nanobottom sensed the terrain shift and adjusted, and they straightened. At least the rain had stopped. With night coming, the temperature was dropping. On a patch of black ice, they'd have been swimming in the river.

"Nice touch," Day commented, looking totally unruffled at the near miss.

"Thanks."

She tilted her head. "So, you think I'm devious?"

"I think you're not above using the power of your position when you have to. Same as me."

"I don't abuse that power."

"Didn't say you did. But, you said it yourself: When it comes to something like the death of a Mountie, then you do what you have to do. Is there a line *you* won't cross, Day?"

113

"Isn't that a bare-all question?"

"I showed you my weakness."

"And here we've hardly gotten on a first-name basis."

"We're far more intimate than mere first names." He waited a beat. "Benton thinks you've claimed me into the pack as your mate. You did lick me."

Her lips twisted. "It seemed necessary at the time. You won't be mentioning that at the Mountie depot, will you?"

"Not a syllable." He shot her a glance. "See? There are advantages to working with a floppy brim."

"Good Lord, I didn't think that term was known out of the corps."

"I treated a delusional Mountie once. He kept calling me that." He grew serious, remembering the man who had died. "You didn't answer my question."

"No one's ever asked me before," she said, bracing her foot on her seat. "Anybody who knows me, including myself, knows my answer. I won't break the law. I may manipulate within it, but I won't compromise it. It's too important. Why?"

"Because I don't think anyone knows the answer until they've been pushed to the limit. Have you ever reached that moment? Have you ever had to give up everything you cared about to keep to your convictions? What would you do, Day, if the only way to stop a virus release was to break the law—say by letting Juneau go free? And, what would the decision do to you?"

He was surprised when she didn't answer promptly. Instead, she rested her chin on her knee and her teeth caught her lower lip. "I don't know. You're right, my beliefs haven't been that sorely tested. I'd like to trust that I'd stand by them, but given that scenario . . . Have you ever been tested like that?"

"Once." When he'd chosen between his people and the rest of Canada. He had stood beside his beliefs, then.

Could he do it again? And what if the choice meant losing Day?

"Maybe," she added thoughtfully, "such moments aren't about defining your limits. Maybe they reveal what you hold most dear."

They finished the last kilometers in silence, broken by Lian's appreciative whistle when he parked outside Scree's complex. "He's guarded by a cold plasma shield. Scavenging's more lucrative than I thought. What's the lowdown on him?"

Day pulled up the history she'd downloaded. During the worst of the plague years, with over half the population dead, too many buildings and homes and vehicles had languished, unclaimed and decaying: a magnet for looters. The ravaged structures had spawned vermin, become a breeding ground for the hovering specter of lawlessness. Important raw materials were lost.

In response, the government had licensed the scavengers. Given them territories to patrol and assistance to protect those territories. The result was reclaimed goods to be distributed—taxable goods—and the recycling of vital materials no longer able to be imported. The job had proved lucrative. A respectability had grown for the scavenger union, and caches like these for the men themselves.

"Scree's family were transplanted Québecois. They've held an exclusive scavenge contract for this area for the past hundred years," Day read. "A territory almost completely wiped out when the viruses hit."

"In other words, there were a lot of empty shops and buildings to plunder."

"They've paid for the luxury. Everyone in the family has succumbed to an infection. Scree's the last, and so far germ-free."

"Explains the phobia."

115

"The list of people who wish him dead explains the cold plasma barrier. He has a reputation for ruthlessness, high prices, stock no one else can obtain, and convenient accidents for people who oppose him. So far, the Mounties have nothing but suspicions. Nothing proved that we can even level a fine. I'm the first Mountie he's met in the skin for"—she scrolled down the file—"five years."

"Damn, woman, you are persuasive."

"Yes, I am." She turned to look at her wolf. "Benton, you ready for a little romp?"

The beast gave an excited yip.

"You'll let him loose?" Lian asked.

"Only in deserted areas like this. He needs to run and hunt." Once out of the sled, she opened the back door for Benton. He bounded out, sniffed a circle around the trek sled, her, and Lian; then he raced down the empty street, his tail waving. She watched until he was out of sight. The wolf was wild and needed to roam, she knew that, but she never conquered the remnant of fear that she would lose him.

"I hope he's learned cats and dogs aren't part of his food chain."

"Yes. Mostly."

"Does he ever not come back?"

"I've never had to go searching for him." Her nails dug into her palms, and she forced herself to stop gazing into emptiness. "That sniffing circle fixed the area in his scent memory. He'll be back at the sled before we are." She prayed that, once more, saying it would make it true.

The fierce wind whipped her braid around her neck and drove a puddle of water against her ankles. She tucked her chin down, shielding herself, and jammed her hat on her head, holding it there with one hand. Official business meant the hat stayed on.

A sour scent, like rotting meat, permeated the plaza

116

where they'd parked. So deep had it soaked into the bricks that not even a gale could wash it clean.

From the corner of her eye, she saw Lian unlock the holster of his Distazer.

"I'm linking us in to Winnipeg comm." She activated the comm patch behind her ear. "If Scree plans a double cross, he'll wait until he's met with us. Until he can blame it on someone else."

Lian flipped the safety off his Distazer. "Trouble rarely waits."

She nodded. Smart man. She should have realized a plague hunter would be as suspicious of a trap as a Mountie.

"We've got you linked, Day," came a voice in her ear. "You sure you don't want backup closer?"

"The plague doc's got my back."

"Can he handle it if things get nasty?"

She glanced at Lian again, at the easy way the Distazer rode his hip, at the chiseled lines of his face, and at his set mouth. "Yeah, he can. Besides, Scree knows he's coming. Anyone else might scare our lad, whether he's got something to say or not."

"Your call, Inspector. What's your code for trouble?"

"Banzai." Everything she'd learned about the legendary Banzai said the woman would have been a loyal partner in tight spots.

The voice in her ear laughed. "Been listening to the Voice of Freedom?"

"My wolf has."

They reached the cold plasma shield surrounding the collection of buildings that were Scree's home, warehouse, and original source. The energy field shimmered faintly blue, like the center of a flame. Except the plasma wasn't hot. Or cold.

She touched the barrier, testing. Prickles, akin to a foot

awakening, spread across her palm. It was nothing but a warning to step back. Instead, she pressed deeper, testing how far the shield went, inserting first her hand, then her arm into the ionized gas.

"What the hell are you doing, Day?" Lian asked.

"Testing the depth. I've got to see if I can get through this. If I turn my thumb down, pull me back." She stepped forward, and the prickles became tingling. Pain replaced the tingles. The farther she penetrated, the longer she contacted the plasma, the more the energy disrupted her cells and the worse the pain got. Within seconds, her arm was encased in agony, frozen with marrow-deep cell bursts.

Sweat dripped in her eyes and ears. Her throat closed around a groan. *Go faster.* Fortifying breath. *Run forward.*

Not run. The plasma barrier thickened, and the run became a slow-motion torture. Legs. Torso. Face. Only one hand remained free.

The pain! Vision disappeared. Ripping torment shredded her muscles, annihilated her senses, exploded individual cells. It dominated every thought and breath. She couldn't make it through. Couldn't test another millimeter forward.

But she couldn't pull back. She opened her mouth, tried to form the words for aid, but her voice wouldn't obey. Focusing on the tip of her little finger, the single body part that didn't scream, she tilted it. One, two centimeters—

It was enough. Her partner grasped her hand, his fingers a cool antidote, and he jerked her backward. The plasma undulated in a blue wave as she pulled free, reaching out as though seeking new prey, new captives.

Day bent over, cradling her arm, which had been in contact the longest, against her belly. She held it up with her hip, for she had no control over it otherwise. Biting her lip, she held back moans. Her lashes blinked back tears of pain. "Thanks," she gasped.

"You're welcome." Lian slung his med kit off his back,

then pulled out an injection band. Wordlessly, efficiently, he took control of her arm, bracing it in his palms. Had she wanted to, she had no ability to resist, even though every nerve fiber screamed against the movement and the touch. Letting her lean against the heat of his body, he strapped the band around her wrist. The nozzle pressed against her pulse.

"What . . . you giving me?" she forced out.

"Endorphins for the pain." He dialed in a code, then pressed a button.

Even with the backdrop of pain, she felt the medicine's sting as it was shot straight into her vein. He pressed another code, and she felt the pressure of another drug, less stinging this time, as the endorphins did their job.

"A tissue-repair cocktail," he said before she could ask. "Free radicals, ascorbic acid, tocopherol."

"Vitamins?"

"Sometimes old remedies are best." He began to massage her with long, slow, impersonal strokes from wrist to shoulder to neck. "This helps distribute the meds, and keeps blood feeding the tissues with oxygen. Can you wiggle your toes? Lift your legs?"

"Yes." She complied while he ran his thumbs over her face, bringing the blood flow back to her cheeks and lips. Eyelids. Throat.

Endorphins might be helping with the pain, but they did nothing to counter the effect his stimulating touch had on her skin. Her equilibrium vanished, leaving her dizzy.

"Sure you just don't want to hold my hand?" she asked, trying to quell the jumpiness in her stomach as he laced his fingers between hers.

His hand tightened briefly; then he resumed the easy strokes. "You found my secret." He matched her light tone, but he didn't look at her, gazing instead at her arm. "Been looking for every excuse to touch you since we met."

Oh, Lord, so had she. Involuntarily her fingers curled,

119

brushing against his hand that circled her wrist. The tension in her stomach became a hard knot. "Feels good," she admitted with stark honesty. "You have talented hands, Dr. Firebird."

He looked at her, then. "So I've been told."

There was lightning in those raincloud-colored eyes, a heat that she wasn't ready to acknowledge. Especially not now. Reluctantly, she pulled her arm from his grip. Their wrists met. Palm slid across palm. Despite the injected endorphins deadening her nerves, she felt his skin. Their fingers pressed tip to tip, lingering a second longer than necessary before she was free.

She worked her arm, now merely numb, rotated her neck, did a couple of knee bends, testing the muscle repair. The reestablished blood flow substituted her inadequate body heat for his. "Thanks," she said again.

He fisted his hands on his hips. "You know the effects of a cold plasma shield. You could have lost your arm if you'd stayed in longer. Why the hell did you need to know the depth?"

She looked at him, serious. "Because, you can penetrate a cold plasma shield if you can endure the pain and the shield is thin enough. I don't like walking into dead ends. If we have to retreat, I wanted to know beforehand if this was an option."

"It isn't, is it?"

"No. We wouldn't survive the passage. If we're getting out, it will only be through an established portal."

"Damn." A moment later, he grinned at her. "You telling me you can't scale a ten-meter energy fence, Daniels?"

Lian, she was finding, had a graveyard sense of humor: the ability to find absurdities in a grim situation. She laughed softly. "It's you I'm worried over, Firebird. You'd likely need a boost."

He eyed the fence, then shook his head and let out a breath. "I guess we're stuck doing it your way: civilized

and legal. Shall we enter Scree's lair and be done with it?"
He nodded to the lone post topped with a virus swipe and
a keypad, the only sign of where the entrance was located.

Day gave a final experimental shake to her arm, pressed
talk on the post's keypad, and then announced their arrival
to the disembodied voice that answered.

"Swipe your thumbs across the virus scanner," came the
reply.

In turn, they wiped their thumbs across the oil-slick-
colored square beside the keypad. Their skin epithelials
would be analyzed for viral RNA and DNA, a common
practice in public gathering places, although not as common for private residence. Anyone infected or carrying was
denied entrance. They waited in silence for the process to
complete.

At last, the entry post chimed. "Enter," bade the disembodied voice.

The shimmering blue barrier pulled back, leaving a rec-
tangle with a clear view into the grounds. Day and Lian
walked in, and the fence closed behind them.

"Hope you practiced your high jumps," Lian murmured.

Three burly men joined them before they could walk
farther. Two placed themselves on either side. The third
stood in front of them with his hand out.

"Weapons."

Day crossed her arms. "No. We keep our weapons."

"No one armed approaches Scree. He don't allow it."

"Then we have a problem, because a Mountie never
gives up her weapon. Even to overzealous guards. Scree
knows that. So, tell him that I'll be leaving now, and the
Regina escort will be arriving in ten minutes." She pivoted,
and as if cued, a distant howl punctuated her move.

"Wait." The head guard touched a finger to the earpiece
he wore. "Scree says come on in."

"I thought he might," she murmured.

Day glanced around with interest as they were shown to

a brick building on the far side of the compound. Before the plagues, these grounds had held a prosperous collection of stores and restaurants. Some of the buildings still stood, crumbling testaments to a culture of consumer excess. Tiles beneath her feet had once been a colorful mosaic. Now they were merely cracked and faded.

An eclectic mix of relics littered the grounds, items too big or awkward to fit beneath a roof. Immense anchors and propellor blades. Piles of sheet metal and odd-sized lumber. Stacks of bricks and concrete blocks. Brass pipes. Everywhere was clutter and the scent of rust.

They were led to a soot-covered building with the word TERMINAL etched above its doors. More recovered goods were piled haphazardly. Pots, pans, misshapen candles, bottles, jars, furniture, odd-looking objects she had no idea of the purpose. Items of little value, except as replacement of highly damaged goods, as far as she could see.

Then again, Scree likely wouldn't keep the valuables—or the illegals—out in plain sight.

Their footsteps echoed with hollow, empty thuds, and a shiver coursed down her spine. Everything here was spoils from a time of horror. Most was impersonal, merely gadgets and goods, valuable for the nostalgic factor or as a source of replacement parts and raw materials. But, every so often, stuck amidst the functional, was something achingly personal.

Like that doll.

Day halted and picked up the toy, which had been stuck without thought between a brass kettle and a mangled box containing a commode cover. She smoothed the doll's brown curly hair and tidy pinafore. An ancient pair of spectacles—made odder because no one had to wear them anymore—perched askew on the nose.

The doll wasn't new; it had been taken from the box. But, it had obviously been cared for. Day's throat tightened. Everything about the doll spoke that some little girl had loved it—from the clean, buttoned clothes to the jaunty blue bow tied in the hair to the small bracelet fastened around the wrist.

Suzannah, read the etched bracelet.

Was that the name of the doll? Or of the little girl who'd fallen victim to a bioterror virus?

Lian stopped beside her, his arm brushing hers as he reached out to set the metal-framed glasses straight on the doll's nose. "She's very rare. Most dolls and stuffed animals were burned, for fear they harbored a microbe."

Their guard tilted his head, listening to an unheard voice. "Scree says bring the doll."

So, that answered the question about whether they were being watched. He'd probably seen her adventure with the plasma shield, too.

"He's giving it to you as a gift," added the guard.

Day smoothed a hand along the toy's pinafore, so sorely tempted she ached. Something about this lost doll tugged at her, a symbol of all that was gone, all the pain the country had endured. Then, reluctantly, she put it back on the shelf, setting it carefully upright. "I'm here on official duty," she said. "Thank Scree for his generous offer, but I can't accept a gift."

"Day . . ." Lian began.

She shook her head, not wanting to hear whatever he planned to say, whether it was sympathy or a suggestion. "This doll's a survivor. She'll find a second home. And someone to love her." She faced the guard. "Take us to Scree."

Chapter Eight

They were led out of the Terminal and down a glass hall, where a brief dose of sunburn-hot UV light sterilized their clothes. At the end of the hall, the guards ushered them into a knob of a room formed by featureless walls. Ten meters above, a prismatic glass ceiling admitted the last of the day's sun in a colorful light show on the walls. No, Day realized suddenly; the color changes weren't from the sunset, but embedded in the nanoform walls themselves. The only solid decoration was a baroquely ornate, three-meter-tall fountain, whose circulating water came from the miniature penises of marble satyrs. The room air was tinted pink and scented by an exotic musk that was already giving her a headache.

Interesting display of wealth. What interested her more, however, was the man seated by the fountain. There were no pictures of Scree as an adult in the files. She knew he was thirty-four, a decade older than herself. If she hadn't known that, though, looking at him from a distance she would have guessed him barely past twenty-one.

Until she got close enough to see his black, hard eyes.

And the polymer sensor that replaced his natural nose.

His hair was cropped close, and gloves covered his hands. Beneath his faddish crotch-torn denim he wore a biohazard skin suit. His sallow skin was exposed only on his face. He was seated in a steel chair; leather straps dangled from its arms and legs. Hell in Halifax, that was a twentieth-century torture device—an electric chair!

The two metal folding chairs before him were obviously meant for her and Lian, and just as obviously not meant to encourage a prolonged stay. Behind them, the door closed with a whoosh, sealing them in the sterile room. The first guard planted himself at the door. She assumed the other two were just outside. So, that's the way Scree played the game. She settled her hat firmly on her head and stiffened her shoulders.

Scree didn't rise as she and Lian approached. "*Bonjour, Monsieur Scree*," she greeted him, holding out her hand. "*Merci de nous rencontrer.*"

"I prefer to use English for business. French is for pleasure."

"As you wish."

He gave her a genial smile, lifting his gloved hands. "Forgive me—I never shake hands." Languidly he waved toward the empty chairs. "Please sit."

She lowered her hand, then perched on the edge of a chair. Lian, she noted, chose to stand, leaning one shoulder against the wall as he unbuttoned his carbon-mesh lined jacket. The casual air was an act. She could almost hear his mind registering the scanty details in the room, including the single exit, the surveillance lens in the upper corner, and the fact that Scree rested his hand near a Distazer almost concealed beneath one of the chair arms.

"What can I do for you, Inspector Daniels?" Scree's voice was bored, breathy, and annoying.

Day tried to find one thing about the man that didn't

irritate her. She failed. Everything about him—from his obvious decadence to his drawl to his gold-dusted eyebrows—rankled. Swallowing her irritation, she vowed to keep the proceedings civil and by the book. "I'm investigating the death of Luc Robichaux. You've heard of him?"

"The Mountie? Who has not? Surely, you don't believe I had anything to do with such a heinous crime?"

She didn't bother with an answer. "You trade with the No-Borders."

"I deal with anyone who meets my price."

"What have they purchased recently?"

He shook his head. "My customers are people, not faceless groups. I do not ask affiliations."

"Then give me a name."

"I have an extensive customer list. You'll have to be more specific."

"Interesting fence you've got out there," she said instead, after three heartbeats.

"It is not a fence. It's a cold plasma shield."

Good, she'd erased a touch of that smug assurance with her abrupt change. She saw it in the flick of his eyes, the worry about where she was heading. "You just put it up last year."

"It's not illegal."

"Didn't say it was. Expensive though." She leaned forward, bracing her elbows on her knees. "Yet, you paid fewer taxes last year. Odd purchase for a man with declining income. Or do you have an untaxed source of funds?"

"I had sufficient to cover the costs." His smile, and his assurance, returned. "My income fluctuates from year to year. I ordered the fence five years ago; there was a delay in putting it up. I simply met my obligations like any fiscally responsible citizen."

"I'm sure your supplier was grateful."

"He was. Ask him. Likely you have his name," he said drily.

"That I do, and I already talked to him." From the corner of her eye, she saw Lian push away from the wall and begin a slow prowl of the room. He had pulled one of his lab chips from his med pack, and as he circled he glanced at it.

Scree also noticed. He cocked his head toward Lian. "Dr. Firebird, Inspector Daniels didn't say what department you're from. You're not RCMP. Blue earrings are not regulation, I believe."

Lian appeared not to have heard. He frowned at his screen, one hand against the nano walls.

"Dr. Firebird is assisting RCMP as a civilian investigator," she explained, curious about what her partner was up to. At least he wasn't interfering with her. She aimed the conversation back where she wanted. "That cold plasma barrier, how deep is it?"

"Deeper than you can breach."

"How deep?"

"Two meters." He steepled his fingers. "Do you have an order of command for all these questions, Inspector?"

So, time had given him a chance to start thinking again. "No," she admitted truthfully. "But, I'm investigating the death of a Mountie. Any concerned, innocent citizen would desire to assist however possible."

He got the point. She had a hell of a lot of latitude in this.

"I would be delighted to help. If I had any information. I don't."

"Are you sure about that?"

"Get to the point, Inspector."

She leaned forward. "Your fence is ten meters high and two meters deep. According to local tax records, your property line not surrounded by water is 536 meters. That's 10,720 cubic meters of cold plasma delivered to you. You paid for 10,800 cubic meters."

"Your numbers are estimates."

"My numbers are good. What did the remaining dollars pay for?"

"Get an order of command. If you can, Inspector."

"Oh, I can," she said softly.

"Cold plasma dealing is perfectly legal."

"But cold plasma weapons aren't." She allowed all her irritation, all her futile anger out. "Luc Robichaux was killed by a cold plasma ligature. He died in agony, choked by his own cell debris. You had the plasma; you recently paid a tidy sum to a Winnipeg weapons maker. See where I'm going with this?"

"I'm a supplier. I'm not responsible for how the goods are used."

"So, you did sell a plasma ligature." She pressed on, ignoring his protest. She could see the sweat. "I'm only going to ask you once more. Who did you sell it to?"

"And if I don't remember?" he drawled.

She shoved to her feet and pivoted. Pressing her hat onto her head, she stalked to the door. "You'll be hearing from me."

"Jem," he said abruptly.

The Shinook leader? At last, they were getting somewhere. She spun around.

So did Lian. "You're lying."

She bit back a frustrated curse. *Stay out of this, Lian.*

"No." Scree looked at him. "I sold the plasma weapon to a buyer who called himself Jem. Shinook AIN. I didn't ask what he wanted it for."

Lian closed the distance to Scree in three steps.

"*Lian,*" she warned. Damn him for interfering, for inserting himself into her interrogation.

"Maybe you should have asked." Lian held out his hand. The lab chip he held was blinking red. "Inspector Daniels neglected to mention that I'm from Health Canada. A plague hunter, to be exact."

Why would he tell *that* to a germ phobic?

"What?" Scree's sallow skin turned pale.

Lian thrust the lab chip closer. "Know what that blinking light means? Ebola is in this room. It's a nasty, hemorrhagic virus. Blood weeps from skin. Death by exsanguination."

There was nothing languid or decadent about Scree's shriek. "Where is it?"

"Health Canada never did find the natural host. Could be something in that contraband you're hiding behind these nanowalls."

Day frowned. After all Scree's precautions, how could anything infected have been in here?

"What did you sell to Rupert Juneau?" Lian demanded.

Rearing back, Scree shook his head. "I didn't—"

"Sure you did." Lian waved the lab chip. "Rupert Juneau. No-Borders. What'd they buy? You know what groups you're selling to."

Scree gave a wild glance toward the guard, who called up data on a handheld.

"To the No-Borders? Crampons. Ice picks. Titanium line. Spider silk vests and molecular heat suits," the guard answered flatly, then rattled off an address in Moose Jaw.

Mountain climbing gear for extreme weather, sent to the same address as the tobacco drop. Day filed the facts.

"Sold to—" The guard paged down. "L.J. Malachite and Jem of the Shinook. That's all we know." He snapped off the handheld.

"I don't believe you." Lian's jaw set, and his words were like chips off the icy floes in the river outside. His gray eyes held no compassion. "You know more about Juneau."

The guard's gaze flicked toward Scree, as if seeking instruction.

"No answers?" Lian closed in, his face plastered so near to Scree's, they could share breath. "Maybe this will jog your memory. I'm a crazy plague hunter, remember? We have contact with bizarre diseases." He brought up the blinking chip. "Could I have brought the Ebola in here through your defenses?"

"What have you done?" Scree bent over, gagging. "*Mon Dieu*, I'm cramping."

"What do you think it would take for me to decontaminate the room?"

Day's ears buzzed with fury. She could not believe what she'd just heard. Lian had just threatened Scree? With the vile Ebola? If his words weren't quite a threat, they were a first cousin to one, and that was enough. Scree's goods weren't infected; Lian had somehow planted the virus.

She doubted it was truly dangerous—Lian wasn't *that* crazy—but that didn't matter. She herself might wiggle within the law, but even with scum like Scree certain boundaries weren't crossed. A threat with Ebola was one of them. If she put the pressure on Scree now, he'd be demanding a conviction trial faster than she could open a comm.

Hell in Halifax, Lian had just screwed up her interrogation. Damn him. *Damn him!* She stalked over to Lian and gripped his wrist. Breathing heavily, she jammed her hat down on her head and glared at him. "Stand down, Dr. Firebird. You will decontaminate now."

"When he—"

"Decontaminate!"

He silenced, his jaw working as he stared at her. Smart man. He caught the rage vibrating through her.

"Fine!" He keyed in a code, swept the instrument around the air for another sample. The red light turned green. "I was mistaken. My equipment was faulty. The sensor needed to be reset."

From his bent-over position, Scree stopped examining the skin beneath his sleeve. He tilted his head to look at them. "What are you saying?"

"He's saying there's no contamination," Day answered through a tense jaw. What the hell kind of game was Lian playing at? "It was an equipment malfunction."

"Are you sure?"

"Doctor Firebird?" She didn't even try to warm her tone.

"I'm sure," Lian snapped back. "There is no contamination."

"How do I know *you're* not lying?" Scree demanded.

"Because I'm a plague hunter. I live on 'kines and T-helpers and antibodies. I'm not infected. Besides, any hint of active biological contamination here and I'd have slapped on an immediate, official quarantine. Check your own sensors."

The guard reopened his handheld, then nodded. "Our sensors are clear."

With a jerk, Lian retrieved a cytokine spray from his pack. "The latest and most powerful immune booster in Health Canada. To ease your mind."

Scree looked at it with suspicion.

Lian made an exasperated sound. "Open your mouth, Inspector." He sprayed it toward her, then toward his own open mouth. "Nothing in it but 'kines." He handed Scree the canister.

Scree clutched at it and directed two sprays into his own mouth.

Day straightened, swallowing down the bitter tastes of cytokines and failure. "I apologize, *Monsieur* Scree, for my colleague's inattention to the details of his equipment. We thank you for your assistance. Will your man let us out through the plasma?"

"Yes. Yes." Scree took another spray, then straightened, finally regaining some composure. He ran a finger across his brow. "I trust I won't see you again."

"No. Again, the RCMP is grateful when our citizens cooperate. Good-bye." She started to hold out her hand, then changed her mind.

Utter silence accompanied her and Lian to the plasma shield. Outside, once the guards retreated behind the barrier, she reactivated her comm two-way. "We're out. I'm disconnecting; backup can stand down."

"What happened in there? The plasma barrier interfered with our relay."

"We got all we could use." With that, she turned off the comm and took a deep breath. It didn't help either her anger or her deep disappointment.

Night had fallen, and a cold, dark wind eddied around Day's boots. Benton waited at the sled, looking extremely satisfied. He bounded up to her and Lian, then stopped and sat on his haunches, ears back. He gave a low, confused rumble, as he looked between the two furious alphas.

"What was that all about, Day?" Lian sounded as angry as she felt. "We had him—"

"We'll talk about it when we're out of Scree's surveillance range." She held out her hand. "I'm driving."

"Like hell." With a jerk, he opened the back of his sled for Benton, then rounded to the other side and slid in.

Day's hands shook as she gestured her wolf into the sled. "Inside." At his hesitation, she ruffled his fur. "It'll be okay. You won't be cooped up long."

Just you and me, she thought as Benton jumped in; then she got in the other side.

Lian took off, speeding. They'd driven about fifteen minutes when she pointed to an old turnoff beside the river. "Stop there."

He jerked into the abandoned park and turned the sled off.

Day grabbed her hat, flung the door open, then got out, heading for the footbridge across the river. The Winnipeg Depot was on the other side, a few blocks past the bridge. "C'mon, Benton."

Unfortunately, Benton kept his haunches planted in the sled. Traitor. Lian was the one who followed her along the river's edge. "Where the hell are you going, Daniels?"

"None of your damn business. This partnership is finished."

"You don't have the authority."

"After that fiasco, I'll find the authority."

"He was talking. Why did you curl tail?"

She spun around. She could barely see him, the night had turned so black, and the few meager lights of the city didn't penetrate the overgrowth of trees at this abandoned park. His hands were buried in the pockets of his open jacket and he'd freed his hair so it whipped about him.

She spread her feet and laced her hands behind her back, holding her hat. Spine stiff, she glared at him. The powerful wind tugged her braid, but she didn't move to tame it. "You interfered with my investigation."

"You weren't getting anywhere with your questions."

"I was getting exactly where I wanted!"

"You were leaving."

"He thought I was going to get an Order of Command."

"Big threat. Bureaucracy would have tied you up for days. Weeks maybe. By then, we could have a full-blown epidemic on our hands."

"It *was* a big threat. Investigating the death of a Mountie? I'd have had the writ like that." She snapped her fingers. "And I could have made it as broad as I wanted since he was obstructing me. I could have closed down his operation, and I would have, too."

He leaned forward, hands at his hips. "Then why didn't you get the Order before walking in there?"

"Because the threat is more effective in this case. I need specific info—on Luc Robichaux's death, the No-Borders, and the virus. He's a peripheral to all those, so once I get rid of his posturing, he tells me the truth. In turn, I don't look deep at anything else he's doing. Unless I'm forced to get an Order."

"My way was more direct."

"Your way was illegal!"

"You didn't think to clue me in on your plan, *partner*."

"Scree knew what it meant when I was walking out the door. I knew it. You would have, too, if you paid any attention to the law."

Lian was silent a moment. "Was I also supposed to figure out that Luc Robichaux was killed with an illegal plasma ligature? That's not in the official report."

"I'm not used to working with a non-Mountie!" Dammit, when had she gone on the defensive? "We agreed I was in charge of criminal investigations. You ignored that."

"He was blowing smoke in your face, and you were inhaling it."

She pressed her lips together, fighting for the calm she needed, deliberately slowing her heaving breath. She hated this. But his interference could compromise the investigation. If Scree pressed a complaint because of Lian's threat during her meeting, then both she and Lian would be pulled off this case. She would not risk failure because of him.

Moreover, he'd used a biological threat, and that was unconscionable. "The room couldn't have been contaminated. Not with his precautions. How did you bring in the Ebola?"

He stopped pacing and stared at her. His eyes were unreadable in the darkness—not that she was good at reading him anyway. "Is that what you think happened?"

"Doesn't matter what I think."

"It matters to me," he said enigmatically. "But, if you don't know that, or don't care, then there's nothing to talk about. C'mon, Day." He jerked his head toward the sled. "We've got to catch the Connect back. We've got some new leads to follow."

He just didn't see! She put on her hat, her eyes stinging. The tears were whipped up by the biting wind, she told herself as she swallowed around the clog in her throat. From long practice she erased expression from her face, then tried to purge emotion from her chest.

Use the law. There was only one way she knew to work independent of him, to prevent him from derailing her case.

"Dr. Julian Firebird, you are removed from the investigation into the death of Luc Robichaux. You used a biological agent to interfere with an officer of the law investigating the aforementioned death. Under the authority invested in me by Parliamentary Emergency Law 238, Section 5, sub paragraph d, you are hereby arrested and judged guilty."

Chapter Nine

"My whole career is about combating disease, and you're arresting me for using biological weapons?"

"Not exact—"

"Damn it, Day, you can't do this." Lian slammed a hand against a tree trunk, his simmering anger fed by her accusation. How could she? Yet there she stood, every centimeter the Mountie: hat on, spine stiff; coat unbuttoned and her white shirt gleaming in the moonlight. No, not accusation; she'd already judged him guilty. "I don't have time for this." He strode toward the sled.

"Are you resisting arrest?" She blocked him. Gaze steady, she held out her hand. "I'll take your weapons."

Damn if those unique eyes didn't bewitch him. Green and hazel. Guileless. Intriguing. Fascinating. For a moment he thought he saw a flicker of pain inside them and felt her fleeting regret.

The touches of humanity quickly erased. Her face held no expression except cool determination, and now her eyes held no warmth. There was no hint of the moments of shared laughter and danger and the intimate conversation they'd shared on the sled. No hint she knew her scent still lingered on his skin and her taste on his lips.

Green and hazel. Camouflage colors. A woman's body hiding a robot's mind.

He pushed away. "You are not taking me into custody." The thought of a jail repelled every part of him—the claustrophobic, the plague hunter, the shaman. He strode past her.

"Stop!" She sounded furious.

With only a wave—why argue with beautiful marble?— he stalked to his sled, giving a quick whistle. "Out, Benton. Stay with *her*." He'd take his sled, let someone know where she was.

A second later, his feet whipped out from beneath him and he landed face first on the hard ground. The shock drove the air from his lungs. Dizzy. Cold. Wet. Lightheaded. Unpleasant sensations rang through him. Pine needles jabbed his cheek; stones dug into his chest. A knee to the small of his back pinned him down as Day yanked his arm back.

"Don't resist," she demanded. "It's only—"

"Like hell!" His survival instincts kicked in. Before she could snap on restraints, he jabbed back his free elbow, tempering the blow at the last second so he wouldn't break her rib or arm. Still, she grunted at the contact. Furious and not afraid to play dirty, he reared back and twisted his arm from her grip.

She didn't give up. Hell, Day didn't know the meaning of the word *surrender*. Winded but not incapacitated, she hooked his elbow and pushed it toward his shoulder, going after the restraints again.

Using every bit of his twenty-five-centimeter and thirty-five-kilo advantage, he tossed her off, aiming to land on top of her. She rolled away, scrambling to get to her feet. He lunged forward and grabbed her ankle, pulling her back down and dislodging the Distazer she'd drawn. He shoved it out of reach. Her boot kicked the side of his head; his grip loosened from the impact. She sprang upright. He did, too.

She was trained and proficient, but so was he, and he had the size advantage. He should be winning this handily.

Except she had advantages, too. Assets like agility and flexibility. And a maple scent that drove him *loco*. Assets like, despite his anger, he did not want to hurt her.

Their breath rasped into the night. Warily they circled, each looking for an advantage, an opening that neither was likely to yield. The weight of his carbon tube dagger pressed against his hip, a way to finish this, yet he didn't draw it. Not a weapon for bluffing, its only uses were to maim or kill.

He could do neither to Day.

Oh, hell, she was edging toward her Distazer.

Benton bounded in, tail wagging, obviously thinking this was a strange new playtime for the pack. Suddenly, Lian had a wolf in his face, paws on his shoulders, and a wet lick on his nose. He staggered to keep his footing as Day ran forward, Distazer in hand, looking for that opening.

Except Benton turned and sprang on her with a joyous yip. Down she went, knocked on her back with a thud. She went limp beneath the energetic, wrestling beast.

For one, brief, ignoble moment, Lian wished he were the one on top of her; then he took off toward his sled. Except, he could not stop himself from looking back, from making sure she wasn't hurt.

She hadn't moved. Benton straddled her, nudging her with his nose. Was she unconscious? He grabbed his med pack from the sled, then raced over. She was pale, her cheeks sans all color, and her chest moved in shallow, gasping respirations. At least she was still breathing. Could she move? Was she injured?

"Day, you'd better be alive and well," he muttered,

kneeling beside her. Benton straddled her, nudging her with his nose. Lian urged the wolf aside with his shoulder, as he lifted her wrist to check her pulse. Faster than he liked, with a filliping beat. Likely the beast still sitting on her chest wasn't helping matters.

"Move, Benton. Let her breathe." Lian patted the ground beside him. Benton glanced between them; then, with no countercommand from Day, he got off and sat where instructed. Lian leaned over his patient to attach a diagnostic chip.

Searing pain was his only warning before the Distazer shot robbed his arms of all ability to move. A second later, his elbows were locked together in a stasis restraint. The restraint's electron impulses prevented muscle contraction, and thus movement.

He'd worried for nothing. His patient was more than capable of taking care of herself. "I didn't think you had such a deceptive talent," he muttered.

"I had a good teacher." She winced as she sat up, rubbing her shoulder.

He refused to feel sympathy. Still, he had to admire such single-minded determination.

Her Frisker located both his Distazers. She tucked his weapons into her pocket, then nodded to the sled. "Let's go."

He got awkwardly to his feet, disdaining her helping hand. The carbon tube dagger still hidden in his holster might cut his restraints. Or a comm to Health Canada would have him out—

"You'll spend the night in a depot cell," she said, "then be out at O six hundred tomorrow."

"Under twelve hours? For a biological threat?" He stared, incredulous.

"I tried to tell you, but you were too pig-headed to listen. I charged you with obstruction of an investigation. Scree has twelve hours to lodge a complaint about your threat.

If he does, you'll be in jail and the complaint will go no further."

He was missing some nuance here. "No charge of using a biological weapon? Why? Not that I'm complaining."

"Because I do think I know enough about you to believe you'd never put someone at risk. You just made Scree think you would. Whatever you did, it was noninfectious."

"But you *do* think I laced that room." He glared at her. "What happens when I get out?"

"We work our separate cases. Comm as necessary." She lifted her chin. "I work better alone. Maybe you'll admit that now."

Alone? No. Lian rebelled at the thought. No way he was abandoning her and this partnership. He had twelve hours to figure out how to convince Day of that fact.

To Day's relief, Lian didn't argue further with her. Silently, he got back in the sled, although he refused to let her assist him, and she winced inwardly when his head barely missed the edge of the door.

The Winnipeg Depot was a short distance away, but the trip there was the longest she'd ever taken. And the silence was the noisiest she'd ever known. Lian looked out the window, surprisingly calm in the shadow of his earlier anger.

Day missed the passionate man, even if he had almost bested her in their fight. Duty, tonight, was a very stark companion.

The Depot was crowded, by Canadian terms. Besides the six staff officers, four field Mounties were in the station. Each was processing an arrest, meaning their nabs required jail time; fines were processed by remote. Day knew about half the officers and constables well enough to bend an elbow or two, and most of the others she'd met at least once. One of them took charge of Benton, and Day heard the constable beginning to regale the crowd with one of the Benton legends that had sprung up in the corps. Multiple cheerful greetings followed her as she ushered Lian forward. She responded in kind, feeling a familiar kinship with these people who put their life on the line to protect their home and way of life.

Sort of like a plague hunter.

It wasn't a comforting thought when she'd just arrested Lian for trying to do that, too—albeit in an unacceptable way.

She made one detour: to the handheld inputs officer. "On the common-location bulletins add Jem, leader of the Shinooks."

"Will do. All Mounties on the lookout. Any DNA samples, images? Description to aid?"

"Just the name. Possibly armed and dangerous. Detain, then link to my comm. I'll direct from there."

As soon as she and Lian reached the inner level, she unfastened his restraints.

He lifted a brow. "Not afraid I'll run anymore?"

"Procedures. Once restraints are on, I can't take them off until now."

"Procedures. Of course." When she reached for him, to work his arm until the motor activity returned, he stopped her with an abrupt, "I'll handle it."

"As you wish." With that, she bent over her handheld to enter her report. "What did happen? Was Ebola there?"

"Yes."

"You laced something?" Her heart clenched and her fingers flattened on her handheld.

"No." His tone drew her glance. "That area was decimated by an outbreak of Ebola. It's a hemorrhagic disease; blood coming out of all orifices. Spreads viral RNA all over the place. Our equipment has gotten so sensitive that even this many years later we can still detect residual fragments in the air or on blood spattered surfaces. That's what my chip picked up—long dead, non-infectious remnants, which are nothing to worry about. Normally we calibrate our chips to be less sensitive; otherwise we'd have too many false positives. I altered the calibration."

The surge of relief left Day weak. He *had* interfered. And resisted arrest. Beyond that, though, he'd done nothing more than let his machine detect what was already there.

"And technically," he added, "I didn't threaten Scree. I posed a hypothetical question."

"But you did interfere with my questioning, and in a way that might have derailed our investigation."

He started to speak, but when he pressed his lips together and stayed silent, she bent back to her handheld and finished entering in the arrest—interference with an investigation, no mention of the virus. Then she stiffly rose to her feet and gestured to the guard. "He'll take your personal effects and return them when you leave. Goodbye, Lian." With that she laid his trek sled key on the desk, pivoted, and whistled for Benton. She walked out, back straight, unable to respond to the cheerful good nights of her colleagues.

Not when, for the first time, leaving after an arrest felt so wrong.

With winter's approach, dawn came late to the north. The sun hadn't yet reached the horizon when Day steered her sled into the fast-running river. The night sky had faded to charcoal, though, and the change would help her negotiate the foam-capped rapids ahead. Sled lights had a deceptive way of reflecting off the river, hiding the shadows of buried obstacles.

She avoided the spear of a log, then hit the first of the rapids. An eddy slapped her sled, causing it to buffet back and forth. The nose dove down, and the back end swung forward, jerked by a circulating current. Deftly, she pulled out of the whirlpool and slipped past a boulder breaking through the river's surface.

Behind her, Benton whined. The wolf didn't like traveling on rough water; he got motion sickness. "I know, big fella," she called back when the first series of rapids eased. "Not nice. Sorry, but there's no other choice. Not if we want to visit Trafalgar."

He whined again and laid himself flat out, his muzzle on his paws. Unfortunately for Benton, the numerous rivers and lakes were the easiest—sometimes the only—way to reach the Yukon. The unforgiving land had been virtually uninhabited before the plagues, and since it had become only more inhospitable. What wasn't thick forest was peaty tundra or jagged rock outcroppings.

The sled careened through a foamy rapid, sending them meters upstream to calmer water. Its nanobottom adapted easily to the changing current. Better than the wolf. Day hoped the medicine she'd hidden in his breakfast would keep him from throwing up this time.

She stifled a yawn as she eyed a new set of rapids rising ahead. Last night had been sparse of sleep, even by her standards. She'd left Winnipeg in a rented sled, caught the evening TransCanada back to Moose Jaw, then taken the next Connect west to Edmonton in her own sled. Once there, she'd headed north. Fort Chipewyan was too far to make without stopping, but she'd wanted to cover the by-land kilometers at night. The plan had been to camp on the riverbank for the tail of the night, allowing Benton a chance to roam and her to recuperate by solitude and sleep, then maximize the daylight hours available for water travel.

Solitude, however, had been unbearable. It had left her with only her voice and thoughts—well, excepting Benton's moonlight howls. Once again her sleep had been disturbed by the enigmatic plague hunter she kept misjudging. She'd had to wait until after seven until it was safe to leave, an hour after Lian's release. Too much time to think. And feel.

She braced for the next series of rapids, glad for the distraction. The buffeted sled jerked and pulled, trying to yank the steering from her hands. A spray of water hit the shield glass, blinding her until the silicon reconfigured and shed the droplets. One series of rapids led into another, demanding all her attention, all her strength. Now, this she understood. Action. Despite her sore body and the drag of fatigue, she laughed, relishing the physical challenge of keeping her sled heading forward.

Benton gave her an annoyed glare before closing his eyes.

Lian, Day couldn't help thinking, would have enjoyed this.

The sun finally crested the horizon and began the day's climb when, three hours later, the sled plummeted down the last rapids and out into the smooth, narrow mouth of a lake. Not that a sunny day seemed likely. Leaden skies forecast rain—or snow—and the air felt thick with chilly moisture. The lake mouth widened to a placid expanse. The surrounding firs gave way to an open patch blanketed with red-and-yellow lichen, spears of grass, and thumbs of granite.

Day maneuvered the sled handily around the boulders that rose out of the lake, then let the sled putt forward, giving Benton respite from the motion while she grabbed a quick meal of energy bars. Stretching out her feet, she relaxed except for an eye out for the occasional travel hazard. Immediately her mind returned to last night, like a bear nipping at a caribou herd.

At first, she'd attributed her restlessness to the hard ground and her recent lack of time in the wild; to the nighttime drop of ten centigrade degrees and the unfamiliar canopy of leaves blotting out the stars. She didn't bother with regret over her recent decisions. Not her arrest, not even her anger at Lian's interference. Those things hadn't disturbed her sleep and made the isolated landscape more desolate than soothing.

No, it was the man, the plague hunter himself, who'd destroyed her sleep.

The stark truth was, she had misjudged him. *And she missed him*.

She'd had lovers before. Not many, she was choosey, but enough that she knew what she liked. Physically fit men. Good and honest men. Solid men. Those were the men she respected and liked. The rare times she'd thought about any kind of permanent connection, she'd always seen a Mountie in the picture.

Until claustrophobic Lian had plunged down a dark tunnel with her. Since then, he'd exasperated, challenged, and excited her. The way they'd talked in the sled—for the first time since she was six—she'd opened a piece of herself to a non-Mountie.

Lian matched most of her criteria. He was fit and tough. His heart was good, she'd come to believe.

In place of the shared *esprit de corps*, though, he offered something new. Something that left her confused and unsure, two emotions she'd spent a lifetime trying to conquer. *Passion*. Pure, unadulterated passion, which left her weak-kneed and craving the taste of him. They'd barely kissed, yet somehow the plague hunter had awakened a wild need for something more than a life filled only with the law.

Impossible—even if she hadn't made such hopes moot by arresting him. Lian was not a Mountie. From her adoptive father who had given up so much for her to the colleagues who supported her, wept with her, and guarded her back, Mounties were her family. With them, was where she *belonged*. She didn't want to lose them.

But they wouldn't understand a liaison with a plague hunter. The rivalries and rumors between the two groups ran too deep. She'd even muttered a few futile curses herself when Health Canada had taken over two of her cases. And botched one.

Even her job would be that much harder. True, she worked alone mostly, but without RCMP confidence and backup support when she needed, she'd be less effective at keeping the peace. And her G-1 would probably disappear.

She sighed, glancing around, hoping the beautiful majestic land could soothe her and remind her where her loyalties lay.

This land north of the fiftieth parallel might be barren of humanity, but like many other places in Tri-Canada, the wildlife had thrived in the absence of human encroachment. A herd of caribou spread across the tundra surrounding the lake, driven here by the greater northern snowfalls. A pair of hawks and a lone condor soared in the clouds, while sparrows and wrens fluttered closer to ground. Ptarmigan and grouse waddled through the brush. Up a spar streamlet, she saw a crane wading in the shallows created by a beaver dam. A pair of swans drifted beside her. She'd heard geese used to flock to these waters, thick as pebbles. But they'd been susceptible to one of the viruses, and had been wiped out, extinct since 2083.

She opened the top of her sled, enjoying the unfettered breeze, even if it was glacial cold. The scent of spruce and moss filled the snow-ready air. Benton rose to his feet, nose twitching.

"You smell a marmot? Or a moose?" she asked, ruffling his fur. He gave a low growl in response.

She supposed he needed to be doing some hunting, so she pulled over to the side of the lake. Without a word from her, Benton sprang from the sled and disappeared into a pack of Canadian spruce.

Idly, while she awaited his return, she read a little more about Banzai Maguire, the fighter pilot whom the Voice of

Freedom claimed would return democracy to the UCE.

Day didn't suppose she and this Banzai would ever meet, but she had a hunch if they did, they'd have a few things in common. Two women in physically-challenging fields, charged with protecting their respective countries? That much alone would be enough for a congenial night of tales over beers.

An ancient image unearthed by a voice fanatic and purported to be of Banzai, scrolled across Day's handheld. The female fighter pilot circa 2006 A.D. stared straight ahead, solemn, her helmet tucked beneath her arm. On the sleeve of her flight suit was sewn the old flag of the USA, its stars and stripes glowing in red, white, and blue pixels. A flag the UCE no longer recognized as the symbol of the country.

Banzai had been dropped into a world where her family was long dead, her squadron and her duty no longer existed, her country was unrecognizable. Every familiar, external support was gone. Even the flag had changed.

"What do *you* hang on to, Banzai?" Day whispered. "What shapes *your* days and gives purpose to *your* life? What do you hold most dear?" The hum of an engine caught her attention, and she glanced up to see a plane making graceful loops overhead. "Do you want to fly again? I wonder what you'd think of a plane like that one."

She snapped off her handheld and watched the plane make a tighter loop. It looked to be one of the newest vertical take-off bush planes, gaining popularity since they'd solved the landing problems and found a substitute for rubber gaskets. Trek sleds could still go more places, but these planes were three times faster, so some people preferred them. If they could afford them.

Most of the planes were loaded with equipment. Things like heat sensors and UV scans. If anyone was looking for her in one of those, she'd be an easy pickup on heat scans, out on the open lake like this.

Her eyes drifted shut, and she pushed the seat back in preparation for a quick nap. But her internal clock said she'd only gotten five minutes before the engine grew louder and disturbed her rest. She opened her eyes and saw a bush plane bearing down on the lake. Whether it was the same one she'd seen a few minutes before, she couldn't tell.

She gave a whistle to Benton. Something about that plane disturbed her. Maybe the steady drone or the unswerving line directly toward her.

Or the gun barrel pointed out the window.

Hell in Halifax, a pressure cannon! Whistling again for Benton, she scrabbled at her belt for her matrix filters. She slipped them into her ears just as the first heavy pressure put an ache in the back of her throat. Benton loped out of the trees, a rabbit in his mouth. Normally, she didn't let him in the sled with his lunch, but in this case, she'd make an exception. Fortunately, the pressure cannon hadn't been set at a frequency to disrupt his hearing. Yet.

"C'mon, boy."

At her call, Benton leaped into the sled as she started the engine. She slammed down the shield glass, stuck two filters into the wolf's ears, then shoved the sled into reverse. Full throttle, she headed across the dangerously open lake, aiming for the outlet half a kilometer away. If she could get there, the bulk of trees would shield her against most scans.

Blood pounded against her ear filters. To give the plane above proper warning, she flicked a button and the top of the glass shield displayed the Mountie crest.

The gun fired again, this time an explosion of directed pressure that rattled the sled. Pain sliced through Day's eyes, and a red haze clouded the edge of her vision. Another explosion struck, rattling bolts and glass, but the sturdy sled held together.

Apparently the people in the plane had no qualms about opening fire on a Mountie.

Out here on the lake, she was the proverbial sitting duck. Her attackers could fire at will, and they were not amateurs. Were there any other options besides that stream ahead? Right now it was still her best choice. The lake was mostly underground fed; few streams led off of it, and the only ones she was sure were navigable were the one she'd come in on and the one she was heading for. That outlet was still her best choice.

Heart pounding, she took the sled off automatic and put it on a manual. A high-pitched whine protested the sudden release of dampers and controls. She jammed her foot against the accelerator, pressed it past the max point of computer control, past the safety zone. The engine groaned, but it was tuned finer than the national orchestra and kept up the fiery pace.

Shock waves pounded her until she could barely see. Stiffly she rotated her shoulder, unable to bend her aching neck, to check behind. Blood haze impaired her vision, but she saw enough. The plane was gaining. She coaxed out another couple of kph's velocity. The exit stream. She was going to make it!

Thick conifers signaled the end of the tableland. There the trek sled had an advantage: the plane couldn't fly in the narrow, covered channel. And the trees interfered with their sensors.

The plane cut its speed, dropping from above until it flew almost level with her sled, putting her in the direct line of their fire. And this time they were using rapid-fire ion rifles. Of course, that meant they were in direct line with *her* weapons. She fired, two quick bursts that caused them to pull back, even though she didn't think she'd done any damage.

She dove beneath the canopy. The sudden contrast from

cloudy to dim-as-twilight blinded her and sent a shaft of pain through her eye. She squinted, trying to focus. In her rearview panel, she could see the plane hovering at the entrance to the river.

It sent one last shot after her, a whining missile that skimmed the top of her sled, missing her by mere centimeters.

The river curved just ahead. She could—

The missile exploded in front of her, a phosphorus-white flame that filled her sight with white dots as she drove straight into the explosion.

Halifaxing hell, what was that? She spun the sled into the curve, easing the accelerator to avoid a crash. The engine began to knock and clank. The stench of burning rubber and oil billowed out on a plume of smoke.

She swore. Something in that explosion must have pierced her engine. Which meant the shooter would be coming in after her and she'd be sitting here dead in the water.

Swiftly, she shoved back the shield glass. "Grab your rabbit, Benton, we're abandoning ship!" She collected her emergency pack and weapons, then set the automatic controls again, overriding the crash sensor. Maybe this would fool them, at least long enough for her to disappear. She waited until the sled curved around the bend, out of sight, and then she and the wolf leaped over the side.

"C'mon, Benton!"

The cold water stole her breath, and bruised her every bone and muscle. For endless moments she tumbled helpless, her only sense the emergency kit gripped in her hand, until at last she regained her equilibrium and with painful strokes made her way to the riverbank. Benton paddled gamely beside her, the bloody rabbit still in his mouth.

Behind her, Day heard her sled crash into the bank on the other side. A waste of a fine vehicle.

The fiery explosion knocked her forward into the trees. She kept running, never looking back.

The low-flying plane skimmed the canopy of trees and hovered over the plume of smoke. How long would it take for its sensors to determine there wasn't a human amongst the wreckage?

Not long enough. The whine of the engine deepened as the bush plane began a slow circle outward. Searching for her.

Day followed its progress by the engine pitch, unable to stop long enough to peer through the thick trees. Louder and higher meant closer. On each arc that neared her, she dove with Benton beneath the thickest bushes and choked off all motion. Lying rigid, holding her breath so not even lung movement gave her away, her body across the wolf to keep him quiet, she waited until the engine noise faded and deepened.

Each time the plane circled away, she and Benton scrambled to their feet and sped through the boreal forest, with Day blessing the thick cover that interfered with all tracking technology. Benton seemed to understand the urgency and the danger, for he loped quietly at her side, matching her in either speed or stillness.

On occasion, she felt the joint-rattling shock of a pressure cannon or heard the snap of an ion rifle as the searchers attacked some hapless animal with the unfortunate luck to show on the heat or motion sensors.

Her pack bounced on her back, bruising her spine. The already cold temperature outside dropped beneath the trees and pinched the skin of her nose. She felt as though steam was coming off her, though. Every muscle, ligament, and tendon in her body ached, but she still kept running.

Despite her progress, each widening circle brought the plane closer. The pronged shadow swept across the trees like a funeral veil, so close she felt the chill at her back as it blocked what little sun got past the upper branches. That time, they nearly passed above her. If they came directly overhead they might even spot her without sensors.

The plane was beginning the downward arc of its circle, heading straight for her. A small stream lay ahead. At least it wasn't cold enough that the water and the mud had frozen. Day and Benton crawled down the bank, keeping beneath the awning of trees and coating themselves with the mud and leaves. Maybe the camouflage would cut off enough of her body temperature the heat sensor couldn't detect her.

And if anyone had invented a sweat detector, the stench of the mud would surely foil that one as well.

The drone of the engine inched closer. Day reached down and unfastened her holster. Slipping her Distazer out, she laid her chin on Benton's neck and waited.

Chapter Ten

Lian found Day five kilometers from the crash site. Through the thick boreal forest, he caught a glimpse of her on the ground. Back to a tree, she sat with legs bent while she dabbed at her hands. Only the roundness in her shoulders hinted at her exhaustion. She had her knit shirt off, leaving her dressed in the incongruous mix of boots, bone-repair plaster on her ribs, pocketed black taiga pants, and a skimpy sport top made of a shimmery fabric that shifted subtly between red and black.

The air held a damp, bitter note, and when a stray breeze rustled the treetops, a shudder coursed across her bare shoulders.

His medical eye wasn't pleased to see she'd obviously broken a couple of ribs, while his hormones didn't need the vivid reminder that she had generous curves and wore sexy underwear.

Her Distazer was balanced on her knees. He wasn't so foolish this time to think the pose meant she was unready or unaware of his approach. Frozen moss crackled beneath his footsteps, and before he could tell her it was him near-ing, the Distazer leveled at his chest. Her back straight-ened, and her head lifted—and she almost hid her wince of pain. "Inspector Daniels of the Royal Canadian Mounted Police. Identify yourself."

"It's me, Day." He wove through the trees until she could see him clearer.

He saw more details of her, too, and he didn't like what he saw. Her braid was coming loose and pine needles com-pleted her disarray. Face smudged with mud, eyes blurred with fatigue, a purpling bruise marred her shoulder. The scratches she'd been tending on her hands oozed blood.

"What are you doing here?" she asked.

"Partners, remember?" He knelt beside her on the cold ground, then draped his coat over her shoulders.

Benton, snoozing beside her, opened one eye, gave a growl of welcome, then fell back asleep.

"I distinctly remember taking you off my case."

"Yes, well . . . that was an illegal command, since you and your case were assigned to *my* investigation." He swung his med pack off his shoulder.

"I was afraid you'd figure that out."

"Fortunately, I'm not like you, and I won't stick you in jail."

"You're angry?"

"I was royally pissed until my brain started working again." He picked up her wrist, amazed at the delicacy for someone as sturdy as she, and sent a prayer toward the spirits asking for their guidance in his task.

She tugged back her hand. "I'm just a little banged up."

"You look worse than Benton's dinner."

"Thanks for the pep talk."

"You're the one who wants honesty. Any objections to a second, *professional* opinion to your diagnosis?"

She hesitated, then shook her head and held out her arm. "I won't apologize for my earlier actions."

His fingers overlapped, testing her pulse while he counted her respirations. "Didn't expect you to. I didn't like what you did, didn't agree with it, but you're too much of a stiff brim for anything else." He spoke mildly, but didn't bother with subtlety. "Good thing I'm beginning to like that about you."

He let go of her wrist, fastened a diagnostic chip against her throat, then sat back while it worked. Before they went any further he wanted to clear one thing. "You were right, Day."

"About what?" She looked suspicious. He'd have laughed at her wariness if it hadn't been a subtle sign of her doubts.

"Sitting a night in a jail cell gives you time to think." *And to realize when you've been an ass.* "I agreed you were to handle the questioning, and I should have trusted you to do your job. But, when I heard Scree lying to you about the Shinooks, and you seeming to take it in—"

"He wasn't lying."

"He was, but I'm not trying to start another argument. What I'm saying is: I'm sorry for not trusting you, and, hard as it may be, I won't interfere like that again." Unless she was in danger.

"You're lucky I'm feeling a mite chipped here; it makes me more willing to be accommodating." The stiffness left her shoulders, as though she could no longer fight her fatigue. "Apology accepted."

"And I accept yours," he said with a brief smile.

"I don't remember apologizing." She laughed, then winced.

"Are we partners or not, Day?" He wanted no misjudgments this time. "I've already said I'd give you the space you need. Will you meet me halfway? No more arresting me or some other stunt to sabotage us. We're stronger together."

One of last night's revelations. Along with the disturbing recognition that this unlikely woman was scraping away his isolation and cutting through his layers of defense. Even now, her heat wrapped around him with a seductive whisper, promising that he was no longer alone. It was an illusion though, for this time could only be a brief interlude where their divergent paths ran parallel. A time with a job to do.

She didn't reply right away, and he was glad she gave thought to her answer, for agreeing meant a small but fundamental shift in the way she had always worked. If he could not have her trust, he would at least have her cooperation.

At last she nodded. "You're right. I have been looking for ways to break us apart. If you're willing to try, so am I. It won't happen again. We're partners."

Partners. The word settled inside him like an ember of life-giving fire.

"And I do owe you an apology, too." She laid a hand over his, and the muscles in his gut tensed. "I should have told you my plans. I'm sorry. Next time, I'll keep you informed."

"Apology accepted," he echoed. Yet, inside him an expectant spark winked out, and a piece of him drew back from her. It hadn't been the apology he needed. And that hurt more than he wanted to admit.

He fixed his attention on the diagnostic chip, the familiar protective mantle of remoteness numbing the pain.

"Good." The diagnostic chip chirped, and he glanced at the readout. "So far so good. Let me styptic those gashes." With economy of motion, he applied a stinging gel to her bleeding cuts, holding her hands impersonally, not touching her anywhere else. "How'd your ribs get broken?"

"I leaped from my trek sled into the river."

"Damnation, Inspector, you were lucky it wasn't a broken neck. Had a yen for a polar swim?"

"My choices were limited. Either that or rendezvous with some shooters who took out my engine."

"Who'd you make angry?"

A specter of a smile crossed Day's face. "Besides you? Someone with access to a fully loaded bush plane." As he shone his penlight into her eyes, testing pupil reaction, she jerked her head away and said, "I'm seeing fine."

"I doubt that, since your pupils are dilated and the light hurts your eyes. How'd you get away?" If he kept her talking, maybe she'd forget her Mountie grit long enough to let him examine and treat her.

"The crashed sled distracted them. The trees, rocks, and wildlife around here interfere with heat scopes and infrared sights, so I headed for the thickest underbrush."

"That explains *this*." He plucked pine needles from her hair, then flicked caked mud off her forehead. "Why the mud?"

"Hides body heat." She frowned. "How did you find me? They gave up after two hours."

"I'm more persistent." He wrapped another tissue-repair plaster around her swollen wrist.

She gave him an askance look. "Canada's got a lot of land—"

"For locating a grouse-sized Mountie? I know."

"Grouse are pudgy."

"And you're definitely not," he agreed, scanning her this time with an appreciative male, instead of medical, eye.

The comment brought a flush of color to her pale cheeks. He was having a hard time keeping that uncivilized piece of him—the one that persisted in seeing her as a sexy woman, not a patient or a partner—under control. Sitting this near to her, touching her, even if she did stink of tundra mud, he got distracted by the curve of her brows and the softness beneath the delicately shifting colors of her undershirt. Her energy, subdued right now beneath pain and fatigue, but still more vibrant and powerful than most women he knew, crackled across his skin.

"Okay, so how did I find a petite Mountie? You told me about your plans to go to Wood Buffalo before we left Moose Jaw. It wasn't hard to figure out which rivers you might take, and the oil smoke from the explosion was a huge hint. After that . . . well, I'm a good tracker." He smiled at her. "It helped that you had the wolf. Benton hasn't a clue about hiding his tracks. He crapped at least twice in the five kilometers I trailed you."

She laughed, then broke off abruptly, grimacing and holding the plaster at her side. "The nanobots haven't finished the job."

"They repair bone, but there's still damage to the surrounding tissue. It'll hurt for a while."

"I still don't understand how you could find me when my pursuers didn't."

He hesitated. She'd probably get angry again. Except, he wanted to start out fresh with her, working together. That meant a few explanations.

Besides, hurting as she was right now, he'd never have a better time to weather her wrath. "I got a GPS trace on your position."

"You got out of jail, said, 'I want a trace on the arresting officer,' and the depot did it?"

"Not exactly." He laid a hand against her hip, needing to touch her, wary of her response. "After your Car Town disappearing act, I figured you might try to ditch me, so I requisitioned a wireless tracer. As a plague hunter, I have the authority—" He plucked the tiny transmitter off her pack. "—to trace even a Mountie. On the ground, the trees don't interfere as much," he added sheepishly.

For a long moment she stared, gape-mouthed; then, to his relief, he felt her amusement. She shook her head. "Damn, Lian, you *are* good."

"I keep telling you that. One more test." He put his cardioscope against her sternum, braced her with his hand, then listened to her amplified heartbeat as he watched the display. Yet it was the silk of her undershirt, smooth and cool beneath his palm, that captured him as he asked her to breathe in and out.

"Doesn't the diagnostic chip check all this stuff?" she asked.

"I still like to listen. Now shush and breathe."

She stayed quiet until he put the scope away. "What's the verdict, Doc?"

"Banged up, but otherwise fine."

She laughed. "Didn't I tell you that when you first sat down? Can you hand me my shirt?"

Reaching out, her hand brushed his. The touch was a scorching arrow, straight to his groin. She froze, her fingertips resting against his, her eyes narrowed. So she had felt it, too, this inexplicable wildfire between them. Slowly, her hand shifted; not away, but to interlace their fingers, though she didn't close her grip.

He had to hold her; the compulsion was as strong as the need to drag in a breath of cold air. His hand splayed against her back.

"Diagnostic chips don't relay this little anomaly in your physiology. When I do this . . ." He urged her closer, testing her willingness. Bending slightly, she tilted until her barely clad breasts neared. Silky underwear covered the sturdy ridge of her back muscles and the steel of her spine. The contrast, softness over strength, roused a hard need. He swallowed against the ash taste in his mouth. "When I touch you, your pulse speeds up. And your heart skips beats."

"I've never had another physician say that," she murmured, her green-and-hazel eyes locked with his. She slid forward, her legs shifting gracefully to the side so her hip rested against his. "Must be your bedside manner."

159

"Complaining?" The backs of his fingers stroked her jaw, clearing off a smudge of dirt before resting at her nape. His thumb tested the pulse at her throat. Rapid it was, and strong. His chest and gut tightened, and his heartbeat raced to catch hers.

"Do I look like I'm complaining?" She leaned forward, her breasts brushing his arm. They left a fiery trail.

With a muttered oath, he closed the physical gap between them and kissed her.

The north was no longer cold, but steamier than a sweat lodge. The taste of Day was sweet as maple sugar, spicy as a smuggled pepper. Desire. Heat. Punch-in-the-gut need. The rioting, mingling emotions dug deep and stripped away Lian's thin veneer of control. Wild demands rose inside him. An imperative to make love. The urge to stake his claim. To leave his scent. To make her his, though he recognized she would never belong to him. Not independent, in-your-face Day.

Deliberately, he lightened the kiss with a brush against the corners of her mouth. Left, then right. Her hands laced through his hair; her thumbs ran across his earrings, sending a shudder of desire coursing through him. That low ache felt swollen and tight, but now was neither the time nor the place for relief.

Instead, he contented himself with a slow exploration. His lips traced from the tip of her nose to the point of her jaw, while he stroked behind her ear. He nipped the soft skin of her neck, then blew on it.

"*Lian,*" she breathed. "Are you always this indirect?"

"No," he whispered back, leaving anything more to her imagination.

She pressed forward, and he gathered her closer, hearing her gasp. Followed by a grunt of pain.

Her injured ribs! Or her shoulder. Or her arm. Lian swore and gently set her back, sanity and training returning in a rush. How could he have forgotten how beat up she was? He laid a hand against the healing plaster. "I'm sorry, Day."

"Damned ribs," she muttered, pain creasing her forehead. Then, a moment later she asked, "Got any more of those tea leaves you gave me for the shoulder?"

"Not with me. I may have to start carrying them with you as a partner, but I've got endorphins."

"No more pain cocktails. They make me woozy."

They sat forehead to forehead, letting their breath and hearts return to normal. Cold air intruded; a snowflake fell on his cheek, then another. Day shivered and moved back. Without a word, Lian handed over her shirt, and she awkwardly shrugged off his jacket, put on her shirt and coat, and buttoned them.

"Yesterday, I promised myself this wouldn't happen," she said with a sigh. "It feels right and seems so inevitable, but there's too much between us. And against us."

"Neither one of us is planning for something permanent," he said. They both rose to their feet, stamping their boots to circulate their blood. He slanted a glance toward her as he bent to repack his med kit. " 'Be it all. Do it all.' Isn't that your motto? Think of it as starting to learn next season's skill early."

She laughed softly, then gathered her things. When she righted herself, she was but a few centimeters away. Unable to stop himself, he traced the curve of her jaw. His fingers tingled with the contact, and his heart contracted with a rush of excitement and wariness.

What the hell was he doing, starting this again? He clenched his hand into a fist and pulled back.

Though the trees cut the breeze at ground level, the west wind moaned through the upper branches, and the trunks creaked as though they mourned summer's passing. "We don't want to be sitting this close to the crash site if your friends decide to come back," he said.

"Where's your sled?"

"Back at the river, so we've got a trek ahead."

Day glanced up at the darkening sky. "Then we'd better push forward." She whistled for Benton, who bounded up, circled Lian, sniffing, then gave a yip of delight. The wolf looked satisfied that his pack was at last at full strength.

But as the three of them returned to the sled, Lian was well aware that all was not right. Despite his apologies, he still kept one secret: His Shinook heritage. But until he had better evidence of their involvement, or had no other leads, he couldn't lead Day there. Not as long as his promise forbade it. And not with that outstanding warrant to capture and detain Jem.

The next hours blurred for Day. The strenuous hike back to the river, the perilous sled ride through more rapids, the endless mix of trees and water—unchanging, yet each kilometer different—the collecting flakes of snow on the trek shield, the brief stops for necessity and to change drivers: all melded into a mass of body aches and unresolved questions.

Farther north, the trees thinned into tundra. Without their interference, she commed the Mountie post, relaying the attack and the loss of her sled.

"Comm me when you have info on that bush plane registration," she finished. "If you can't reach my number, send it to the Wood Buffalo depot. We're nine hundred kiloms out, and there's more forest to go through."

"Do you need medical assistance, Inspector?" Mountie command asked.

"No, I'm fine. Nothing that a bone-repair plaster and my doctoring partner can't fix."

A pause came from her comm. "I thought you'd put him in jail."

Was she surprised that tidbit of gossip had made the rounds in less than a day? She glanced over at Lian, who was engrossed with his handheld, seeming to pay no attention to her conversation.

Like hell he wasn't.

"He's still my partner," she answered briefly, then closed off.

She maneuvered the sled across the open tundra, the glint of moonlit sedge and ice-crusted puddles like diamonds in the twin headlight beams. Lian's sled handled as smoothly as her own. Not surprising, since his life probably depended upon it.

Her fingers tightened around the steering, the loss of her own sled painful. When she got her hands on those bushie owners, they'd have some paying up—

With a sickening lurch, the sled dove right. The abrupt jerk nearly ripped the steering from her hands. One headlight angled into utter blackness. A sinkhole!

The sled's nanobottom whined as molecules shifted, and Day fought to find solid purchase. Thank God they'd only skimmed the edge. At last she righted the sled, then glanced beside her. Lian was frowning and running a thumb along an eagle feather he held in one hand. He hadn't even looked up. Hadn't offered advice or seemed concerned. Apparently, he'd meant what he said when he apologized for not trusting in her.

Fresh cold air streamed in from the window opened a crack beside him, ruffling his loosened hair. Flakes of snow dusted his pants. Against the night, his profile looked almost feral.

Their hours of travel had been broken mostly by conversations reviewing the case, planning their next moves. Occasionally they drifted into getting-to-know-you conversation. He had a fondness for Saskatoon berries. They shared an appreciation for Indian flute music. He rooted for the CHL's Calgary Flames. Her team was the Regina Boulders. They'd played a few minutes of hockey trivia—

she'd won that challenge handily—and compared scars. He'd won that by baring a long slash across his ribs, courtesy of a knife-wielding plague victim who'd thought Lian was a giant germ.

She'd discovered he had a nanotat. The bird, tattooed in brilliant hues of red and yellow on the skin above his heart, flapped its wings with slow majesty while the feathers fluttered like flame.

The rest of the time, when he wasn't driving, Lian tapped meditatively on a small drum or worked. Even her work ethic paled beside that dedication.

Or was he avoiding her? Every time she edged too intimate in their conversation, he'd shut down. Become annoyingly close-mouthed and distracted.

With other riders only a few centimeters away, she'd never had trouble isolating herself. Yet with Lian, her ears attuned to his breathing, she knew when he was asleep and when he was merely pretending. She felt each brush of his arm as he input new data on his handheld. His fresh sage scent permeated the sled.

"What are you working on?" she asked at last.

"Checking references to Citadel whenever I can get an Interweb connection, and computer modeling the virus DNA and protein coat for infectivity. Not that I'm making much progress. The sample from Robichaux's hat was too fragmented for much beyond identifying we've got a new strain. I need more virus to work with." He banged his head back against the neck rest. "I can't believe I just said that. The last thing I want is more virus. If we never saw this bug again, I'd be ecstatic."

"If it's coming, we need to be prepared."

"Except I'm running blind." He ran a hand through his hair. "I *hate* not knowing, but the computer models are based on too many assumptions. We can't even broth antibodies."

A stanza of flute music sounded on Lian's handheld, and he turned away.

"Excuse me while I take this. My sister calls."

He read, then sent back a long message, and when he'd finished, he was frowning.

"Bad news?" she asked.

"My brother has disappeared on another of his hunting trips, and my young sister, Aveline, frets over him. However she, too, is stubborn. Can you believe? Despite the coming snows, she persists on a journey to her child's father, saying I told her to go. I did not tell her to leave. She should simply have told me his name and left that to me."

Okay, some definite frustration there, Day thought, hiding a smile, her sympathies firmly with the unseen Aveline. She had only been dealing with Lian's sometimes autocratic ways for a few days; Aveline had lived with a demanding older brother all her life.

"Your voice changes when you talk about them," was her only comment. She didn't really understand the details of what sounded like a complex personal life, or feel like she had the right to offer anything but a sympathetic ear.

"Because I think in my native language and translating."

"I thought you were in exile," she wondered aloud.

"Yes, well, some do contact me, through comms and holomessages."

"Not the same as face-to-face though," she guessed.

"No." He rubbed his cheek, looking fatigued. "Traditions are hard to maintain alone."

The sled lurched again, finding the edge of another hole, breaking off their conversation. Behind her, Benton growled, an indication that he would soon make known his protest at being shut in the sled. "We'll have to make camp soon. This lichen is hiding some treacherous sinkholes, and night beams can't detect them. Besides, Benton needs his night hunt, and we could use a few hours of solid sleep."

"I don't like stopping in this open an area." He glanced around. "How about that granite outcropping?"

"Agreed." She turned the sled toward where he pointed, not seeing the rocks at first. One thing she had discovered, Lian's eyesight was keener than hers. Or perhaps he was more attuned to the land, for he'd chosen well. The overhangs would secure them from overhead view; the rock slabs would protect their backs.

Setting up camp was a simple matter of moving the sled seats back for more room and unfurling the compact blankets. When she opened the sled, Benton leaped out. He took his identifying circle then raced into the night, accompanied by a lurch in her heart and her silent prayer for his safe return.

They settled in for a needed nap. The snow hadn't yet started to fall. It swelled the clouds and muted the air with a dull mist. Against the featureless background, the interior of the trek sled seemed an intrusion of polymers and dials.

Day turned in her seat to face Lian. He looked natural against the backdrop of wild nature. His eyes were closed and his breathing steady. She took the chance to study him, this man who had caught her attention and reminded her of forgotten sensuality.

She liked the look of him, had from the first moment in the bar. She liked the thick brows and the steady gray eyes and she especially liked the blue earrings. She liked the chiseled cheeks and the whip-lean body. There was an earthiness about him, a sense of primal contact that was rare—like he wasn't just one man, but an essential thread in a larger canvas of nature.

As if sensing her scrutiny, he opened his eyes. For a long moment they studied each other in the dark, the only light the colors of the panel of control dials. He lifted his hand to stroke her cheek and jaw, a wistful touch as delicate as the brush of bird's wing.

Something had changed between them. Some undefinable, subtle shift. A recognition they'd misjudged each other. A growing sense of trust. An admission of their mutual desire. All these danced them closer, yes; but something else, darker and divisive, was there too, now. This close to Lian, his fingers warm on her skin, his breath near to mixing with hers, Day could almost feel his glimmer of disappointment snaking through her. The heat between them still simmered, ready to erupt, but it was as though a carbon dagger had severed a few of the gossamer strands joining them.

"Navigating this partnership is harder than shooting those rapids," she said, testing.

"But you got through those, and we'll figure this out," His hand lowered, and suddenly her cheek and neck felt the bitter touch of winter.

"What's different?" She was a trained observer, and she remembered the moment she'd first noticed the change. Now, in deepest night, she had the courage to ask. "Earlier, when we were apologizing, everything was fine. Then you shut down. Why?"

"Just keeping to my own business. Isn't that what you want?"

The honest streak in her stopped her automatic "yes." The rest of her acknowledged that she was being unwise to prod him.

She took in a breath, catching the wisp of sage, and licked her lips. She could face down a 'tail head jumped up on 'mines, but opening Lian's shell of reserve . . . "No. I've never had trouble separating personal and professional before, and professional always comes first. But, there's something about you . . . A door's opening inside me. I'm not sure I want to walk through it. Fact is, I'm scared spitless to walk through it, but I've never backed down from a challenge in my life, and I'm not backing from this one.

So, I'll ask you again. What happened? Was it something I said?"

"More something you didn't say." He shook his head. "Never mind, it's better this way."

"I just bared my insecurities, and all you can do is babble back riddles?"

"Day," he warned, "I'm about to forget that a trek sled is a lousy place to make love, and that I'm exhausted and you're hurting. I have but a single thread of self-control stopping me from coming over there and kissing you. And unless I was misreading the signals, you'd be kissing back."

"The fact that I reek of muck doesn't have anything to do with this laudable self-control, does it?"

"I'm too much of gentleman to mention it." His laughter faded. "Hell, Day, you want the bald truth? I want to make love to you so bad, I ache with it. I want to be your lover for however long life's wheel gives us. But, it's not going to happen tonight." He rolled over, turning his back to her, wrapping the blanket around him.

"Because we're partners—and, technically, you're my commanding officer?"

"You conveniently ignored that last night. I guess a lawless plague hunter could, too." After a moment's silence he added, "When we make love, Day, we both know it will be an interlude, a moment out of time and duty with no rank and insignia."

She stared at his back, a curl of heat in her belly. "How do you know a trek sled is a lousy place to make love?"

"Hmmm?" he mumbled.

"How do you know a trek sled is a lousy place to make love? Have you tried it?"

"Yes." He craned his neck to look at her. "What does that have to do with anything?"

"Just curious."

"You haven't?"

"No. I think I should learn that as next season's skill."

He gave a bark of laughter. "Day, you are constantly surprising me."

"Maybe that's why we have this crazy attraction. We never know how the other's going to react." She tugged his shoulder, leaning over him to stare into his face. "Why did you pull away?"

"Are you always this chatty in bed?"

"At this rate, you're never going to find out. Was it because I arrested you?"

"No." He rolled to face her, his gray eyes shadowed. "You believed I could use a live virus."

"I have to make snap judgments all the time in my job, and in this case I made the wrong one. I admit that. I didn't trust you, and I'm sorry."

"I know we haven't been partners long; there's a lot we don't know about each other. But the fact is your instinct was that I'd do something so heinous. And you didn't change until I *told* you different."

"I didn't put it on your file. I gave you a tiny sentence. I apologized." She toyed with the end of her braid. "What more do you want from me?"

"Maybe the impossible." He met her eyes. "I want your shoot-on-the-run reaction to be that I'll do the right thing. Not necessarily the legal thing, but the *right* thing. And I want you to let me do it. I'm not sure that you can give me that trust." Without another word, he rolled back, leaving her wondering whether he was right.

Chapter Eleven

Trafalgar Daniels lived in an abandoned ranger camp. Lian and Day drove around the herd of bison munching tundra sedge, and reentered the thick forest that had overgrown any cleared area that once housed the collection of cabins. True to his nature, Trafalgar had claimed the settlement as home when he retired, citing "too much damned civilization" to the south. His only neighbors in a hundred kiloms were now bison, whooping cranes, wolves, caribou, and several million ducks and swans.

While Day searched for the tree notches Trafalgar left to direct any visitors to his home, Lian concentrated on maneuvering their sled between the trees and the falling snow. Each kilom passed, each taste of clear air and each breath of fragrant spruce, fed his soul.

He opened the window of the trek sled, relishing the cold and the deep silence. He loved the wilderness, when the sky above and the earth below surrounded him with snow and solitude. An unfettered need called him to taste, to touch, to experience the raw, primitive nature outside the sled and inside himself. To become one with the wind and to chant the songs and play the drum as the shaman he had once trained to be.

Except surrender to this alluring solitary wild was not enough. Lian rubbed the back of his neck. He needed this union, and he also needed the communal fires. He recognized that now.

In the cities, the middle world, the world of man, he had existed, not lived. There he stood amidst the bustle, yet always isolated. The separation had come so gradually, his mind had ignored the loss, but his soul had been hollowed by the choices of necessity and the reality of his work.

He clenched the sled wheel, swept by a pressing ache of loneliness made keener now by the urgency of his mission, which held a tantalizing promise of the end of his exile, and by Day. His connections to his people had faded to a gnawing ache in the intervening years. But his puzzling, chaotic feelings for Day were sharp and immediate. They made him wonder for the first time whether he was not limited to only two choices and exile could mean something had more than denial.

He glanced over at her. Day, with her sweet scent and silky hair. Her courage, stubbornness and honesty. With her as his partner, for the first time in almost seven years, he no longer felt isolated.

He smiled, faintly. If she heard his whimsical thoughts, she would likely think him half mad. At this moment, she was drumming her nails against the dash.

"I wish Trafalgar had a comm," she fretted, pointing out another small identifying mark on a tree.

"Why do you call him Trafalgar and not Dad?" he asked.

She perched one foot on the seat and rested her chin on her knee. "At the quarantine camp, adults were blurry images to me. Someone giving me an injection. Hands putting a bowl of soup on a table. A woman in a bright red dress . . ." She broke off abruptly.

"What?"

"Just remembering. I thought the dress was pretty until I realized the red was blood. I didn't know which ones were my parents. No one bothered to tell me names, so any adult was Mom or Dad. When I went to live with Trafalgar, I finally felt like I had a dad. But . . . 'Dad' was the men at the camp. So, I just started calling him Trafalgar, and the name stuck. Trafalgar didn't mind; he's not much for sentiment."

Day, too, had known deep loneliness, Lian realized. It was that which made the Mounties as important to her as the Shinook were to him. The shared emotion was a common bond between them, but it would also tear them apart one day.

But that time was not today. For now, they were partners.

At last they pulled into a wide spot between the trees that held a collection of cabins. An air of abandonment hung over the camp, although the three buildings were in good repair. Maybe it was the bison wandering between the porches. Or the lack of smoke from the chimney. Or the lack of lights, despite a morning smudged by snow.

Trafalgar's home was cold and empty. The ex-Mountie wasn't at home.

Anything unusual?" Lian asked Day, who stood, hands at her hips, a frown on her face. She surveyed the room, which held a desk, stuffed chairs, and a battered Chesterfield.

"Not that I can see."

"Does he often just pick up and go?"

"Yeah." She prowled the room, and he could feel her clutch of worry. "Trafalgar's got a special knack for knowing when things aren't right. He wanders around and keeps an eagle eye on the land. He's a bit paranoid, so some people dismiss his warnings, but he's got a real instinct for trouble. He sees connections and details other people miss." She paused at the desk.

To Lian, Trafalgar sounded like the Mountie version of a shaman.

"This chuck keeps popping up like bad eggs." Day tapped a nail against the lone paper on the otherwise clean desk.

"Who is it?" Lian joined her. The paper was a fuzzy picture of Rupert Juneau, probably taken by the surveillance eye at Flash Point.

"Trafalgar must have printed this from the Wood Buffalo Depot holo. Why?"

"Is there a note on the back?" People used to holoimaging never thought about the backside of paper as a place for noting information, but Trafalgar might have.

She turned it over. "There is. 'Dear Day. I hope you will be by soon to see this. Remember that enclave I mentioned?' " She looked up at Lian and explained, "Trafalgar told me he found some camp in the mountains that he thought was suspicious. A guerrilla training camp or something." She glanced back at the paper, her gaze skimming it as she summarized. "He saw Juneau there when he discovered it a couple of weeks ago. He's gone back up to investigate."

"You think we should follow him?"

"Yes." She looked up again. "Luc Robichaux and I were investigating the No-Borders. The No-Borders are planning some disturbance to get the borders opened, and power grid captain Juneau is helping them. Now Juneau shows up here at some camp that's got Trafalgar worried. We'd be stupid not to check it out, no?"

"Does Trafalgar say where it is?"

"Grand Cache, just north of Jasper." She kneaded the back of her neck, looking weary. "That's another ten-hour trip. We might have time for a quick shower—"

"No. We're not driving." He flipped open his comm, and

within minutes he had auth for a bush plane big enough for them and Benton. "The plane will pick us up in three hours, drop us off as close as possible to the compound. A tech will follow with my sled."

"You got a bush plane? That fast?"

"Health Canada, the only agency better funded than you Mounties. And I *am* a plague hunter." He grinned.

"Why didn't you do that earlier?"

"I did." His thumb traced the line of her jaw. "If you hadn't left Winnipeg so fast, you could have ridden with me. How do you think I caught up to you? I only took the sled to get where you were. So we've got time and then some to wash off this taiga mud."

"You want a shower, too?"

"Definitely."

"While I shower, check the kitchen for supplies. Trafalgar keeps a huge stock, and he won't mind us raiding it."

Lian's hand dropped and Day left, the Mountie back in her straightened shoulders.

While he waited, he did as she suggested, replenishing their food stores, then stopped to glance over the old-fashioned photographs Trafalgar had amidst his collection of antique books. The pictures were all of Day, a catalogue of her growing up: from a scrawny, big-eyed, half-starved child glaring at the photographer—that one must have been taken soon after she'd been found—to a laughing girl on a swing; to a poised adolescent dressed in shimmering finery.

One photo was taken on Day's graduation from Royal Canadian Mounted Police training, and was the only picture of someone with her. Lian picked it up to look at it. Two stiff-back Mounties, complete with hats and regimental shirts, stood with arms around each other, beneath the Canadian flag. Day, and the older man was assumably Trafalgar. Surrounding the pair, like a close-knit family, were the other graduates and their guests.

Gently, Lian put the photo back. That was Day's world; the place she belonged.

"Shower's yours." Day strolled in, toweling her hair dry, looking fresh-scrubbed and smelling like wild-berry soap. She wore loose shorts and a knit undershirt, giving him his first real look at her legs. Fatigue, attention to duty—everything, vanished, replaced by a kick of desire. Those soft-skinned calves of hers sparked a riot of fantasies.

Not yet, he reminded himself. She was shiny clean, and he reeked of a night in jail.

But he couldn't bring himself to look away. Not when her walk was a pleasure of feminine sway. "Who made your spirit guard?" he asked raspily, nodding to her anklet of woven leather and gold beads. Anything to distract his pounding blood.

"That Cree shaman we talked about. Your mentor. It appeared on my doorstep seven days after I rescued his granddaughter."

"Edgar would do something like that."

Day leaned one hip against the desk. "When you shower, leave your clothes outside the door. I'll throw them in the sonic cleaner with mine."

Both of them stripped down? Spirits bless him, Lian didn't think he'd have the strength to resist. He finished showering in record time, then threw on a clean pair of recycled denims and headed back to the main room.

Day was engrossed at the desk, absently braiding her hair. Her handheld was on, with a holomap of southern Canada coloring the air above it. She had books piled in two stacks and pored over bound yellowed pages.

"What are you doing?" he asked.

She started, gave him a fleeting glance, then returned to her study. "Help me look."

So much for any hope of a more satisfying way to spend the remaining couple of hours. He pulled up a chair beside her and straddled it. "What am I looking for?"

"Citadel."

"Citadel's just a legend. A place where the borders open."

"Maybe not just legend. Bart told me that's where the No-Borders are planning their demonstration. We know they bought equipment for snow mountain climbing, so that pinpoints it to the Rocky Mountains." She pointed to the handheld-generated map. "That's the area highlighted in red."

"Still a lot of kiloms to cover for a place we don't even know exists. There's no reference to it in the GPS databases."

"True. But, I got to thinking: What if Citadel does exist, eh? What if, for national security, a government wanted to hide a route between the two countries? Erase all record of the landmarks? What if it was taken *off* the databases?"

"And these days, if it's gone from online, it's as though it never existed." Excitement rose as he finished her line of thought.

"Exactly."

"How would the No-Borders know where it is?"

She shrugged. "This militant faction is mostly expatriates. Maybe they had family who tried to cross back. A story passed between generations. The point is, if it exists, then likely it was once on a map. Trafalgar collects old books, so I pulled out his atlases and maps to see if I can find Citadel referenced in one."

"Which stack have you completed?"

She pointed to the smaller one, so he pulled the top book off the pile and got to work. The process was painstaking. In each reference book, everything encompassed by the highlighted areas had to be examined—towns, rivers, mountain peaks, monuments. As he worked his way through the documents, Lian's vision blurred and his trapezius muscles knotted. He was rotating his shoulder to

work out the kink when he spotted the faint green print in
the brittle topographical map.

Citadel.

Nerves ablaze, he noted latitude and longitude, then
plotted the coordinates into his handheld. Right in the middle of their highlighted band. "Day, look at this!" he said
tightly.

Day spun. "What?"

"Here. This mountain peak, right at the border, is called
Citadel."

"It commands this narrow pass." Day peered over his
shoulder, and her finger traced the contour lines south.
"Which drops into this valley. An escape route through the
mountains for those fleeing the plagues or a backdoor for
smuggling into Canada. And Citadel is the guidepost." She
overlaid the holomap image onto the paper. Where the old
map showed the mountain peak and the pass, the holoimage was a solid wall of rugged rock.

Citadel had been erased.

"What do you wager we find a cold plasma barrier right
here?" Her finger traced north again and stopped at the
narrow pass. Her voice hardened. "If I don't find Luc Robichaux's killer at Trafalgar's mysterious camp, then I'll find
him here at the No-Borders demonstration."

Lian stared at the pixels of light, barely listening as Day
commed to have complete topographical and climatic data
as well as information about installations in that general
area relayed to her handheld. With the holoimage over-
laying the map, he recognized some of the nearby landmarks. Citadel was on traditional Shinook lands. His
people never went there, however, for it was nearly inac-
cessible and the lands forbidden. Citadel was on the site
they called *Okeyu H'ea*, Rocks of Death.

Was there substance to why Jem's name kept cropping
up?

* * *

While she waited for the data, Day leaned back and stretched her arms overhead. They had over an hour before the bush plane would pick them up. Her stomach rumbled, reminding her that food should be a part of this interlude. Food, and maybe a nap.

"I'll get us something to eat." Lian pushed to his feet, tension radiating from him though she didn't hear a whisper of his movement.

"I'll get our clothes . . ." She stopped as she was suddenly reminded that she sat in little more than her underwear.

Not that Lian was overdressed, either. She'd been engrossed in her work and hadn't really looked at him since his shower. Oh, she'd been skin-tingling aware of him— teased by his outdoorsy scent and his heat—but she'd kept her eyes trained on the maps.

Now, she drank in her fill as he faced her. Damn, but the man cleaned up good.

Lian wore only a pair of faded denims low on his hips. Nothing was beneath the denim but man. A patch of black hair bisected his chest, arrowing straight down. His nanotat glowed gold against his dark chest, the wings of the phoenix performing a slow, sensual beat. His hair was brushed back, but still loose and still damp. Hard of body, hard of mind. Her mouth went dry, the shock of a wildfire running through her. This was a no-nonsense man honed by a dangerous career and caring heart.

A man she wanted, regardless of what their future held, she admitted. She was tired of denial.

At last she stood and accepted the inevitable. "I'm not hungry for food," she told him, and held out her hand.

His eyes narrowed and his nostrils flared as he registered her invitation. Civilized male stripped away as he stalked toward her. "Are you sure, Day? This is an interlude, a time with no—"

"We have an hour," she said.

"We'll never have *enough* time." His voice was husky with need. He ran a thumb across her knuckles, while his other hand caressed her cheek. "But for now, an hour will do."

At his gentle strokes, a flush spread across her, tightening her chest, hardening her nipples beneath her shirt. He smiled, looking both the wolf and the warrior as he saw.

"You can't hide from this any more than I can." His hips pressed against hers, so that she had no doubts about his state.

"What happened to 'I'm exhausted and you're hurting'?"

He grinned. "We're cleaned up and we're not in a trek sled." With the back of his free hand, he brushed the sensitive tips of her breasts—a touch of exquisite torture that roared through her. New sensations, a new definition of passion, all brought by Lian.

"My heart's skipping that beat again, but I know the cure." She lifted on tiptoe and kissed him. His lips were firm beneath hers, his mouth a fiery invitation to her tongue. He tasted of mint. He smelled of the outdoors.

With a groan he gathered her into his arms—being gentle, she knew, because of her various injuries.

"I'm sturdy," she whispered. "I won't break."

"I don't want to hurt you."

"You won't," she answered, although a piece of her wondered. Not her body, but there were other wounds he could inflict, other possible hurts she was newly discovering might be even more painful. "You won't hurt me," she repeated, for her own assurance.

"Not by my life would I," he whispered against her neck, in Native Common. Then he reared back. "Come outside with me, Day."

"It's freezing out there!"

179

"You've never made love in the snow, either. Have you?"

"Actually I have. That's how I know it's cold."

"Then we'll make sure you're warm." With an economic motion, he slipped on his boots, knelt down, and slipped hers on her feet. "The trees will shield the wind, and there's nobody for a hundred kiloms in any direction."

"Isn't the cold, um, inhibiting to masculine parts?" She'd been in a male-dominated profession long enough to have heard plenty of stories about the aftereffects of diving into cold lakes and the reasons for cold showers. And that one episode in the cold—too brief and unsatisfying with her partner's complaints about frozen bits.

Lian grinned. "I don't plan to be hanging out in the cold for very long."

"Boots and my underalls, a fetching combination." She struck a pose, feeling a little silly.

"They are to me. Especially the boots. They remind me that you're a strong woman, and my people value female power. Not just in fertility but in constancy and endurance. To us, female strength is an aphrodisiac."

It was the first time he'd referred to his people like that. Cree, she assumed, since he'd studied with the Cree shaman.

He ran the tip of his middle finger up her arm to trace a pattern on her shoulder. "The underalls are nice, too. They let me see your shoulders—always a personal turn-on." He buried his face, giving her a trailing kiss at the juncture of her neck and shoulder, igniting the nerves there. "Just looking at you, Day, scenting you, is enough to make me hard. Do you want me?" he breathed.

"Yes."

"Then I'll compromise with an open window."

Somehow the need was a fundamental part of him, she realized. She laced her fingers with his. "I have a better idea than frozen moss."

Detouring only to collect blankets from the sled, they raced to one of the other cabins. Trafalgar had modified the interior into an anteroom and a sauna, filling the building with the fragrance of cedar. She didn't stop there, however, leading Lian out back to the true marvel: the back porch.

The hardwood forest encroached clear to the steps, forming three other walls. A solid view of trees was unbroken, except for the sand path leading to a small lake. The porch was cushioned and the overhead beams were decorative. The sky was their roof. The sun, at its zenith, poked through the thick clouds with warm wintery rays. Falling snow drifted through the beams of wood, briefly dusting her and Lian before melting away.

She inhaled deeply. The air was clear, redolent of spruce and promises.

"It's outside, but it's warm." Lian's amazement was evident.

"Radiant strips." She pointed to the narrow grid surrounding the porch. "To heat the open area. Sauna. Jump in the lake. Back here to relax. It's not indoor warm—"

"It's perfect."

The world seemed far away. Outside of their voices, only the wind generated sound. It was rustling the autumnal trees' lingering leaves, while their branches creaked and snapped at its touch.

Standing in her boots, her shorts and tank, her hair coming undone, her skin tight with the run through the cold, her breasts tight with need, her heart racing, and her insides afire, Day turned to Lian and opened her arms.

He joined her. She caught him about his waist as he bracketed her face with his hands. When he leaned down, she raised on tiptoe to meet him. Their lips met in a kiss that started gentle, his mouth sweet on hers. His fingers feathered across her cheeks, and the tingle filled her throat, sparked in her chest.

181

She slanted her mouth, and the kiss deepened. Her tongue tasted the mint of Lian's lips, felt the ridge of his teeth, caught the nectar of his breath. With his long, slow strokes from her shoulder blade to her hip and back again, her body felt jolted to life. Her skin was as sensitive as if it had been massaged with fluffy cotton.

She tunneled her hands through Lian's hair, the thick strands clinging to her fingers, and stroked his neck, so sturdy, the cords at the side taut. Unable to break from the kiss, unwilling to part from that necessary touch for even a second, she gave him small sips across the jaw. His pleasured groan told her she was doing this right.

Outside the porch, deep in the thick woods, she heard a long, joyous howl. Maybe Benton was also celebrating life.

Their hands raced in frantic strokes. Tongues met, and legs entwined. Desire exploded, a nuclear burst of energy between them. Day pressed closer, eager with need, tilting her hips to rub the erection pressed against her belly.

"Slow down," he choked out. "We've got an hour."

"Forty-one minutes," she murmured against his skin.

"Hmm?"

"Chronometer implant."

"Either way, we have time." He drew back, running a hand across her hair. "I want to explore you, learn you. Find out what you like."

"I like when you touch me." She lifted his hand to her mouth and kissed each knuckle. "You have magic hands. When you touch me it's a straight connection, nerve to nerve. Sparks and tingles. I've never felt anything like it."

"A rare gift I have." He laughed. Then he renewed the kiss and she was lost to common sense, lost in sensation.

Her hands fumbled with the zip of his recycleds, uncharacteristically clumsy, but at last she got it undone. As she'd known, beneath the denim was only skin. She pushed the cotton down his legs, and he stepped out of the pants, toeing off his boots in the process.

The cold didn't affect him. He sprang free, full and ready. She knelt, then leaned forward and took him in her mouth while her hands braced against his lean hips. Her tongue wrapped around him, tasting, licking, sampling, then flicked across the tip of his sex.

He jerked back. "*Day!*"

"Enjoying?" she murmured.

"If I've got talented hands, then your mouth is Premiere League."

"A rare gift *I* have," she echoed.

He laughed, then retreated. Reluctantly, she released him.

"Come here, woman. I think we need a slight cooling, or we won't need all thirty-nine minutes."

"Thirty-six."

Still, she followed him to the edge of the porch, not protesting when he stood behind her, both of them facing the forest. He lifted off her shirt. She noticed, even naked and aroused, he still took care with her shoulder and ribs. She hooked her thumbs into her shorts, ready to push them down, but he stopped her.

"Leave them on," he whispered against her ear. He eased the two of them onto the sand trail, just past the radiant barrier. "And the boots."

The snow was coming down harder now, harbinger of the shortened but intensified wet winters that now characterized this land. Large flakes ambled their way to the barren limbs of trees and the ground.

"Hold out your hands," he commanded in a low voice.

Curious about his intent, she obeyed, content for now. Flakes fell on her feverish palms, melting and cooling. Lian stood behind her, his arms and scent surrounding her. He warmed her all over—her back where he pressed tight against her, arms where he excited her with easy strokes, neck where he kissed her, shoulder where his hair brushed against her. All was warm but her hands catching the snow.

His arms and hands were dark against her pale skin. His voice, darker still and purring, surrounded her. He whispered sensual commands, teased her with what they could do, told her what he felt when he touched her here. Or there. Or here.

He rocked his body against her, stroked and stoked her, excited her until the snow and the trees were but a blur.

The contrasts, the faint air of dominance, the inability to see more of him than his hands or to touch more than his arms, shot through her, leaving her weak-kneed and panting.

He crossed her hands across her chest so that she cradled her own breasts. Her cold palms tightened her nipples to hard buds, as he eased down her shorts. Then he surrounded her again. He pressed a finger to the juncture of her thighs, on her swollen bud, slipped a thumb inside her. So hot, his touch. His skin. So cold, her own hands.

The tension of release built in her.

Yet she didn't want this alone.

She leaned back against his chest, his skin a fiery touch against her cheek, and looked up at him. "Inside me, Lian. Now."

"Yes," he groaned.

With a deft movement, she toed off her boots and turned in his arms. His expression was near-savage, and his gray eyes weren't chrome or rain clouds. They were liquid lead, molten.

He braced against the smooth bark of a birch; his hands circled her waist. "Nature, in all her savage wonder," he murmured. "This is where we need to be."

His muscles bunched and he lifted her, as though she weighed no more than a computer chip. Still not stopping

GET TWO FREE* BOOKS!

SIGN UP FOR THE LOVE SPELL ROMANCE BOOK CLUB TODAY.

LOWEST PRICES EVER!

Every month, you will receive two of the newest Love Spell titles for the low price of $8.50,* **a $4.50 savings!**

As a book club member, not only do you save **35% off the retail price**, you will receive the following special benefits:

- **30% off** all orders through our website and telecenter (plus, you still get 1 book FREE for every 5 books you buy!)

- Exclusive access to dollar sales, special discounts, and offers you won't be able to find anywhere else.

- Information about contests, author signings, and more!

- Convenient home delivery of your favorite books every month.

- A 10-day examination period. If you aren't satisfied, just return any books you don't want to keep.

There is no minimum number of books to buy, and you may cancel membership at any time.

* Please include $2.00 for shipping and handling.

NAME: _____

ADDRESS: _____

_____

_____

TELEPHONE: _____

E-MAIL: _____

_____ I want to pay by credit card.

__ Visa   __ MasterCard   __ Discover

Account Number: _____

Expiration date: _____

SIGNATURE: _____

*Send this form, along with $2.00 shipping
and handling for your FREE books, to:*

Love Spell Romance Book Club
20 Academy Street
Norwalk, CT 06850-4032

*Or fax (must include credit card
information!) to:* 610.995.9274.
*You can also sign up on the Web
at* www.dorchesterpub.com.

Offer open to residents of the U.S. and
Canada only. Canadian residents, please
call 1.800.481.9191 for pricing information.

If under 18, a parent or guardian must sign. Terms, prices and conditions
subject to change. Subscription subject to acceptance. Dorchester
Publishing reserves the right to reject any order or cancel any subscription.

his easy movements, he pulled her atop him.

Dizzying seconds later, she straddled him. "Whoever knew a plague hunter had such strength?"

"I find myself well stimulated." With one hard, primitive thrust, he seated himself deep inside her. "Take it from here, Day."

She braced herself against the tree, her arms above him, her legs around his hips as she began to move. Her mouth joined his. Their kiss exploded inside her as his scent enveloped her. Quick, wild, lost to all sensation but desire, she moved faster. His hard chest slid against hers, rasping her breasts and belly.

Had she ever thought making love in the snow was cold?

His fierce erection swelled inside her. She tightened around him. The falling snow melted within an instant of touching their fevered flesh. Raw and explosive, an orgasm shuddered through her, rapid and unstoppable. It shook her to her core. Lian shouted, something foreign and guttural, and he joined her.

There was no aftermath, only more need. They stumbled backward, into the radiant heat, and then down to the blankets. Day's palms craved Lian. Her frantic touches grew less practiced, less gentle. More needy and demanding.

She bent over him. He took the invitation and wrapped one breast in the moist heat of his mouth. His tugs and sucks sent a shot of hot plasma straight to her groin, where he was still buried and again growing. Stray snowflakes drifted onto her back, caught on her lashes. Again the contrast of heat and cold, dampness and dry-mouthed wonder.

Lian slowed, teasing her other breast with equal skill. Lower-and-lift: she matched his rhythm of rebuilding, topping the roiling desire with exciting precision. The coil of coming completion grew tight. His hips joined hers, then pushed her, demanding more—all. Precision disintegrated. Frantic, hot, surrounded by the Canadian wilderness and the fragrance of cedar, they moved together. Partners.

His hands grabbed her shoulders. Exquisite tension. Unbearable need. The coil exploded, even as he gave a tremendous thrust, bursting again inside her. Their hips came together without finesse, only an eternity of desire.

She sagged against his hands, and he slowly lowered his arms until she rested against his chest. She lay there against his strong muscles, with her ear above his heart. His heartbeat was steady and solid, and she found herself attuned to the rhythms of his pulse and his breathing. His arms enfolded her, and they lay together in the warm glow of satiation.

She couldn't find words, couldn't think of a thing to say in the wake of explosive sex and rising questions.

What did they do now? She had no guidelines, no rules, after sleeping with her temporary partner. Not that they'd gotten to the "sleep" part.

Lian's hand ran down her spine. "Your braid's come loose."

"I'll fix it."

He looked at her. "You're thinking. You're doubting."

"No, I'm not," she said honestly. "I don't believe in regrets. I do believe in plans."

"This isn't that hard."

"It's not that easy."

"It *is*. We're lovers, now, for as long as we want to be. We still have a job to do, one that takes precedence. Everything else . . . we'll just figure out."

Was he as calm and assured as he sounded? She smiled against his chest.

Probably.

"How long?" he asked, his fingers idly combing through her hair.

"Eleven minutes," she answered, instinctively knowing what he asked. "Is that time enough for again?"

"It can be. But, right now, regretfully, no. After all, it is cold out here."

She laughed, and he rolled over and pulled her beneath him. All he did, though, was kiss her nose and then sit up. He held a hand out. When she grabbed it, he pulled her upright, then swung around to sit behind her. He slid the elastic off her hair and began rebraiding it.

"I can do that," she protested lightly, not quite sure she was ready for this kind of intimacy.

"I know. Let me anyway."

There was something soothing about his fingers combing through her hair, his deft braiding, so she relaxed and let him finish. He knew what he was doing, too, weaving the strands into a tight plait.

"Where'd you learn to braid?"

"I used to braid Aveline's hair."

"I know so little about you," she whispered. He had a brother and sister. The remainder of his family was dead, he was banished from his home. So little to know about the man who'd just made love to you. "Not your Nation, not why you are exiled. Nothing."

"You know what's important. You know who I am now." He kissed the back of her neck, his fingertips caressing her jaw for a brief last moment before he pushed to his feet. "Your braid is finished and the plane will be here soon."

She lifted her brow as they dressed. "Defining the limits?" She wondered what they were.

"It's not you." He ran his hand across the back of his neck. "I don't often speak of my people while I'm no longer considered part of them. When I do, it's uncomfortable. I'm sorry."

She lifted her hand. "No apologies. I respect your boundaries." She understood the difficulty of talking about something cherished and lost. "As you said," she added, "this is just an interlude."

187

So, why did it hurt to say that? Gamely she pressed on. "Besides, we're down to one minute. Dr. Firebird, it's time to get back on the job."

"Understood, Inspector."

Their interlude was over.

Chapter Twelve

The bush plane let them off in a meadow five kiloms from Trafalgar's mysterious compound. Unfortunately, those kilometers were straight up. Even sleds couldn't go there.

The mountain loomed above them, a giant crag of the Rockies tempered at the lower levels only by stunted trees poking out of its coat of snow and a trail cut two centuries before. At the top were treacherous glaciers. It was beautiful, majestic, and dangerous.

Feeling the thrill of challenge, Lian settled his gear on his back and adjusted the pack straps. Each moment in the wilderness soaked into him, like rain on parched ground.

Beside him, Day made a small, resigned sound. Making love to her had not cut his acute awareness of her, nor had it made him want her any less. If anything, the feel of her wrapped around him and the taste of her had made the need keener.

He glanced over at her. She stared up the mountain, gripping the straps of her pack. Falling snow coated her in a layer of white. "What's the matter?"

"I don't like mountain climbing. It's too—" She shook her head, as though unable to explain, and sighed again.

The sound scraped through another layer of his isolation. If he could have spared her this he would have, but this was a possible criminal investigation, so Day was in charge.

"I can do it," she concluded. "I just don't like it."

"You could send another team up."

"No, I'm in charge of finding Robichaux's killer. Trafalgar thought this camp was connected, so this is my responsibility."

Day had opted for a low-key, two-man approach since there was no evidence—beyond Trafalgar's claim—linking a legal cult to the No-Borders. Still no sign of the ex-Mountie, either. A worrisome fact if the compound turned out to be a front for a hostile camp.

While Day contacted the nearest Mountie depot, Lian tuned his comm to her frequency—a precaution in case he had to call in the backup.

"We're heading up," she reported. "Have you got our position?"

"You're on our screens," the depot replied.

"I'll keep the GPS beacon blipping, but I'm turning off comm. If this snow continues, the Graetzel cells may not recharge. We'll check in every four hours."

"Backup's on its way if you're a minute late, Inspector."

"Understood," she replied and flipped off the comm.

She and Lian donned their goggles, the front shields tempered to keep cleared of snow, and strapped phosphorescent algae lights to their ankles. When dusk fell, the glow would light their footpath without spreading warning of their approach. Last, they each locked one end of a single microline around their waists, connecting them with a thin filament of carbon tubes and spider silk. The microline, flexible, nearly invisible and virtually unbreakable, would be a lifeline in the event of a fall.

Or it could tether them together in death if they both failed to anchor.

"Ready?" Day asked, preparing to lift her face protection into place.

"Almost." Lian bent forward, cupped her cheek with his glove, and kissed her lips—bare skin to bare skin for the last time until they finished this trek. For one wonderful moment, she returned the kiss.

Then, they parted in unison. Without another word, they raised their face protection and started up the mountain.

At the lower altitude, the trail retained elements of long-ago grooming, with spars of wood delineating the route. The spruce and fir soon thinned to stunted scrub. The ground would be rock and drying grasses if they could see it, but the persistent snow had laid a mantle of white over it all. At least at these elevations the snow was drier, and so far they hadn't had to contend with the trickier ice.

Benton stayed nearby, matching their steady pace. They walked mostly in silence, saving oxygen for the exertion of the climb, relaying only necessary information. Yet the silence was companionable, not strained. Lian realized. Day was a woman he could share even moments of solitude with.

As they reached the higher altitudes, the air thinned and vegetation disappeared. The scents of evergreen faded, until the air seemed devoid of everything except cold. Their breathing was labored, since neither Day nor Lian was acclimated to the elevation. They paused once for him to give them both an infuspray of heme-booster and artificial oxygen. The temperature had dropped, too, he realized, as he bared a patch of skin for the spray. When the sun dropped the final distance below the horizon, the temperature would fall to arctic levels.

He glanced at the sky. That time wasn't too far off, either. "How far away are we, do you estimate?"

"About a kilom. Do you see any lights?"

"No. I don't smell or hear anything, either. Machinery. Oil. Voices. Song. Nothing. You said this compound was registered to a religious cult. Are they antitech?"

"Not that I know. They call themselves Shadow Canada. I think they're Voice of Freedom followers—except they've decided the revolution will come on an astral plane, not in the physical world."

Lian gave a snort of irritation. Belief in spirit guides and lost pieces of the soul was as fundamental to his upbringing as learning how to survive a snowstorm on a mountain. But that didn't mean he'd ever dismiss the dangers of the corporeal. "The world's problems are very real, very physical. Astral revolution won't do much good against dictators." He shook his head.

Day seemed to agree. "Oh, I know. Either way it's not our concern."

"It will be," he found himself preaching. "If what I've read is true, this brewing revolution is one Canada can't ignore. We'll either rejoin the world as a strong, independent nation or we'll be eyed as a resource to be plundered." He believed that true for the Shinook, too. Of necessity, his people had turned away from the world, but times changed. If his people didn't adapt, they might not retain their independence.

"What if the borders stay closed?"

"They won't. They're already leaky, Day."

"Well, until they are officially opened, it's my job to uphold the border laws."

"And if the laws are changed?"

"I'll enforce the new ones, and do my damnedest to keep my country secure." She sighed. "We've got other concerns, right now. The cult moved here a month ago to 'be closer to the origin of the Voice,' and to build a temple to Banzai Maguire. They keep to themselves but, from what I understand, they took their handhelds, power generators, and Distazers. So, even taking into account the distance to go, the snow, and the twilight, we should have *some* sign there's a settlement up there." Day rubbed her arm. "I don't like this. It's too eerie."

A serpent of apprehension slithered down Lian's spine. "I've been feeling that, too. Let's see what's up there."

"Tyranny, like hell, is not easily conquered."

The ancient quote wisped through the empty camp like tarantula silk.

Day recognized it. It was the same quote the boys on the Moose had played. So, maybe there was somebody here. Still, everything about this felt wrong—from the darkness to the lone voice to the silence encompassing that single sound.

Settling her hat firmly on her head, Day detached the microline from her waist. She drew her Distazer and, from the corner of her eye, she saw Lian do the same. She raised her fingers to her lips, a gesture of silence for Benton. She shouldn't have worried, at least about him making noise. The wolf was slinking backward. Something dangerous lurked in this camp.

She touched Lian's hand, drawing his attention, then gestured to the comm patch behind her ear. He caught on at once.

"What frequency?" he mouthed.

She signaled, and they turned the comm units on to a local setting. Her gut tightening, she slid through the hole she'd opened in the old-fashioned barbed wire, listening as she tried to locate the direction of the voice. Her thin breath formed a steady white mist in the chilly twilight, while her nostrils puckered from the lingering trace of something in the air.

"Sterilization chemicals," Lian's voice sounded in her ear.

"Do you realize what this is?" she asked, unable to suppress the shiver of revulsion coursing through her.

193

"An abandoned quarantine camp."

"Why in hell would they choose that? Do you suppose they deked us?"

"I don't think this is a hoax. I think it's something we weren't supposed to find." He ran his scanner through the air. "At least the air is clean—but we'd better protect ourselves."

She took standard precautions, a dose of her cytokine spray, then risked turning on her light; the algae strips weren't giving enough light to see beyond a meter in front of her feet. The torch's white beam danced across buildings as she searched for any signs of occupancy. A light. A smell of cooking. A grunt of sex.

Buildings, only. No people. Not even a dog or a cat.

"Nothing on this side," Lian said.

"The days of our deliverance draw nigh." The sexless, mechanized Shadow Voice sounded again from speakers attached to a rickety pile of bricks.

The camp's onetime hospice house. She recognized the faded green Chi symbol painted on the side. Oh, God, she didn't want to go in there. People who went in a hospice house didn't come back out.

"I'll check it out," Lian said. "You check the dorms and see if a temple's there." He flashed his light against the dark buildings set far back in the compound. Obviously, he'd seen her hesitation.

Nothing. There was nothing between the hospice building and the dorms. Not even a footprint in the snow. She stiffened her shoulders and straightened her hat, refusing to give in to childhood fears. "I think we need to follow the voice."

"Join the revolution," the impassioned voice said as if it had heard her.

"Like hell," she muttered back. She admired Banzai and the ideals the pilot represented, but that Voice gave her the creeps.

A distant howl added Benton's disturbance to the following silence. Dinnertime, but still no stirring. Not even a dog. Every collection of humans had a dog, didn't they?

Getting that stomach-gnawing feeling that this was more than a case of a few harmless culters—or even just a violent No-Borders camp—Day fired up her Distazer; then she stepped onto the porch of the hospice house, the warped wood creaking beneath her boots. Lian followed, his back to her, his focus behind them, ready for an ambush.

The chemical smell was stronger here, and Day's stomach roiled against the acrid, unpleasant scent. After wiping the grime off one of the windows, she peered into the building. Apparently, the cult hadn't been too keen on cleaning things up.

It was too dark inside to see details, but she saw no shadows of movement either. She lifted her goggles to the top of her head, then shone her light in, illuminating the small, empty anteroom.

A picture had been painted on the door leading to the infirmary. It was a fantasized portrait of a woman wearing a white skin suit, dark glasses, and boots, with a dark helmet of hair and impressive breasts. She was surrounded by gold beams and the word *Banzai,* written in different handwriting and colors.

The Banzai Maguire temple. Day wrinkled her nose in distaste. This stylized Banzai was a distortion of the image she'd seen on her handheld.

Guessing the source of the voice lay behind that door, she tucked her light away. Fitting her Distazer into her palm, she sidled inside, giving her eyes a moment to adjust to the gloom before she trod noiselessly to the rear door. Behind her, she heard the hum of Lian's Distazer powering up. Lifting her weapon, she pressed her lips together against the sickly odor.

"Oh, damn." Lian's voice rang in her ear as she slammed back the door. "Day, that smell. It's—"

"C-X gas," she finished, grinding to a halt with planted feet. Her lip curled as she lowered her Distazer. "Hell in Halifax."

Half a dozen naked couples writhed on the room's lushly padded floor, engaging in various acts of copulation. Quite vigorously and energetically did they apply themselves to this "worship." The Voice of Freedom spouted its exaltations from the walls, while huge holoscreens displayed scenes of clouds and rainbows and the stylized Banzai. A heap of robes and footwear filled one corner. The room held no furniture, although there were some intriguing-looking devices.

They hadn't heard or seen anything on the journey here because the neon-lit room was sealed to prevent the escape of the gas.

Ah, hell, what a disappointment, Day thought with irritation. No hostile No-Borders. No weapons cache. Just some folks pulling on a disguise of religion as an excuse for a group grope. No one here would have a clue who'd killed Luc Robichaux.

A copulating cultist scooted sideways, reaching blindly for one of the myriad spray canisters littering the room, his partner still pumping atop him. He directed the valve toward his mouth for a fresh hit. Gas hissed out. The man inhaled a long drag, dropped the canister, then rolled his partner over for a new penetration.

Virility in a can. Apparently the myths around C-X gas had some validity. Amazing stamina, incredible aphrodisiac. Its adherents claimed even the scent was a turn-on.

She wrinkled her nose. Couldn't say that it did anything for her.

Although, there was that nice tingle growing just about womb height. She pushed closer to Lian. Damned fine-looking man, he was, eh? The look he gave her back was definitely interested. She could read the signs.

Loosening the buttons on her coat, she lifted on tiptoe. With a quick movement, she discarded his transparent mouth shield—when had he put that on?—and before he could retrieve them, she kissed him. Slow and languid, so she absorbed whatever it was he was trying to say.

At last, he gave in, his arms wrapping around her as he joined the powerful kiss. When she pulled back, he was smiling and his fingers left a trail of fire along her neck.

"The gas . . ." he choked out, the words at odds with his smile.

"I know we have to get out of here," she agreed, opposite the eagerness of her body to stay.

"Tell me about it."

She glanced down. Yep, they were definitely affected by the gas. Yet neither moved away, as though the gas had disconnected any muscles or nerves not related to sex. Lian toyed with the end of her braid, his knuckles brushing her breast in the process.

Day shook her head, trying to clear the light-headedness and extinguish her rising desire. That was the gas muddling her emotions. Partially.

That kiss felt powerfully good.

Somehow, she found herself running a finger across the electric-blue rings in Lian's ear and teasing his lobe with her thumb. His face turned hard with need.

Wrong. This was wrong. A measure of sanity returned. Maybe the air from the anteroom was diluting the gas.

"No," she gasped. Damn it, she was a Mountie. *Do it all, be it all* did not mean giving in to mindless urges, to coupling under the effects of some sex-aid gas. With great effort, she lowered her hand and forced a step backward. Lian, too, clenched a fist and dropped her braid. He inched closer to the door.

One of the cultists noticed the open door and muttered angrily to his partner and his neighboring celebrants. Several others joined the disgruntled chorus as the gas continued to seep out the door and the fresh air started diluting the room.

Another thing she'd heard about C-X gas, Day remembered, as her mind cleared a little, was that it created rabid cravings. If those cravings weren't satiated by sex, the craving morphed into violence.

Just what she needed. A mob of angry, frustrated bone snakes coming at her. "Leave," she ground out. "Let's let them finish. Nothing illegal here."

"Agreed," Lian said tightly, his voice rough-edged.

She found it easier to move those last centimeters to the door. Suddenly, though, everything about Lian stiffened—what wasn't stiff already, that is—as he reached into his pocket. Whatever he found there turned his expression harder. And angrier, his mouth pressing into a thin line. Was he succumbing to the drug's hormone-fueled rage?

Like the cultists behind him, angrily getting to their feet.

Without warning, Lian grabbed her arm and yanked her out of the room, then slammed the door behind them. Backing her against it, he ground into her, hip to hip in a carnal touch that sent lightning bolts across her, not all of them gas-generated. In a swift move, he bent down and gave her a raging hot, highly abbreviated but arousing kiss. Before she could respond—still deciding between returning anger and passion—he lifted from the kiss and held his hand out toward her.

She squinted to focus on what he held. His lab chip.

The light was blinking red. *Virus.*

Two short. Two long. The pattern from his office. The new strain.

He moved the chip closer to her mouth; the red deepened.

Exposure.

Chapter Thirteen

Lian saw Day turn white and brace a hand against the door.

He forced back the arousal from the gas and the cold nausea that had stunned him when he'd felt the faint vibration of the lab chip and seen the blinking light. The light he'd seen too many times. The light he'd prayed he'd never see again.

Exposure.

He was a plague hunter. He was supposed to plan for these things.

Earlier, when he'd entered the compound, he'd slipped on his mouth shield, level-one nostril filters and biohazard gloves. A plague hunter's usual precautions.

He'd unwisely thought Day was doing the same when he'd ordered protection. He'd forgotten. Since Mounties never handled biocontamination cases, their precautions were designed for quick application and brief exposures— cytokine sprays and level-two filters. Efficient enough for viral particles, not gas molecules. Between the dark and the search, it wasn't until they'd gotten into the room that he'd seen those precautions didn't include a mouth shield. Instead, she'd taken off his and kissed him, allowing him to inhale a good portion of the gas, too.

He was still painfully hard from that erotic interlude.

Even as the thoughts ran through him, he was grabbing two air-foam packets from his pack. He laid one over Day's mouth. "Breathe that. Twenty seconds," he commanded before he applied the other to his lips. The packet of antiviral air would clear out their lungs of both virus and gas. It would also help Day regain her equilibrium.

Breathing hard, she clutched her stomach as though she was about to vomit, and he knew she'd despise the weakness in herself once her initial shock faded.

She was a hyperimmune. Her exposure was brief; his briefer. She would survive this. *They* would survive this. He had to believe that. To trust it.

As he sucked in the antiviral air, his mind cleared. His erection mostly subsided. He was still semiaroused, but it was a manageable state. He saw Day's eyes starting to focus, and when he checked his viral scanner, the light was green. None of the virus had escaped the sealed room.

When the packets were empty, he pulled out two thin jumpsuits. His and Day's clothes were impregnated with viricidals, but he had a feeling there were some stray dangerous body fluids in that room. The jumpsuits were an extra layer of protection—against bioterror agents or strains. He handed one to Day. "Put this on."

"Shouldn't we be going in there, stopping that virus? Helping those people?"

"We have to protect ourselves first." It was a harsh rule, but necessary. Protect yourself first, because you were no help if you got infected. "Do you have biohazard gloves and filters?" he asked briskly, keeping her on task. The filters would also block the C-X gas.

"In my pack." Without waiting for his command, she

rummaged around for them. "Sorry about discarding yours. Do you have extras?"

"Of course."

"Of course. Doesn't everybody carry multiple sets?" she muttered as she found hers and put them on.

Good, Lian thought, the snappish Day was coming back.

"Two more steps. Open your mouth." He held up a canister.

"I took my cytokine spray when you suggested protection."

"This is an improved formula, so stop arguing and open your mouth."

This time she obeyed, and he sprayed the immune enhancer in her mouth.

"Yuck. It tastes like hot metal." She made a face as she replaced her mouth shield.

He loved hearing her complain. "Don't be a chipmunk."

"A chipmunk?"

"A timorous creature." He pulled out a tube of MAB gel and squirted the camphor-smelling ointment onto any possible exposed skin on his hands, face, neck, wrists, ankles.

"I must be getting over my shock, if I can feel insulted."

He tossed her the tube. "Monoclonal antibodies. Put 'em on and rub 'em in. Feeling anything about the fact that you were all over me?" he teased.

"When I have time, I plan to be utterly embarrassed."

"Damn, and here I thought you might be wanting another whiff of that gas. Sans virus, of course."

"In your dreams, Firebird." She gave him a hot look.

He returned it. "Got a feeling they're going to be mighty vivid tonight, Daniels."

"Do all plague hunters get this chipper before going into a biohazard scene?"

"What? Mounties never crack jokes before they pile out of the depot, off to quell rioters?"

Her lips quirked. "Point taken."

She rubbed in a last bit of gel and tossed him back his tube, then her smile faded. They were protected, the banter was finished. They both knew what came next.

"What are the steps to stop and contain that virus?" she asked, donning her biohazard gloves.

"Locate and eliminate the source, if there's one other than a human vector. Keep everyone inside and cooperating until I can administer air packets and cytokine sprays. Foam the room, then seal it. Establish quarantine. Treat any infections."

"Do you have all the supplies you need?"

"Enough to get started. Give me a sec to comm Health Canada for an airdrop."

When he'd finished the quick call, she said, "I'll make sure the crowd cooperates. You do whatever you need to clear that virus."

"They could turn mean."

"I'll handle it. Whatever happens, you keep doing what you do best." She paused. "Unless they shoot me. Then you might want to clear out."

"Day!"

She put a finger to his lips. "Mountie humor. Trust me, Lian, to do my part."

He hesitated, then nodded and slipped his goggles in place. Day matched his action, and together they stepped into the room, sealing the door quickly behind them.

"These are the times that try men's souls." The broadcast Voice of Freedom still exhorted action. The couples had gone back to their orgy.

Day jammed her hat on her head, then planted herself at the door, chin up, feet apart, hands on hips, back straight. Lian saw her gaze skim the room, ready.

He gave her a quick thumbs up, then studied the situation. No one showed symptoms of smallpox. The virus's normal incubation period was ten to fourteen days, although a genetically altered strain could be different. Day had said these people were alone together for a month. Which meant if one of them was the primary source, they'd have been dead by now. So where was the external source? The C-X gas was his best guess, given that the air inside the room was ripe with the virus while the outside was clear.

He began collecting C-X gas canisters and setting out room air-purification packets, picking his way around naked butts and flailing limbs. Despite his earlier teasing, a faint flush of embarrassment touched his cheeks that he and Day had succumbed, even briefly, to this sordid spectacle.

What they shared, whatever it was, was private and deeply personal, not this mindless exhibitionism and carnality.

By this time, some of the group had noticed him. A murmur of protest, of discord, arose. Not bothering to look at the speakers, he worked with rapid efficiency. Eliminating the external source of the exposure came first. Purification did little good if the virus kept spewing into the room. So far nothing was contaminated except the air and the mouthpiece of two canisters. Although he couldn't *prove* whether virus in the canisters had infected the lungs, or the breath from infected lungs contaminated the canisters, at least it didn't rule out his theory of infected canisters.

He prayed this was the cultists' first exposure to the infection, that he'd caught them in the initial stages of incubation. He could save most of them then. Once the symptoms manifested, the survival rate plummeted.

The cultists were louder now. "What the eff do you think you're doing?" came a shout. "Dudes, he took the C-X." Someone shoved his knee.

"Revolution, my fellow citizens of the world. Return to freedom and democracy." The damned voice was still spouting its rhetoric.

Day snapped into action, striking the speaker with a

well-aimed laser, silencing the mechanized voice. Silencing the crowd, too, at least momentarily.

"I'm Inspector Daniels of the Royal Canadian Mounted Police," she called out, her weapon sweeping the room. "Do you have a problem, citizens?"

The crowd turned toward her. Naked, snarling bodies untangled and stalked toward Day. A few delayed enough to don robes and slip on footgear. "He's taking our gas?" one demanded.

"He's Health Canada. Under National Emergency Code 451, section 3, paragraph L he is authorized to examine a possible health hazard in your temple."

Wise woman, she stayed away from the V-word. Hearing Health Canada was enough to frighten people. Say "virus," and nasty things started happening. "Plague hunter," meant a riot. Still, these chucks were too hopped up on C-X to care much about what she said. They turned back to him, wanting their orgy gas back.

"I'm in charge here," Day's voice rang out again, pulling their attention back. "If you have any questions or complaints, come to me."

"We got complaints." One of the men, a bear of a fellow in all respects, grabbed a set of bondage chains and started swinging them over his head. This one hadn't bothered with a robe. "The gas ain't illegal for personal use, so get the hell out!"

Lian tried, unsuccessfully, not to glance worriedly at Day as he quickened his pace around the perimeter claiming the final canisters. What was that in the corner—a surveillance eye? Some voyeur was holoing tonight's little meeting? He retrieved the eye before beginning the decontamination. The process might ruin any useful information they could get from the device.

His gaze shied back to Day. He didn't doubt her abilities, but his more primitive instincts kept demanding he protect. The bear of a man stood close enough that his impressive erection jutted into her ribs. Other men backed him up, an encompassing, threatening circle. A head shorter than any of them, Day didn't back away a centimeter. She lifted her chin—standing stiffer, if that was possible—and met her challenger eye to eye. Only Lian saw her fingers tighten around her second Distazer.

Some of the women, Lian noticed, were toying nervously with their robe belts. Day's steady presence was starting to affect their mood.

"Sir," Day said, "we are not here because of your gas. We are investigating a complaint about emissions. This is one of the laws I am charged with upholding, just as I am charged with maintaining your safety and your rights."

"See how safe you feel with this!" The man swung his chain, threatening, close.

Lian pulled his Distazer, then abruptly stopped a fraction of second before firing. Let her do her job, Day had demanded. He slammed his weapon back in its holster, just as Day grabbed the man's chain.

"Sir, perhaps you did not hear me. *I am a Mountie.*"

"Yeah, you're a stiff brim all right."

Lian found the last canister, then checked his monitors. The purification packets were starting to clear the air. Once the people were done, he'd use the Decon Foam 550 to finish the decontamination process.

"No honest Canadian citizen attacks a Mountie," Day continued. "The gas is not illegal, as you so rightly pointed out. As soon as we finish our inspection, you may resume your activities."

As a plague hunter, when he came into an unsettled situation, he often dealt with panic and disintegration. Day, though, actually seemed to have grabbed their attention and a measure of their respect. Some of the men backed down.

Not all, though. The bearlike man jerked his chain free. "Attacking a Mountie is against the law. The law is your shield, your protection against anarchy. Are you intent on breaking the law, sir?"

Lian clenched his fists, admiring her bravery even as it twisted his gut to see her in danger. Still, he stood back, denying every particle of his training, ignoring every masculine protective instinct, to honor his promise of belief.

If that chain touched her, however, no power on this land would save that man.

Lian activated an individual air packet and held it to the mouth of the nearest cultist. "Keep that there and breathe," he advised in a low tone. To his surprise, the woman did. He continued on to the next, still keeping an eye on Day.

"C'mon, Dude Quint," said one of the men, now flaccid. "Leave her be. She's a *Mountie,* and a cub-sized one at that."

One of the women chimed in, "Let them do whatever. The sooner they're done, the sooner they're gone. We've got a lot of nights."

Slowly, Quint lowered his chain. Day grabbed it looking perfectly calm. Lian tensed. The surrender was coming too easy.

Without warning, Quint's arm, the one without the chain, rammed forward, a beefy fist aimed at Day's throat.

Lian snapped out his Distazer.

In a blur of speed, Day responded. She tugged the chain. Spun. Swept her foot. The next thing anyone knew, Quint was face first in the padding, his arm stretched in a painful lock across his back. One of Day's boots crushed his buttocks. Her other boot was between his legs, the toe pressing against the man's sagging genitals. She faced the room, Distazer in hand.

"Quint, you are under arrest for attacking a Mountie. If you so much as twitch, tonight's will be the last C-X party you ever enjoy." She pressed her boot forward, making her point. Every man in the room, Lian included, winced.

Day's gaze swept them all. "Does anyone else have any

complaints about this inspection?" Utter silence met her question. "Good, I will expect your fullest cooperation."

Damn, but she'd done it. Gotten them under control. Lian kept unobtrusively to the back, amazed as each cult member took an air packet. Still dazed by the gas they were, he guessed, and respecting Day.

"Who's in charge here?" she asked.

After a moment's hesitation, a pale young man came forward. He had leader-size equipment; but totally naked with a wisp of a beard, he didn't look in charge until he straightened his shoulders and met Day's eye. "I'm the Head Dude. Paul."

A dark-skinned woman joined Paul, tightening the belt on her robe before handing him a matching garment. Her body was even more impressive. Was size a criteria for joining the group? Lian wondered idly as he circled the room, dispensing cleansing packets.

"Call me M'ya," said the woman.

Day acknowledged the greeting, although Lian noticed that she kept her gaze firmly on their faces. "Do you have someplace I could lock this man?"

"There's a storage facility with a bolt," Paul offered.

"That will do. Now, before anyone leaves this room, you each need to receive a preventive from Dr. Firebird."

The cultists glanced at him with collective suspicion, and Lian gave them a brief wave, Distazer still in hand in case they had any thoughts that Day could be overcome.

"What's going on?" asked M'ya.

"We'll talk about it in the morning. When Dr. Firebird finishes his tests and you've had a chance to . . . recover. One more thing, no one is to leave this compound unless I or Dr. Firebird give you permission. This order has the full weight of the Royal Canadian Mounted Police and Health Canada behind it. Anyone ignoring it will be sentenced to the full punishment decreed by law. Is that understood?"

Some of them were beginning to notice the biogear he and Day wore, to realize there was more here than a simple emissions violation. But Day's presence kept them calm.

Paul glanced around the group, then nodded. "Yes."

"You have our cooperation," added M'ya. "Just tell us what you want."

"A place to pitch our tent."

As far away as possible from the group sleeping quarters, Lian amended silently as the cult members began to line up in front of him.

He finished distributing air packets, then circled again with cytokine, still praying he'd caught them early enough to abort the infection. "Have you used any other canisters of gas before tonight?" he asked one woman, a petite redhead.

"No, this was our first," she answered, flushing.

"Anyone come or gone from the compound since you moved up here?"

"Only Mr. Juneau. He moved us in, then left until he brought fresh supplies a couple of days ago."

Trafalgar was right: Juneau *had* been here. Why? What the hell was a UCE border official doing with a Canadian sex—?

The thought broke off as he noticed the flushed cheeks of several other cultists. Tension spread deep to his bones.

"When did Juneau leave?" he asked the redhead, forcing his voice to stay steady.

"Yesterday morning."

Thirty-six hours ago. If Juneau knew about the smallpox, then he'd have been way the hell gone before it was released.

"How long have you been in this room?"

"Two hours."

Viral exposure occurred between thirty-six and two hours ago, if the virus was in their first breaths of the canisters.

The redhead wrinkled her nose. "My throat's getting scratchy."

"How long's this going to take?" complained another. "I'm tired."

"Open your mouth," he told the redhead tersely. When she complied, he shined his light inside, sweeping the beam around her mouth and down her throat.

There it was: the characteristic rash. Her throat was red and inflamed. He bit back an oath, buffeted by rage as his light shone on a single blister embedded in the skin. The first of many.

Smallpox. Less than thirty-six hours post exposure and they were symptomatic? This was the most rapidly virulent strain he'd ever encountered.

He grabbed virucides from his pack and gave himself a quick injection, then strode over to Day. Without a word he injected her, too. Hyperimmune or not, he wasn't taking risks. She stared at him, traces of fear widening her eyes. She didn't need to be told the deadly enemy they faced— or that all hell was about to break loose.

He tossed her the cytokines. "Give everyone a dose while I start injections."

Her chin stiffened, and she nodded before starting her assigned task.

Although he'd have wished her anywhere but here, he sent a small prayer of thanks to the spirits for her grit and strength.

A piercing shriek rent the temple. The redhead was screaming and pointing at Paul. On his face were pustules, the dreaded herald of smallpox.

"The compound's clear. No other signs of infection."

Day joined Lian on a ledge of rock, watching black smoke smudge the night sky. The burning pyre of jump-suits and other items not suitable for the Decon Foam glowed like wolf eyes. She handed him back his scanner. While he'd been absorbed with his patients, he'd asked her to make sure they'd contained the virus.

"Good. We stopped it. Smallpox doesn't survive long in the open air."

"I did find something else, though. A lab for the manufacture of C-X gas. It's an odd quirk of the law—the gas is legal to use, illegal to manufacture. This isolated cult made a nice cover, with the added perk of sampling the wares."

Lian didn't respond to her weak flippancy. Even in the uncertain light, she could see the lines of exhaustion marking his face. "How many did we lose?" she asked gently.

"Three. Paul, Quint, and one of the women. A couple more are in critical condition. The others have stabilized. One was injured when he panicked and tried to escape. Health Canada's airdropped a cold plasma quarantine barrier around us. Two didn't come down with any symptoms, so they're keeping watch for me tonight."

She closed her eyes, offering a brief prayer for the dead.

He knocked a fist against his palm. "I can't believe I let us get exposed."

"Your sensors read negative until we entered that room. Besides, you didn't *let* me get exposed. I used the wrong precautions." His silence told her she hadn't convinced him. "I mean that, Lian. I'm an adult, a Mountie. You aren't in charge of me. My actions are my mistakes."

He stared straight ahead, elbows braced on knees, his face concealed by his laced hands. "I can't change the fact that I'm responsible for putting us at risk. I'm the one in charge of infectious issues on this assignment, and I didn't do my job. I also can't stop worrying about you."

"I can take care of myself," she said uneasily.

"My worry isn't about your abilities. Trust me, those I've learned to have a healthy respect for. But there's a lot of trouble brewing." He tilted his head toward her, the fire a hot glow on his cheek. "I can't help worrying about you, wishing you were safe."

The fire snapped and began to die to embers. Around Day and Lian, the compound was finally quiet. Except Day didn't feel quiet. Despite the fatigue weighting her shoulders, the enforced delay gnawed at her gut. "How long are we in quarantine?" she asked.

"The cultists will have to wait until all the lesions dry up. You and I? Depends whether we have immunity. I can use the equipment in the C-X lab to run the test. We should have the answer in about fifteen minutes."

"Let's take care of it, then." She had to know just what the consequences of her actions tonight were. How much time did they have left? As they walked through the cemetery-like quiet of the compound, she asked. "What's our best case scenario for the quarantine?"

"Four days. Even with immunity, I have to make sure we won't be asymptomatic carriers."

Four days. Four days were a brief bit in the course of a lifetime, but they were too long for her to be out of commission. Damn! She pressed her fists against her thighs, trying to stop the trembling in her hands, and faced the hard decision square on. *Be it All. Do it All.* Focus on what needed to be done. "I have to comm headquarters for a replacement on the Robichaux case." Her friend, Rich, would do a good job with her case. Maybe even get the G-1 from it.

"Don't," Lian said abruptly. "Not yet."

Her eyes narrowed. "Is that an order, Dr. Firebird?"

"No. Not exactly. I'm suggesting—asking—you to wait until morning, Day. After we've had some sleep. And a chance to talk first. We've done everything we can tonight. The virus is contained and I've alerted Health Canada to

211

take the necessary precautions. I'm too tired for anything else right now. Six hours, a nap, and a conversation. Is that too much to ask?"

She didn't know what would be different in the morning. This was not something she could keep from her fellow Mounties. Not by law. Not by the bonds of fraternity.

Still, she wasn't sure she'd be able to form a coherent sentence any more tonight. Or worse, keep the raw emotion out of her voice when she turned over the case. "I'll wait until morning," she agreed.

"Thank you. And talk to me before you comm."

"Fine." He wasn't going to change her mind, but the least she could do was listen to whatever he had to say.

At least there was no residue of C-X gas inside the lab. Everything was spotless and redolent of alcohol and bleach. She wrinkled her nose as she perched on a stool and held out her arm. "If I never smell another chemical again, I could be quite happy."

With practiced efficiency, Lian drew off blood for the test, then took three more vials—one for here, two for Health Canada—in case her hyperimmune system had formed active antibodies. When he finished, he pulled the needle from her arm, then stretched the muscles in his back and yawned. "I'm so tired, I'm surprised I could find your vein."

Day rolled down her sleeve. "I feel like I've been sucking pond water."

"You awake enough to draw off *my* blood for the test?"

"If you walk me through the steps."

He did, and managed not to even wince when she had to stick him three times before she found the vein. While the blood ran through the analyzer, they sat in knotted silence, holding hands, waiting for the result. Death or life?

At last the chip beeped.

"What's the verdict?" she asked, her chest tight.

Lian let out a long breath as he looked at the reading.

"Immunity. Active antibodies for you, passive immune globulins for me. We won't come down with active disease."

Day loosened her fist, unwilling to admit until that moment just how scared she'd been. She'd faced death as a Mountie. Never did it frighten her like the deaths she'd seen too many times in a quarantine camp. How did Lian do what he did? She would rather go down in a blaze of Distazer fire tomorrow than be brought down by a tiny microbe.

Life surged through her veins, banishing fatigue. Tonight, she was alive.

Lian wrapped the precious vials of Day's blood in a padded container, then they stepped outside the lab into the cold night and deep shadows. The single light across the compound where the cultists lay sleeping and healing did not reach this far, and snow clouds covered the stars and moon.

"We'll have a better chance of finding Trafalgar when it's light." He laid a hand on her shoulder.

"It's annoying when you read my mind like that."

"Only because I'm worried, too." He massaged the taut muscles of her neck, intending to give comfort. The soft hair of her braid brushed against the back of his hand, hitting right at the tiny gap between his glove and sleeve. With the simple touch, a laser-strength charge of desire careened from his hand to heart to groin.

Suddenly, he needed her. Needed her vibrant strength. Needed to know that life and passion existed in the midst of horror and death. Needed to not be alone.

"You still feeling the effects of that gas?" she muttered.

"Can you read my mind?" he asked with a lilting laugh, running his fingers in a demanding circle down her spine.

She slanted a glance his way, first at his face, then lower. "A grouse could read your mind right now, Lian. Men aren't exactly subtle."

Too bad women, even ones as straightforward as Day, could be. He felt as if he were running blind right now. Good thing he'd never minded it before.

He tossed his goggles to the ground. The snow fell on his face, but he didn't care. He needed to see her without barrier. All that mattered was Day, his need for her that seemed a never-ending thirst. His hand splayed between her shoulder blades, and he moved forward until their bodies touched. Despite the confining grip, they both knew she could be free if she wanted.

"You aren't turning back, Day?"

"No." She lifted her goggles, then raised up on tiptoe.

Their lips met, and desire meteored through him, an unstoppable conflagration that burned away all pretense. With a growl, he ripped off his gloves, then pulled her tight against him. His hand cupped the back of her head, holding her still for his kiss. She gripped his shoulders, holding him just as fast.

Their kisses turned deep as their tongues met and dueled. Her leg wrapped around his calf, pushing her sex against him. Feeling, sweet feeling! Ah, she tasted of maple. The heady musk of her feminine desire overrode the antiseptic scents of decontamination chems. She surrounded him. Enveloped him. He tried to stroke her, but met the thick pads of her winter gear. He tried to run his hand through her hair, but the goggles perched atop her head barred his way.

"Damn cold," he muttered. "All these clothes."

"Adjust," she demanded. Her fingers worked his coat open. "I am." She slid her hands inside—sometime, she'd discarded her gloves—clasped his waist, slipped her hands into his pants, cupped his buttocks and moved her hips against him, pulling at him from the rear.

It was an open invitation. With a feral noise, Lian buried his face beneath the high neck of her shirt. Nipping, sucking, licking her soft skin. Probably marking her. Good. He didn't care. Marks would heal before they left. Besides, he *wanted* to mark her, to stake his impossible claim.

With a quick tug, he pulled her shirt from her waistband, then tunneled beneath each layer—coat, shirt, knit shirt, thermasilk liners—until he found her warm, full breasts. With tingling, frantic palms, he kneaded them, then flicked his thumb across the nipples, bringing those to turgid attention.

All the while, his kisses continued as he bent to her neck, and she kissed the side of his ear, his temple, any patch of skin within reach. Frantic with need, they met and stroked and demanded as equals.

"Now?" he asked.

"Rock face," she demanded.

He walked her backward, quick steps to the nearest mountain. She had his pants undone by the time they arrived. Hers soon followed. With a grunt, he lifted her up until she was eye level. Their eyes met, locked, and she braced back against the stones as he drove upward inside her hot wetness. Fully inserted, he stopped while she gripped his shoulders and embraced him with strong legs. Then, he pushed up, farther, deeper, impossibly harder, feeling himself swell. A rapid pounding rhythm—deep, deeper—drummed inside him, and she clasped him, her muscles working every part of him. Every thrust of his, she met. Her breath came in short pants. He could barely suck in air. The snow drifted harder, coating their faces and lashes and shoulders.

It wasn't subtle. It had no finesse. It was what it was: raw, primal sex. The inexplicable, impossible need of one plague hunter and a law-bound Mountie for each other.

With a final thrust and a guttural shout, Lian exploded, coming home to her feminine heat. Day's fingers tightened on his shoulders, and her body went taut as she gasped out her own release. The tension encased them, one endless yet too-short moment of oneness, of nothing but each other, before it disintegrated, leaving them both gasping.

Lian wrapped his arms around Day, almost unable to stand. She, too, held him as their breath mingled and slowed.

Earlier they'd had an hour. Moments ago, they'd had mere seconds. Now they had the remains of the night. Yet he couldn't move.

"We ever going to do it inside, Lian?" she asked.

"Tonight."

"I don't want to sleep in one of those buildings."

"I don't care where we sleep. As long as I'm with you."

She didn't answer right away. Instead, stiffly, she moved away from him, and they both righted their clothes. She looked at him.

"My tent holds two. I'll get it set up, eh?" With that she pivoted away; and stiff-backed, braid mangled, she marched to their discarded packs and equipment.

It was all the invitation he would get from Day.

It was all the invitation he needed. Humming a little, he joined her.

Chapter Fourteen

Day woke to daylight, slobber, and the aroma of sizzling grease.

The daylight came from the open tent flap and dazzled her eyes, meaning the snow had stopped, at least for now. The slobber came from Benton, who stood in the doorway licking her.

"So, you decided the compound was okay," she said, ruffling the wolf's fur affectionately. She really hadn't spent any time with Benton lately, other than the time cooped up in the sled, which didn't count. "Let me get some clothes on, and I'll play with you a bit." She shoved his head. He got the hint and backed away. Grimacing as the cold hit her bare skin—the sun might be out, but that didn't mean the air was any warmer—she quickly slipped on her clothes, boots, and coat, and exited the tent.

The sizzling came from an open fire and frying pan with round slices of back bacon. Though the sun was well up, no one else was around except Lian, who sat on a rock by the fire, studying something on his handheld. He hadn't been awake very long, she guessed; otherwise his absence from the chilling sleeping bag would have roused her.

"Help yourself to the bacon," he said without looking up.

"Thanks, I will. How are your patients?"

"Improving. They all made it through the night."

"Good." She left to take care of necessities, then came back to the fire, Benton jumping at her heels. She grabbed a piece of the bacon and munched it while she and the wolf chased back and forth. At last, breathless and laughing, the altitude giving her a little headache, she dropped to one of the stones beside Lian and took another piece of meat.

She studied Lian a moment, enjoying the sight of his sharp profile and incongruous blue earrings. Last night they'd slept in each other's arms, not making love, just holding each other in a tender, poignant embrace. In addition to passion in his arms, she'd discovered caring.

This morning, however, she was relieved to be back to business, back to the work she needed to do. It was easier ground to tread, and Lian seemed to understand that.

Easier ground, that is, if she didn't have to comm HQ. She took another bite of bacon, delaying the unpalatable task. "I haven't had fresh bacon in ages. Thanks."

"Everything I have is concentrated." He looked up. "Thank Trafalgar when we find him. I filched it from his stock."

The reminder that they hadn't yet found Trafalgar sobered her. While she hadn't expected to find him in that scene last night, she couldn't rid herself of the feeling he was nearby. Trafalgar took care of himself just fine and wouldn't appreciate her fretting about him. Still, when she finished breakfast, it was time for a thorough reconnoiter.

She reached into her pack for two energy bars and tossed one to Lian. "My contribution to breakfast."

"I always wanted a woman who could cook."

218

"Glad you appreciate my finer points." She saw the ready flare of heat in his eyes, but knew he wouldn't act on it now, and neither would she. For there was something else pressing. "You wanted to talk, Lian? Before I comm the Depot?"

He laid down his handheld. "Don't do it, Day. If you bring in a new investigator, then you'll have to fill him, or them, in on everything, including this." His hand swept the compound. "And the news of this outbreak must be kept contained."

"I have to tell the RCMP. I can't drop my murder investigation for four days without informing them. And the smallpox? Health Canada may have jurisdiction, but the Mounties have to know, too. We *have* to be prepared." She held back nausea as the breeze shifted and she caught the faint acrid aroma of burnt fabric from the contaminated robes. "How can you expect me to keep quiet?"

"Because it's the best thing for Canada," he said, his voice hard.

"No." She reached to her comm patch. "A secret like that is not only illegal, but it would abuse the trust my fellow officers put in me. I couldn't betray them like that. How could I work with them afterward?"

He grabbed her wrist before she could turn on the comm. "Just hear me out."

"Let go of my wrist first," she warned.

He studied her in the sunlight, then nodded and opened his fingers. "All right, partner. Here's the offer. I'll lay out how I see the situation, based on my experience. If you'll listen without judgment before you make your decision, then I'll accept it. If you decide you have to designate a new investigator into Robichaux's death, I won't stop you."

He couldn't stop her if she truly put her mind to comming. But, last night she had said she would give him time to explain, and she owed her partner that much at least.

His argument would have to be awfully convincing, though. "Go ahead."

"This is what we know. Luc Robichaux was killed by a cold-plasma ligature when he was discovered at the No-Borders meeting, and someone at that meeting carried a trace of smallpox virus, which was transferred to Robichaux's hat. If we find out who was at that meeting, we find our killer."

"That's why we were following the No-Borders links." The action planned by the militant expat No-Borders to open the borders. Two buyers calling themselves L.J. Malachite and Jem purchasing mountain climbing gear for extreme weather. This mystery of Citadel.

"Right. Your piece of the puzzle. But focus on the other piece right now. My area, the virus. I've had a chance to start modeling it with the raw samples here. It's an undocumented, highly virulent strain, with nucleotides similar to other genetically modified viruses. Yet, it shows up again in a compound where the people have been isolated for a month, and there's no other outbreak in Canada. Which means the cultists weren't infected before they got here. Perhaps it was already here, then. A mutated strain *might* be more resistant to degradation. If so, where was it? The air outside that room was free of virus and so far all other scans are clean. So, where did the virus come from? It's not part of a resurgent epidemic or a latent contamination." He paused and took a sip from his water canteen. "To me, everything points to a virus which has been deliberately engineered, then planted. Here. By an individual. Who? According to the cultists, they've had contact with only one man. Rupert Juneau."

Day shook her head. "His name's cropping up way too often for someone who's supposed to be on the other side of the border. There might be something here we could get his DNA from. To put into the national database."

He nodded. "There is; I asked around this morning. M'ya

has a sample of his DNA. According to her, he is not only handsome, but a talented lover," he added dryly.

"How did she—Oh, it isn't his . . . ?" Day wrinkled her nose.

"A strand of his hair," Lian answered with a faint smile. "Left on a pillow. I already started to process it. You can upload it when it's done."

"Thanks. Now, back to Juneau's role." She was coming to some conclusions about the man, but she kept them to herself. She was in listening mode.

"He's working with the No-Borders. He comes to a place that's been isolated for a month, and thirty-six-hours later they have overt smallpox from a unique strain of virus. He's UCE. This virus had to have been made somewhere, and it sure as hell wasn't a Canadian lab. I think he planted it here."

The clutch of fear Day hated grabbed her stomach. "Juneau could be planting more virus as we speak."

"Yes."

"I was hoping you'd give me a reason why that conclusion was impossible."

"I wish I could. I'm not being cavalier about this, Day. I've put the Health Canada commissioner on alert and notified the other plague hunters. They'll take all precautions. If there's a whiff of infection elsewhere, they'll know about it and will go into action. But right now, we're stalled. To stop this virus, we need to locate Rupert Juneau and we need to find out *how* he infected these people. You've already got search alerts on all Mountie handhelds for both Jem and him. Tomorrow you'll have Juneau's DNA. Anyone spots them, you can galvanize every Mountie in Canada and I'll be on comm to Health Canada. Until we have that exact location, though, Canada will be a hell of a big place to search. So, Health Canada waits. I'll comm the Prime Minister, but I think she will agree with my recommendation that the news goes no further for now. After all, if I can prove this is from a new, UCE source, she can still make her announcement that Canada is virus free."

"How long do you plan to keep this hidden?"

"My gut says that we have a little time. Until Juneau chooses to act, we're safe."

"When will he act? And how?" Was Lian thinking along the same lines as she was?

"I don't think Juneau wants a widespread virus release. I think he's working with the No-Borders because he's planning something to coincide with their action at Citadel."

She thought of the information that had been downloaded to her handheld. Maybe they did have a little time. Weather data confirmed there wasn't enough snow in the area near Citadel to require the serious equipment bought from Scree. She pointed to the hospital. "If Juneau's planning something at Citadel, why this?"

"To test the virus? To confirm the effects without endangering his own people or releasing it prematurely? If Trafalgar hadn't clued us to this compound, everyone here would have been dead and the virus destroyed before we knew about it."

Trafalgar. She couldn't delay any longer. Comm, then reconnoiter. Nothing Lian had said was enough to change her mind. "I think everything you've said is right so far. I'll even accept Health Canada decisions about the smallpox. You have the expertise there. But, you've given me nothing why I should ignore my duty to the RCMP. I don't *want* to turn over my case, but it's what I have to do. There are things to be done out there, like interrogating L.J. Malachite, the guy who bought the gear from Scree, which shouldn't be put off."

"I know I'm asking a lot for you to put your investigation on hold because mine is stalled. But I want *you* to stay on as sole investigator. For one thing, our cases are inextricably entwined. To solve Luc Robichaux's murder, you have to work with Health Canada, and I don't think anyone else could do that as well as you have, Day. That's a compliment, by the way."

For the first time since they started talking, she smiled. "Thanks."

"And, two: because every person who knows about the virus adds another risk of this getting out. The people at Health Canada who know deal with this all the time, but outsiders, even Mounties get unpredictable when you say the word 'smallpox.' Did you ever see the old vids? The ones taken during the first plague years."

She shook her head. "I've read about them, studied the history though."

"You need to watch the actual vids, see it firsthand. They're chilling." He turned his handheld on, and the vids started scrolling across. "Watch, Day."

She watched, and her gut knotted. Mindless panic. People reduced to survival instincts, fleeing when there was no place safe to flee. She fisted the hem of her shirt, trying to hold back the trembling and nausea as she saw children abandoned or trampled. Border-crossers shot. Vigilantes hauling out suspected carriers for execution.

Scene after scene of the unthinkable. A shudder passed across her shoulders. In some scenes she saw her valiant comrades brought down by mobs. In two others she saw Mounties give in to the panic and start spraying the crowds with bullets.

She sat numb, horrified, as Lian moved the handheld off her lap.

"It wasn't Canada's finest hour," he said quietly, "although I'm not sure any other country would have reacted better. The thought of going back to those days scares the hell out of me."

"We won't. We've learned. We've grown."

"Have we? Remember the news last month? A woman died in her home and wasn't discovered right away. From

223

the smell, her neighbors decided the house had been infected so they burned it down, not caring that her niece was inside. The niece is still recovering from the burns and has lost her job, even though it was determined the woman died of natural causes. And that crazy coot who was slaughtering chickens? Killed because a mob thought the blood was from a hemorrhagic fever." He shook his head. "Canada's stronger now, but we're still terrified. We're brittle. Word of this virus gets out it'll be chaos, and I don't know if we can survive panic again. Give me four days. Even from quarantine, you can do a lot; comm and Interweb connections are good here. Any hints that something's moving in that time, we call in all resources. But not until then. So, what's your answer, Day?"

Once Lian had challenged her whether she could make the right choice instead of the legal choice, and she'd thought the decision would be a given. Especially if she wasn't sure what the right choice was.

Lian was sure. He had no hidden agendas here. The only reason he was doing this was because he wanted to protect Canada and stop that virus. He wouldn't keep silent if he thought people were at risk. Everything he said made sense. But his right choices weren't necessarily hers.

She hated uncertainties. She liked dealing with the law, where everything was clearly labeled right or wrong.

Except even the law had ambiguities and judgments, she was learning.

What do you hold on to, Day, when everything else is gone? What do you hold most dear? Being a Mountie? Or keeping people safe?

She stole another glance at the vids, at the panic and destruction.

"All right," she said, shredding one part of her soul to save another. "I'll keep quiet."

* * *

Wisely, Lian didn't try to go with her when she began her reconnoiter for Trafalgar. Halfway around, she was confiding to Benton that she didn't think they were going to find anything inside the compound. "We'll have to go up the mountain—" Her words cut off as she saw something she'd missed last night in the dark.

A splotch on the white bricks of the building furthest out. Heart pounding against her ribs, she ran over to it. Yes, it was . . .

"A handprint," she breathed. From dried blood. She held out her hand, testing the size. Bigger than hers, about the size of a hand she'd held for twenty years. "Trafalgar? Look, Benton, another smear." Frantic, she started to follow the smears, then halted and ran back to her pack.

She'd learned last night: Blood meant precautions.

"Lian," she shouted. "Trafalgar. He may be hurt." She threw on all her protective gear and slathered her exposed skin with quick swipes of the MAB gel as she raced back to the trail, Lian at her side. He already had his gear on from his work at the hospital.

She followed the smears to the rear of the compound, where a wire door in the fence hung useless and open on its hinges. There she lost the trail in the snow. "Do you see where it went?"

"There." He pointed to a patch of crushed lichen.

Between the two of them, they trailed the signs up the mountain into a small meadow. Blood pounded in Day's ears, and her breath came in needy pants as they circled, looking for where to head next. All of a sudden, Benton took off at a howling run and scrambled up a rocky face into a small cave.

Day followed, barely able to see past the black spots in her vision. She fumbled at her waist for her Distazer and her light, and with quick leaps joined Benton in the cave.

The wolf stood over a heap of cloth. A heap of cloth

225

with a red-and-gray-haired head. With a cry, Day dropped to her knees. Hands trembling, gulping back a sob, she pushed back the blanket.

Trafalgar! Oh, God, he was so white, so still. Her icy fingers tried to reach for his pulse, but she couldn't feel anything.

"Let me." Lian's calm voice intruded on her grief, and he slipped his hand beneath hers. "Let me do my job, Day."

Everything in her protested. *She* wanted to save Trafalgar, like he had saved her. Trained to action, she needed to do something. She couldn't sit by idly. But she knew that Lian had skills beyond her first-aid training, skills Trafalgar needed. She sat back on her heels, bracing her fists on her thighs.

When Lian pushed the blankets back the rest of the way, she saw Trafalgar's blood-soaked flannel shirt and useless tears started rolling down her cheeks. Angrily, she brushed them away, but she couldn't stop them.

Instead, she scrambled to her feet. Clutching her Distazer, she did a quick survey of the cave, making sure there were no hidden surprises or waiting ambushes. She glanced over her shoulder. "Is he . . . How is he?"

"He's alive, but his pulse is thready. He's lost blood, and the cold hasn't helped." Lian's steady voice was counterpoint to his quick, assured movements. But she saw worry etched between his brows.

"Should we take him back to camp? It's warmer there."

"Let me stabilize him." He pulled a blanketlike pouch from his pack and handed it to her. "Put this on his legs and lower torso, then press the red square in the corner."

Glad to have something to do, she complied, smoothing the blanket in place with care. When she pressed the red square, the blanket began to radiate heat.

She knelt back, taking Trafalgar's hand in hers. Lian's glance flicked toward her, but he didn't say anything or futilely try to stop her.

The diagnostic chip strapped to Trafalgar's chest was running through a series of lights and clicks. Beneath his opened shirt, an ugly-looking gash spread across his abdomen. Sniffing, Day gulped back the bubble in her throat. Above the point of the gash was a different stab wound, which radiated red streaks. Even as she watched, the streaks spread, a millimeter closer to his heart.

"What is it? Blood poisoning?"

"No." His jaw tightened, and she saw him reach in his pack for something. "That stab wound is from a K-tipped blade. K-tips form clots in the blood, gradually clotting all the way back to the heart. If I don't stop it soon, the cascade of coagulation will be too far gone to stop." His hands deftly packed a slimy paste into Trafalgar's wound.

"What's that?"

"Leech-saliva unguent."

"Oh my, God, you're killing him!" At the height of the plagues, hysterical citizens had laced boundary waters with genetically-modified leeches, using their potent saliva as weapons against illegal crossings. Anyone encountering the leeches bled to death.

Lian shot her a fierce, angry glare. "Don't trust me at all, Day? Well, don't worry. I won't kill him," he snapped, then returned to his work.

"I'm sorry. I know, but this seems so . . . unscientific."

He didn't answer her right away as he finished packing the wound and began to make tiny pricks with a scalpel along the line of red. At each prick, he added more of the unguent. Then, he took some sort of wand-looking equipment out of his pack and rubbed it slowly across the skin, his fingers testing the direction. He was directing the medicine toward the clots, she realized.

Ancient remedy meeting modern medicine.

"Leech unguent is a treatment known to my people. Modern medicine isn't always the best. You have a problem with the concept?"

She swallowed hard, realizing her unthinking reaction had insulted him. "No."

"Then go get me some water. I'll have to wash it off soon."

"Understood." She stood, pivoted, and left.

Trafalgar was a big man, and he hadn't shriveled any in retirement. When Lian deemed it safe to move the patient, he and Day struggled down the mountain with the stretcher. He wasn't willing to risk exposing the sick man to any of the cultists. The journey was a nightmare of jostles and lurches, but they finally settled Trafalgar into a clean room at the compound.

Lian worked to repair the reopened gash: more artificial endorphins to mitigate the shock-stimulating pain, another application of leech unguent to reforming clots. Day stood behind him, gulping in air, breathless from high-altitude exertion. Worry radiated from her, searing his back, as she expected him to work miracles.

"Is he going to be okay?"

"I think so," he lied, as much for Trafalgar as for himself or Day. Unconscious patients could still hear, at some level, what was said around them, and he wanted Trafalgar hearing only positive beliefs. But the truth was, he didn't like the weak blood pressure or the man's ghostly pallor. "He's sleeping. He was strong and healthy before this. He'll come through."

"Professional opinion or feel-good encouragement?"

"A little of both," he allowed himself to admit. He sat back, having done all he could for the moment. Yet the blood pressure monitor continued to show a dangerous hypotension.

"He doesn't look good," Day choked out. "Isn't there something else we can do?"

"No . . ." His denial faded. There *was* something else. A

ritual that had leached out of his life over the past seven years and been rediscovered these past days. Strange, that it would be Day, a *wasichu*, a practical Mountie, who was the catalyst. "With your permission, I could seek guidance in the otherworlds."

"You mean, pray for him?"

"Yes. No." He struggled to simplify and explain something he'd studied some years to understand, yet was no longer instinctive. "My people believe in a multidimensional universe. Worlds above and below us. Nations around us, not just of men, but of bison and pine and granite. Sickness, too, isn't simply physical. Pieces of the soul may be lost if the spirit is in disharmony."

She stared at him, then drew him away from the bedside. "He's not going to make it, is he?" she whispered, so low he could barely hear.

He shook his head, unwilling to voice the words and give them power.

All stiffness went out of her. She braced a hand against the wall, as though it were the only way she could stand, and her cheeks paled. Then her jaw set. "You have my permission for anything, *anything*, that might help him."

Lian collected what he needed. He no longer traveled with all the tools of ceremony, but he had the basics. Ideally, this would be done outside, but the civilized physician in him rebelled at moving Trafalgar back into the cold. Instead, he turned up the temperature in the room, then removed his shirt and shoes, and loosened his hair. He washed his hands, remembering to thank the waters for their cleansing gift. Beside the bed, he set a small copper bowl holding sage leaves. He lit the leaves, letting their fragrant smoke fill and cleanse the room.

Crouching next to Trafalgar, he picked up his drum and began the rhythm and the chant.

How may I help this man?

229

Drum slower. Breathe deep the smoke. All other sensation was lost except the flickering life beneath his palm. Deepen the trance. Open. Humility.

How may I help this man? His mind wandered to the upper world, seeking his animal guide, the firebird. Nothing. None came to answer him. His mind wandered further and he delved deeper, seeking guidance in the caress of the north wind or the sound of the river. A blue-eyed wolf peered at him from beneath a spruce, but the wolf refused to come nearer; instead, it bounded away when he approached.

How may I help this man?

The spirits had no guidance for him.

At last, the physical world intruded. Lian's arm cramped from the long drumming; the sage smoke died. Day sat next to him, he realized, as her warm scent replaced the sage. Failure dehydrated his mouth, already dry from his chants. Drops of sweat beaded his forehead as he bent. Inside, he was hollow, his body a brittle husk.

Hesitantly, Day touched his shoulder. When he didn't respond, she began to knead the back of his neck. He shook his head, answering her unspoken question and shaking off the sympathy.

"Thank you for trying. Trafalgar does seem to be sleeping a little easier."

Lian opened his eyes, squinting a bit, though the light was dim. Immediately, his gaze went to Trafalgar. The inhalations and exhalations did seem a little less uneven, although that could be wishful thinking.

Sometime during the ritual, Day had also laid a hand on Trafalgar, just above where Lian held the man's wrist. He stared at it.

Day.

Had the spirits given him an answer? The wolf, blue-eyed like Benton. *How can I help this man?* Perhaps it was not his destiny to help more. His physician's skill had started the healing process.

Perhaps it was up to Day, now, to finish what he had started. Day, whom Trafalgar needed. Day, and her nourishing roots to the family of Mounties, a nation formed by affection and trust, not blood.

"Talk to him, Day," he said, rising stiffly to his feet. "Our voices are heard, even by the one who can't speak back."

"What should I say?"

"Anything, everything. Memories. What you are doing today. Give his subconscious something to ponder. Remind him of the future."

She took Trafalgar's hand and began talking. Lian brought a chair over for her, making her more comfortable.

And so, through the long afternoon and the longer night it went. Lian continued to check on all his patients. He worked on the virus he'd isolated, characterizing and modeling it now that he had a better sample. He brought Day food and drink, bullied her into a brief break to see to her own needs. When her voice scratched, he gave her soothing honey water. When her fingers cramped, he massaged them.

All the while, Day talked. About anything, about nothing as he had suggested. Boys who had hijacked Mac the Moose. Benton's latest antics. Her Japanese brush work. The trek up the mountain. She talked about her past. She talked about putting her name in for the Gretzky Cup hockey tickets lottery, promising to share them with Trafalgar if she snagged a pair.

She bared her soul to Trafalgar, and to Lian.

At last, she talked about Luc Robichaux's death and the No-Borders and the viruses. Lian added his own bits, filling in gaps, expanding and clarifying the picture, for himself, for her, for the unconscious Trafalgar. They speculated, about Juneau's purpose, about time and place and action, and about Citadel. They planned their next steps.

The only thing they did not mention was each other.

What had happened yesterday was private, for them alone.

The deep night held hours of escape, an interlude of worry and exposure and joining detached from the rest of the world. Tomorrow would see if they had helped or lost. Tomorrow would bring back all the actions and necessities of their work. But, in the deep night, Lian joined Day in that oversized chair, holding her in his arms, while she struggled to keep talking. He stroked a hand down her hair, suffused with a contentment that he didn't remember ever feeling.

She dozed, and while she slept he filled the gap with his own tales. He dozed, too, his cheek resting on the top of her head as he held her and listened to her. In those hours, he learned more about Day than he could have discovered in a lifetime.

Eventually, the tension and time took their toll, and he and Day slept entwined.

Lian woke with a start, aware of Day's hand on his thigh, of her hair tickling his nose and her breath across his bare chest. Of his thumb on her breast and his unruly arousal. He blinked. Enough sunshine got through the snow to hit him in the eyes and awaken him. Morning.

Trafalgar!

His glance spun around to the bed.

Trafalgar stared back at him, green eyes startlingly clear, red brows knit. "Who the hell are you?" he rasped. "And why're you holding my daughter like that?"

Rupert Juneau kept a home on the Canadian side of the border furnished with all the fine things he enjoyed. He'd made himself a very tidy sum and accumulated a lot of luxuries by turning a blind eye to the Canadian No-Border smugglers, but it wouldn't do to have too many questions being asked in the UCE because he sported a lifestyle beyond his usual means. As the UCE's chief engineer for the plasma grids and a cold plasma expert, he had no trouble powering down pieces of either the UCE or the Canadian barrier whenever he wanted to cross, and he came here often to indulge himself.

Tonight, however, he was not pleased. He downed half a glass of ale and glared at the blank holoscreen. The Mountie and the plague hunter. Those two were turning into a damned nuisance.

His sweet situation threatened to sour if Canada stayed virus-free and their Prime Minister negotiated for the quarantine to be officially lifted. Open borders meant free travel and the end of the need to smuggle. He fingered the gold box on the table next to him. The end of his lifestyle, influence, and power.

His plan to remedy that should have been a straightforward operation. He enjoyed playing many roles while he was in Canada. Experienced lover. Easy confidant. Sympathetic expatriate supporter. It had been a simple enough matter to incite a group of rabid No-Borders, to convince them the pace of government was too slow. Listen to the Voice of Freedom. You should be free to join with your brothers and your relations. A grand gesture, a broadcast to the world was needed.

Such fools. They thought the plan to blast open the power grid, to broadcast the first symbolic open exchange of goods was theirs.

Everything was set. The date: In ten days. The place: The legendary Citadel.

Except the grand gesture would become a horrific tragedy, witnessed by the world. It would be proof that viruses still plagued the north. The borders would slam shut, and it would take more than a lifetime to open them up again.

But things had gone wrong from the moment his

genetically-engineered virus mutated. The mutation made the antibodies he owned worthless, and he wasn't about to unleash a scourge until he knew he was safe. So far, his lab contact hadn't come up with a replacement.

Then the Mounties had started interfering. First he'd had to kill the one who stumbled into his meeting with the No-Borders. The man had heard too much.

Next thing he knew, he had a female Mountie on his tail. Damn woman had spread his picture all over Canada, forcing him to lie low. How she'd found out about the virus and brought in a plague hunter he didn't know. He glared again at the holoscreen. Now, tonight, when he'd planned to verify the virus worked as fast as he needed, the doctor had destroyed his surveillance.

Pain stabbed his ribs as he shifted in his leather chair. He downed his ale in one gulp, then poured another glass. The wound was compliments of yet another Mountie, the one who'd interfered at the cult compound. At least he'd taken care of that meddler.

Damn Mounties. Maybe once this was over and he was sitting pretty again, he'd look into spreading a little infectious panic through them.

His comm sounded. It was his cohort at the biolab, well-paid in both money and smuggled Canadian medical advances.

"I may have a solution," the scientist announced without preamble. "That Mountie. She's a hyperimmune."

"Hyperimmune? What's that?"

"She makes antibodies to everything."

"And she's just been exposed to my virus." Maybe, with a little adjusting, things were beginning to fall back into place. He leaned forward. "What do you need?"

"A sample of her blood."

"You've got it. How long will it take to broth the antibodies?"

"You'll have your antisera within a week after I get the

234

blood." The scientist coughed delicately. "I've always wanted to study a hyperimmune."

"You make those antibodies, and you'll have her. Your own personal lab rat."

He turned off the comm, then leaned back and laughed. The green light was shining. He was sitting pretty again. Though he'd have to wait until they left quarantine to get her blood; he wouldn't risk getting infected.

The front bell rang. He checked the outdoor camera, then smiled when he saw the visitor wrapped in thick fur. His hand rubbed appreciatively against his groin. The night had definitely taken a turn for the better.

His lover came in, and the two of them tumbled to the silken bed. Juneau spent the evening pampering and pleasuring his lover well. After all, tonight he played the role of a generous, experienced man. This contact was too valuable to treat like he treated the common whores.

He made the requisite promises, and tonight his indulgence paid off.

Much later, after his visitor had left, Juneau leaned back against the satin sheets and fine-tuned his plans with the information received. In less than two weeks, the borders would be closed, the plague hunter would be destroyed, and the lab rat Mountie would be sorry she ever crossed him.

Chapter Fifteen

Three days later, Day sat in the sunshine with her father. Trafalgar had made steady progress, and when the snow finally stopped, except for a few idle flakes, he insisted he'd been cooped up long enough, he needed to get outdoors. Surprisingly, Lian—who'd been more protective than a mother bear with cubs—had agreed. As long as Trafalgar didn't overdo it. So, here Day and he sat, Trafalgar soaking in the anemic rays, her making sure he stayed bundled. Neither one of them tolerated idleness well, however, so they were working together on her case, bouncing off theories and avenues of investigation. In Trafalgar's mind, work never came under the category of overdoing it.

Day had been surprised at how much tedious gruntwork she'd been able to knock out with a handheld and hours that she didn't have to devote to other tasks.

She'd delighted her supervisor by catching up on her delayed paperwork and cleaning out her overflowing comm box. She'd absorbed a lot of information as reports about the No-Borders' activities, an assessment of UCE and Canadian troop strength along the border, stories of the initial plagues, updated news flashes, and the latest virus research reports had all scrolled across her handheld.

"You find anything to back up my theory?" Trafalgar asked, nodding at her open handheld.

"Nope. Doesn't seem to be any relationship between scenic icons like Mac the Moose, The Giant Loonie, the Sausage Statue and No-Border gatherings."

"Hmmph, thought they might be trying to destroy a few good Canadian symbols."

"One of your suggestions did pan out. I found out an interesting fact about Citadel." She'd been stymied getting data on Citadel since everything about the area seemed to have been erased on the Interweb. Information abounded for the kilometers around it, but the mountain itself seemed to be a black hole for facts. None escaped. Until Trafalgar suggested she look deeper into the expatriate No-Borders, at what they did when they weren't being criminals.

"One of the No-Borders repairs Interweb relays, and he did a job recently that took him somewhere into the mountains near Citadel. One job he never talked to anyone else about." And the node would be one of the least defended by actual troops due to its inaccessibility and vanishing act. Hard to justify sending squadrons of troops to a site that doesn't exist.

"Add that to the information from that cold plasma dealer about where a node would have to be based on distance between the other nodes—"

"Yup. You've got the technologic equivalent of the mother lode sitting up on Citadel: An Interweb relay and a cold plasma node. Remind me to tell Lian when I see him next," she added. She'd also dug up some frustration, which she wouldn't share with Lian. Not a single lead to the Shinook had panned out. Despite Lian's belief they weren't involved, she'd followed the occasional lead to mostly useless information. If anyone even knew their location, they weren't talking to her.

"He's a good man, Day, but he's not for you."

Trafalgar's sudden comment startled her, for she'd thought he'd dozed off, but she didn't pretend not to know whom he meant. "That's not your decision to make," she said easily.

"I know, just voicing my opinion. He's not like us. He doesn't revere the law like we do. I can sense it. Over time, things like that start to matter."

Revere the law. Day dug her gloved hands deep in her pockets and buried her chin in her coat. Neither she nor Lian had spoken again about her decision. That it was the right one didn't mean she'd forgotten, that it didn't prick her. "Have you ever broken the law, Trafalgar? Knowingly and willfully?"

"Nope." He caught a drifting snowflake in his hand. "There have been times when I've had to choose between conflicting laws, choose which was most important. Other times, I admit, I've turned an eye to infractions, remembering our purpose to protect and serve. But have I broken it myself? No. How can I uphold the law if I don't honor it?" He closed his fingers around a snowflake. "Why? Have you broken one?"

"Would you arrest me if I did?"

"If I weren't retired, yes. And anyone else involved, if it was dangerous to society. Would I need to?"

"What could I have done up here?" She waved a hand around the stark mountains.

"Joined this cult?"

"Like either Lian or I would. A sex cult?"

"I don't know. Since I'm going to be staying up here recuperating after you leave tomorrow, I just might give in. Don't hold much with that Voice of Freedom, but that Banzai woman—she looks like my type." Lines of humor crinkled around his eyes. "Maybe she'll show up. I figure, since she's over a hundred and seventy, I'm more than young enough."

Day burst out laughing, pleased to see a bit of the old, raunchy Trafalgar back. Even though his comments reminded her that she'd be leaving him tomorrow.

One of Lian's fellow plague hunters was coming to finish overseeing the cultists' convalescence. There was a fresh grave in the graveyard, but everyone else was recovering. Rapid detection, quick treatment, and isolation had made a huge difference.

For her and Lian, the quarantine would be lifted tomorrow. Their four days were up, and their blood evidenced no lingering virus. They were free to go.

They planned to leave at first light. Down the mountain, a bush plane would airlift them to Calagary. It turned out that of Lian's interesting contacts one happened to be Bible Bob, who had finally agreed to meet with him. Not only was Bible Bob a source for black market aerosols, he was father to L.J. Malachite: rabid No-Border, patron of Scree, the escaped smoker from Flash Point, and a compatriot of Rupert Juneau.

"I hate to leave you," she said, capturing Trafalgar's hand in hers. He was still too weak to move out of the camp.

"I'll be fine. That plague hunter crony of Lian's will keep a fine eye on me and those cultists. We'll watch Benton for you, too, till you're done in the city."

"Thanks."

His fingers tightened around hers. "Don't be stirring up an avoidable tempest, Day. You always did have a knack for finding troubles. Remember when I first came into the quarantine camp?"

"I believe I kicked you."

"A good left to the shins. Hurt, too. You thought I was one of those plague hunters, who'd bring more sick people to the camp but wouldn't take you out. You were brave, then, but you were also wild and scared. You've learned to harness that, to look for the kinds of trouble you can fix. Don't be forgetting your duty comes first. If you keep true to your calling, you'll be happy."

Trafalgar thought she needed someone who shared her duties and loyalties. Day was beginning to think she needed someone who also awakened her heart and shared the wildness that dwelt inside her.

Someone who could laugh when he made love in the snow.

Lian stopped to speak to one of the surviving cultists, and she saw the hint of the firebird nanotat beneath the open neck of his shirt. His hair was pulled back with a cotton tie, and he wore a series of narrow braids fastened on his right wrist.

There was one other troubling kerfuffle in their relationship: She might not be the right woman for him.

"You're up for a G-I promotion, Day. It's an honor we've both wanted," Trafalgar reminded her softly, perhaps seeing where her attention fastened. "A liaison here, in quarantine, is one thing. Outside? He'll distract you. He'll hold you back."

Her throat closed around a bubble of remorse. Trafalgar had been passed over for the G-I because of her. Did that mean she had to lose Lian for him?

She shook her head. "Just tell me you'll love me no matter what my choice."

"Of course I love you, Day." He hugged her, but he didn't speak the words she needed.

Day was glad when Lian perched on one of the rocks in front of them, interrupting the uncomfortable silence that had fallen between her and Trafalgar.

"Are you going to order me inside, Doc?" asked Trafalgar querulously.

"Not unless the snow gets harder or your temperature

sensor turns blue." He pointed to the dot attached to Trafalgar's hand, then stretched out his legs. "Who attacked you?"

"Rupert Juneau."

Juneau again. Day leaned forward, glad Lian had finally decided his patient was well enough to talk. "What happened?"

"I heard about this new No-Border cult couple of weeks ago, so I came to check them out. When you circulated Juneau's picture, I remembered seeing him here and came up for another reconnoiter. He was delivering those canisters. I followed him. He snuck a surveillance eye into the temple, then left. Apparently, I'm not as stealthy as I once was. He ambushed me. Did *that*." He pointed to his wound. "I got him, too, though, so he hightailed it out of here. I had enough strength to crawl into that cave before I collapsed."

Lian pushed to his feet. "I have to get back to work. Don't stay out here too much longer, Trafalgar."

At least the work he and the Winnipeg lab had done the past few days gave a better picture of the virus. Not that it was a pretty image, Day thought. Airborne transmission, highly contagious, rapid onset, a very tight window for effective treatment. The only bright spots were that it was destroyed by sunlight, and humans were the only biological reservoir. So, if they could keep quarantine to prevent human-to-human spread, the virus would die in an open environment.

Inside the canisters was another tale, however.

The light blinked on her comm. She activated her voice link. "Inspector Daniels."

"This is the Moose Jaw lab. You asked us to let you know about any matches for the unidentified DNA sample at the Luc Robichaux murder scene." There was an edge to the man's voice, an eagerness she'd never heard in the science-minded tech.

Her fists clenched. "You found something?"

"Yes. The DNA from Rupert Juneau you just added. It matches."

A match. Her fist clenched; she was so furious, she shook. She forced a breath, forced herself to stay calm. "Thanks. Patch me in to Central Comm.

"Will do, Day. Nail that bugger for us."

"I plan on it." When Central came on, she ordered upped the all-comms-alert on Rupert Juneau, DNA and holoimage attached, then concluded with, "I want everyone on the force searching for this puck."

Day disconnected, then leaned her head back, grateful for the cool wind blowing across her cheeks. Her insides churned. She had an ID. She had the murderer.

"What's up?" asked Trafalgar.

"Rupert Juneau's DNA was in Robichaux's wound." The words were like lead drops in her stomach. "He killed him."

Lian shook his head. "That bastard."

Trafalgar added a few other colorful curses.

"My sentiments exactly. But it's only a matter of time before I catch him."

The next day, in Calgary, Lian and Day hired a suite at Hedon—the latest of several new luxury hotels cropping up around Canada, ready to serve a population emerging from austerity and starting to crave indulgence. The rooms offered every amenity—from a virtual media experience center, to a bar stocked with beer and ale, to a bubbling spa bath, to a personal massage service.

Day ran an appreciative hand over the silk brocade upholstery. "I'm glad we left Benton with Trafalgar. This fabric wouldn't withstand his claws."

"The front desk wouldn't have been pleased to see him, either."

She inhaled the delicate floral scent of a spray of real lilies and fireweed. "Health Canada expense accounts must be more generous than the RCMP's."

"This is from my personal account, and don't even think about offering to share the fees," he continued rapidly, silencing her with a finger on her mouth. "It's already paid for, and I can well afford the night. This is my gift to you. And, very selfishly, to myself." He leaned down and kissed her with languid thoroughness. "I want to make meticulous love to you. To luxuriate with temperature control and downy comforters and aromatic candles."

She laid a hand to his warm chest, her heart thumping against her throat. "I was going to ask how you got a reservation. I heard this was booked for a year from opening. And with the Flames season opening against the Moose tonight, Calgary is filled with hockey fans."

"I went to university with the owner. *And* I successfully treated his wife, so he feels kindly toward me." Lian came up behind her and wrapped his arms around her waist. He kissed the side of her neck, sending a spark shimmering through her. So she was startled when he asked, "Day, do you have your hat with you?"

"Always." She touched the small envelope on her holster. "It's folded up in here."

"Tonight, at the market, don't take it out. Whatever happens."

"I'm not planning on arresting Bible Bob."

"Where we're going tonight, you might see some illegal goings-on. You're going to have to ignore it, all of it, if we're going to find out what we need. Can you do that? 'Cause if you can't, I'll go in alone."

"Ignore something illegal? You're asking me to make a habit of it here," she said with a trace of bitterness. Turning in his arms, she stepped back. "Is overlooking one transgression not enough?"

He gripped her shoulders. "You made a hard decision, but a necessary one. That does not make you a habitual criminal. Or unworthy to be a Mountie."

That hit too close to something she refused to examine. "I'm getting annoyed how you keep thinking you can read my mind. I'm a damn good Mountie, and I know it."

"I know it, too. Which is why I'm asking you: Can you see a black market and not make any arrests or levy any fines?"

"Afraid of losing your illegal sources?"

"Afraid of what not turning a blind eye will cost us."

"I know what to do, Lian." At least this time, her duty was clear, for now she could ignore the festering questions and doubts. " 'During undercover operations, an officer is to focus on the objective at hand. Paramount is maintaining the safety of officers, informants, and civilians, and assuring the successful outcome to the mission.' Mountie Handbook, page 103. It means no arrests while undercover unless securing the primary target." She lift her chin. "Just like you told me, don't always assume you know what I'm going to do."

"Damn, woman, did you memorize that entire handbook and its statutes?"

"Yes. It's part of the job."

He laughed. "And have you memorized our cover that well?"

"You have doubts?" she asked, amazed as always at how he both challenged her and made her feel so . . . happy. She enjoyed sparring with him, hummed with the anticipation of joining him on that downy bed. And she found she liked both as much as she liked the thrill of promised action after the inactive days of quarantine. "We're Lian and Day. After investing your earnings, we're an up-and-coming, new tech-money couple in Calgary's fast-living elite. Hmm, are we eyes-of-God-wed, legally contracted, or shacking?"

"Shacking."

"You ever been married before?"

The nanotat, its edge visible at his collar, glowed a bright gold. "No. My people don't believe in divorce. You?"

"Nope. Never the time. Never a man who gave me the inclination. So, here we are, out for a night of indulgence. Massage and tingle skin wrap and decorating our nails and nipples. Full sensory holos in our private theater. A full-bodied ale with fresh-caught salmon. Of course, at each of these stops, for the right price and the right contacts, we might find a few unpublicized extras. Am I forgetting any of the night's entertainment?"

"A trip to Bible Bob's to start."

"Ah, yes. He'll whip us up a carafe of perfect caf-blend, although I must admit I'm a bit jaded in that regard. It will be hard to beat the one I had in Moose Jaw."

Lian grinned at the reminder. "Bob also supplies more exotic fare. 'Tails if you need a little stimulus. LS-4 for some vivid dreams."

"Prialude for a twelve-hour erection?"

"Cantifly, the all-night aphrodisiac for your woman."

She hooked her little finger at the point of his jaw and urged him closer. "Lian, if you even think about serving me one of those concoctions as part of our cover, I *will* whip out my hat."

"Wouldn't dream of it, Inspector." He leaned down to kiss her nose.

"You still haven't told me where this market is located."

"I know. You aren't telling the Mounties ahead of time. And we're going in with comms off. These people will spot the law a hundred yards away. If we're made, we get nothing from Bible Bob."

"So, what do I wear tonight?"

"Leather and tech. And make it sexy."

* * *

Lian gave a low whistle when Day came into the hotel sitting room. "You should go undercover more often."

"I never get tagged for the duty. The commander says I don't act the part." She frowned at her reflection, her loose hair swinging across her leather-clad behind. "You sure this is right? I thought a medical black market would be more . . ." She wrinkled her nose. "Retail."

"Trust me, you'll fit right in." She would not, however, go unnoticed. To be anonymous, to slip in and out, was no longer possible. One look, and Lian still hadn't gotten his breath back. Or stuffed his tongue back in his mouth.

The woman was sexy as hell. Oh, he'd known she had a sexy way of walking, sway-hipped and confident. They'd been together a lot in recent days, and in those precious moments when she'd been naked with him, he had adored the generous appeal of her body. But, outside bed, he'd seen her dressed only in sturdy taiga pants, boots, sweaters, and heavy coats.

Never like this. No man would pay him or his activities any mind tonight; they'd be salivating over Day. He frowned. Maybe this wasn't such a great idea.

He'd told her leather, tech, and sexy. He should have remembered Day never took half measures.

Her black leather pants were so tight they looked as if a nanobot had built them from her skin. Her top—a black knit with thin straps, a low neck for one hell of a lot of exposed shoulder, a silly, sexy bit of lace peeking out from beneath—somehow managed to be both demure and titillating.

This was also the first time he'd ever seen her wearing obvious makeup. Red lips. Gold glitter on her cheeks, brows, and lashes. To complete the outfit, she had her Distazer strapped to her thigh. He figured she had a few other weapons—although where she'd hidden them he hadn't a clue.

She grinned at his obvious surprise. "Tech enough for you?"

Gold flashed from her head, and Lian asked, "Did you do something to your hair?"

"Took it out of the braid."

"That much, even I can tell."

She lifted the top layer, and he could see the underneath strands were a shimmery gold. "Got an under-shampoo." She lifted a glittery brow. "You're not looking so cold yourself. I like that smoky silk. And the leather pants. We match."

He neatened the cuff of his gray shirt. "You fill yours out better."

"I wouldn't say that," she purred, her eyes lowering.

"You keep that look, and we're a couple of hours late for our appointment."

"Only a couple of hours?"

In answer, he grabbed her by the hair, feeling just a bit savage. With a tug, he tilted her head back. With no warning or asking, he kissed her. It was hard, primitive, one hand wrapped in her hair, the other delving beneath her shirt.

Her leg wrapped around his calf, and she matched every thrust and stab of his tongue. When he stopped and would have moved away, she grabbed his shoulders and pulled him back.

At last, when they were both breathless and aroused, he murmured against her lips, "Your call, Inspector. The bed, the floor, or Bible Bob."

She pulled back, breathing heavily. "Damn, why'd you say Inspector?"

"Guess that means we're going."

"We'll save the floor, the bed, and that hot spring tub for later."

"Promise of a Mountie?"

"Promise of a lover. For now, though . . ." With quick motions, she had both pairs of their leather pants down. She aimed him backward until he bumped into the chair, then her hands urged him to sit. Quick as a promise, she was straddling him. Lowering. Impaling herself on his rigid staff. "We have the chair. Make it fast and good."

He did.

Chapter Sixteen

Hockey was a national obsession. From October to April, the scores, league standings, and player stats and antics dominated Interweb chats. Gretzky Cup playoffs were front-screen news and the source of impassioned debates. Canada League home openers meant a day off for the city. Hockey attire—minus the skates—remained a fashionable style, and models sported the hockey haircut. Day had broken up more than one "discussion" that ended with drawn weapons.

The game was so embedded in the national psyche that Canadians even overcame their post-plague phobias to gather and watch in person. Tonight's game—an intense rivalry between the Calgary Flames and the Manitoba Moose—even brought out those without tickets, who came to share the pregame madness and display their support for their chosen team. The gold and red of Calgary or the blue and bronze of Manitoba fluttered from coat lapels and toques and earlobes and brow piercings.

All those people in one spot, bank credits in pocket.

Game night was a rare opportunity for entrepreneurs to hawk their wares directly to the customer instead of relying on Interweb sales, and they took full advantage. Eye-catching kiosks and elaborate port-a-stores littered the streets surrounding the Calgary Saddledome Arena.

Day strolled through the crowd next to Lian, his arm draped across her shoulders with masculine ease. A shout from the fringes made her jump, and only Lian's hand kept her from spinning off after it. The knot in her stomach tightened.

This mass of humanity was making her uneasy. There were enough people that, despite the night being cold enough for visible breath, she didn't need to button her coat. Too many people—men mostly—lingered for a second or third look at her. Admiration was nice, but not in such big, anonymous doses.

She fingered the edge of her holster. She wasn't accustomed to being in such congestion. Usually people gave her shooting room, once they caught sight of her hat.

Except they were undercover tonight, and she wasn't wearing the hat.

At least Lian's size helped them move through the throngs. He seemed particularly adept at avoiding contact with knots of people—the touch seemed to bother him, too. Once she felt his muscles tense, and he pressed a hand to his Distazer. With an abrupt twist, he steered her away from a tangle of hard-edged men, whose stealthy trade vanished as they caught her watching them.

"When do we get to the black market?"

"We're there."

She glanced around, surprised. She'd imagined the Calgary black market to be seedy unsalvageable buildings manned by furtive men in tatty clothes. Not these attractive shops. "All of these?"

"Not that I know. Just a few I've dealt with."

Keeping their cover that they were a shacking tech-pro

couple, she draped herself on his arm. Despite the unease, despite the knots in her stomach, she couldn't help but notice she liked Lian with her. She liked the hard muscle beside her, the twisted leather and jade on his wrist, and the new look of his hair: thin braids, two on either side. With her heels on, she discovered, she was able to look directly at his mouth. She traced his talented lips with her decorated nail. "How do you know which?"

"Not a chance I'm telling you that, Inspector," he said with a grin. A moment later, he added, "This is Bible Bob's establishment."

Another surprise in a night rapidly filling with them. From the name Bible Bob, she'd expected a religious slant to the shop: saint statues, disks of sacred texts, chemical-induced trips guaranteeing to see Jesus, a church of perpetual praise. Instead, she found a blatantly secular display of glowing white and aqua tubes in abstract shapes that could have been either women's breasts or fish.

FOOD REDEMPTION was the brightly lit name. Inside, it smelled like fresh bread and apples.

Bible Bob's advertised specialty was exotic food. Reclaimed cans, salvaged from the Atlantic-buried cities of Dartmouth and Halifax, and said to contain delicacies never before tasted. Rare Canadian treats like the Saskatoon berry, cod tongue, and caribou-digested lichen. One of the high, lighted shelves housed genetically engineered soy that was reported to mimic foods lost since the quarantine. Pineapple. Bananas. Coffee. Cinnamon. Monitor menus hinted at other choices not displayed.

"Have you ever tasted real chocolate?" she asked Lian, eyeing the dark brown package.

"Once."

"I read people used to believe it cured disease and altered mood."

"I don't know about curing diseases, but I did enjoy it."

"*Bonsoir,* Mademoiselle, Monsieur. *Bienvenue.*" A saleswoman, her wild hair shifting between blue and green, greeted them.

"Bible Bob is expecting us," Lian said, before she could start her spiel.

"Who shall I tell him is here?"

"Lian and Day."

When she disappeared, Day gestured to the incongruous note in one corner: the religious items she'd expected. "Religious paraphernalia and exotic food? Those two match about as well as my eyes."

"I think your eyes are harmonious."

She made an annoyed face. "You know what I mean."

"Bible Bob started out an Interweb preacher, sharing the gospel with all who'd listen, and apparently he was compelling at it. Meanwhile, the son, L.J., running ads beside him, was hauling in dollars selling food, under the banner of: Feed the Belly, Redeem the Soul. Eventually they got this port-a-store. Said they were bringing religion directly where it was needed most."

"Hockey games?"

"People have been known to express a few prayers here. Bible Bob stands outside the shop preaching now and again. Draws a crowd when he does."

"So which one's driving the sled on all of this?"

"Bible Bob's preaching and enjoying the perks. L.J.'s everything else."

Like the No-Borders and their illegal imports. "So, Bible Bob's our conduit to L.J.?"

"He's getting worried. L.J.'s into something too illegal, or dangerous, even for Bible Bob to ignore."

She glanced around. "Must be a hell of a something."

Bible Bob—at least that's who Day assumed the rotund, white-haired, white-bearded man was—glided over to them, his cheeks shiny with sweat.

"Put him in a red robe," she muttered, "and he's Father Christmas."

"Don't be fooled," Lian said in a lower tone. "He's about as benevolent as an arctic gale."

"I'm rarely fooled into not expecting trouble." She stuck out her hand to the man reaching their side. "Mr. Bible Bob, I'm—"

"Not so obvious." Bob cut her off with a whisper. Then, in a louder voice he said, "Yes, we have a catering service. For how many?"

"Ten," answered Lian, obviously playing into the game. "If you'll follow me."

To her surprise, he led them not to a private spot, but to a delicate desk in the heart of the port-a-store. "Business done out in the open draws less attention." He answered Day's unspoken question, barely loud enough to hear. "And many voices can mask one from surveillance." He pulled out a book, pretending to take their order. "L.J.'s part of this group—"

"No-Borders," she interjected. "Are you part of them?"

"No!"

Probably it wasn't his first lie tonight.

"Just listen, because I'm gone in five minutes. I overheard L.J. talking to two of them the other night. I didn't like them, and I didn't like what I was hearing."

"What did you hear?" she asked.

"Who was he with?" added Lian.

"I recorded their meeting on a data dot. Anything I'm willing to tell you is on that."

"Does your son know about this? The data? And that you're giving it to us?"

Bible Bob gave her an annoyed look. "No."

Obvious lie number two. What she couldn't figure out was whether he was sweating because he was betraying his son, or because he was betraying her and Lian. But, why agree to talk if he only wanted to set them up?

Because someone else was paying or threatening him.

253

Her edgy nerves fired to alert with a kick-boot dose of adrenaline.

"I didn't trust sending it through online—impossible to keep secure. That's why I agreed to talk with you, Lian. So you could alert authorities. But I want something in return."

Lian's foot pressed against Day's, warning her to be quiet. "What?"

"Charges dropped against my son."

"I don't have that authority."

"But, you know how to get these things done." He was looking at Lian; obviously he didn't know she was a Mountie.

"I can't make any promises, but I'll do my best."

Bible Bob gave Lian a steady look, then nodded. "You've been a man of your word. I'll have to trust you. The data dot's in my safe. Leave, and come around the back so no one sees you." He stood and held out his hand; then in a loud voice said, "I'm glad we are able to serve you. Thank you so much for coming."

Reluctantly Day kept up appearances and shook his hand.

As Bible Bob scurried to the back, she whispered to Lian, "Am I the only one who thinks he gave in way too easy when you didn't promise him a thing?"

"Nope."

Moving in unison, they went to the rear of the store, where private cubicles hinted at some business not on the handheld menus, then passed through a door that fit almost seamlessly into the reflective rear wall.

There were no pleasing scents here. The room was musty and dark, lit only by three green algae strips. Beyond the thin green light, they could see nothing but velvet blackness. Day's wariness thermometer shot up ten degrees.

Bible Bob was flicking off the holoimage of a crackling fireplace, which concealed his safe. Store voices followed them through the open door. At the sound, he spun toward them, hand out.

Day shoved him against the wall, drawing her Distazer in the same motion. Holding him with a hard hand on his shoulder, she glanced down. His hand was empty. No weapons.

Bible Bob swore—a rather nasty curse for someone who lived by preaching—and threw Lian a frantic glance. "What does she think she's doing?"

"It looks like she's aiming a pulse at your throat, Bob." Lian was eyeing the cryptlike room.

"I think we need to start chatting," Day said. "Like you telling us what you're really planning."

"This isn't how these things are done. She's crazy."

"Wrong. I'm the crazy one. She's a Mountie. She's just suspicious."

"Nobody said anything about a Mountie!"

"I don't tell you everything. Day, could you see fit to release Bible Bob now that you've got your point across?"

Day backed off, releasing his shoulder but not lowering her weapon. Good cop, bad cop still worked, and it was a bit of fun playing the bad cop for once. "Yeah, I'm a Mountie, and you know how cranky we get at the thought of being led into a trap."

"It's not a trap. I swear." Bible Bob flicked a handkerchief out of his pocket.

Day came within a hairbreadth of firing her Distazer before she realized he was only mopping sweat. Of course, Lian's dagger now pointed at his throat. Bible Bob froze, his handkerchief hanging limp.

"You'd be wise to warn us when you're pulling something out of your pocket," Lian told him. "I'm a paranoid plague hunter, remember?"

"Yes, yes, of course."

Lian stepped back, and with a twist of his wrist, his dagger disappeared.

There were advantages to a partner who read her mind and reacted as swiftly, although she'd best not be getting used to it. After this investigation, she was back on her own. The thought brought an unpleasant ache, an echoing sense of loss so swift and unexpected it caught her off guard.

She swallowed, forcing her attention back to the duty at hand, knowing she'd have to visit it later.

"So, what's tonight's story?" she asked Bible Bob, adding a conciliatory note even as she surreptitiously scratched on her comm patch the sign for "This situation stinks like dead fish." There was no answer. Must have shielding back here, preventing a connection to the Calgary RMCP Depot. Behind her, Lian powered up his Distazer. He was hearing the same warnings.

"I'm getting out the data dot for you. Now, from my safe." He'd learned to warn them about his movements.

She tensed as he laid a thumb on the DNA ID, and held his eye to the screen for a retinal confirmation. Beside her, Day felt Lian's muscles knot, waiting for an attack.

The safe opened with a soft sigh. It looked empty, except for a few canisters in the back. Catching her glance, Bible Bob quickly notched shut the door, hiding his cache from her, then reached in.

She clicked her Distazer safety off, sparing a glance for the battery. It was full.

A soft hum came from Lian's weapon. His dagger dropped again into his palm.

Slowly, Bible Bob pulled his arm out from the safe.

Day pressed down the nail-shaped heels of her shoes, converting the footwear to runners.

Bible Bob closed the safe . . . and held out an empty hand.

No, not empty. In his palm was a small black disk. The data dot. As he'd promised.

From the corner of her eye, Day saw Lian's shoulders relax.

"Take it." Bible Bob dropped the dot into her hand. Carefully, she tucked it away. "Now go. I have nothing more to say."

"The RCMP thanks you for your assistance."

They exited the store without further incident. Day paused and took a deep breath, as tension retracted its claws. Seemed she'd misjudged Bible Bob. "Where to next, Lian? Got any desires? A little shopping? The hotel to read the data?"

"I've got desires." He laid a hand on her behind, urging her forward. "The—"

A brilliant light jabbed her eyes, blinding her with white, excruciating pain. Day grabbed for her Distazer, but found herself spun around and shoved face first against the side wall of Food Redemption, back in the shadows where the assault would be hidden. A foot shoved her legs apart, a hand ripped her arm up her back, and a hard body held her flat and immobile.

"Lian—" she shouted.

The man behind her pressed a sonic pricker to her throat. One quick shooting pain contracted her trachea, silencing her. All she could manage were thin gasps, enough air to keep herself conscious, but barely. A sharp whine cut the air, followed by a couple of thuds. She heard Lian grunt. God, had they shot him?

"Cooperate and the plague hunter lives," oozed a voice behind her. "Nod once if you understand me."

Her vision had big holes in it. The chuck behind her had her effectively immobilized with her face against the wall. One good push and he'd break her nose. Or one good snap and it would be her neck. And what had they done to Lian? Cooperation seemed the best option. At the moment.

She nodded, using the motion to free her head slightly.

She pulled her glance as far left as she could, straining the muscles in her eyes, until she saw Lian in a similar pose. The man holding him was hidden by night, dressed all in black, and his face was distorted by an overlaid holoimage. Probably her captor was similarly disguised. No ID-ing there, but she assumed one of the two was L.J. Could the other one be Jem? Or Juneau?

Blood dripped down Lian's collar from a slash in his neck. Frost invaded Day's bones, as she realized that a few centimeters to the left, and they'd have gotten his jugular. He also had a swollen knot on his cheek. The Distazer pressed against his throat emitted a steady hum, meaning it was on a low current, immobilizing Lian's muscles.

A pinprick stung her arm. "A dose of LZ3. Insurance for your cooperation," murmured her captor as he locked her elbows together into stasis restraints.

Whatever drug he'd given her had a quick onset. Her eyelids drooped, as if a pair of hockey skates had been hung across them. Her head floated above her shoulders. She bit her lip, dug her nails into her palms, hoping the small pains would keep her coherent.

Her captor spun her around to face him, but she was still off balance with her legs spread and her shoulders pressed against the wall. Her dizziness wouldn't have allowed her to escape, anyway. That, or the rainbow haloes around her nose and hands.

A tight band wound around her bicep. A tourniquet? A larger pain radiated out of the crook of her arm. A needle. In her vein. Taking her blood?

The man's face was distorted, unrecognizable. But, the dark hair . . . Hadn't she seen that somewhere?

"*Inspector Daniels.*" A faint voice came from her comm patch, vibrating in her ear across the muzzy thoughts. At least, she thought it was her comm and not her imagination. "*Do you need assistance?*"

She couldn't answer. Could barely decide who was talking as the drug took hold of her mind.

"Say Banzai if you are all right."

She wasn't all right. She bit her tongue to keep from mumbling.

"Backup will be there in five."

She only had to hold on for five. She licked her dry lips with her thickened tongue. Tried to swallow. Blinked. Saw Lian tense. "Juneau?"

"We meet again, Inspector," answered the man taking her blood.

"Juneau? Robichaux's killer! All officers to the scene!" Voices pounded in Day's eardrum.

Juneau finished drawing off vials of blood. He loosened the band on her arm, then jerked her forward. "Let's go."

"She's still conscious," said his companion. L.J.?

"She's small; she'll be out in the sled." He dragged her toward his trek sled.

"Small . . . but . . . wiry," she mumbled. She'd stay . . . awake. Show them.

"She's already seeing paisley bunnies."

"Paisley. Rats." She bit down hard on her cheek, fighting the drug.

"What should I do about him?" L.J. shoved Lian.

"Kill him."

"Noooooooooo!" Day screamed. With a wrench that sent searing pain up her injured shoulder, she lurched forward, knocking into L.J. before she dropped to her knees.

Lian's foot jammed backward, an explosion of power right against L.J.'s kneecap. Day heard the crack of bone, the scream of pain, as distant echoes.

Blood and sweat assaulted her nose. Pain raked across the back of her hand as Juneau got in a shot. Her bound hands found the tiny Distazer strapped inside her coat. Thousands of hours of shooting practice took over. By instinct, she leveled one shot—

—at nothing.

Juneau had vanished into the crowds surging toward the hockey arena doors in preparation for the opening face-off.

Day scraped her comm. "Juneau. Dark pants. Shirt. Holomask."

"Not much to go on, Inspector."

"Running toward Saddledome. Daniels out." She rolled to her side, her last bit of strength gone, barely conscious. "Lian."

Blood oozed from his neck. Sweat coated him, and he shook as he pulled his med pack closer. God, he was dying. Her hand flopped onto his wrist. His heartbeat was strong against her palm; hers was hammering against her ears. He'd taken so many doses of the Distazer. "You lost blood," she accused, as her eyelids finally gave up the fight. "Do you hurt?"

"I'll live." He pressed an infuspray to her neck. "How are you?"

"I'm tough."

His fingers laced through hers, an anchoring touch in her rainbow blindness. "That's an antidote to the LZ3. You'll be feeling better in a couple of minutes. Hallucinating less, too."

"I was enjoying the rainbow," she joked.

Another voice added to the buzzing in her ears. Bible Bob, screaming. "L.J.! Lian, do something!"

"You're more important," she muttered. She had little sympathy for someone who'd just been using a Distazer against her partner. Her lover.

"I have to help him," Lian said softly.

"I know."

Before he left her, he ran a thumb across her knuckles, and she began to believe again that he was still part of her. "Juneau hurt you," he said quietly. "I've never wanted to kill someone so much in all my life."

"But you don't do that." She glanced at L.J. One of Juneau's shots had caught him in the chest, and his harsh gasps were slowing. "Save your patient, Doctor."

While Lian worked, she kept a blurry eye on him and his patient, her Distazer dangling in her hand. Lian might follow the Hippocratic oath, but she didn't. If she had to lose her informant or her lover, it was not going to be Lian.

Lian worked on the gaping wound in L.J.'s chest. The holomask image had faded, leaving a younger-looking version of Bible Bob.

"Will he live?"

"Probably."

"L.J. Malachite, you are under arrest," she grunted at the youth.

Their backup came, taking over the care of L.J. as he was transported to medical, Bible Bob at his side. Juneau, however, had escaped.

Failure had an ugly taste.

"It's not your fault," Lian said in a hoarse voice, looking exhausted. He braced his hands against the asphalt, showing again that uncanny ability to know what she was thinking. Or feeling.

"We were caught unaware because I was thinking of you and that hotel."

He cupped her cheek gently, though his face was fierce. "Don't you dare blame yourself. You took thirty seconds to be a person, a woman. That's not a crime, Day." His thumb traced her lips. "Don't you ever think what we share is a crime."

"It interferes with my duty."

He shook his head. "It's passion. That passion is what makes you so good. If you cut off your emotions, eventually you'll find yourself drying up inside. You'll lose the fire not only for your own life, but the fire to protect others."

"You sound like you know."

"I'm discovering it."

"Don't sound so happy."

"It could end up taking me away from you."

She closed her eyes. When she stopped seeing paisley bunnies, she might remember to ask what he meant.

Chapter Seventeen

Day half opened her eyes, drowsily savoring the sight of a starlit, naked Lian joining her in their hotel room spa. Steam swirled around him, smudging the harsh lines of his face, and the blue-tinted water concealed the scars and fresh wounds that gave character to his lean body. He moved easily to her side and hoisted himself onto the faux rocks. After adjusting their surface to increased softness, he leaned back and stretched out. With a sigh, he closed his eyes.

"You like your water hot," he murmured.

"I can adjust the temperature, if it's too much."

Without opening his eyes, he shook his head. "No. It feels good. Relaxing. Perfect for a cold night."

The spa was outside, on their private patio. Day leaned her head back, snow drifting onto her lashes. Despite the few flakes, ever present now that the snows had started, the sky above was clear enough to see stars. With no other lights as competition, not even in their hotel room, the constellations shone in brilliant clarity.

And the fresh, wintry air counterpointed the steamy water of the spa.

But, the peace was an illusion. Especially when the night had gone so wrong. She'd lost Juneau. She'd almost lost Lian. The data dot Bible Bob had given them was useless, an ordinary surveillance record.

"Let it go, Day," Lian murmured. "For one night, let it go."

"How can I? When so much is at stake?"

"Because you need to mend. We both do."

He carried burdens, too, she recognized. Did he need this interlude as well?

"Your body, your mind, and your spirit need to be whole. Use the remains of the night to join them—then tomorrow we'll start anew." He took her hand and laced their fingers together in a simple gesture that caught her breath.

The imperfect night was made bearable.

Mend. She laid her head back, matching his relaxation—at first only in her body's pose, but soon the quiet seeped into her muscles and nerves. Time drifted without measure as the healing, soothing waters bathed their damaged bodies. Except for their fingers, they didn't touch, but each time Lian stirred, the water lapped against her with a warm little caress. Clean sage wafted on the humid air, surrounding them both.

"How are you feeling?" Lian's low question blended into the steam.

"Better now."

"Shoulder? Ribs? Cheek? Back?" Slowly he detailed her injuries and scrapes and pulled muscles, each now healing, she assured him.

"How about you? Neck? Chest? Cheek? Legs?"

"I'm fine." He chuckled. "No—in truth I'm in a sorry state if I'm naked with a beautiful woman in a spa, and we're spending our time cataloguing injuries."

"In the showers at the Mountie depot we've been known to compare scars."

"Yes, but I'm assuming in that venue you aren't having thoughts like mine."

"Depends upon your thoughts."

"That I'd like you to lean over and take me in your mouth. Or straddle me and take me inside you."

He said the carnal words so easily, so relaxed, it took her a few seconds to realize exactly what he'd said. When she did, she smiled. "You're reading my mind again."

"Uh-uh. I'm feeling too lazy to move," he said after a moment.

"Me too."

His thumb traced a lazy circle over her palm, and though he said nothing, the gentle gesture was an intimate one.

Baring her body seemed so easy and natural with this man.

Baring her heart, her soul, was much more difficult. Emotions made her uncomfortable. They contained so much vulnerability. There were no guidelines or parameters or standing operating procedures to follow with your heart.

Despite her claim that she would make her own choices about Lian, she couldn't get Trafalgar's warning from her mind. *He's not the man for you. He's not a Mountie, and that will come to matter.*

She wasn't used to being indecisive, but with Lian her feelings were too murky for her to make a decision. They disagreed soundly on many issues. Their approaches to life were so opposite, how could they ever find something that would last beyond this explosive passion? His differences challenged her long-held beliefs and confused her.

Yet, she'd come to believe she needed just that.

Part of her heart was already Lian's, she realized. She swallowed against the tug of that aching yearning for him. She wanted to share her life with him. God help her, her hours and minutes were so much richer in his company.

Still, she was a Mountie. Those beliefs and values had formed her, shaped her to the woman she was now. Whether she wore the hat or not, she was a Mountie, and she felt like she had betrayed that foundation with her doubts and her actions.

The snow was falling harder, thick wet flakes that melted when they touched the water.

Would her feelings also melt when exposed to the heat of disapproval from everyone who had been her life up until now?

Everyone except Benton, of course. The thought brought a smile to her heart.

"Is this new territory for us?" she asked, feeling braver in the darkness and the steam.

Lian didn't answer. Perhaps he too had doubts, fears. Part of him remained remote and untouchable, confusing. She opened her eyes to find him watching her. "You didn't answer my question."

"Because I don't know the answer. I was waiting for you to look at me."

"Do you know the answer now?"

"No. I can't change your doubts. I also know I can't make any promises. Will tonight be enough for you, if that's all we have?"

A single night to feel? Not as an officer, but as a woman. The way only Lian made her feel. Perhaps it was an illusion, but with him she felt loved. Not for what she accomplished or represented, but simply for herself, with all her abrasiveness and her quirky sense of humor. Her flaws and her fears, her strengths and her desires.

His hand still held hers.

"No," she said, suddenly realizing that simple truth. "Tonight won't be enough."

His fingers tightened around hers. "Honest. Succinct."

"But, I'll accept it if that's all you can give. You're still avoiding answering me."

"There's another claim, one I can no longer avoid."

God, but that hurt. Even though she could not, would not believe he spoke of another woman. He was not a man who betrayed someone he cared about. "Who?"

"Not who? What. A nation."

Just as he could not be part of her Mounties, she could never be one of his people. Both of them were too bound by their pasts to join their futures.

Yet, tonight was a moment out of time. No past shackled them for now.

Tonight, there was no future to haunt them. She wouldn't let it.

"Maybe the new territory for us is living in the present."

He lifted her hand and kissed her knuckles. "Yes, let's enjoy each moment. Have you soaked enough?"

"Enough that I feel like warm noodles." She accepted his withdrawal, knowing it was merely a piece of the night's natural rhythm. "And speaking of noodles, I ordered room service while you showered. It should be here in ten minutes."

He bent his head back, slicking his wet hair with his hands as he did. "Then we should get dressed, at least enough so we don't shock our waiter. Ready for the mad dash through the cold?"

"This is Canada, Lian—we embrace the cold, not dash through it." Slowly, she rose from the spa, savoring his hungry regard as she bared herself to him. Water drops joined snowflakes. Hot and cold on her skin. Invigorating. Challenging.

Lian stood to meet her. His body and face were taut, and there was something primitive about him of a sudden. He looked sculpted of ice, and a natural part of the elements.

She felt alive and needed, and she lifted on tiptoe to kiss

him. The swift hard kiss melted the layers of snow beneath their feet and was broken only by the rumbling of her belly.

Lian smiled against her lips. "I guess we should wait for room service."

By mutual accord, arms around each other, they strolled through the winter to their suite. She broke from their embrace. "I'll get dressed."

"Nothing too confining or difficult to remove."

"Do you have anything with fur?" she teased in return.

When she rejoined him a few minutes later, she found he did own fur, a soft vest of wild ermine, left open with no shirt beneath. He was barefoot, and his recycled denims were riding low on his hips.

He tilted his head to study her as she entered, then twirled his finger. "I've never seen you in a skirt. Let me see it move."

She did a quick pirouette, the skirt flaring. It and her top had cost her a good portion of a pay period, but she'd been unable to resist the combination of silky sturdiness and beauty in the smoky nano-formed fabric. Tonight, it clung to her damp body like a multishade, silvery moss.

Lian had lit the thick vanilla-scented candles supplied by the hotel, adding their rich aroma to the evening. When he turned on the suite's music system, a jazzy electric sax filled the room. "That's different than your usual fare of drum and flute."

"No reminders of the past. Twirl again. I like the way your braid swings."

"You don't want me to loosen it?"

He'd left his hair undone, she noticed, and she gave in to the sudden temptation to comb her fingers through the soft, thick strands, smoothing her hand behind his ear. He rotated his head, letting her fingers glide across his scalp on a caress.

"I want whatever is most comfortable to you."

"I like the braid." In truth, she was more comfortable

with that little reminder of order, for life with Lian was chaotic and unpredictable.

"So do I. I like the way it swings across your behind. I like *this*." He took it in his hand and brushed its tail across the swell of her breasts. The caress awoke her body, already heated by steam, and when he turned the braid to tracing his own lips and smooth chest, she gave in to the urge to follow, delicately outlining the line of his jaw and the corded strength of his neck. Her fingers faltered at the gash in his neck, healing thanks to his skill and the aid of tissue-repair catalysts.

"I almost lost you tonight," she whispered, haunted by the specter of loss, of an irretrievable gap in her soul.

"And I could have lost you." His hand fisted around the braid. "Plague hunting is finally, blessedly a dying profession. Soon, I can focus on new things. But you put your life on the line every day."

"Couldn't you live with that?"

"You're who you are, Day."

"That's not an answer to the question."

"Yes, it is. If I had my choice, I would wrap you up and protect you from any hint of harm." His face was harsh, his words stark. "But I also accept who you are, whatever you are. All of you."

A soft knock announced the arrival of their food. They waited in silence while the waiter laid out plates of fresh-caught walleye, delicately sauteed with caramelized maple sugar, mixed greens with Saskatoon berries, and whipped potatoes.

Dinner was a companionable interlude. The past was set aside. The questions for tonight had been answered in the spa. The uncertainties for the future were tabled. For this half hour, as they replenished their bodies, they were simply Lian and Day.

At last, as she blotted her lips and fingers on the linen napkin, Lian rose and put his hand out. Day's stomach knotted. Flesh that had cooled since the spa reheated with a pulse of fiery blood.

"Would you like to dance?" he asked, surprising her a little.

"Yes."

The jazzy electronica was still playing on the media system. Lian drew her into his arms, then executed a neat twirl before leading her into the complicated steps of the bellagio, a classic in the electronica dance craze.

He was good. She was, too. They moved in unison to the swings and sways and footwork. She had not danced in months, and she'd forgotten how satisfying it was to be with a skilled partner, bodies fluidly united in the program of steps. She had one brief falter when he switched slightly on the sequence, swinging her left instead of right.

"Smooth," he complimented. "You recovered well."

"Warn me of the change next time, and I won't need to recover." Her smile softened the mild rebuke.

"Impulse. Can't warn you about that. You just have to go with the flow."

"I'm learning how." *With you.* "How did you know I knew the bellagio?"

"Your file said you'd won a competition. I figured that was one season's skill. Know any other dances?"

"Most of them. Where did you learn?"

"Old girlfriend."

"Couldn't have been that old—the dance isn't."

"She's not important," he said impatiently, twirling her in the final dip of the dance.

A new tune began, but they didn't resume. Instead, he hooked his fingers into the knit straps of her top. Slowly, so slowly, he lowered them, capturing her arms at her sides, baring her breasts with the same motion.

"Is this when we start that slow lovemaking?" she teased.

"We started two hours ago." He nuzzled her neck, still painstakingly lowering her shirt.

They had, she realized. The spa soothing sore, tight muscles. The food filling physical spaces. The dance, the conversation. All of it was intimate lovemaking.

Her shirt reached her elbows, and she pulled one arm out to hold him near. Laying her cheek against the soft, white fur of his vest, she absorbed the steady rhythm of his heart. "I think that erratic heartbeat of mine is back."

He laid his palm on her chest, his large hand covering the curve of her breast, and smiled. "I think you're right."

"Is it dangerous?"

"Only to my peace of mind." Bracketing her face with his hands, he lowered his mouth to hers.

The kiss was like the spa—slow and steamy. A tremor ran down her spine as his tongue touched hers. She pulled her other arm free and traced the shell of his ear. He groaned and pulled her closer. The soft fur on the tip of her breast, the hard muscles beneath the fur, the taste of butter, and the scent of sage—sensation drowned out thought.

The kiss softened to nips and tastes, to gentle pressure and slow strokes of tongues. Her breath mingled with his as their bodies started an intimate dance against one another. Her arms, her lips cried for more as they kept the slow, throbbing pace. Never lifting, never parting, a build to completion, exquisitely sensitive as each cell fired to life. Her shirt and skirt bunched around her waist, and with a languid gesture she undid both and stepped out of them.

With caressing hands, she finished unfastening Lian's pants and slid them down his legs. His erection jutted forward, thick and heavy as her hand closed around the hot staff. Her thumb caressed him, circling the tip with her nail, and he groaned against the top of her head.

"Come with me," he demanded.

"Outside?"

"Not this time. Remember? Down comforters."

The bedroom windows were open, she noticed dimly, but she didn't mind the cool touch on her heated body. With a steady, unrelenting hand, Lian urged her onto the bed with him. Down comforters and pillows swallowed her in their silky softness.

Lian followed her down, sprawling atop her, sinking her deeper into downy softness with the hard, lean length of his body. Later they could explore other positions, but for the moment she reveled in the blanket of his strength and his demanding kiss. Her hands skimmed his hot flesh, memorizing the contours of his shoulders, his waist, his buttocks.

He lifted a little, shifting his weight off her. She missed the pressure, she found, until he replaced it with his mouth. A line of fire burned down her throat as he kissed his way to her breast. He took her in his mouth and teased the taut nipple with his tongue. Pressure built, and he moved to her other breast, then her rib cage, her belly button.

As he explored her skin, she could not stay idle. Her hands circled freely over him, casting off the fur vest and kneading the strong muscles of his back. When he kissed her eyelids and brows, she tugged the lobe of his ear between her teeth, then ran her tongue across his earrings, whispering, "I like that."

All the while, he murmured soft words in return. He told her that he liked the curve of her shoulder, that he planned to suck the brown tip of her breast, that he found a woman with a nipped-in waist and legs curved with muscles incredibly sexy.

As she gasped her approval of a caress, touched him where he asked, directed him with her response, his foot ran a lazy pattern up and down her leg.

What he was doing with her might not be legal, it felt so good.

It was definitely right. Every bit of her skin was afire with pleasure.

"Open your legs," he whispered, and when she did, he pressed his thumb against her hot little button. Beautiful red fireworks set off inside her. Sinew and blood joined in racing pleasure.

Then, without warning, he hooked his leg around hers. With a strong, lithe movement he flipped her over, getting the drop on her because the move was so unexpected and she was feeling pliant.

Startled by the dizzying reversal, she reacted instinctively. Counterattack. Muscles bunched. Palm flat to chop. Only at the last second did she pull back, remembering this was Lian, her lover.

She pulled in a long breath, her heart racing and not from passion. "Damn it, Lian. I could have hurt you."

With her face down, he covered her once more. His teeth were on her neck. "The beast claims his mate," he said.

Her lover. Her alpha mate. Her crazy, plague hunter partner.

"What the hell are you doing?" she demanded.

"You were getting too complacent. Too ready to come."

"Isn't that the point?"

"Not yet. We're prolonging this."

She remembered his earlier promise. Slow, and all night. She had thought that meant multiple orgasms, not one long, exquisite, breathtaking, torturously delayed journey to a single joining.

"And I was getting too excited," he added.

"You were too excited?"

He nudged her with his hips, his erection pressing against her cleft. "Never have any doubts, Day, about your total appeal to me."

She considered her position. With the down cushioning their joined weight and her head turned on the pillow, she could breathe easily, she discovered. His weight, his body, his mouth held her. He knew what he was doing and was strong enough, skilled enough to carry through.

His hand began to caress her side as his lips and tongue teased her neck.

Maybe she'd wait a little before getting free.

"Do you want me to move?' he murmured against her hair.

"Yes," she answered, curious about what he'd do.

His hips moved. His legs nudged hers apart, so he rested between them, pressed tight without joining her.

"That wasn't what I meant."

"I know," he answered with a lilt of laughter, loosening his embrace and rolling to his side.

"You have a strange sense of humor."

"So I've been told."

It was her turn to startle. With her arm and leg, she rolled him forward, sliding atop his back, mounting him as he had mounted her. She brushed away his loosened hair, then bit his shoulder, a touch harder than a love nip.

"Ow," he protested mildly.

"We alpha females like to bite."

"Good. Have your way with me."

She learned the curve of his shoulder, the taste of his breath, the way his nipples became hard nubs when she caressed him; the shape of his lean waist and the friction of the hairs on his legs. On the back of his neck, where normally his hair covered, she discovered a small mark.

"What's that?" she asked, tracing the lines—a series of curves above, horizontal waves beneath.

"A brand."

Her fingers stilled. "Someone *branded* you?"

"It's the mark of transition, given by our shaman to a male who is *wichasha*, worthy to join the men of the nation. The design is the symbol of my people: wind and wing."

This was the part of Lian separate from her, the past she didn't understand, the piece of his soul that kept him remote and would take him from her. Yet he had embraced the whole of her. Could she do any less?

She leaned forward and kissed the mark.

He rolled to his side, drawing her into a new embrace, and the loving renewed. Desire rose to new heights the second time. His hands delighted her with their caress. His mouth pleasured her with teeth and tongue and lips and the breath of tantalizing words and the taste of loving.

How could such a hard man be so caring?

It was what made him a good plague hunter and a good physician, this duality. It was what she loved about him.

Day's heart skipped, and her breath caught on a stab of pain. Loved. She'd fallen in love with him. A man who was not her future.

But he was her present. She opened to him and shared everything that she was, took everything he gave, for she did nothing by half measures.

Be it all. Do it all.

At last, they joined, both shouting their joy, with the Canadian night gusting over them and the scent of wild sage surrounding them, and the distant bay of a wolf serenading them. Afterward, they held one another, lying side by side, and drifted to sleep.

During the night, the wandering wolf wailed his plaintive call, while the clouds of winter blotted out the moon.

But they were fast asleep and did not recognize the omens.

Chapter Eighteen

He had to tell her.

Lian leaned against the rail of the pedestrian bridge and stared down at the rushing waters of the Bow River. He had come to the small island behind him for his morning ceremony. Overgrown with trees, the snow broken by two hardy yellow chrysanthemums that had yet to succumb to winter, the island was a piece of wilderness within the city. His vision had never been clearer.

Clarity, however, did not mean the path was easy. So, he paused on the bridge, sorting through the dilemmas ahead and awaiting a private comm.

He had hoped the data dot from Bible Bob would give him and Day new threads to follow, but the preacher had played them false. The Shinooks now remained their sole lead to Juneau. After learning Citadel was on their land, Lian could no longer deny their possible involvement.

A brown, brittle leaf fell from a nearly denuded tree into the river. The current caught it, sweeping it away from its island home.

The metaphor was not lost on him. If he'd needed a sign that he'd been too long separated from his people, he now had it. Although he still loved them, he no longer knew their hearts. He'd believed none of them would partner with Juneau. The evidence pointed otherwise.

His comm buzzed, and he answered it at once. "Madame Prime Minister."

"Dr. Firebird, are you alone and on scramble?" Her voice, as usual, sounded crisp and focused.

"Yes." Always.

"Were you ever able to prove the canisters were infected before the cultists started breathing on them?"

"No." He still had no proof what had happened there.

"What's your progress?"

When he finished summarizing for her, she made a small *tsk*. "So, you still have no direct confirmation of this complex web you've fashioned. The connections are tenuous at best."

"I feel in my gut they're right."

"We're basing an awful lot on your gut, Doctor. Anyone else I wouldn't trust like this, but you've been my best hunter. You're a hard man who doesn't hesitate to make tough decisions."

"I appreciate your confidence."

She paused only a moment. "I have to ask. You've been at this a long time. Longer than most. Are you absolutely sure this virus is from a new external source? Not one just lying dormant? I know your situation, and a new epidemic would keep you from your people even longer. Could you be misjudging? Seeing a conspiracy where none exists? Not believing that our age of isolation should continue?"

It was a fair question; he'd already wrestled with the doubt himself. "I'm sure it's engineered. This is a threat we can and must stop."

"You'd better be right. In eight days, I'm scheduled to announce that Canada has beaten its bioterror viruses. If you haven't found irrefutable proof of an external source before then, my announcement will instead be the infection at the cult. Not only will confidence in my administration be shaken, but we'll be back under quarantine and border negotiations will collapse. I think you understand the further implications."

Chaos. Panic.

"Find me that source, Doctor. Until then, this virus is strict need-to-know only."

"Understood, Madame." The comm ended.

Cold mist eddied about his feet, obscuring the tide of the river. He looked up. Enough of the old city high-rises had crumbled that he could see the vast prairie surrounding Calgary. The flat land stretched to the far reaches of the country.

Ah, but he loved the sight of that open land.

He turned, bracing his elbows against the rail. Prairie in this direction, too, but beyond were the mountains, concealed by thick clouds, but still there, majestic and solid.

The morning mist circled his legs, sucking away his heat and leaving an empty shell. His chest felt as brittle as the dried leaves. One week. The Shinooks would not talk of such matters through comms, but he had promised, if he set foot on Shinook land, he was done being a plague hunter. Yet, until Juneau was stopped, it was a promise he could not honor.

His vision today had shown him a possible way, with the intercession of another Shinook, and he knew the man to ask. His fingers gripped the bridge as his chest tightened around the empty ache of his heart. He would return to his people. But with the end of his exile still tantalizingly out of reach, the taste of that promised reunion was bittersweet.

Also, fate, in its whimsical manner, had granted his pressing need to return to his people at the very moment when he found his heart lay elsewhere. With Day. And there was no place within the Isolationist Shinooks for a *wasichu*. Especially not a Mountie who had no jurisdiction on the First Nation lands.

Once, he had sacrificed his bond with his people to keep his world safe. For a few days with Day, he had even glimpsed a tantalizingly new future—one where he accepted his exile and strode forward with her. Now, he would be called upon to again sacrifice, this time his love for Day. Spirits grant him the strength to make the choice again, for he knew he could not do it alone.

He wasn't sure when he had fallen in love with the stubborn and honorable Mountie; he knew only that she occupied the largest part of his fresh-sewn soul. A soul that would remain broken when he eventually honored his vow to his people.

For the longest moment, he could not take that first step off the bridge.

When he did, he was startled by the *kek-kek* of a red-tailed hawk. No, two hawks. They soared in looping dives high above him, talons out in a wild aerial display of mating.

Hawks were monogamous, mated until death.

Were the spirits telling him there was a third path? If Day remained steadfast as a hawk?

Day awoke, instantly alert. She stretched, enjoying the slight fatigue of well-used muscles. Lian had left the bed half an hour ago, and she admitted to a twinge of disappointment that he hadn't yet returned to her, although she knew he took time alone each morning.

Still, he'd been in a strange mood before leaving. He'd awoken before dawn, restless and edgy. Prowled the room like a caged wolf before slipping out.

While brewing a pot of tea, she ran through her exercise regimen, starting with the dial-in weights she carried in her pack and ending with a series of push-ups. She showered and dressed. At last, her hair bundled on her head, dressed in her pants and knit shirt, she padded out of the bedroom into a still-empty suite.

She missed her pack: Benton and Lian. She'd gotten used to being with them. When her stomach rumbled, she decided she needed to get out of the four-wall confinement. She could grab breakfast from the muffin kiosk downstairs, then try to make some headway with that list of bush plane registrations on her handheld.

She was sitting on a park bench across the street from the hotel, taking the first bite of her walnut muffin and powering up her handheld, when Bible Bob sat down beside her. Between the muffin and the handheld, she'd been too slow on the draw.

Bible Bob clamped a hand over her Distazer.

"Don't shoot me," he said. "All I want is fifteen seconds. I gave you the wrong data dot."

His hand lifted from the Distazer. She eyed him warily. "What do you want?"

He held out his hand. On his palm was another data dot. He turned his hand over, dropped the dot onto her thigh, then got up to leave.

"Why are you giving us this now?" she called after him.

"Because, despite what L.J. did, Lian saved his life. Tell him thank you." He disappeared into the park, leaving her staring after him.

The suite was still empty when she got back. Disappointed, but not willing to wait, she loaded the data dot into her reader, then flipped on the holoimaging.

Three men hung in the air of the hotel suite. Two of the images were clear; Bible Bob used good surveillance equipment. However, he'd altered the recording to smudge the image and voice of the third man. L.J., she assumed—to ensure his safety.

Good equipment, but the preacher didn't know much

about placement of the cameras; one of the three men kept his back to the eye. All she could tell about him was that he had long dark hair and a lean build—from the back, he resembled Lian. The third man she knew quite well. Rupert Juneau.

The conversation was difficult to follow with most of L.J.'s contributions erased. Since he was the lead for the No-Borders, a lot of detail was lost. The third man stayed silent throughout.

Day swore as they wrapped up the meeting. Apparently they planned to neutralize the border guards, then exchange a symbolic trade—cytokine canisters for cigarettes. The third man made a disgusted noise at L.J.'s choice of cigarettes, but he'd let it stand. The action was to be broadcast over the Interweb, and somehow they seemed confident that the world would be watching.

"Give me a date," she muttered.

The third man finally spoke. "You just do your part, Juneau, and have those shields down on the UCE side."

Juneau's lip curled. "The borders will open, Jem, and the world will be watching."

Jem! It was Jem! Damn, Bart had been right, and she'd let Lian talk her out of pursuing that angle. She snapped on her comm, still watching the holorecording unfold.

The hotel door opened with a click. "Day, I have to—" Lian began.

She waved him silent as she spoke into her comm. "This is Inspector Daniels. Upgrade the eyes-out bulletin on Jem, the Shinook leader. Arrest warrant, hold in isolation. Download to my handheld anything you've got about the Shinooks."

Lian stiffened, coming slowly into the room, his gaze locked on the holoimages.

"That's Jem," she whispered to him. "Bible Bob gave us the real data dot as a thanks for you saving L.J." She turned her attention back to her comm, giving the few details of

Jem she could garner: His coat as he put it on, the length of his hair as he lifted it out of his collar. The cords of his neck. The holoimage blinked out. Wait, what was that last image? "Hold on," she told comm. "I may have more."

"Day—"

"I saw something," she interrupted Lian. Something her instincts said was important.

He put his hand over her comm. Not watching the holo, he watched her with a feral look in his eye.

"You saw *this*." He swept back his loose hair, exposing the back of his neck and the brand she'd kissed last night.

The design is the symbol of my people.

A sudden understanding made her blood ice. Her gaze swung back to the holo. To Jem's bared nape. And the image branded there.

The stylized wing and air.

Her gaze locked with Lian's, she raised her comm. "Belay that last. That's all the information for now. But keep that arrest warrant active." Slowly, she lowered her hand, feeling as stiff and weary as an old maple. "You're Shinook."

"Yes."

At least he had the guts not to deny it.

She raised her gaze skyward. "How did I not see it? I didn't want to see it. You've been misleading me all this time. Protecting your people."

"Like you would protect a Mountie."

Her insides felt like raw meat. "It's not the same thing, Lian. You lied to me, and those lies put people in danger."

His face hardened. "Judging me again, Day?"

"I have to. I'm trying to protect *everyone*. So, are you done evading? Do you know Jem?" She gestured to the frozen image.

"What will you do with him?"

"Arrest him and throw the book at him. Change your answer?"

Lian stared at the image instead of her. "I don't recognize that man from the back."

"Another lie to protect your people? You're Shinook." She had to keep repeating it, to remind herself of how thoroughly he'd deceived her. That's what happened when you started caring, and caring for the wrong person: You lost your common sense. "Are you telling me you don't know the leader of your nation?"

"I've been in exile for seven years. There've been changes."

"You've kept in touch." She held up her hand. "I don't know what to believe from you anymore."

"You knew what to believe last night. Then you were believing your heart."

"Do *not* bring this back to me. This was your deception."

"Don't you care why?"

"No," she lied. She didn't dare care, didn't dare believe in anymore extenuating circumstances or fuzzy, gray areas. How could she do what she must if she did? Hadn't Trafalgar taught her there were those who maintained the law, and then there was everyone else? Your duty was to protect and serve, to do it all and be it all, and ultimately the only one you had was yourself.

Her throat filled. Except she hadn't wanted to end up like Trafalgar: living in an isolated cabin, alone; traveling the country with only suspicions as companions. She'd had a taste of something different, and she'd liked it and wanted it all. Do it All. Be it All. The motto had acquired a new meaning and a new depth.

It seemed fate had another twist in mind.

Trust, once lost, was hard to find again. And the missing pieces of your life might never be restored.

Damn, but loving hurt.

She set her jaw against the yawning ache, pulling herself from the spiral of self-pity. Whatever life threw at you, no matter how much it hurt or how much of you it took away, you had to go forward.

She had a job to do.

Blindly, she reached for her hat, the one she'd thrown so carelessly to the side last night. She flicked her braid over her shoulder and straightened her spine. "It was given to me most emphatically that you are in charge of this investigation. However—"

"Going to arrest me again?" He asked casually, but there was nothing else casual about him. He was utterly still, though Lian was normally one of the most edgy, restless men she'd ever known.

"Don't tempt me." She certainly had grounds. But she could no longer take refuge behind blindly citing the law. This investigation was filled with too many of her own choices, judgments, and mistakes. She pivoted, preparing to leave the scene of the crime, the place where he'd stolen her heart.

"Running out again?"

"No." Her one thought had been to get out of this room before she shattered, but his question gave her pause. "I'm going to find someone who will tell me where the Shinook are," she said at last. The claim was bravado only, no one of the Shinook would take a Mountie into their midst, but it was a place to continue her investigation. A place to do her duty that she'd denied too long.

"I'm the only one who can lead you to the Shinook. To Jem."

"Why would you?"

"You're still my partner. That's our final lead, and I'll do what I must stop that virus."

Partner. Her fists tightened. "Why should I believe you?"

"You have to figure that out yourself." He stared again at the frozen holoimage, and something inside him seemed to shut off. It was like a final candle extinguished at a campsite, leaving only the black of a moonless night.

"Do you know where Jem and the Shinook are?" she asked after a moment.

Why was she still believing in him? Perhaps because, despite the betrayal and the doubts, she believed that single last statement. He was first and foremost a plague hunter.

"Yes. But I have to see someone first. If you're coming with me, pack your things and be ready in an hour."

That deadly, remote chill still surrounded him. She had to choose, without a hint that he cared one way or the other, what her decision would be.

Except the wings of his nanotat were a hint; the firebird namesake was flapping wildly. He cared. Perhaps too much.

When he saw where she was looking, he grabbed a shirt and threw it on, concealing the revealing mark. Just as he concealed the brand of his people, the people who had exiled him, the people he was returning to.

"I'm coming." There was no other decision to be made.

He paused in the doorway to the hall, his hand gripping the jamb. "Day . . ."

"Yes?"

"Lela washtae che la ke."

"I don't understand." He'd spoken not in the Native Common she understood, but in Shinook.

"I know. But that doesn't make it any less true."

And with that crazy enigmatic statement, he disappeared.

Lian was looking for a smuggler and a fight. He took the shortest route to Kahane's, the one through Calgary's seediest neighborhood. Bricks and siding from collapsed buildings had been used to reform the area in a warren of alleys, which no longer resembled any known map. Clandestine transactions, potent cocktail mixes for everything from oblivion to frenetic energy, wagering, illegal trade—all of it could be found here.

He almost hoped the ghetto reputation for danger held true. Energy coursed through him, itching for release. If he couldn't find it with Day, then he'd be glad to vent frustration onto some hapless villain.

The lead-colored clouds overhead, swollen with unreleased snow, matched his uncertain mood. After all they'd shared, after all he'd thought that he had her trust, this morning had proven once again that, in her core, she didn't believe in him. She never would.

In one sense, he should be glad. It made what came next easier. But there was nothing glad about the rip in his heart.

You put people in danger. As though he hadn't spent a lifetime trying to keep the nameless, faceless Canadian population out of harm's way.

Truth was, Day was looking for an excuse to close her heart. Truth was, he had been looking to give her the chance.

Neither one of them was a good candidate to form a lasting relationship, no matter how much he wanted to make it possible.

If only he couldn't still smell her sweet scent and taste her lips. If only his skin didn't remember her holding him. If only his spirit didn't still long for her teasing laughter.

A pair of thugs stepped out from between a rusted Citroen and a pile of sheet metal. He tensed, automatically assessing them and their weapons. Swaggering machismo and the armament to back it. But they were flicking their fingers in nervous twitches and their feet were tapping. Their rapid breath blossomed in thick vapor. They were sweating, too, despite the frigid air. Definitely hopped up on something, but past the point of its making them faster.

"What you doing in this alley?" said one, sneering.

"Looking for Kahane."

The two exchanged glances, then apparently decided not to let Kahane's name spoil their intended fun.

"We're his bodyguards," lied the spokesman. "You'll have to pay us to get through to him."

"Yeah," giggled the other. "Bodyguards."

Lian smiled and flexed his fists. "No," he said simply. "Have it your way."

They came in with fists first, and they were even clumsier than he expected. Must be some potent 'tail they were tripping on. Truly, the art of mixing illegal substances was a lost technique.

Still, one landed a sharp punch to his gut. Breath expelled, Lian gasped for air. The other clipped his cheek. His vision wobbled.

Clumsy and crude, but still dangerous.

He lashed out, in instinct and anger. Frustration gave power to his return kicks. His hands dealt blows one side of lethal, and his Distazer blasts were of pinpoint precision.

Adrenaline numbed all his pain.

The fight was swift and satisfying, and over too soon.

"Where'd you learn to snap like that?" one asked feebly.

"Wrestling with wolves." He reached into his pack and tossed down two packages. "The brown one will stem the blood. The hypospray will help your pain."

As he wound through the alleys, he moved his jaw back and forth experimentally. It wasn't broken, but from the pain in his eye, he'd have a shiner. At least word seemed to travel fast through the underground; no one else tried to stop him.

The clouds finally released their burden, and icy needles pricked his cheeks as sleet fell. The cold, however, felt good on his scraped knuckles.

The stealthy sound of a boot on metal caught his ear. He ducked behind a rusting Dumpster, welcome adrenaline pumping again, and pulled his Distazer. Breath held, he waited for the boot to appear, then spun out, grabbing his would-be assailant and pressing his Distazer to her throat.

"Why are you—?" He broke off with a curse as her Distazer rammed his sore ribs, and he recognized the body in his arms. *Day!* He stepped back, releasing her and holstering his weapon. "What the hell are you doing following me?"

"Had a hunch you might do something crazy. Although a stroll through Calgary's most notorious ghetto exceeded even my expectations." She put away her Distazer and fisted her hands on her hips, glaring at him.

"I felt like plunging a fist somewhere." He scowled at her. "Go back to the hotel or the sled, Day. Wait for me there."

Day shook her head at his request, the clutch of fear that forced her to follow him increasing. Deep in her gut unfurled a crazy notion: Whatever happened from now to the end, betrayal or not, they had to see it all through together.

"Who are we seeing?"

"My relation." He turned his back on her and strode away. "And this will go better without you," he added bluntly.

She kept up with him. "Leave me, and I'll just follow. You know I can track you through here."

His smile was cold. "I wouldn't be so sure about that. I haven't deliberately tried to lose you before."

"I'm willing to gamble." She rose to her full hundred-and-sixty-centimeter height. "Besides, you need me to protect you against people like that." She jerked her head back toward the fallen muggers.

"I don't *want* you here."

She flinched. So, the trust between them had shattered on both sides. But Lian's remoteness had already proven that. Why did it keep hurting? She tucked her chin into her coat, telling herself that the sting in her eyes was from the wind.

"My cousin is Kahane," he added, striding off again.

The skin over her spine tightened. Kahane? One of Canada's most successful smugglers. An idol of the No-Borders, even though he didn't belong to the organization. And the Mounties couldn't touch him, because he operated solely on AIN lands, and by centuries-old treaties the Mounties had no authority on those lands. Out here, he was a beloved philanthropist who aided the orphans of the plague.

She shoved icy hands into her taiga pants pocket and caught up to him. "I left my hat back with my gear."

"Doesn't always stop you."

"Kahane's home is, by law, part of the Shinook lands. I have no authority there; I will abide by that law."

At last he nodded. "Let me handle this."

"Like you let me handle Scree?"

At last she got a brief smile from him, before the remoteness fell back. "I'll expect better behavior from a Mountie than a plague hunter."

"Why do you need to see Kahane? Does it have something to do with your exile?"

Without slowing his pace, he gave her a sidelong glance. "I thought you didn't want my explanations."

"I'm listening now."

He ran the back of his hand against her braid a moment, before he pulled back and stuck his hands in his pockets. "Shortly after I became a plague hunter, I returned to my family for a visit. During that time, the epidemic found us, and many died. Including my parents and two older brothers." He broke off, as though unable to continue.

Dear, God, this just kept getting worse.

At last he began again, his voice rough. "The elders thought I brought the destruction, and I could not convince them otherwise. So I was banished for as long as I remained a plague hunter. I gave my solemn vow to abide by their decision. We need to talk to them, but since I am still a plague hunter, I need the intercession of a Shinook to meet them. Especially accompanied by a Mountie."

She forced in a stab of air. My, God, how she had mis-judged him. She'd been preaching duty and brotherhood and service to a man who had given up everything he held dear in order to practice those ideals.

As they talked, they finished traversing the ghetto with-out further incident, the streets gradually turning cleaner and more kempt, the houses repaired and pleasant. Now, Day stood in front of a house that had once been a grand mansion, surrounded by an ornate iron fence. The mani-cured lawn was colored by bright yellow, long-stemmed bushes in the front, but the stateliness of the manor was warmed by a profusion of outdoor play equipment. As their boots crunched up the gravel path to the house, Day allowed a brief whistle of admiration. "Nice orphanage."

"It won't make up for losing their parents, will it?" Lian asked quietly.

"No, it won't." The sting of pain surprised her. She'd come to terms with her orphaned status a long time ago.

Lian must have heard the hollow note in her voice, for he reached out to her. Then he tightened a fist and drew back, perhaps remembering he no longer had the right to touch her.

More pain.

They reached the front porch, but before Lian knocked at the door, it opened. A woman built like a padded iceman barred the entrance. No hint of welcome graced her face. "Do you have an appointment?"

"No," Lian answered. "But Kahane will see me."

"That's what they all say." She started to close the door.

He retrieved a chain from his pocket; letting the pendant dangle. "Do you recognize this?"

That stopped her. Even Day recognized Kahane's per-sonal totem—the raven clutching an eagle feather—dan-gling from the chain. The guard held out her hand, and he handed her the totem.

"What about her?" She angled her head toward Day.

"She's with me. Be sure to tell Kahane it is *Dr. Firebird* who wishes to see him."

"Wait here."

Icy snow absorbed the hints of daylight poking through the gray cloud cover as they waited. Day shivered against the cold and the anxious press of time. Her arm, where Juneau had taken her blood, itched. Her instincts itched, too. Mountie instincts that told her things with Juneau and the No-Borders were coming to a head. Female instincts that told her she wasn't going to like the next hour.

The door opened, and the woman they'd seen before gestured them in. "He'll see you in his office. Down that hall, and third door on your left."

Although the house wasn't clamorous, high-pitched children's voices could be heard throughout. Day and Lian passed two classrooms, each with three or four kids inside receiving their lessons. Two boys careened down the hall, nearly knocking into them before swerving at the last minute.

As they drew up to Kahane's office, an uneasy feeling—like she was under hostile observation—tiptoed up Day's spine. She glanced around, seeing only a solemn-looking girl of about six with wide eyes and two braids, peering around the corner.

Lian noticed her, too. "Is that how you looked when Trafalgar found you?" he asked in an unguarded moment.

"Not exactly. My braids were messy. And I kicked Trafalgar."

"*Dr. Firebird?*" Kahane opened the door.

Day had seen pictures of Kahane, so she was prepared for the tattooed black lightning bolts across his darkskinned cheeks. She also knew from files that he was slight of height and weight for a man. The dossier, however, hadn't told of his charisma, or of the shrewd calculation in his eyes as he glanced between them.

"Who's your friend?"

"My partner. Inspector Day Daniels of the RCMP."

She held out her hand. "Pleased to meet you, Mr. Kahane."

"Just Kahane." He didn't take her hand, and he stared at Lian. "Why are you bringing a Mountie here?"

"She recognizes the sovereignty of your home."

That appeared to mollify him, for he jerked his head toward his office. "Come inside."

The little girl sidled along the wall, inching closer, her brown eyes still locked unrelentingly on them. Her chest heaved in panicked sobs as she reached for Kahane.

The man knelt beside the girl, who clutched his hand in a fierce grip and spoke to her in a gentle voice. "Celia, these people won't hurt you." He glanced up at them. "She scrutinizes everyone who comes to visit. She doesn't speak much; the therapists say she's afraid of being hurt. Her sick parents were killed by virus-phobics."

The girl was staring at them, dry-eyed, her chest still working with terror.

Day's heart squeezed with memory, with a short sympathetic fear. She stopped and, without getting closer, she crouched down until she was eye-level with Celia.

"I'm not going to take him away," she told Celia, gazing steadily at the girl sidling backward, tugging Kahane. "Neither is my companion. And you can trust me. Do you know why?"

The girl stopped her retreat, all the answer Day needed. Slowly, she pulled out her badge and showed it. "I'm a Mountie. Do you know what that is?"

A faint, imperceptible nod answered her.

"A Mountie's duty is to protect and to serve. He will be safe today. You have my promise on that, and the promises of a Mountie are never given lightly."

A small nod again, then the gaze flicked toward Lian.

"Dr. Firebird, too. Kahane is a relation to him. He, too,

is sworn to the nation and its people. Do you have a hand-held?"

When the girl nodded, Day took a thin disk out of her pocket and handed it over. "That's my contact number. If Kahane is ever threatened in this home, call me and I'll make sure someone I trust comes out to investigate. So, are we approved to go in?"

Again that slight nod; then the girl sidled back.

Kahane was looking at Day with confusion. "Celia gets hysterical with strangers. Her tears won't stop until they go away. What did you do?"

"Reassured her, at least about us. She's not afraid of being hurt. She's terrified of *you* being hurt. Of losing you. So, she watches everyone who comes near you."

"How do you know that?" Kahane asked.

Day brushed her hands on her pants. "I recognized the fear. The first two years with my adoptive father, I was numb to my own pain, but I was terrified something would take him from me." She unclenched her fists. "I still don't like to lose things."

"Thank you," Kahane said simply, nodding to the woman who came to take charge of Celia.

And as Day watched the pain that crossed his face as the little girl walked away, still staring back at him, she knew that, even without the laws of some treaty, she would never have arrested this man in this house.

Inside his office, Kahane offered them chairs. Day accepted, sitting a little to the side, so she could watch both men. This was Lian's bailiwick.

Lian, however, did not sit. He paced in quick short strides, driven by an internal restlessness. "I would visit the Shinook land."

"You're returning at last?" Kahane's delighted smile faded, and his lips tightened. "Yet you come here as plague hunter?"

"I have no choice. The Shinook have information Inspector Daniels and I need, but my final task is not complete. I come as Dr. Julian Firebird, requesting a favor."

"Tell me what you want. Thanks to you, I haven't been exiled. That's a gift I can never repay."

"You were not exiled because your presence did not bring the specter of death."

Kahane gave a neutral shrug. "What is the favor?"

"Will you, as an active member of the people, request the council meet with the Inspector and me on a neutral ground? We request information and permission to visit the peak called *Okeyu h'ea*."

Okeyu h'ea? Citadel?

"You should not have to do this," Kahane said fiercely. "The elders were wrong."

Day saw a flash of pain cross Lian's face, quickly hidden behind the stoicism of a plague hunter.

"They did not anticipate my duties would keep me away for so long."

"You know the condition they will demand."

"That at the completion of this task I honor my vow."

"Will you?"

"Yes." Lian paused at the window, looking outside instead of at them, a man apart. "I will honor my vow and return to the Nation."

Day's lungs froze in her chest. He was going back to the Shinook? He planned to settle in a place where she had no possibility of staying, where she would never be accepted and never have a role. He had told her their time together was an interlude. Now she knew why.

She gripped the chair arms. Why did that hurt? She'd already decided there was no future with them. He'd already decided that she would never trust him as he needed.

Kahane joined Lian by the window and laid a hand on his shoulder. "You are not a man who can cut yourself off from the world. You will wither."

Day's hands shook, but she bit back the denials, squelched the urge to leap up and demand a different choice from him. The Shinooks were isolationists. They brooked very little consort with others. They were self sufficient and proud. As she had no place there, how could Lian cut himself off from the world like that?

As if he'd heard her jumbled thoughts, Lian shook his head. "Changes can be made. Must be made. I will try. But if not . . . My roots are there. I miss them."

The simplicity of his answer told her how important this was to him.

Lian lifted a hand, forestalling further argument. "My decision is made. Will you contact them?"

"And if they ask when you will fulfill the vow?"

He looked at Day, his face emotionless. But his gray eyes burned like molten lead and, above the edge of his shirt, she saw the bright gold nanotat. "The prime minister has given me eight days."

Eight days to find a killer? To be together? They only had eight days left?

Lanced by pain, her chest so squeezed by loss that she could barely exhale. Day forced herself to stay upright. Stiff spine and straight shoulders. Do *not* give in to the pain. Her gaze locked with Lian's. Her ears buzzed so with the race of blood that she barely heard Kahane talking on his comm, although she wouldn't have understood anyway, for he spoke in Shinook. Messages were relayed back and forth, separated by long silences while decisions were made at the other end. Instead, all she knew were the stark taut planes of Lian's face and the unspoken heat of his eyes.

At last, Kahane nodded and turned off his comm. "The council agreed," he said, speaking in English—she guessed in deference to her.

"To what?" asked Lian, breaking away to turn to his cousin.

"Because of your vow to return within eight days, Dr. Firebird is welcome on Shinook land during that time, and the inspector may come with you. They will meet with you at Gash Canyon."

"Thank you."

Kahane grasped him by the forearm. "It's good to have you back, my cousin."

As the two said their farewells, Day's thoughts spun, circling around two very final, crazy words.

Eight days.

Chapter Nineteen

"Benton!" At the trek sled, Day gave a delighted scratch of the wolf's neck. "Thanks for bringing him," she told the Health Canada tech, who'd delivered him.

"Trafalgar claimed the 'damn wolf is driving me crazy with his mooning howls and his sudden starts.' That's a direct quote."

She laughed. "I figured."

"He wants to talk to you." The tech gave her a handheld code, then left with a jaunty wave.

"Trafalgar?" She stared in astonishment at her screen, unable to believe he'd answered "You're using a comm?"

"I wanted to see you," he said gruffly. "You know that wolf of yours is plain *loco*."

"Benton always does that when I'm away."

"Still, I'm thinking I'll get some gear and snoop around. You never know what he might have sensed up here."

"You're not supposed to be hiking."

"Two days on my back is my limit."

"You'll reopen your wound."

"Skin fits like new." He lifted his shirt to demonstrate his healing wound.

She gave up. "Just be careful."

"That Health Canada doctor did a fine job of stitching me up."

"He is a good doctor," she agreed, turning to watch Benton frolicking with Lian. Her dark mood lightened at seeing the wolf leaping about in joyous abandon, while the doc laughed—laughed!—as he ruffled Benton's fur.

When had she last heard him laugh?

"You're a Mountie, Day," Trafalgar warned her in a low voice. "Up for that G-1. Don't forget that."

She swallowed the hailstone in her throat. "I never forget that, and I'm a damn good Mountie." Despite her mistakes, she *was* a good officer.

Lian finished his romp with Benton, but when he looked at her the bland mask was back. "Ready to go, Day?"

"Ready." While Lian promised Benton a run outside of Calgary to persuade him into the sled confines again, Day turned back to the handheld, touching the air beside Trafalgar's beloved face. "Bye, Trafalgar. No excuses anymore. I'll expect more comms in the future."

"That I will, Day darling. Take care of yourself." He returned the borrowed comm to its owner without turning it off. Her last view of her father was Trafalgar already striding in the other direction, his shoulders hunched against the wind as he returned to his duty without a second glance.

Unlike Lian, whose gaze she felt as she steered the sled out of Calgary. She refused to look at him, not wanting to see cool emotionlessness where once there had been a fire that warmed her soul.

The winter snow started in earnest as they left Calgary. Thick, gray, and icy, it isolated them, all sound blotted out by the staccato of ice against the sled and the buffeting arctic winds. For a while all her attention was on keeping the sled moving and in the right direction, as she refamiliarized herself with the controls. At least Lian's sled maneuvered with the ease of a spoon through warm syrup, and by the time she started climbing into the mountains; she soon felt comfortable enough that her uncomfortable thoughts returned.

In the trek sled, she couldn't escape. Couldn't escape the subtle sage or the sound of his breathing. Couldn't escape that sheer, bone-deep awareness of him, so much more potent now that she knew intimately what his body felt like against hers.

At least here, he couldn't escape either.

She took a deep breath. "Lian, about this morning. What I said—"

"Your reaction was understandable."

"You're being too calm about this. My God, we made love one night and the next I'm accusing you—"

"Of putting people in danger. I heard you."

"Would you stop finishing my sentences!" She knew those snappish words would come back to haunt her. Saying she regretted them the moment they left her lips wasn't going to help, however. "What I was going to say is, I didn't even give you a chance to explain."

"No, you didn't."

His words were brief, blunt, and final. Lian opened his handheld and began to work, effectively shutting off the conversation.

Except she refused to be cut off. If direct tactics didn't work, try a wraparound. "What are you working on?"

"I scanned in Trafalgar's old topomap and am using it to plot a route up Citadel. The Winnipeg lab, by the way, sends their thanks for those most recent tubes of your blood. They're making progress on cloning the antibodies, although the process proved tricky. I've got enough with me for a couple people. They could vaccinate a dozen more. We may have to hope there are other hyperimmunes to harvest blood from. And pray the exposure is limited."

"If I have to provide blood for all of Canada, I'm going to end up as dry as a sheaf of winter wheat."

"Not you, Day." His voice held grudging respect. "You can survive anything."

"This cold withdrawal of yours is tearing me apart." There, she'd said it. She'd admitted that, for once, she could not Do it All, Be it All if it meant losing him. "Is it because the first thing out of my mouth was that stupid accusation? I was angry at myself for not following my instincts and pursuing that lead faster, for not arguing with you about something I felt in my gut. You wouldn't deliberately put anyone in danger. I know that."

"This time the accusation had a grain of truth. I might have just done that—put people in danger to protect others important to me."

"You would not do that."

"Don't, Day. Don't go soft on me. Not now."

Day stiffened, tightening her belly around its hollow ache. She'd been taught not to give up. She'd given up on Lian before. She wouldn't make that mistake again.

Not when she smelled his scent of sage. Or when she remembered how he touched her and called her name. Not when she knew that despite the sometime hardness and ruthlessness of the man, the essence of him was a big heart.

She jerked the sled to a stop, then turned and grabbed his hands, lifted them to her cheeks. "Isn't there any other choice?"

"Once, I hoped so." He kissed her knuckles. "Now? No."

"I can't accept that." Only now, as she faced truly losing him, as the yawning gap made her ache with need, did she admit how much she wanted him.

"What about us?" she demanded, feeling a tremor run through him, as though he absorbed every emotion she felt. "Not Canada. Not the case. *Us*. Is it all lies? Just a romp in the night? An interlude?" She grabbed another breath, fighting dizziness. "Because it wasn't for me."

Her chest heaved, trying to relieve the tightness with thinner air. He stilled, searching her face. Looking for something? Waiting for something? She couldn't tell.

He must not have found it, for he lifted her hands from his shoulders. For a single, too-brief moment, he squeezed her fingers; then he released her.

"What would you have me do?" he asked quietly. "Abandon them? Forget my sacred vow and my duty? Let Juneau release his scourge?"

The questions hung between them, filling the ensuing silence.

Her shoulders dropped and she sat back. "No."

She had to respect his choices and decisions, as he had learned to accept hers. Just as he would never have asked her to abandon the Mounties, she could not ask or beg him to abandon his people again.

She started the sled back up. She hated to lose anything, but as the trek sled headed toward the Shinook settlement, with each passing kilometer she was losing Lian.

They agreed that Day would drive the first shift southwest toward the heights of the Rockies and Lian would take over the second shift when they neared the Shinook lands. Lian knew it would be easier for him to find the route to take, to recall landmarks he hadn't seen in seven years, if he was driving. At the moment, though, they stood outside the sled, preparing for the first shift, letting Benton roam.

The snow hadn't diminished. Icy needles stung Lian's cheeks and froze any exposed flesh. At least it was still daylight. With luck, they would make the Shinook settlement before nightfall.

Despite his decision, the thought was not a comforting one. Still, there was no other choice. They were out of

301

leads. L.J. was still comatose. Juneau had disappeared. Finding Jem from the data dot and what he was planning was their last hope.

Going home was both right and inevitable.

The howling wind cut through his shirt, yet he didn't close his jacket. The cold he welcomed; the winter—it was no more wild than he.

Right and inevitable? Every moment was hell.

He couldn't force himself back into the sled and start those final kiloms that would drive an irrevocable wedge between him and Day.

Day rejoined him. "Are we far?" she shouted above the wind.

"Couple of hours."

She leaned closer, the words whipping from his mouth. "Somebody could be around the next drift, waiting to ambush us, and we wouldn't have a clue, would we?"

"Uncomfortable thought."

Her multihued eyes were the brightest part of the afternoon as she leaned close to him. Snow coated her brows, and he wiped the ice off with his thumb. Beneath the chilled skin, he could feel the heat of her.

He couldn't resist. His fingers tunneled beneath her braid, and he traced the line of her jaw. One last touch.

"Don't." It wasn't wise.

He didn't hear the word above the wind, only saw the motion of her lips. But, he knew exactly what she meant, for it echoed his own thoughts.

She made the first move. She stood on tiptoe and kissed him. He joined her, tasting that sweet maple flavor and teasing those soft lips one more time.

"You confuse me," she shouted.

"While I always know exactly what's going on in your mind." He skipped the backs of his fingers across her hair. Hard as it was to leave a lifetime of work, cutting himself off from Day, especially when she showed these rare moments of vulnerability, was worse. He could barely see or hear past the pain.

Benton came bounding back, distracted by chasing selected snowflakes. A patch of blood and a tuft of fur told them that he had a full stomach again. All was right in the wolf's world.

The humans were having more troubles than a belly full of rabbit could help, however—although they both could imagine some positive points to bounding naked in the snow.

Day might have made the decision that he was not for her. He had not. But, he had made a decision, nonetheless.

His kiss this time was lighter. "We'd best be going."

Seven years had changed the landscape in minor ways, but the formations of granite were timeless and eternal. To the forces of erosion, seven years was but a blink.

Lian recognized it all, memories descending on him with a rush. His muscles remembered each necessary turn of the sled. His hands and feet made adjustments to speed by instinct. He needed no map or thought to guide the way through these mountains, which were as familiar to him as his own face.

He sent the sled down a narrow trail, which hugged the edge of the mountain. Tufts of bear grass and jagged boulders poked through the steep, snowy slope downward. If he should misjudge the trail, nothing would stop their precipitous descent. Still he pushed on, guiding more on instinct than on recall.

"How are the power cells holding out?" Day asked.

"With the overcast skies, they haven't recharged," he admitted. "But we should have enough power to make the settlement and recharge from the generator."

"Can I help you look for landmarks?"

"This part I recognize. See that spire ahead? We have to go through Gash Canyon to that. The spire marks a passage through the mountain to a protected valley. The settlement should be there."

"If they're not?"

"Then we're there until a sunny day recharges the cells."

"Well, it will give us time to come up with a new plan."

One of the many things he liked about Day: She wasn't a whiner.

Benton shifted until his face hung over Day's shoulder, probably trying to see out past the ice coating the sled sides and roof. At least the defrost elements kept the front and back clear.

He gripped the wheel tighter, his heart accelerating. It was his damned claustrophobia kicking in, he knew. The sled was taking on the attributes of a coffin.

At the spire, he turned the sled into the canyon. Iron-striped walls rose on either side of them. Not helping the claustrophobia.

"Great place for an ambush." Day said, peering upward.

He heard the same note of unease in her voice as he felt. Not just his claustrophobia, then, since she didn't suffer from it. "Anything specific sparking that comment?"

"You mean beyond the tall walls with no exit except behind us? No."

He didn't see any evidence of any traps. That didn't mean they weren't there, though.

They were in the narrowest part of the canyon. Rock ledge overhangs blotted out what little sky they might have seen, if there had been any sunshine to light it with. Sleet rapped sharply against the trek sled windows. Despite the excellent insulation, a draft of cold permeated the interior, stirring the hair at the back of Lian's neck.

Benton growled in his ear. The wolf was eyeing a brace of grouse fluttering above a scarlet-branched bush. Lian angled the sled in that direction.

"What set those birds fluttering?" Day asked, following the same train of thought.

"That's what I'm aiming to see."

A rumbling shook the earth. Behind him, Benton growled again. The trek sled began to shimmy and slide backward as the ground vibrated and resonated.

Lian swore and revved the sled forward, listing as he angled to the far edge of the narrow canyon. Benton yelped as he bounced around.

"Sorry, fella."

The rumbling became a roar. Pelting thuds against the sled exterior drowned out the pouring sleet.

"Avalanche?" Day shouted.

"Rock slide."

A boulder crashed in front of them with a spine-rattling jolt. More followed, landing on all sides. One grazed the sled, and the side window cracked. A screeching whistle joined the cacophony as icy wind burst into the sled.

They were directly below a collapsing mountainside. Led neatly there by a flock of grouse.

A two-meter rock speared the ground in front of them. Lian yanked the sled left.

"Aim ten degrees right," Day shouted, bracing her hands against the dash.

He steered automatically to her command, then saw what she had—a crevasse splitting the ground and widening with each impact. The sled skimmed the rim, then grabbed the frozen ground to propel them away. They spun down the canyon, aiming for the spire and the thick shelter beneath the mountain. He shut off the heater, needing every ounce of engine power. Dust, snow, and ice billowed behind them, blotting out the landscape and any hope he had of seeing further traps. Or who might set them.

Day leaned forward, peering through the debris and snow with infrared binoculars. "The spire's at O two hundred!" she shouted over the din, pointing.

Almost there.

Rocks tumbled down the slope. A loosened scrub tree

caught on the roof. Ahead, a ledge of rock cracked. Shattered stone dropped in daggerlike shards, stabbing new cracks into the glass.

A low pounding shook the sled, an ominous rhythmic bass. Growing louder. Growing closer. Half the side of the mountain was descending on them.

Directly toward Day's side of the sled.

They wouldn't reach the tunnel before it hit!

Lian swore and sent the sled scrambling up the cracked wall of rock. Twisting direction, he put the rear of the sled toward the massive slide.

"Benton! Forward!" he shouted to the cowering wolf.

After a single glance behind, Day shoved her seat forward, pulling the seat-back down at the same time. Reaching over, she shoved Benton's haunches forward. The wolf scrambled between them into the front seat.

With a tail in his face, Lian spied the opening. He shoved harder at the already flat-out accelerator.

"Come on!" he urged the engine that had never failed him. The machinery protested with a loud whine.

Rocks slammed their rear, crumpling the back of the sled. The impact shot them forward.

He twisted the steering. The sled scraped against the side of the tunnel; then they were in! Some rocks followed, pelting the sled from behind. Most, however, clattered harmlessly against the face of the mountain.

The engine died. They were stranded in the dark depth of the tunnel.

Dust and snow settled. Cold at once began to take over the sled interior. The din of the rock slide ended, leaving Lian's ears ringing with silence. The last power drained from the cells, and the headlights cut off. Unbroken blackness surrounded them.

Lian held tight to the steering wheel, hating the claustrophobia nibbling at his self-control.

"Day?" He reached out blindly, finding only Benton's fur. "Are you okay?"

"Yeah." She coughed. "I got grit in my throat. And wolf slobber down my neck. Hell of a driving demonstration, Firebird. How you holding up?"

"Fine."

He heard her scrambling for something. A second later, he blinked as she shone a light in his face.

"Claustrophobia's a bitch when you're stuck in the middle of a mountain, isn't it, Firebird? Let's get out of here. Benton, get your wet nose out of my ear."

He could just see her within the circle of light, her braid askew, her face pale with cold and worry. She made a face at him, and he couldn't help but laugh, easing a little the pain in his chest. "We'll have to walk to the settlement. There will be people and equipment there to move the sled and clear the exit. Take what you and Benton need for a night."

Reluctantly, he forced himself to look away from her and gather his med pack. When the wings of claustrophobia beat again, he kept them at bay long enough to fumble for his light, then exited the sled.

Day had circled around. Her pack was on her back, her braid dangling easily atop it. Her light held steady against the ground, and her hat was jammed tight against her head. Benton trotted at her side.

She was so beautiful, this outdoor Canadian Mountie. Not even his sometimes anger with her or his churlish hurt at her doubts could erase his love for her.

If only things had been different, he would have fought for her, never let her go. Convinced her what he knew was right between them.

She took his hand, then shone her light toward their route. A warren of rooms greeted her, the inside of the tunnel as cellular as a sponge. "I'm sure hoping you will

307

pull yourself together to guide us through this."

Again, he had no choice. For Day's sake, he couldn't give in to fear.

Fear of any kind.

"This way," he said, holding tight to her hand. "Just talk to me as we go."

"Okay. How about a joke? When the Almighty was portioning up the land of the earth, he was telling an angel of his plans. 'I'll give this country high mountains and fertile land. Wide-open spaces, clear air, fresh waters, a population to make me proud, an abundance of wildlife. And, I'll call it Canada. Is this not good, eh?' The little angel gazed up at the Almighty. 'But, Lord, is it fair to give such blessings all to one country?' The Almighty lifted a finger. 'Ah, but you should see the neighbors I'm going to give them.' "

Lian laughed again, his thumb rubbing against her palm. Laughter, the touch of her, staved back the darkness as he forced himself to examine the closing walls and ceiling of the maze for the signs of passage.

"So, you got any jokes?" she asked.

"Not a joke exactly. Do you know what the definition of a Canadian is? Someone who can make love while standing on hockey skates."

"I heard it was someone who knew how to make love in a canoe."

"Well, there's also the makes love in a kayak version."

"Or the makes love in an igloo version."

"We've done snow already. But I'm game for any of the above."

"When we get out of this tunnel, we'll see if you're Canadian, Dr. Firebird."

He lifted her hand to his mouth and kissed her knuckles. "You know I am," he whispered.

The mouth of the cave took shape in front of them. With the light and the fresh air, his claustrophobia faded. He stopped before they reached the exit. Standing at the edge of the light, he took her hands in his. "Explanations, Day. Why I got so defensive at Scree's words, the reason I couldn't believe the Shinooks were involved. It's simple. I'm their leader. *I'm* Jem."

Chapter Twenty

The cave walls tilted in on Day. She squinted, trying to pull the world back into focus. "I don't understand. How can you be Jem? That wasn't you on the data dot."

"One of the questions I intend to get an answer to."

"Why didn't you tell me?"

"You wanted Jem brought in for questioning, issued a warrant for his arrest. I couldn't risk jail again. Not even for a single day."

She deserved that doubt, perhaps. She had given him little reason to expect anything else.

Without another word, she scratched her comm, opening channels. The connection was faint from weather and mountain interference, but it had enough strength for her message. "This is Inspector Daniels. Cancel that warrant for the arrest of Jem. It's a frame job. Someone else is using the name. No, I don't know who. Yet." She signed off, then spun around, startled as a shadow crossed the mouth of the cave.

Four men blocked the entrance. Four hard unsmiling men, dressed in leather and soft-skin boots and brandishing weapons.

Instinctively Day grabbed her Distazer, but Lian stopped her with a viselike grip around her wrist. He took her gun.

"Don't! These are my relations." He spoke in Native Common, hard for her to interpret. Except his meaning was helped along when he handed her Distazer to their unwelcoming committee.

One of the men gestured for them to follow.

"It has to be this way," Lian whispered as they left the cave.

She forced back a useless protest. No officer of the law ever willingly gave up a weapon; she felt stripped without its comfortable weight. Despite the protection of the valley, a wicked wind slashed across her. She clamped a hand over her hat, holding it in place.

"State your purpose," demanded one of the men, a commanding warrior with a hawklike nose and long, dark hair like Lian.

"Dr. Julian Firebird, assisted by Inspector Day Daniels of the RCMP. We have been given permission to question the members of your nation."

The warrior inclined his head in acknowledgment, his dark hair swirling about his shoulders. "Hakan of the Shinook welcomes you."

One of the younger men stepped forward. "Julian Firebird of the Shinook, do you honor your sacred vow?"

She'd misjudged their solemnity, Day realized. They were not threatening; they were engaged in some kind of formal ritual she didn't quite understand.

"I do, Taku, cousin to my family." Lian held out his hands, crossing them at the wrists. "I have begun one task which I must complete. I have been granted eight days, then I rejoin with the people to lead them to the future."

311

Hakan gestured toward Taku, who handed him a leather rope, which he held above Lian's wrists. "The symbol of your sacred pledge."

Day's chest tightened, and her heart fluttered against her ribs. She pressed her lips together, knowing she could not interfere even if this felt wrong. Instead, she kept her hands steady at her sides, feeling the comforting weight of the Distazer in her coat. Jurisdiction be damned if anyone harmed Lian.

At the sight of Lian bound, Benton stalked forward, growling, hackles raised. Day, too, planted herself at his side, massaging the cold from her fingers. Whatever drama was played out here would include her and the wolf.

Hakan raised his brows. "Your companions, Jem, aren't too happy."

Lian turned to her, his bound hands flicking her braid back over her shoulder. "I know what I'm doing, Day. Trust me in this." Then, he leaned over and whispered, "Unless they shoot me. Then you might want to clear out of here."

He was quoting the words she'd said to him at the Banzai temple when she'd asked him to let her do her job. He had kept his promise then and not interfered. Now, he asked the same difficult task of her.

Her jaw tightened, and she lifted her chin. "Understood."

The heat in his eyes flared, then extinguished. He crouched down until he was eye level with Benton. He wrapped his bound hands around the wolf's muzzle for a moment, then ruffled the fur. "Stand down, Benton. Stay with Day. She'll need you. You can go back to being alpha wolf."

Lian rose and faced his escorts. "We need our sled brought to the settlement and the tunnel entrance cleared. Provide Inspector Daniels with whatever tools and supplies are necessary to repair the sled. She's in charge of that in my stead."

Day saw a flash of resentment tighten Taku's face. "We take orders when the council yields authority."

Hakan's hand tightened around his rifle. "Keep a civil tongue. Is it not enough that I, a member of the council, do not counter him?"

A mask slid onto the younger man's face. "It shall be as ordered."

So. Day thought, not everyone welcomed the prodigal's return. Not surprising. After seven years away there were bound to be those who no longer readily accepted Lian back.

She followed the small group deeper into the valley, Benton butting her leg. The wind was still frigid, and their boots crunched on the layer of ice forming atop the snow. Footing was treacherous, despite the level surface, and she found breathing harder at this altitude. She walked stiff and determined not to let any of the them see weakness or a hint of the stitch in her side.

Instead, she kept her gaze firmly on Lian. His hair was blowing in the wind, and she could see his brand alternately revealed and concealed. The planes on his face were taut and stark in the cold air. There was a wildness about him, which made him seem more a part of Benton's world than she could ever be. Or maybe it was an attachment to the sky and mountain, a broad understanding that she approximated with her ties to her Mounties.

They came around a ridge, and the settlement spread out before them, the end of their journey.

"Lian," she called, refusing to call him Jem.

He stopped and turned to her. With a single step, she closed the gap between them. Gripping his tense shoulders, she lifted on tiptoe—dammit, he wasn't making this any easier; he could at least bend his head—to look more directly into his eyes.

"There's a blessing said upon graduation from the Cadet Academy. 'Go now with the courage to lead, the strength to protect, and the heart to care.' If that is what it takes to make a good Mountie, then you would have made an excellent one, Lian Firebird." She gathered him in her arms, for he could not hold her with his bound hands, and kissed him—at the edge of his mouth where she could reach.

He leaned down, his mouth and nose buried against her shoulder. He drew in a deep breath, then whispered, "*Lela washtae che la ke,*" too low for anyone but her to hear.

The same phrase he'd used this morning.

He stepped away, and the sick twisting in her gut told her it was the last time he would allow that intimacy between them. He turned his back on her and strode into the settlement, shoulders erect, hair framed by the two narrow braids he had taken to wearing, the wild wind whipping about him as it pushed him away.

She rose to her full height and followed. Hakan, behind Lian, glanced back at her, then snapped his head toward the patrol. Two of the men blocked her.

"This is not for you, *wasichu.*" They weren't hostile or harsh. Simply stating an obvious fact.

Why did doing the right thing have to hurt so much?

"I won't interfere," she said quietly. "I would like to see and understand."

Lian glanced back and said something she didn't understand. They stepped aside.

"He asked me to interpret." Taku remained beside her to translate the Shinook language for her.

Lian was greeted with quiet warmth, welcomed back to the nation. He responded gravely and formally, without the irreverent flashes of humor that often underpinned his comments. Despite Taku's attitude, Day saw most of the tribe regarded Lian with respect.

Suddenly, a young woman, maybe slightly younger than Day, raced into the circle surrounding him. She handed the infant she carried to one of the elder women, right before she launched herself at Lian, hugging and kissing him. At last a smile broke across his solemn face.

"That is his sister, Aveline. She is very glad to see her brother, after seven years," Taku told her drily.

"So I see."

When they broke apart, Aveline reached for the infant and placed it in Lian's arms. Despite the bonds, he held the child with a natural ease, looking down with blatant love. Gently he cooed to the infant, who responded with a gurgling laugh.

"His nephew, Perren, whom he has never held."

The ache of seeing Lian holding the baby, as though it were his own, surprised her. "What is she saying to Hakan?"

"She berates him for binding Jem's hands, but he says that Nation law demands it until the council removes the restraint."

"What happened seven years ago, Taku?" Lian had told her a little, but she still didn't understand it all. "How could he be leader, yet exiled?"

"His father was our chief, the lead voice in the council of elders. With two older brothers, Jem instead trained as shaman. And doctor." There was a hint of distaste in Taku's voice. "He came here from a *wasichu* village, and the plague followed him. He claimed the infection was already here, but the elders did not trust him. It was that which led to his exile and the vow demanded of him. Even though, with the deaths of his relations, he was our leader. The council has commanded in his stead."

Taku looked at her with hard eyes and added, "He left in the wake of our destruction. Now Jem must confirm where his first loyalty lies."

"Lian sees his people as part of a bigger world," Day whispered, her throat so clogged she could barely speak. Standing here in the cold, alone, with nothing in her eyes but Lian, and for the moment no purpose or duty to distract her, she finally understood.

He'd asked her for the trust his elders had not given him. A straight-from-the-gut, first-thought-in-your-brain confidence that he was doing the right thing. Instead she'd rebuffed and doubted him at every turn. Only too late, too feebly had she begun to give him that necessary basic belief.

Only to fail again this morning. Because she had feared trusting him, loving him, would sever her from the Mounties, and she did not know if she had enough fortitude to risk that.

A younger, less harsh version of Lian joined the brother and sister. He stood with thinned lips, not joining the exuberance. "Who's that?" Day asked.

"Yves, Jem's brother," said Taku.

"He doesn't look very happy. Did he take over as chief?"

"No, he was adopted and could not. Still, in Jem's absence he has taken on duties that would have fallen to Jem. Now, he must step aside from them."

Looking at Yves, Day wasn't sure she agreed with Taku's casual dismissal of the about-to-be displaced brother. Ambitious people didn't give up so readily.

Had Yves been desperate enough to send a rockslide at them?

Or maybe a member of the council?

She glanced around the settlement for the first time, curious about what they might find here. The settlement was a mobile one, she realized. Lian had said his people honored their nomadic traditions, but their homes had little relationship to spartan trailers or ancient tepees. Situated on the versatile bottoms similar to the trek sleds and with thin, nano-fabricated walls, they could be moved by towing or by their own engines. The scattered dwellings weren't large, but they looked comfortable and well maintained.

The walls were awash with designs that lent a colorful splash to the white-coated valley.

"The council arrives," Taku said quietly, breaking into her thoughts.

Day straightened and flicked her braid over her shoulder. She stared straight ahead, just as Lian stared straight and proud at the elders of his nation. Taku's voice sounded in her ear, so quiet in his translation that it was as though she actually understood the words of Shinook.

Hakan and four others stood in a semicircle in front of Lian. "You were exiled, Julian Firebird," one said.

"You gave a solemn vow to the spirits," added another. "Do you honor it?"

"Yes. When I complete my final task. I assist this Mountie—"

The collective attention drew toward her. Day kept her back straight, her eyes fastened straight ahead. She forced her breath steady despite the thin air, and refused to shiver in the cold.

"—in her quest for the murderer of her colleague."

"You have been given eight days, then you will give your service to the Shinooks," the third council member said.

"Yes." Lian lifted his bound hands.

The fourth raised a knife and, after seeing the others nod, with a swift stroke cut through the leather. There was a moment's silence; then Hakan began an undulating cheer.

Hands still raised, Lian turned to face his people.

But Day saw, if no one else did, that his gaze held but one place.

Her.

Her hand lowered to Benton's furry head. She stared back, stiff with cold and pain, at the man who had just been lost to her. Tears seeped from her eyes, only to freeze on her unmoving cheeks until they were coated in ice.

*   *   *

"The rock slide was a stupid move!"

Rupert Juneau kept his face pleasant as the Indian strode out through the snow, not revealing the bitter taste of his near failure or his anger at the rebuke. "I'm sorry. I took a chance. The rock slide got away from me. You said you needed them kept here."

Of course, *his* plan had been that once the sled was immobilized, it would be an easy task to capture the Mountie. Instead, they'd gotten away.

"I don't want him on a funeral pyre. I told you I would get you the Mountie."

Juneau bit back the reply he wanted to give. What made him good at what he did was two things: his patience, his ability to adapt. He'd waited a long time for this plan to come to fruition. He'd made adjustments in it before, taking advantage of new information, handling new problems.

And it never hurt to have one or two alternatives waiting.

"When?"

"I'll send word. Soon."

"Excellent." He slid his hand beneath the fur sleeve. "Can you stay?" he purred, pleased when he heard a catch of breath.

"No. I'm expected elsewhere." The denial came on a soft sigh.

"Pity."

With a swirl of fur, his Indian lover disappeared into the snow.

Juneau stretched out his hands toward the meager output from his bush plane heater. The waiting was almost done. Just a few more days he had to deal with these arrogant Canadians.

Just a few more days and he'd have the woman. The plague hunter would be destroyed. Canada would be too busy trying to protect itself, with the borders slammed shut again, to pay any attention to his activities.

The next evening, Day set the wrench to the side and stretched the kinks from her shoulders. The trek sled was fixed. One border troop had been vaccinated and sent to Citadel. With no more vaccine, though, they wouldn't send more. Health Canada stood by, ready to act. The remaining plague hunters were gathering.

They just needed two pieces: a time to act and the source of the virus. If they could identify "Jem," he could give them the answer. Unfortunately, she was no closer to that than she had been two days ago. And she hadn't spoken to Lian yet to know if he had discovered anything.

Unlike him, however, she had no excuse for staying here. In truth, she was chafing at the inactivity. It was time to leave.

"Is the sled ready?" Lian's sister, Aveline, joined Day, like she had several times before in the past two days. Her baby, Perren, scrambled from her arms over to a sleeping Benton. The wolf opened one blue eye as the child tumbled over his paws. He licked the baby's cheek, then with a snuffle settled back to sleep, ignoring Perren climbing on his back.

"I believe he thinks of Perren as a cub," Aveline observed.

"Likely. He disappeared last night and was looking rather mellow in the morning. I'm thinking he's found a lady wolf on the side."

"Why has he not joined her then? Wolves are faithful to their mates."

"Perhaps he hasn't yet decided which pack he belongs to."

"A male always chooses the pack where he is the alpha."

"Then maybe he has some unfinished business here."

319

Aveline shrugged, a gesture that Day was discovering could mean anything from disapproval to excitement to hesitation. The woman was pleasant enough; when she forgot her agenda, they actually had some interesting conversations. Day had begun to learn more about the Shinook culture; tidbits she appreciated, for they prevented her from making mistakes like failing to greet a council member whenever she met one, or filling conversational gaps with chatter.

She'd never sat in companionable silence with so many different people for so long a time in her life. It could be very peaceful.

However, Aveline obviously had a biting desire to make it understood that her brother was at home with the Shinooks. Her conversations were laced with tidbits—how much she'd missed her brother, how warmly he'd been welcomed back. How he had healed Eliha with a stern warning not to keep drinking the willow bark tea.

"I've seen you talking with Taku, learning our language," Aveline said, in one of her characteristic leaps of topic. "You speak with everyone. Why?"

"I'm a Mountie—asking questions is what I do."

"Yet you respect our ways."

Day gave her the universal shrug back.

"There's a communal ceremonial dinner tonight," Aveline said suddenly. "Hakan would like you to sit at his side."

"Can't Hakan ask me himself?"

"This is not the way it is done."

It had become one of Aveline's most common phrases. A not-so-subtle reminder that Day was the outsider.

"When Jem decides who he will ask, I will also convey that request."

Day busied herself putting away the tools. A stab of pain to her lungs made breathing hard, and she refused to show Aveline the barb had hurt. She recognized the ploy. Lian had shown no interest in another woman, she knew, but the thought hurt nonetheless.

Suddenly, she sat back on her heels and decided to ignore the stricture against staring at someone. She was tired of games. "Aveline, stop hiding what you want to say in wolf terms or stories about the nation. I know what decision Lian—"

"Jem."

"He will always be Lian to me. I know his decision. In two days I have not gone near him. The sled is fixed. I'm leaving tomorrow, so if you've got anything to say to me, say it outright. Because this is the last chance you'll get." She made a final adjustment to the sled, then wiped off the last nanopen and put it away.

"You're leaving?" Aveline fingered the beaded jade necklace she wore.

"First light."

"Will my brother go with you?"

"I don't know. That's his decision, not mine."

They had a job to do, and she trusted Lian to do his part. She just wasn't sure how he intended to do it.

"Are you going to the dinner?"

"With Hakan? Tell him, thanks but no, thanks."

"At all?"

"No." Even if Lian wasn't sitting with another woman, she couldn't bear to see him and know he was out of her reach. Her body still craved him. She had a feeling she had a lot more restless nights ahead of her, when she prowled through the woods, as feral and instinctive as Benton. She didn't need to be reminded of what Lian looked like, how he smelled, or the way he moved with a quick, economic grace.

Aveline pursed her lips, as though coming to some decision. "My brother is not happy."

Day didn't stop arranging her pack. "I've stayed away from him. What more do you want from me?"

"He never stops looking for you. Oh, it's not obvious, but I know."

She would not be drawn out or back in. Time to go on the offense. "You haven't seen him in seven years, yet two days and you're an expert on the psychology of Julian Firebird?"

"No. But I know about men."

"Yeah, well, I've got a job to do."

Aveline scooped up her son, who had gone to sleep against Benton. "Then I shall say good-bye." She moved off.

Benton got up, yawned, and stretched. Coming over, he gave Day a nudge. She ruffled his fur. "Let me finish loading the sled, then I'll come play. Go get your dinner."

Benton gave an agreeable woof before bounding out.

Alone again, Day blew on her fingers. The snowfall had heralded the start of a bitter cold spell with bright skies and a biting wind. The trek sled was in a three-sided covered porch, out of the wind, but not the cold.

When she finished stowing gear in her travel kit, she put on her gloves. Repairing the sled was precise work, too precise for gloves, but the warmth felt good now.

"My sister giving you a hard time?"

Chapter Twenty-one

Day spun around, leaving her heartbeat behind. Lian stood in the open side of the garage, casually leaning his forearm against the edge.

Her mouth felt like dry ice. He looked good. Different, but good. He wore brown leather pants and a white shirt beneath his lamb's-wool coat. His hair had the two braids with four jade beads. Instead of thick boots, he wore soft, fur-lined moccasins. Updated moccasins, she realized, since they didn't absorb any of the dampness of the snow.

"Do I pass?' he asked, making her realize she was staring.

"You'll pass. You're looking good, Firebird."

"You look fine, too—especially for someone who's not sleeping."

"I never sleep; I nap. And is nothing secret around here?"

"Very little." He came forward.

"Thanks for your help with the sled." In the hours when she'd taken a break from mechanic duty, she'd come back to find the work had progressed, and she imagined she recognized Lian's touch.

"It's my sled. It's my responsibility to keep it working well."

Responsibility. They were both bound by their responsibilities and duties. She looked away, busying herself with pulling the last of his gear out of the back of the sled. "Are you finding the answers you need?"

"The answers I need, maybe. Not the ones I want."

"How?"

"The shaman traditions and ceremonies are natural, like I stayed part of them all my life."

"You did—I could see that. You just practiced them different."

"My relations . . . they are not so familiar. Or comfortable."

"Yeah, people tend to be pesky that way." She stored her pack in the sled. "Maybe because you never abandoned them. They abandoned you."

"That's an odd way of looking at it."

"Sometimes it takes an outsider to point things out." Even before she turned from the sled, she knew he stood beside her. The heat of his body, the sage of his skin wrapped around her with a caress she had so dearly missed.

"Why are you taking my things out of the sled?" he demanded.

"I thought you'd be staying . . ." She turned to face him, drawing to her full height, determined not to yield a centimeter.

"Wrong. We have a job to do."

"I'm leaving at first light tomorrow, heading over to Citadel. I haven't found anything useful here; I can be of more help there. But you need to stay here to follow through finding the man impersonating you. If anything develops, we'll comm."

His pursed lips told her that he knew she was right, and that he didn't like it. "You'll need this." He held out her first Distazer.

Gratefully, she strapped it to her thigh. "Thanks. Have you made any progress?"

They moved out of the garage to a rock outside, keeping their backs to the mountain, watching for anyone listening.

"A little. Not about the rock slide, but I've been trying to figure out why someone here might have gotten involved in this crazy plot."

"I've noticed there's a spot of smuggling going on among the younger men," she said drily. "Like, the bead pattern on those moccasins you're wearing is Montana Shinook."

He grinned at her, completely unrepentant. "They're comfortable."

"Just don't wear them off of tribal lands or you'll be facing a fine."

"Better than jail time." He hooked his arms across his knees. "I've been thinking. The Shinook smugglers would be glad for the borders to be open. They're mostly interested in obtaining the goods, and legally would be a lot less risky. But 'Jem' could be in it for another reason. Our hereditary lands cross what is the political border between the UCE and Canada. 'Jem' could be wanting the border opened in order to reunite with our cousins."

"A traditionalist? Well, that narrows it down to about everyone in the group. Except you. Who are your chief suspects?"

He ticked off five names.

Day thought a moment then said, "I've been trying to piece together movements, people who might have been gone from here during the times we know Jem was meeting with L.J. Our lists overlap by three—Hakan, Yves, and Taku."

"Any one of them would have the resources and the daring."

She snapped her fingers. "Gather them together and tell them everything."

"You mean about the virus and Juneau?"

"Yes. What do we gain by keeping silent?"

"The PM has ordered it."

"We've only got six days, Lian. Juneau knows we're here. He knows we're after him, that we're mobilizing the border."

"I'm not sure 'Jem' will believe us. Or that he's not in too deep to pull back."

"But we might plant the seeds of doubt. At the least we'll warn him what's at stake." She moved close to him.

Lian nodded. "Yves is out hunting, and we should wait until he returns." He didn't move away, seeming content to spend these stolen moments with her.

"How did you get the name Jem?"

"My given name is Julian, but during my childhood I was called Jules."

"Jules. Jewels. Morphed into Gem," she guessed.

"I took Lian when I left."

"It suits you."

"I think so, too."

"Still, you look like you belong here."

Not that he had lost his hard edge or that the veneer of civilization had thickened, but the restlessness, the edginess he'd had before, was muted. Though they hadn't spoken, she had watched him. She'd seen how the people were accepting him back, deferring to his decisions. Some were eager, some cautious, but none of them questioned his right to lead. Even some members of the council had seemed grateful for his guidance. Other Shinook settlements spread across the lands had commed, requesting he spend time with them as well.

Given time, he would settle in well here. She swallowed hard, knowing this was their final night.

"Belong here? Yes, I do," he said at last, tilting his head

to look at her. His fingers trailed along her jaw. "And no, I never will completely. Because you won't be here. I've missed you, Day. Missed holding you, talking to you, being inside you. I've missed smelling and tasting you. I've missed your stubbornness and your smile and your logic and your passion. I will always miss you."

She gripped the edge of the rock. "Don't make this any harder than it has to be, Lian. Let's keep the focus on stopping Juneau."

"That's tomorrow. Tonight, will you share my bed?"

One last time to embrace him, to sleep with his arms around her? The mere thought brought an ache to her heart so fierce that she could scarcely breathe. Yet, she could not refuse this final chance to love him. Unable to speak, she merely nodded.

His fingers tightened around her nape.

A child ran up to them, gesturing and chattering with excitement, breaking off their near-kiss. Day caught a few words, including *waphiye wichasha*, Lian's honorific, and *lacrosse*, before Lian laughed and tousled the child's hair, sending him off.

"I've been asked to referee the lacrosse game," he explained. "The child was apologizing for not asking me to play, but then the sides would be uneven. Too bad, as I haven't had a good game in a long time." He gave her a speculative look. "Do you play lacrosse?"

"I've played. Not my best game, but I acquit myself passably. Why? Oh, no—you're not thinking of asking me to play? I thought with your people, only the men played."

"The warriors. Traditionally it was a war tactics game. I'd say you qualify as a warrior. C'mon, after sitting in a shed all day, the exercise will do you good."

She shook her head. "I don't know if they'll accept me as a player."

"We'll ask them." Taking her by the hand, he led her to the open playing field. She tried to ignore the speculative looks at their clasped hands, concentrating on the players warming up instead. This was no gentleman's version of the game; there weren't even any marked sidelines. Two goals seemed to be the only rules.

Lian strode onto the field, his hair blowing behind him, speaking too rapidly and complexly for her limited vocabulary. Instead, she studied the two teams' reactions. Well, they didn't all walk off the field, at least. A couple were hostile. Hakan was openly accepting. The others were cautiously neutral, as far as she could tell. In other words, they weren't opposed to her attempting to play, but she'd have to prove herself.

Lian rejoined her, as there was some shifting of players on the field. "They've put us on opposite teams. Figured a woman and a man who hadn't played in seven years were both liabilities." He began stripping off his shirt, and she noticed several other players matched his action. He grinned at her. "I made sure you were on the team that keeps their shirts on."

"Thanks," she said drily, smiling back despite the flutter in her stomach. She'd never seen Lian look so lighthearted. So happy.

Hakan captained her team, and he put her on outside defense. Probably he was trying to find the place she could do the least damage. Lian, she noticed, was on offense. The game began, and she forgot about Lian, about Juneau, about last nights. Not having to play on the skins side was the Shinooks' only concession to her gender. They attacked her side of the field immediately, testing how weak a link she was.

And they soon found out she knew what she was doing, when she sent the ball spinning downfield to Hakan, who promptly buried it in the goal. She grinned at Hakan, who gave a wild yell in return. As she strode back to her position, she could almost feel their level of respect, and acceptance, rise a notch.

Her focus became running, scooping up the ball, and protecting the goal. The fast-paced, hard-fought game demanded everything she had. Sweat poured off her, and her legs and arms began to ache. Her shoulder started to burn but she pressed on, refusing to admit defeat. She was going to prove to these Shinooks what a Mountie could do. She gave up two goals, one when Lian outmaneuvered her for a clear shot, much to her disgust. But she also saved others, and her team also scored again when Taku banked in a shot.

The game was almost over—they played until the last sunbeam disappeared beneath the horizon—when the skins team began the final run down the field: a last, full-strength effort to score and break the tie, their lead scorer moving the ball with blurring speed.

From the corner of her eye she saw Lian running to the far side. Day shifted ground, just as the ball was passed to him. With that sure instinct, attuned to his movements from the first moment when they'd trailed Juneau in the tunnels, she leaped. And batted down his straight-on goal shot.

Her jubilant Shinook teammates mobbed her, staggering her with their celebration. Day gasped for breath amongst the press of sweaty bodies; then suddenly, she found herself tugged out of the mass. Gratefully, she pulled in air, as Lian cleared a space around her.

"Good game, Daniels," he said, breathless, his hand resting at her waist.

"Thanks."

"Remind me not to believe you the next time you say you play passably."

She grinned at him, feeling as happy as he looked. "Next time, you'll remember a Mountie's definition of passable."

Lian had thought he knew these men, but he knew them by labels only. Hakan—his friend, cheerful, loyal. Yves—

his brother, hot-tempered, righteous. Taku—his cousin, youthful, earnest. Yet, if he could not figure out which one had taken his name and made a pact with a demon, then did he truly know them? Too much had been lost in the years apart.

They were gathered in the meeting hall, the crackling fire in the central stone fireplace now dying. Yves had come back late from hunting, so the hall was empty except for their quiet meeting. The three Shinooks looked at Lian with a mix of curiosity and suspicion.

From the corner of his eye, he saw Day turn a chair around and settle into it. Scrubbed from her post-game shower, she stacked her hands on the chair back and rested her chin on them, seeming casual, waiting for him, but she'd picked her spot so she could see all three men. She gave a brief nod when she was situated.

They'd decided he should lead the confrontation, while she watched and analyzed.

And acted as backup if necessary.

He perched one hip on the table. "I know one of you took my name, Jem, and used it to obtain gear from Scree and meet with two men, L.J. Malachite and Rupert Juneau." He held up his hand at their startled protests. "Let me finish," he spat. "You are listening now."

Gradually, under his glare they quieted.

"I know you are a member of the No-Borders. That you are planning a violent act to open the borders." He kept a close eye on their reactions, but so far the fake Jem was eluding them.

"You likely know that Inspector Daniels and I are investigating this. Didn't you ever ask yourself why a plague hunter and a Mountie would be working together? This is not a normal investigative team."

He waited a minute to let the question sink in.

"She is seeking the killer of Luc Robichaux, a Mountie. If you had any doubts about the ruthlessness of your associate Rupert Juneau, remember that fact."

"Explains the Mountie," Hakan drawled, "but not the plague hunter."

"Luc Robichaux's hat was contaminated with a viral trace. Smallpox. Genetically modified, so it's not an outbreak of something we've dealt with before." He leaned forward, studying all three. Hakan looked amused, Yves stormy, Taku scared.

"I've seen the effects of it." He turned on his handheld, and a holoimage of the infected cultists rose in front of them. "Fever, blisters. In the worst case, the skin peeled off in great sheets. Not a pretty sight, is it? And Rupert Juneau plans on unleashing it."

Taku looked like he was about to be sick.

"Onset is under thirty-six hours," Lian continued, relentless. "Thirty-six hours to get cytokine sprays and vaccines. Except, the germs spread like wildfire and the antibodies are hard to synthesize. That woman over there, in fact, happens to be our only source. Four liters of blood for seven million people. I don't like the odds."

He leaned back. "Which one of you is Jem? I don't care about your No-Borders. Hell, I was one myself. And I don't think you knew Juneau's double cross. I care about one thing—that virus. We need dates, times, and plans if we're going to stop this insanity."

No answer. He didn't really expect Jem to leap to his feet and confess based on one dramatic lecture. Still, it would have been nice.

He flicked off his handheld. "Think about what I've said."

Yves stalked out without saying anything. Taku looked nervous, but he kept his own silent counsel.

Hakan paused and gripped him by the shoulder. "If I were Jem, I'd tell you. I, too, lost family in the last plague."

"Your sister and mother, I remember." Another loss.

A moment later, Lian was left alone with Day. He sat

beside her. "Any inkling which one's our man?"

She wrinkled her nose. "Not beyond a doubt."

"Where's your leaning?"

She hesitated. "Yves."

"I thought so, too. I'll put someone to watching him. We'll know if he leaves."

Day slipped from beneath the covers. Beside her, Lian reached out a hand.

"Where you going?" he mumbled, his face buried in the pillow.

"For a walk."

"If you'd like some exercise, come back to bed."

She chuckled. "I need to clear the cobwebs. I've told you, I don't sleep much."

"I'll come with you." He rolled to his side.

She leaned over and kissed him. "No, I need this time to myself. I'm not used to sharing so many minutes of my life with someone."

"I don't want to bind you or change you, Day. I just want to be with you every moment we have left."

"I know. But . . . let me have these minutes. I'll go check the sled, see if Benton's returned, then be back."

"If we had more time, I might get used to your nocturnal wanderings." He played with the ends of her braid.

"You might," she said easily, her insides tightening with his casual assumption they could have made a future if things had been different.

She remembered he had said something to her in the hotel room. Now, tonight, she had the courage to ask. "Lian, what does *'Lela washtae che la ke'* mean?"

"It's Shinook for 'I love you.' "

"*I love you?*" Her heart collided with her ribs. "Why not tell me in English?"

"Would you have believed it if I said it in English?"

"Yes!" Would she have? Then? *I will never lie to you in*

Native. He'd wanted to make sure she believed it, she realized. "You could have interpreted it."

"I figured that when you were ready, you would find out what it meant."

"That's a strange logic. Messy and indirect."

"You yourself haven't exactly been forthcoming."

"I love you, too, Lian." Why had she thought it hard to say? Saying it wasn't the problem. The problem was that saying the words didn't solve all the problems facing them.

Yet, saying them and hearing the words gave her hope.

At her admission, Lian sat up with a surge. He gripped her shoulder. "Repeat that."

"I love you. *Lela washtae che la ke.*"

She saw that wildness inside him flare, the passion that overcame messy logic and duty. He leaned over and kissed her, hard and possessive. Her hands bracketed his face as she kissed him back. Then, he urged her back onto the bed with him, and it was a long time before she rose again for her wandering.

"Be careful," Lian mumbled, his fist tightening around her braid.

"You've got guards on the valley. People watching our suspects. I'm a trained professional. I'm safer here than on duty. Now, go back to sleep."

"Don't do something stupid like going off with one of our suspects. Or answering a summons you think is from me. Or thinking you should investigate something alone," he mumbled.

"Understood. I'm just reconnoitering."

She disentangled her braid, slipped on clothes and outerwear, strapped on her weapons by habit, and then let herself out. The winter snows had started again, smudging the low moon and muting the night noises. She drew in a long breath of spruce and cedar, and she tucked her hands in her pockets.

She loved nights like this. Fresh. New. Wandering with

no purpose but to be part of the land. She loved the outdoors, the winter, the wildness of the Canadian interior. Tonight she could believe she belonged here, that it would be possible to find happiness with Lian. If she could only be a Mountie here.

Too bad life rarely gave you your if-only's. All it gave you were choices.

She looked overhead and saw, beyond the veil of snow and the distant beacon of stars, two red lights blinking. Some aircraft speeding toward its home. Who's flying you? she thought, reminded of her journey in the trek sled, when she had read about Banzai Maguire, the fighter pilot frozen in time and lost to all that was familiar. What did a woman like that hold on to when she awoke? Love? Honor? Duty?

Snowflakes drifted onto Day's braid, and she lifted one gloved hand to catch the flakes, their white lace melting on her red gloves. The gloves were still shabby and comfortable and familiar, but beneath, keeping her warm and safe, were the liners Lian had given her.

The cold night wrapped around her like the embrace of an old friend, and her breath formed a cloud in front of her. Was she, too, frozen in time? Was this her moment to wake up and walk out into an uncertain future?

What do you hold most dear, Day? The Mounties, yes. Their ideals were her foundation; she loved and admired the men and women she worked with each day.

But, a new love had also entered her life, one that had awoken her to a new future. Lian, with his stubborn reticence and his passionate heart, held a huge, irrefutable place in her heart. Her love for him lay alongside her love of her colleagues and father. Embracing one did not mean losing the other; they filled and completed her in different ways.

But it was her love for Lian that she turned to now, this was the love that would carry her to the future.

The homes of the Shinook spread about her, quiet and peaceful. The thickening snow hid them from her sight, but she knew they were there. She looked up again, and the red lights had disappeared.

"May you find what you lost, Banzai," Day whispered, "for I have."

For at the heart of her dedication to the Mounties was not reverence for the law or devotion to her colleagues, though both were held dear. It was one sure fact: When she did her job, and did it right, the people she served slept safer that night.

Loving and trusting Lian didn't take that away, it only made her stronger.

All life gave you were choices, and she knew what hers must be now.

She strode forward, returning to Lian. Before she reached him, however, a voice caught her hearing.

Adrenaline pumped through her. Withdrawing her Distazer as a precaution, she narrowed her eyes and listened. Difficult to tell where it came from. No footprints in the snow. New snow could have filled them in. The voice sounded familiar. And unnatural. Maybe from that light. The facts clicked through her mind.

"Just reconnoitering," she muttered to herself as she inched closer. She might love the man, but she was not about to let the man's protective caution stop her from the way she'd always acted.

The light was coming from Yves's window. Now that she got closer, she recognized the voice, too—the Voice of Freedom. She circled the house. No one else was around and up. There were no footprints here, either, except for her telltale ones. She sidled up to the home and peered into the window.

Yves was kneeling and drumming—alone in a room he must use for his spirit walks, judging by the sparseness.

Three stones and an eagle feather were on the floor before him. He was chanting in rhythm with the voice, which pounded from his handheld.

She turned, feeling uncomfortably like she was peeping into a very personal moment. Just then, the voice stopped, and Yves's drumming stopped. He looked up, staring at the window. Did he see her out here in the dark?

"Come in, Day," he said. "I want to talk to you."

That answered that question.

Inside, she knelt beside him. "Why talk to me, not your brother?"

"Because you and I can stick to facts."

"You took the name of Jem? Why?" She figured his invitation meant she had permission to ask, not that she ever waited for permission to do her job.

"For many reasons. It was Aveline's suggestion to conceal my actions from the elders. Because it should have been Jem who united our nation and aided our cousin Ahanu. Because it might get his attention."

"You don't resent that he came back?"

He gave a short laugh. "I resent that he left. I wished I could, too. But I was left, and there was no one else for Aveline."

"What do you want to do instead?"

He looked surprised at her question, as though no one had ever asked him. "I want to be a lawyer. If the borders are opened, and I think they should be, then I want to make sure Shinook strength is maintained. The best way to do that is through the law."

"How can you revere the law and plan a violent demonstration?"

"They assured me the demonstration would be peaceful."

Barely past twenty, he was young enough to be idealistic. "Not with these No-Borders. You didn't know about the virus?"

336

"No! But my spirit guides say my brother speaks true."

As if it took a spirit to know Lian wouldn't lie about this. "When are the No-Borders acting?"

He let out a sharp breath. "The action is planned to co-incide with one of the Voice of Freedom's broadcasts. We're going to piggyback onto the Interweb. A two-pronged attack—hacking into the broadcast and lowering the borders. Then, the symbolic exchange."

"Couldn't you have come up with something better than cigarettes to trade? Like chocolate?"

He rolled his eyes. "Cigs were L.J.'s choice. Where will the virus be?"

"Since they're both inhaled, we think in one of those exchanges. Can you warn the No-Borders?"

"They're commed on a specific frequency, and L.J. was in charge of that."

And L.J. was still comatose. "Do what you can. When is the broadcast?"

"Tomorrow at noon."

"You couldn't have given us more lead time?" She sprang to her feet.

"Day—"

"What!"

"There will also be families there. Expatriates reuniting with their long separated kin. I've tried to comm them, but they've started the journey. We agreed to go in with comms off, so we couldn't be detected."

"Oh, hell in Halifax!" Outside, she raced back to Lian, enveloped by the silence of the night and deafened by her own thoughts.

Twelve hours! They'd barely have time to reach Citadel from here, and this was the closest settlement by far. They couldn't pull in more troops—even if they'd had any who were vaccinated, Citadel was too remote to reach in time.

"Day!"

Day squinted into the night, to see who had called. "What are you—?"

Despite the muffling snow, she heard the scrape of a boot. One single scrape. But most everyone here, except her, wore soft soles.

She spun around, facing the threat, Distazer armed and comm pressed. But before she could shout an alarm, a Distazer blast hit her from behind.

Voice paralyzed, she dropped her own Distazer from a useless hand.

Two of them, and damn, but they were good. That was her last thought before another blast knocked her unconscious.

Lian bolted upright. Pain stabbed his forehead. Blinding, dizzying pain. His heart fluttered before it settled back to its normal rhythm.

A wolf howled in the distance. A long, angry howl that faded to mourning.

Day?

He swore, not knowing how he knew that she was in trouble, but knowing it to his bones nonetheless. He threw on clothes and ran outside, shouting to raise the others. A swift rising williwaw stole his voice.

He staggered forward, following the tracks of her rapidly disappearing footsteps. Straight to his brother's house.

He crouched down, his tracker's eyes scanning the area. She'd gone to this window, then walked away. Gone inside? Here. The snow was scuffled, footprints mangled. An imprint in the snow. A Day's-body-sized imprint. Fearfully, he ran his light around the blurring crater, then ran his scanner across. No blood. No viral DNA either.

The body had been dragged to a trek sled. All footprints were wiped out by the drag marks. He raced back to his own sled, not wasting time trying to be heard in the storm, to rouse the others, then roared out, following the tracks from the valley until they disappeared into the night. He circled, checking with lights and scanners, then slammed his fist against the steering wheel.

He'd lost her. With a howl to rival the missing Benton, he raced his sled back to the settlement and his brother's home.

He threw the entry door open against the wall. Yves raced into the hall.

"What the—"

His curse broke off as Lian slammed him against the wall. "Where is Day? I saw the footprints."

"I'm not fooling around with your woman," choked out Yves.

Lian tightened his grip around his brother's throat. "I know that. Not Day. Somebody ambushed her. Now, where is she?"

"I don't know. I told her about the No-Borders and she left."

"Why should I believe you?"

"Because if you want to get her back and stop that virus we're wasting time."

Somehow he believed his brother. He loosened his hold, fighting against the need for blind action. Go in unprepared and you did nobody any good. Day was a survivor. For sanity's sake, he had to hold tight to that belief. "Quick, tell me what you know."

Before Yves could answer, they heard a whine at the door. Benton?

Lian raced over, only to find the wolf shaking and bleeding on the doorstep. He started to run his hands over the animal. By the spirits, what had happened? The wolf backed away. "Benton, I won't hurt you."

The wolf kept backing up.

"I think he wants you to follow him," Yves said.

Lian followed the staggering wolf, past the tracks where Day had been dragged, over to a secluded corner of the settlement. Benton halted, shuddered, then fell over.

Right next to Perren. The wolf dropped a paw over the baby, laid his head down, then closed his eyes.

Gently, Lian scooped Perren out of the cold. Where was Aveline?

"Lian!" shouted Yves, kneeling in the snow.

Lian raced to his brother, falling to his knees as the moonlight revealed the sprawled body. Aveline.

Blood coated her chest. "Get my pack!" he shouted to Yves, handing him the baby. While his brother ran for the med kit, Lian frantically tore off his shirt, trying to stem the bleeding in a cause his experience told him was almost hopeless. The plasma ligature had cut deep across her chest.

Her fingers were looped around the jade bead necklace he'd sent her, anonymously, upon Perren's birth. Aveline opened her eyes. "Perren?"

"He's fine."

"Benton saved . . ." She wet her lips, fumbling for his hand. "I'm sorry."

He kissed her knuckles. "No, no. Save your breath."

"He said he would bring you back, and he did. He said he would be here for the blessing ceremony. The price was the Mountie. But, he betrayed . . . I'm sorry." Her eyes closed.

"No!" shouted Yves, dropping the med pack.

The brothers worked side by side, united at last in the bonds of desperation.

Chapter Twenty-two

Day hated mountain climbing. Mountains were too lofty. Slopes were treacherous and deceptive. Footing was precarious, especially on icy snow. It was always terrible. This particular climb had hit rock bottom.

She just had to make sure it wasn't her body hitting that rock bottom, too.

Her crampons bit into the snow as she and Juneau trudged across the narrow ledge of Citadel. Fortunately, most of the trip had been through one of the three sloping passes that surrounded the legendary peak, but now the jagged spur of the mountain rose toward the sky on her right. To her left was the steep unbroken downslope covered with ice and snow. One misstep, and the next level ground was a thousand meters down.

It would have been easier if she'd had the full use of her arms, but Juneau had fastened them in front of her with loose but unbreakable stasis restraints. Cut them, and they simply reformed. They took a keyed probe to unfasten.

Of course an ice axe had been out of the question.

Her crampon came down on the edge of a buried rock. The metal scraped granite, and her ankle twisted. She fell, her feet sliding out from beneath her. The impact drove the breath from her lungs. Her face buried in snow, her body skidded over the slick terrain. She was going down!

Desperately, she fought gravity, twisting her head uphill. *Arch your back! Traction, traction. Dig in your shoulders and toes. Elbows. Fingers. Traction!*

Her body jerked. The skid stopped.

The microline connecting her to Rupert Juneau snapped taut above her.

Saved by the bastard.

She lay facedown in the snow, breathing harshly. Dizziness wore black dots in front of her eyes, and she fought back a wave of nausea. Nothing like a brush with death to bring on a nice case of altitude sickness.

A foot kicked her leg, followed by the sting of a Distazer. "Get up," snarled Juneau.

"Not exactly easy to do with my hands tied, Rupert." She rose awkwardly to her feet, digging in her crampons again to keep from slipping as he hauled her back to the narrow trail. She stood unmoving, her body shaking, until a taste of the Distazer sent her forward.

Snow caked her cheeks, but when she lifted her hands to wipe it away, the damned Distazer zapped her again. She'd have spun around and iced Rupert, except he had the weapon, she had her hands tied, and the snow was everywhere. Instead, she bit out, "I'm just clearing snow from my eyes. I hike faster when I'm not blind."

The lack of a punishing prod told her to go ahead. She cleared the snow, but since it was still falling, the effort was a continuous one. Next time, she just wiped her face on her shoulder.

She'd awoken from her attack to find herself neatly trussed in Juneau's trek sled and thoroughly disgusted with herself. When they'd reached the point where they had to climb, Juneau had given her the choice of hiking or being shot right there.

She'd opted for hiking. So far, between her bound hands, the treacherous land, and his arsenal of weapons, she hadn't had any chance to take him down or escape. At least, she hadn't had a good enough chance that she was ready to risk it. Yet.

An elk bull's bass call rumbled through the morning, followed by a wolf howl. A sudden longing for Benton's welcome yip almost made her slip again.

She couldn't tell if anyone was following them. Morning clouds eddied below, obscuring her view of the route they'd taken up. Somehow, though, she knew in her bones Lian would be coming.

The question was whether he would be in time.

The narrow mountainside trail widened, the last flat area before the final steep climb to the top of Citadel.

The summit of the mountain was a ridge formed by three close flat peaks. The Canadian and UCE governments had taken advantage of the unique unimpeded transmission characteristics of the heights surrounded by three mountain passes. One peak held the Interweb transmission relay, one peak held a node of the plasma barrier erected by Canada. The third peak held the UCE node.

The three surrounding passes formed a Y around Citadel. The narrow pass they'd come down coursed straight through Canada and ended at Citadel. The other two passes were mountainous conduits between the two countries blocked by plasma barriers.

Day wiped her face clean again, although she could do nothing about the ice pelting her collar. Or the arctic wind piercing her coat. A loud crack above the constant wind startled her. A piece of ice was breaking off somewhere above.

A headache jabbed behind her eyes, while a trickle of blood froze beneath her scarf. Juneau had torn off her comm patch while she was out. She was on her own.

Except that somehow, this time, she didn't feel alone. Deep inside, she could hear Lian's voice. *You're a survivor, Day*.

She slowed her pace until she was even with Juneau. "So, why are you bringing me along here, Rupert? Not that I'm complaining, you understand."

A prick from the Distazer was his only answer.

Okay, so he was not the chatty villain.

"I'm guessing it's my blood. Antibodies."

She got a harder prick this time. She tried not to flinch.

"Because that's the thing about viruses. They're equal opportunity. No sense of loyalty to the sickos who invent them."

She couldn't stop the groan this time as he charged her again. For a moment she questioned her tactics, as she added quivering nerves and tender ribs to her list of complaints. She drew in several breaths, willing back the pain.

"A virus, you can't control. Bet that put a crimp in the plans. Is it invasion?"

"Nothing so lofty."

Good, an answer. She was making progress. "Oh, hell, Rupert, don't tell me we're dealing with plain old greed here?"

The Distazer again. Stumbling forward, Day grabbed in the air, forcing herself to stay upright.

"Want to keep chatting?" Juneau asked, his sculpted face cold.

"Where's the virus?" she asked.

Her answer was more pain.

"Why'd you kill Luc Robichaux?"

"He was an in-the-way bug who overheard me comm the lab."

A confession. "Rupert Juneau—" The pain started with her first words. She didn't stop. "By the authority invested in me under Canadian law, you are hereby arrested and judged guilty in the death of Constable Luc Robichaux."

The Distazer brought her to her knees by the time she finished. She braced her gloved hands on the ground, sucking in the near nonexistent air, while the burst of nerve stimulation disappeared. Slowly she got to her feet, trying to stay conscious.

Juneau smiled, evil and malicious. "The scientists at the lab are going to love you. A blood source of antibodies and a feisty personality to boot. Maybe they'll even dose you with a little C-X gas and let the guards have some fun."

She hated when people called her feisty. It ranked right up there with cute as a button in the gag factor.

The notion that she was destined for lab-rat status wasn't much of a welcome bit of news, either.

He gave her another dose of his Distazer, without her even asking a thing. She had to stop this maniac, and talking wasn't getting her anywhere.

They'd reached the end of the plateau. Ahead was the final steep climb. In a nightmare of step, push in crampon, keep foot level so it doesn't slip, grip the ice, pull up, step, they made their way up the final incline. Her muscles ached from the Distazer and from the exertion. The bones of her ribs squeezed her lungs. Her knees and ankles felt like jelly.

Day pulled herself over an arête on the Interweb relay peak, then swore under her breath. A brace of No-Borders, bristling with arms, a pile of boxes at their feet, crouched in the rocks, awaiting the signal to go.

A meter ahead of Juneau, she scrambled over the top, then swung into action, kicking out and catching the Juneau in the chest before he could find footing. He tumbled to the side—

—and pulled her with him.

Damned microline.

"He's double-crossing you!" she shouted, scrambling to get to her feet. "A virus—"

Juneau's Distazer caught her throat and silenced her.

Still, she yanked the microline and circled her foot behind her, sweeping Juneau's feet out from beneath him. He dropped, and she pounced on his back.

"She's a Mountie!" yelled Juneau. "Caught her sneaking up."

Unfortunately the No-Borders believed him instead of her, and she couldn't fight them all. At least, not with her hands bound.

Juneau gagged her with his scarf, detached the microline, and then added restraints to her legs. "Watch her," he commanded one of the lesser No-Borders as he shoved her onto a rock. "The rest of you, go take those guards out of action."

No-Borders crawled up the rocks toward the Interweb relay, concealed by camouflage, snow, and rock overhangs. Her brief scuffle had at least alerted the guards around the relay, but the No-Borders outnumbered them. The bulk of the troops were stationed at the plasma-barrier node, in the belief that the No-Borders would invade the control compound to bring it down. The relay was guarded by mostly electronic means, which the well-equipped No-Borders worked steadily and efficiently to overcome.

On the next peak over, at the plasma-barrier node, another fight had broken out. The No-Borders, however, didn't seem to be interested in storming the compound, just keeping those opponents confined.

As the guards were beaten back, other No-Borders moved in to efficiently set up their cameras, tap the Interweb broadcast, and blow open the plasma shield.

Day watched it all in impotent fury. She forced herself to sit quiet, not even wiping the snow from her face as her body numbed. Only her fingers did she keep wiggling and warmed. And only then, when at last her hawk-eyed guard began to lose interest in the boring docile prisoner, did she start the slow process of surreptitiously retrieving the key probe from her pocket, the key she'd filched from Juneau during their struggle.

She had to be ready when her partner arrived.

For she knew to her soul that Lian was on his way.

Lian crouched and ran a hand across the track in the snow. Day had fallen here, nearly gone over the side. His fist clenched against hot rage. The stumbling tracks told him she was hurting.

"Juneau will not escape," Hakan said at his side, also reading the signs.

"They went up that way." He pointed to the arête, now barely visible through the thick clouds settling over the mountain. Icy dampness swirled around them, doing nothing, though, to chill the fire of his fury.

"Then we should go this way." Yves held a small topographical holomap. He pointed to the route between the two peaks.

Lian studied the map, trying to decide where Juneau might have taken Day. The element of surprise was still their strongest asset. "Agreed."

He paused to give himself an infuspray of heme booster—he hadn't acclimated to the heights yet—then nodded to the men with him. They moved out as one, silent and swift. When he prepared to leave to find Day and complete his final task as plague hunter, Hakan, Yves, and the others had joined him. Without questions, the men of the Shinook Nation offered to follow him. He could only take five—Hakan, Yves and three others, for he had limited antibodies—but they had been raised in the mountains, hardened by their austerity, and trained by the unforgiving nature here into a formidable force.

The Shinook plague hunter no longer hunted alone.

The end was in sight. He could hang on to one thought alone: Juneau had dragged her this far; he must want her alive.

* * *

"My fellow citizens. We have a revolution at hand." The Voice of Freedom blasted from the mountaintop. "Let justice be done."

The broadcast had begun.

Snow and mist swirled around Day in cold eddies, leaving her cloaked in solitude. Her guard had grown lax, joining the No-Borders as they completed the final steps of their plan.

She'd gotten her gag off and her feet undone, but her hands were still bound. Unfortunately, the position she was in, she was having difficulty turning the key in the precise direction needed to unlock the stasis restraints.

She glanced up for a quick check to make sure no one was watching her. The No-Borders had set up their equipment in the shelter of a rock face. The only way to approach them was straight on. Foolhardy, even if she was armed. And unbound. And not frozen to her marrow.

"Banzai has come to lead us. She is our spirit, our emblem, the embodiment of our ideals." The voice spouted its rhetoric. The spectral clouds parted long enough for Day to see the giant holoimage cast in the air. The Interweb broadcast had no faces, though, only dramatized scenes from the original, world-shattering American Revolution.

"We're in!" shouted the hacking No-Border.

The broadcast suddenly split. Half was the same scenes as before, with the Voice of Freedom still spouting its claims. The other half was the jubilant No-Borders, dressed in boots and wools, brandishing their weapons. One of them held up a holoimager. Suddenly, blazoned across the snow was their fiery demand—*Free Canada*.

Drums sounded across the Interweb. *Thump, thump*— the sound reverberated through her boots. Across the bottom of the screen more demands scrolled and blinked and flashed. *NVC—No Virus Canada. Open the Borders. Unite with our Brothers. Canuck Pride. Hockey Rules.*

Hockey Rules?

Whoever thought a No-Border would have a sense of humor?

Or maybe cold and altitude were taking their toll. They were all dosing regular on the heme booster infuspray.

Day glanced around the giddy group. Where was Juneau? With the thickening snow, she couldn't see much beyond the immediate scene, and even that was getting fuzzy. She swore. He probably was coming back for her.

She scooted around a rock, barely noticing the sharp points of the granite with her snow-frozen behind. With her teeth, she pulled her coat up and braced it with her bound hands until she could reach the hidden pocket with her Distazer. Luckily, Juneau thought she'd only had one weapon. She nudged open the pocket, then pulled out the weapon with her teeth and set it on the rocks. Setting the key probe beside it, she tried to find a good angle to get her restraints undone.

A smudge in the falling snow caught her eye. She spun, aiming the Distazer. Someone grabbed her wrist, shoved it up, spoiled her aim.

She lashed back with her foot, angling for a knee, pulling back at the final second as she felt heat, smelled sage.

"Damn it, Day, it's me."

"Lian!" Her body sagged as she faced him, and he held her in a fierce embrace. It was one second of sheer joy before she returned to duty. She held out her hands. "Undo me. The key's on the rock."

Through the layers of clothes, he kissed the top of her head. "May we never go through such hell again."

The smudge turned into Hakan, who crouched beside her as Lian ran the key over her bonds. "You almost fried me."

"Good thing your leader has learned a few plague hunter tricks," she whispered back.

The restraints fell. Day winced as her nerves fired back

349

to life. Lian picked up her hands and started massaging back the blood with quick efficiency. She looked around, surprised to see Yves and three other Shinooks surrounding her. Damn, but they moved quietly, aided by the howling wind and dulling snow.

"What about the isolation thing?" she murmured.

"I do things differently." Lian's tone brooked no argument. "We're not a Mountie troop, we don't work by the law—"

"I could wish for no better backup than your relations. You will do the right thing. I trust you." Their gloved fingers closed tight around one another, for one moment; then she looked up at the hard men surrounding her. "Thank you. *Pilamaya ye*. Has everyone received the antibodies?" Anyone who hadn't was heading back down the mountain.

"Of course. Everyone's got Health Canada cytokines, too, and filters on." Lian handed her the same, plus a comm, her Distazer, and her pack. "Juneau left these when he whacked your head."

Felt good to get the second Distazer back in her hand.

"What's the layout?" Yves asked.

She summarized quickly, finishing with, "The No-Borders on this peak are well protected on three sides."

"Nonetheless, our main focus will be here." Lian began directing his men. "That's where the virus will be. On camera. Day, you go—"

She shook her head. "Juneau's disappeared. You go after the virus, Lian. I have to find Luc Robichaux's killer."

Before he could answer, a humongous boom rattled the mountain, dropping them to their knees. Day bent over, shielding her head, deafened as cold plasma vaporized. Electricity crackled and raced down the border barrier, swallowing the shield in a hellish fury. She squinted and turned her eyes from the phosphorescent burning, as the barrier that had separated Canada from the world was destroyed.

The incandescent brilliance winked out, and Day uncovered her head, unable to believe until she saw it for herself. Ionized air raised the hairs on the back of her neck and stung her eyeballs. The end of her braid fanned out with static. Dazed, she saw luminescent clouds of sparks cascade away along the barriers.

The border was gone! She could barely form the words in her mind. The thin, blue barrier that had been both bars and shield was destroyed. The secrets of Citadel were blazoned across the Interweb.

Whether Day liked it or not, whether *Canada* liked it or not, the country was now open. She shivered, suddenly feeling the cold blow up her spine, then gave a grim smile.

Look out world, look out UCE, look out Voice of Freedom, we're back!

And it would be Day's job to help make sure her country stayed safe. *So get back to work, Daniels.*

From the corner of her eye, she saw Lian gesture to the Shinooks, using hand gestures she'd never seen before to direct them. Day tried to use her comm, but between the deafness from the blast and the obscuring howl of snow and wind, her world took on a silent surrealism.

She backed down the rocks, planning to circle, looking for Juneau. A hand at her elbow stopped her, and Lian turned her toward him.

He wasn't stopping her from her duty; she knew that without a doubt. She smiled at him as she lowered her scarf.

Lian pulled down his own, gave her a highly abbreviated kiss, then nodded and strode away.

In that moment—when he had defied the strictures of the tribe to come after her, when he had brought his friends and family for the cause they shared, and when he had trusted her enough to do her job and come back to him—she had never loved him more.

And she also knew, without a doubt, that whatever it took, whatever was necessary, she would Be it All and Do it All with him at her side.

She pivoted and headed toward the crackling, sparkling disintegrated border.

So far the scanner had showed green. Lian crept around the perimeter, closing in on the No-Borders at the relay. Juneau would want the virus to be seen in the broadcast where the message would be undeniable: Canada was still infected.

His hearing was coming back after the plasma blast. He could hear the No-Borders' celebration and the sporadic exchange of weapons fire as one of them caught a shadow of his men or spied a guard.

Six men and four women—hard, somber, Distazers and cytokine sprays at their waist—marched into the yellow misty circle of No-Borders. They set two metal boxes at the No-Borders feet. The cigs. The virus? *Take some puffs, spread the DNA.*

Lian found his hand shaking as he scrambled the last meters through the rocks. Dear God, two of the men were mere teens, sons perhaps of one of the others.

The No-Borders passed out the cytokine sprays, handing them to the UCE contingent, then began opening the boxes of cigarettes. A cheer rose from the camp, as the world witnessed the first open exchange of goods between the Dominion of Tri-Canada and the UCE in over a hundred years.

Still, his scanner stayed green. The virus was here, damn it! Where?

Then, the celebrating began. Cousins long separated clapped one another on the shoulder, their hearty thumps muffled by gloves and wool coats. Faces were examined for resemblance: the eyes of a grandmother never seen before, the same mole at the neck, matching gangly heights in some of the teens.

"We're in place." Hakan's voice sounded over the comm patch, as Lian reached them.

"Back me," he ordered into the comm, then stepped into the circle, Distazer held easy. From their position hidden in the rocks, the Shinooks readied their weapons.

The UCE and the No-Borders cocked their weapons. A face-off. Except, he didn't want a shooting match.

"Hold fire," a man commanded. "Unless he moves."

The speaker strolled into the yellow mist of lights. *Juneau*. The handsome face twisted into a smirk, as though he were privy to some joke none of the rest of them understood. Which he was.

"Day," Lian whispered, "Juneau is here."

She swore. "I thought he'd be slinking back to the UCE."

"Dr. Julian Firebird," drawled Juneau. "Of Health Canada."

At the words Health Canada, one of the UCE women paled. She grabbed a quick spray of cytokine before she lowered the scarf of the boy next to her and dosed him.

Juneau pulled a cigarette from the box, lit it, and then inhaled a long drag. "Why is a Health Canada *plague hunter* here? Is Canada hiding something from us?"

One of the No-Borders coughed. Another bent over, holding his back and wheezing in a sharp, high whistle of pain.

"I've heard the plague hunters are loco," Juneau said conversationally, still puffing on his cigarette. "Get crazy ideas. You've been one for how long, Dr. Firebird? Seven years?"

Keeping his eye on Juneau, Lian crouched by the cigarettes and snipped off one end. With the lab chip he added solvent. No virus. The scanner light still blinked green.

The cytokine, then. Juneau hadn't contaminated the tobacco, the UCE gift. He'd been on this side of the border. He'd contaminated the Canadian gift. Canadian virus all the way. Except—

Everyone from the UCE was still healthy.

"Yours is a sad story," Juneau continued. "Unable to return home until the endless cycle of viruses is over."

Lian grabbed a cytokine canister, tested the spray. Negative. Where the hell was the source?

"Such incentives would make anyone anxious to hide a new outbreak." Juneau stubbed out his cigarette in the snow. "Ready to find any excuse for his failure. Even blaming a friendly neighbor?"

Lian felt the speculative looks pressing into shoulders. Even Hakan gave him a second glance. Damn! He'd been led neatly up here, where his very presence was a condemnation.

"What an ass." Day's voice sounded in his ear over his opened comm. "As if you'd ever do something that stupid."

"No doubts, Day?"

"Not a one ever entered my mind."

For one crazy moment Lian smiled, the horror and the fears wiped out by a spur of joy. Day not only loved him, she trusted him. Straight-from-the-gut, without-a-doubt trust.

Juneau pulled one of the No-Borders into the broadcast. The man was sweating in the cold, his cheeks scarlet with fever. "Look at this man!"

Another, the one closest to Lian moaned. Wind plastered Lian's coat against him. Ice pelted his lashes and his forehead. None was as cold or as howling as the anger inside him as the scanner went black, the green light flicked off, then returned.

Red. *Virus.* Pattern? The new strain.

From the lungs of the No-Borders.

An outbreak was about to take place in view of the entire

Interweb. Men, women, and even children were about to die.

And unless he located the external source, he'd never prove it was a planted infection.

"Look at the sensors!" demanded Juneau. "That's small-pox. And the only place you'll find it is in their lungs." His hand swept across the group.

For one stretched moment, the tableau froze, horrified.

Day appeared on the rocks above them, her Distazer pointed at Juneau, her feet planted and her hat jammed on her head. "Royal Canadian Mounted Police. Drop your weapons. Dr. Firebird has the full support of our agency. Rupert Juneau, you are under arrest."

"For saving my country from possible infection?"

"For *planting* infection. If we test your blood, we'll find traces of *my* cloned antibodies. How'd you know to get them beforehand?"

Suddenly, Juneau shoved the No-Border away, then spun and blasted the Interweb relay. The remnants of cold plasma ignited in a brilliant blue flame. A fireball shot up the supports to the main relay housing. Electricity arced out in an explosion of white, screaming streaks. The No-Border side of the screen turned static.

More sparking currents shot skyward. Speeding upward to the source of the remaining broadcast, the Voice of Free-dom. An arc of electricity, a snap of the screen, then a shattering explosion, and then the voice disappeared, lost in the destruction of the source.

A melee broke out in a frenzied exchange of shots. Screams and sobs mixed with the cacophony of weaponry. Lian dove forward, scrambling in his pack for biocontain-ment. Distazer rays struck his arm, his leg. From the corner of his eye, he saw Juneau slip away.

"Day," he voiced into his comm, "where are you?"

"Above you. Watching your back, partner." The whine

of a Distazer punctuated her words, and a UCE woman dropped beside him.

"Juneau's leaving."

"I know. But my duty is to protect *my* people. I'm making sure you find that virus first. Just hurry up and get to work, before my man escapes."

"Everybody here is under quarantine," he shouted, though he doubted they could hear him. Or cared. The scanner lit bright red with the virus, as No-Borders collapsed with the first deadly symptoms.

The limited access worked to his advantage, keeping everyone confined. What the virus wasn't handling, Day and his men were.

Heedless of the fighting around him, Lian threw his med pack on the ground and grimly set to work. "I'm starting treatment." Even without the source, he couldn't wait. "Don't forget your heme boost, Day. You aren't acclimated—"

He broke off, staring at the No-Border who had collapsed in front of him. A heme-infuspray hung next to the cytokine canister on his pack. Quickly, he tested it.

Negative.

But, the smallpox would only need to be in one canister, not all of them. One whiff was all it took. And no one who worked in these mountains ever tossed rubbish. No-Borders, especially, had learned to hide their tracks.

Swiftly he rummaged through the man's pack, grabbing three infusprays on the bottom. Tested one. No smallpox. Tested the second. None.

Last chance, Firebird. He applied the sensor, then stared, elated and nauseated.

Faint red. A minute trace left. Yes! He had his source. And his proof.

No wonder there'd been no virus in the air until the No-Borders started coughing it out of their lungs. The infuspray had sent it directly to their bloodstream.

"I got it, Day. It was in the No-Borders' heme infuspray. We're biobagging it now."

"That leaves the human vector."

"Hey, you're talking like a plague hunter."

"You're allowed to use Mountie talk."

"Does 'I love you, Inspector' count?"

"I don't think it's regulation," she said, humor lacing her voice.

"By the way, you do know that cloned antibodies can't be identified back to the source."

"Yeah, I discovered that in my reading at the quarantine camp. But Juneau didn't."

Despite the horrors around him, Lian laughed.

Gradually order reestablished. As he kept contact with Day, he worked swiftly, finishing the work he'd trained for. One last time. Biobag the contaminated canisters. Dispense fresh cytokine sprays. Begin treatment.

"You set here, partner?" she commed.

"We're good."

"Then I'm going after Juneau."

Lian glanced around. Things were in control for the moment, with his patients dosed and stable. He handed his med pack to Yves. "Comm me if anything goes wrong. I'm going after Day."

"You think she's in trouble?"

"Day? Nah. She can handle herself. But I'm her partner."

Chapter Twenty-three

She'd lost sight of Juneau in the snow. Frustrated, Day jammed her crampons down as she sped across the summit. Only his rapidly filling tracks allowed her to follow him. But those tracks allowed her to gain on him. She wasn't having to break through new snow.

"Day, where are you?" Lian's voice sounded in her ear.

"Next peak over."

"I'm following you. Yell *Banzai* if you need help."

"Understood."

This third peak was higher than the other two, and when she scrambled over a rock pile, she emerged from the clouds into sunshine. The snow was drier, too, but the wind was stronger. Thankful that Lian had included goggles in her equipment pack, she pulled her face protection up to cover the tops of her cheeks.

And with the visibility, she finally saw Juneau. The bastard was just ahead. She raced forward, taking aim with her Distazer—but he skidded as she fired and she missed. He fired back, also a near miss.

"Damn, he's at the UCE cold plasma barrier."

Juneau reached the barrier. Using a remote control, he opened an entrance, sped through it, then closed the barrier behind him. He turned and gave her a mocking smile.

No, he was not getting away!

The plasma wavered and shimmered. Sparks flicked off the surface, weakened as it was from the cascading reaction from the Canadian explosions. Day didn't even slow down. "I'm going through, Lian."

Her partner's colorful curse came across the comm real clear, but she didn't let it stop her. Praying that the border was weaker now than Scree's shield, she plunged forward.

"This is the UCE," Juneau called. "You have no jurisdiction here, Inspector."

"I don't give a bear's ass for jurisdiction." She hit the edge of the shimmering blue plasma. "Banzai," she muttered, and ran forward.

The tingling rapidly became excruciating pain. Her lungs spasmed under the assault. Blackness curled the edge of her vision. Only's Juneau's shocked look kept her going through the thick poison. That, and the memory of Luc Robichaux.

She burst through to the other side, instinctively rolling down behind a rock as she emerged, knowing Juneau would be firing. She somersaulted, raised herself on one knee, and peered over the ridge of stone.

A wolf howled, a haunting melody for midday. By instinct, she spun toward the sound and fired. Rupert Juneau crumpled forward onto the rock, his weapon plunging down the side of the mountain. Cautiously, she approached him, her crampons biting into the slick snow.

From the corner of her eye, she saw Lian arrive on the other side of the barrier.

Juneau rolled over, holding up a vial. "Stop, both of you. This is concentrated smallpox. New strain. Inhale this viral load and even your antibodies won't be fast enough to keep you safe."

Day stopped, her stomach churning in fear, but she didn't lower her weapon. "Death in service to country is always a risk."

"Are you willing to incur wider contamination?"

Her fingers tightened on her Distazer. "Is it possible, Lian?" she called.

"If it's concentrated. Yes."

"You'll die, too," she said to Juneau.

"I'm already vaccinated. Never play unless you play to win. Lower your weapon, Inspector Daniels. Put it on the ground, and kick it toward me."

Jaw tight, Day did as Juneau said. His threat might not be original, but it was effective. She could see Lian on the other side of the barrier, radiating a barely leashed fury. His Distazer was useless from there—the plasma barrier would absorb the energy burst.

They both knew, however, that Juneau could not be allowed to keep that vial. He had used it once; he would not hesitate to use it again.

As Juneau bent to pick up her Distazer, Day leaped forward, stretching, her fist closing around his, wrapping the vial inside their joined hands. Juneau shot upward, bringing her Distazer around to her throat.

Before he could fire, though, he stiffened. His arm fell uselessly to his side; the Distazer dropped to the ground.

A carbon tube dagger stuck from his shoulder, severing the muscle, piercing the nerves.

Lian, she realized. The dagger could pass through the plasma shield without difficulty. Lian was coming through the barrier, too, though he was showing signs of pain.

Juneau flailed his good arm, the one holding the virus, and his feet went out from underneath him. His weight pulled Day down. Their feet skidded on the icy, treacherous snow. Day grabbed tighter as the two of them tumbled over the mountainside.

She heard a shout—from Lian?—as she fell and rolled across the glacier. A scruffy pine timberline rose up before her. The last thing she did, before she and Rupert Juneau slammed into that unyielding wall, was tighten her hands around that vial.

Day opened her eyes to fur, blue eyes, and bad breath. Her ribs hurt, probably from the wolf sprawled on her chest. "Off, Benton," she croaked.

"You're awake!" Trafalgar reached over and brushed her stray hair back from her face. "How are you feeling, honey?"

"Cranky. Ready to leave the hospital. I'd feel better if this wolf was off me."

Benton gave a cheerful yip and licked her face.

"Oh, yuck."

"C'mon now, Benton. Off my patient." Lian pulled the wolf away. Benton gave another yip, then sat down at the foot of her hospital bed.

"How did you get the hospital to let a wolf in?" She winced as she struggled to sit up. Nope, it wasn't just the wolf that was paining her ribs.

Lian put an arm around her, helping her, then sat beside her on the bed. "I said he was part of your therapy."

"Besides, they were tired of him standing outside howling," added Trafalgar.

"I want to get dressed and go home." Day ran her tongue around her dry lips, her voice scratchy. Lian, being the mind reader that he was, handed her a glass of water, and she took a sip.

"After I check you out," he said. He glanced at Trafalgar.

Trafalgar leaned over and gave her a kiss on the forehead. "When you're dressed, come to the conference room.

361

There are some people waiting, and the commissioner wants to talk to you. Then we can hightail it out of here for Wood Buffalo."

She didn't say anything as he left. Neither did Lian, who clipped a diagnostic chip to her chest, then checked her heart and lungs with crisp medical efficiency.

She'd been feverish, for two days according to her chronometer, awaking in fits and starts, catching up on bits of news. She'd stayed conscious long enough to repeat her arrest of Juneau, who'd also managed to survive the fall. The Shinooks had evacked them, and Lian had sent the vial of smallpox to the Winnipeg labs for destruction. Lian had also told her about Benton and Perren. And Aveline— her seduction by Rupert Juneau and her betrayal. Yves was taking part of that blame on himself. Aveline had met Juneau when she'd sneaked out with him to a No-Border meeting. She'd thought she was helping a lonely expatriate.

"How am I healing?" she asked when the diagnostic chip beeped.

"The redislocated shoulder will take at least two weeks to heal, and the broken radius longer. Your mass of bruises, however, have become an unattractive shade of yellow, which means they will fade soon. Damn, but you gave me a scare out there, woman. Promise you won't go careening down any more mountains."

"Not willingly."

"I guess that's the best I'll get."

She laid a hand on his cheek, amused. "I do love you."

"I love you, too. Before you say anything else, though, the Mountie commissioner is itching to talk to you. Do you feel up to it?"

The top man in the RCMP? "Let me get dressed. Where's my hat?" A few stiff and aching moments later, she was fully dressed. She settled the hat on her head. After she adamantly refused the wheelchair, he helped her down the hall to the waiting room.

Trafalgar, her colleague Rich Tesler and his daughter, and Mounties from the Calgary and Moose Jaw depots all crowded into the waiting room. For the next moments, Day was welcomed back into their midst. Tough men greeted her with tender hugs, their awkward gestures bringing a lump to her throat. Others offered their heartfelt thanks for bringing the murderer of Luc Robichaux to justice. Their acceptance and fellowship enveloped her. She was back home.

She glanced at Lian, who was waiting quietly at the fringes, and she realized that home was no longer where her heart was. And that being a Mountie wasn't about the law or stability or anything so profound. It was about protecting those you loved and served. She knew what she had to do.

Trafalgar clasped her elbow. "The commissioner wants to speak with you. He's on the holo."

Someone had turned on the holopanel, and the commissioner sat in a comfortable leather chair before her. "Good afternoon, Inspector Daniels. Nice to see you about."

She stood in front of the panel, her hat tucked beneath her arm. "Thank you, sir."

"You have the gratitude of the entire force for your efforts in bringing Constable Robichaux's murderer to justice."

"Thank you again, sir. I was doing my duty."

"You may have heard rumors that you were up for a G-1 promotion with the successful outcome of this case."

"It was mentioned, but that was not why I—"

He waved a hand. "No, no, I realize you were dedicated to finding the constable's killer for all the right reasons. I mention it because a slight snag has arisen in the matter of Rupert Juneau." He ignored the murmured protests rising up around Day. "While the UCE has apologized most profusely for his actions and denied all knowledge of his

363

activities, they do claim that, when you arrested him, you had no jurisdiction. You were on UCE territory. Therefore they would like him extradited to stand trial there for smuggling."

Her lips tightened. It was Canadian law she trusted, Canadian justice that should be meted out. "Sir, I arrested him for the murder of Luc Robichaux. That is what he should be imprisoned for. He should get a life sentence without parole."

"With the newly opened borders, the jurisdiction matter is awkward."

"She had jurisdiction," Lian broke in.

"Excuse me?" asked the commissioner.

"What?" asked Day.

Lian stood beside her, close, but not touching. "She had jurisdiction, sir. Outside the government installations, Citadel is Shinook land. Those traditional boundaries are recognized by both the UCE and Tri-Canada. As leader of the Shinook Nation, I have granted her full, law enforcement authority anywhere in these lands."

Day gaped at him, barely hearing the commissioner or her friends, biting back all questions.

"Well, then . . ." The commissioner rubbed his hands together, looking distinctly pleased. "I do believe we can insist that Rupert Juneau serve his sentence here. Imagine, a Mountie with Shinook jurisdiction. Inspector, I think we can reinstate that promotion to G-1 status. That means assignment in Regina, of course—"

"I have to decline, sir," she said softly, still eyeing Lian.

"You can begin— What?" The commissioner did a double take.

"I have to decline, sir. G-1's work out of Regina, and I am requesting permanent assignment elsewhere. I was going to suggest the station at Fort McLeod—"

"That's been closed for years."

"But it's near the border." *And on the edge of Shinook*

land. "In light of Dr. Firebird's announcement, I'm requesting assignment to Shinook land."

"There's no post there. No other Mounties."

"I know, sir. I can report to the Calgary Depot. Someone has to keep an eye on those reopened borders."

"If you're sure that's what you want . . . ?"

She looked at the commissioner; then, steady and confident, she said, "It is, sir."

"Request granted." The commissioner's holo winked out.

Day raised her hand against the hubbub surrounding her. "Give me one minute alone. Please." Then she pulled Lian out into the hall. "Do you have that authority? To give me jurisdiction on those lands?"

"I do now."

"You trust me with your people's welfare?"

"I do now," he repeated softly, his hand at her cheek. "My people will have no better champion." Then he grinned. "Although you might have a spot of trouble with the smugglers for a while."

"I can handle them." Her smile faded. "Will your people accept me? Us?"

"I don't know; we'll have to ask them. Either way, I will have honored my vows to them. And I will stay with you."

Love for him filled her chest, every empty, solitary space inside her. She understood. She wouldn't have loved him like this if he'd been a man who cared less, who could have easily turned his back on his promises. Yet, he had defied the strictures of his upbringing, his very nature, to give her what he thought she most needed.

"I was hoping," he continued, "that you could come back with me. That you could be with me. Even not knowing how they'll react, I'm hoping you'll take a chance on us. I'll lead them, Day, but I'll stand beside you."

"You have given me the greatest gift," she whispered, her hand resting against his cheek.

"Jurisdiction?"

She shook her head. "A plague hunter's great heart. I love you, Julian Firebird, whether you are named Lian or Jem or whatever. And I will go with you to your home. I'll stand beside you, as well." She stretched up, to give him a kiss, then drew back. "Ouch. Even my lips hurt."

"That's from kissing that pine tree." He leaned his cheek on the top of her head. "Good thing you're marrying a doctor. You sure do get banged up a lot, Inspector."

"I do not— Whoa, whoa, back up a sentence." She drew back. "Who said I'm marrying a doctor?"

"Actually, you did. I asked you last night, and you mumbled yes."

"I did not."

"Prove it."

Come to think of it, she did remember something of the kind. "Answering under the influence of painkillers does not count."

He sighed. "Then we'll live together. Just so long as I have you at my side. I love you, Day."

"*Lela washtae che la ke,* Jem."

Trafalgar poked his head through the door and cleared his throat. "Day, some of these folks have to leave."

"I'll wait for you downstairs, with Benton," Lian said.

Before she entered the room to bid her friends au revoir, she laid a hand on Trafalgar's arm. "I know you're disappointed about the G-1, Trafalgar, but I hope you understand. I'm doing what's right. I'm protecting my people, and I'm doing it with someone I love. What's important is that I love Lian."

Trafalgar shook his head.

Disappointment washed through her. "You regretted giving up your G-1 for me—"

"I never regretted that for an instant," he corrected fiercely. "You were the best thing that ever happened to me. What's important to *me* is that you're alive and you're well and you're happy. If Lian is what you need for that, then you have my blessing."

Joy filled her. "Thank you." She leaned over and kissed his cheek. "It helps that I'm the only Mountie ever given jurisdiction on Shinook land, though, doesn't it?"

"That it does, Day, honey. That it does."

The Shinooks were gathered at the communal hall when they arrived. Lian stood at Day's side, his hand on her shoulder, and he faced them.

"I gave a sacred promise that when I returned to these lands, I would fulfill the responsibilities of leadership. Today I accept that duty. The Shinooks have now, and have always had, my loyalty.

"However, I come to you as a man whose soul is now united. Not only with our traditions, but with a face toward the future. Make no mistake, we will honor our past, but if I am your leader we *will* move forward.

"And I will lead with this woman at my side. I embrace her as Shinook and have given her full authority on these lands. That cannot be changed.

"Seven years ago, I was offered a choice. Now I offer you one. Will you accept me, knowing these are the conditions and challenges I lay before you? Or will you exile yourself from me and from her?"

He was risking a second exile, he knew. Risking that they would turn from him. But this time, he would have Day with him, and the prospect was not so heartrending.

"*Full* jurisdiction?" Yves asked. "Over Aveline, too? You would accept the Mountie's judgment of our sister?"

"Yes, I do." He spied his sister in the back. She was still confined to bed, still recovering from her injuries, but she had insisted on coming today. "Aveline, come forward."

Slowly, Taku wheeled her forward in a chair. She looked calm, but Lian could see the uncertainty in her eyes. After all, her last encounter with Day had been a bitter betrayal.

367

Day's decision now was crucial for acceptance in the eyes of his people. If she was too lenient, they would not accept her authority. Too harsh, they would not accept her.

"You have assaulted an officer of the Royal Canadian Mounted Police," Day said.

"Yes," Aveline admitted.

"You are hereby found guilty. Normal punishment is a minimum five years' jail time."

Aveline paled, and there were angry murmurs from the tribe.

Day lifted her hand for silence, and to Lian's surprise the murmurs quieted. "However, I have learned recently that the power of the law is not in simple adherence, but in its justice and its intent. Moreover, at the time, I was not an authorized officer of the law. And I understand that you were misled, made to believe things that weren't true. Therefore I sentence you to six months . . ." The protests rose again, but she ignored them. "One year of hard labor—taking one hour a day to teach me Shinook."

There was a moment's silence as her words sank in, then Taku bent his head back in a shout of joy.

Yves stood up and came to Lian's side. "I accept you, embrace you, as brother and chief of the council of elders." He hugged Lian, then Day. "I embrace you as sister and Mountie."

"As will I." Hakan strode forward to join them.

That was all that was needed. Lian and Day stood together. There would be problems ahead, not all of the Shinooks would accept Lian, but the two of them would meet all challenges side by side in love. Lian—Jem—had returned home.

Two weeks later, Lian finally deemed Day healed enough to resume her normal activities.

No sooner were the words out of his mouth than she stood up on tiptoe and kissed him, setting a hungry fire deep in her belly. "You know what activities I want to resume?' she growled.

"Going out in the trek sled," he answered.

"Not what I had in mind."

"I have something to show you."

"What?"

"It wouldn't be a surprise if I told you."

Half an hour later, Lian drove them to the far end of the valley, then up the fallen rock on the side of the mountain. At last, he stopped next to a rock aerie and got out. Taking Day by the hand, he brushed snow off a rock. They sat beside each other, looking out over the valley.

The Shinook settlement spread out before them, a peaceful spread of homes. The tribe didn't bother with things like lawns or flower beds, but the houses were situated to take advantage of sun or shade, to give views of the last remaining wildflowers or the red leaves of a sumac. Snow covered all but the most sheltered spots, and the dark-bottomed clouds promised more accumulation. The continual drifting was closing paths and trails. Still, today, the sun warmed the top of Day's head, and she stretched out her legs. She was getting to like the mountains.

Lian rested on his elbows, tilting his head to catch the thin sunshine. He didn't look like a man intent on seduction.

"What . . . ?"

"Shhh."

A moment later, she heard a rustling in the snow, then Benton leaped out, running around her and nudging her with his nose. "Benton!" She ruffled the fur on his nape. "Where have you been? I've missed you."

As if in answer to her question, he turned to the rear of the ledge. There, another wolf, a small female, came cautiously forward.

Lian took Day's fingers in his. "I saw her with Benton the day I brought you back here. I call her Lucy."

Day held out her hand. "Hello, Lucy," she said softly.

The she-wolf sniffed at Lian's hand, then at Day's. After a moment's consideration, she gave their joined hands a lick and walked away, regal and proud. Benton bounded after her, and the two wolves disappeared.

"I think she's pregnant," Lian said.

"Benton doesn't waste any time, does he?" Day raised her brows and gave Lian a hot look. "So, why are you . . . ?"

Day's words unleashed the lurking wildness inside him, which found voice in a wolfish howl. Leaning over, he kissed her, and her hands tunneled through his hair as she kissed him back. Slowly he lowered himself until she sprawled across the top of him. He didn't care about the cold snow or the hard rock as long as she was caressing the other side.

He fumbled between them, undoing the fastenings on her pants, reaching inside, and caressing her.

"Ah, Lian . . . Wait"

"You aren't saying no, are you?" He caressed her again. "No—"

"Afraid someone's watching?" Another deep caress.

She shuddered and leaned over him, bracing her hands on the rock above his shoulders. Her braid dangled between her breasts. "Nope."

"Tired of doing it in the snow?"

"Well, I was hoping for hockey skates—" She kissed him, then murmured against his lips, "Logistics. I need to get at least one leg out of my pants."

"Who's stopping you?" The tip of her braid tickled his throat, and he was damn glad of the cold that kept him from exploding right then. Instead, he took his hands from her gloving warmth and unbuttoned her coat, while she freed them both and joined them.

As the pressure built he whispered, "Unite us as one.

Between Mother Earth and Father Sky we complete the circle."

She shouted in release. He thrust upward one more time, his seed freed in a final explosion of desire.

As Day lay limp against him, her breath evening and her fingers playing idly with his hair, he wrapped an arm around her and smiled.

They *were* united; their souls were whole and one.

They lay for a long time, until the cold did begin to seep through his back, then they righted their clothes and headed back to his home.

"The PM's giving a speech tonight," he said. "She delayed it until the matter of Juneau was settled. Let's watch. In fifteen minutes."

They entered his home, and inside he turned on the handheld and surfed up the PM's broadcast.

"Is the Voice of Freedom still broadcasting?" Day asked, leaning her head on his chest.

"Nobody's heard from it since our border explosion. The Citadel relay's back on line, so it's not that. Nobody's sure what happened."

"You know, it's strange. I don't like that Voice, but its talk of Banzai and freedom and the ideals of democracy gave me the courage to change into an *almost*-stiff-brim. I admitted what I valued most about being a Mountie was protecting Canada, and what I valued most about my life was loving you."

"Then I shall be ever grateful to the Voice, and to that woman, Banzai." He kissed Day's nose, then turned to the handheld. "Shh, it's the PM."

The Canadian prime minister stood straight and regal in her red dress, the ancient and traditional maple leaf symbol attached to her podium.

"Ladies and Gentlemen, I'd like to announce that Canada is completely free of the bioterrorist viruses. Recently, a rogue agent from the UCE tried to rerelease one of those viruses, but they were thwarted by the diligent efforts of Health Canada and the RCMP. Just as we will turn back any other cowardly, despicable attempt.

"The UCE has disavowed any knowledge of Rupert Juneau's actions and apologized most profusely. The man responsible overstepped any authority given him, and has been dealt with most severely. UCE assures us this will not happen again. The world will be watching to make sure it does not. As a gesture of good faith, the UCE has powered down their remaining plasma barriers. As have we. The process of border troop reduction has begun."

The prime minister set down her papers and looked straight at the camera. "Ladies and Gentlemen, the quarantine is over. The Dominion of Tri-Canada rejoins the world!"

So, Banzai, Day thought, *If your revolution comes, then look here to the North. Your neighbor is a strong, free nation supporting and living those ideals. And you will have one Mountie waiting at the border to thank you.*

As the PM continued to talk, Day nuzzled closer to Lian.

He laid a hand over her heart. "I feel that erratic heartbeat again."

"Happens every time I'm near the man I love."

He leaned down again and kissed her, gently and tenderly this time.

Day settled into his arms. They would continue to have occasional arguments, but they were secure together, united in their partnership and in their love. For the Mounties and the Shinooks. For Canada. But most of all, for each other.

2176

WATCH FOR THESE BOOKS TO COME!

The Shadow Runners
Liz Maverick
May 2004

The Power of Two
Patti O'Shea
November 2004

And the exciting conclusion of the series . . .

The Scarlet Empress
Susan Grant
December 2004

Spellbound
KATHLEEN NANCE

As the Minstrel of Kaf, Zayne keeps the land of the djinn in harmony. Yet lately, he needs a woman to restore balance to his life, a woman with whom he can blend his voice and his body. And according to his destiny, this soul mate can only be found in the strange land of Earth.

Madeline knows to expect a guest while house-sitting, but she didn't expect the man would be so sexy, so potent, so fascinated by the doorbell. With one soul-stirring kiss, she sees colorful sparks dancing on the air. But Madeline wants to make sure her handsome djinni won't pull a disappearing act before she can become utterly spellbound.

Dorchester Publishing Co., Inc.
P.O. Box 6640   __52486-4
Wayne, PA 19087-8640   **$6.99 US/$8.99 CAN**
Please add $2.50 for shipping and handling for the first book and $.75 for each book thereafter. NY and PA residents, please add appropriate sales tax. No cash, stamps, or C.O.D.s. Prices and availability subject to change.
Canadian orders require $2.00 extra postage and must be paid in U.S. dollars through a U.S. banking facility.

Name_____
Address_____
City_____ State_____ Zip_____
E-mail _____
I have enclosed $_____ in payment for the checked book(s).
Payment <u>must</u> accompany all orders. ❏ Please send a free catalog.

CHECK OUT OUR WEBSITE! www.dorchesterpub.com